Georgiana Kingscote

Lazarus

A Tale

Georgiana Kingscote

Lazarus
A Tale

ISBN/EAN: 9783743350588

Manufactured in Europe, USA, Canada, Australia, Japa

Cover: Foto ©Andreas Hilbeck / pixelio.de

Manufactured and distributed by brebook publishing software (www.brebook.com)

Georgiana Kingscote

Lazarus

LAZARUS

A TALE OF THE WORLD'S GREAT MIRACLE . . . .

BY

LUCAS CLEEVE

"Now a certain man was sick, named
Lazarus, of Bethany."—ST. JOHN xi. 1.
"Now Jesus loved Martha, and her
sister, and Lazarus."—ST. JOHN xi. 5.
"Then said Jesus unto them plainly,
Lazarus is dead."—ST. JOHN xi. 14.
"He cried with a loud voice, Lazarus,
come forth."—ST. JOHN xi. 43.

NEW YORK
E. P. DUTTON & COMPANY
31 WEST TWENTY-THIRD STREET
1897

LAZARUS

"When mourning o'er this stone I bend
Which covers him that was my friend,
From his hand, his voice, his smile,
I am divided for a while.
Saviour, mark the tears I shed,
For Thou didst weep o'er Lazarus dead."

LAZARUS.

CHAPTER I.

THE faint red lights of Jerusalem were twinkling in the distance. The sun had vanished, leaving that strange ruddy glow behind it that, in the East, usurps the place of twilight. On the rose-pink flushings of the sky, tiny, pale yellow stars appeared at every moment, like primroses springing up on a clover field, and, with their appearance, the sky grew a greener blue, to form a fitter setting. The palm trees looked almost black against these jewel tints, and the blue olive trees grew grey, as if about to die, and everywhere was silence, except for distant croaking of frogs, or barking of wild dogs.

Alone, along the road of Jericho that led to Bethany, walked Lazarus, the youngest ruler of the Synagogue, the son of Simon the Leper.

Poetic and dreamy always, to-night he walked more wrapped in thought than usual, for his heart was full of a great unrest. One of the closest observers of the Mosaic Law, as Lazarus was, something to-day had stirred his thoughts with a clashing dissonance he could not account for. A poor Jew had been brought before Caiaphas for failing to pay a money changer. The man's story had been a piteous one of sickness and bad crops, and a terrible overcharge on the part of the usurer; yet Caiaphas had but shrugged his shoulders at the tale.

"Thou hast thy remedy," he had said to the creditor. "He has houses and fields, he owes thee money; take them. Why come to me?"

Something, he knew not what, in the High Priest's tone, had fallen on his ear like a wrong note in a tune. Was this justice? For justice is ever man's measure-tape of right. To Lazarus the words of Moses came back: "If thou lend money to any of My people that is poor by thee, thou shalt not be to him as an usurer, neither shalt thou lay upon him usury."

Something in the man's despairing voice and look had seemed to open out new thoughts of grief to Lazarus. What was bitterness, where was healing for its sting? What was life? Why was life? What was he, Lazarus, doing, walking along that road? Who was he?

Suddenly earth appeared to him as but a hillock, and men mere creeping insects hurrying up and down it. Yet the ancients said that man's soul was immortal. God had appeared to Abraham and Moses. Would He appear again?

Surely David and all the prophets had sung of a Messiah. Surely there must be an ending somewhere to grief and trouble, such as that of the poor man he had seen that morning. Surely there was somewhere a justice not based on human moods, or swayed by human caprice.

Yes, like a flash of lightning on a darksome night,

or the sudden blaze from a log that falls from its place, there sprang up for him a strange new meaning in life. So much did the reflection move him, that he paused by the low wall, and looked back towards Jerusalem, a dark mass, now lying like a gaunt shadow with weird shape across the valley, a faint radiance showing only where the roof of the Temple lay. Absolute Justice! Absolute Truth! Right, real Right, independent of creature. Could they be found ?

Yes, it was possible; he felt it, and as he turned his face upwards toward the sky, and as the cool night air fanned with soothing gentleness his lips, a voice seemed to whisper to his soul: "Seek! Seek!"

Presently, at the turning of the road, from the gloom emerged another figure, and a voice cried out: " Hail, friend Lazarus. I come to sup with thee."

The voice was young and fresh, and vigorous as Lazarus's own, but with a serious vibration in it that spoke of constant introspection.

" No friend I would more gladly see this night," said Lazarus, with truth in every accent; for Nicodemus had been from childhood ever his greatest and most valued friend, and, like himself, was a young and promising ruler of the Synagogue.

" Whence comest thou, Nicodemus ? Thou wast not at the Sanhedrim at all to-day."

" Nay, but if I tell thee, thou wilt laugh," said Nicodemus.

" Methinks 't would do me good to laugh, for my thoughts were sad while thou didst come this way."

Then, lowering his voice and coming close to

Lazarus, Nicodemus whispered: " I went to hear speak this strange Man, after whom the people have gone mad, and I can assure thee, noble Lazarus, that His preaching is no mean thing. Verily never heard I man speak like this Man."

" I, too, have heard rumours of His preaching. 'T is some poor fellow that hath followed in the doctrines of John the Baptist," answered Lazarus. " What preacheth He ?"

" Baptism and Repentance of Sins," answered Nicodemus; " and yet more, He speaketh of Forgiveness."

" Who shall forgive sins but God only ?" questioned Lazarus.

" Methinks verily 't is some prophet from God," said Nicodemus, " and it surpriseth me that neither Annas nor any other of the priests doth take notice of this matter, for seemingly, 't is one of vast importance. About the manner of this Man's birth there are marvellous accounts, and even as a child He did say and do most wondrous things; and His face, I cannot tell thee, Lazarus, how beautiful it is. It hath an expression of mingled purity and power, and it troubleth one strangely to look upon it."

" I will one day come with thee to hear Him," answered Lazarus. " Even but now did my thoughts dwell sadly on the present state of government. It seemeth to me that the old laws of Moses are perverted sadly, and that the world groweth strangely bad, as at the time of Noah."

" Yea, worse; for where were now the righteous man to place within the Ark ?" asked Nicodemus.

" Yet we have kept the laws of Moses from our

childhood upwards," said Lazarus, unable still to break away from the teachings of his youth.

Nicodemus was silent for a few moments. Then he began again, with the air of a man who wishes, while persuading others, to persuade himself: " Yet, Lazarus, it seemeth to me that within the heart there is yet a deeper philosophy of right than the law of Moses teacheth. There is ever an inward burning longing for rest and peace and happiness, as if somewhere the soul could rest eternally."

" So will it be in the resurrection," answered Lazarus.

" Yet that is far off," said Nicodemus. " Methinks that, even in this life, there might be an inward peace with hope, such as this Nazarene doth speak of." Then he stood still, and, gazing down the valley, waved his hand toward the dark outline of Jerusalem. " Mindest thou the words of the prophet, Lazarus ? ' Woe to Ariel, to Ariel, the city where David dwelt! The Lord hath poured out upon you the spirit of sleep, and hath closed your eyes: the prophets and your rulers, the seers, hath He covered. And the vision of all is become unto you as the words of a book that is sealed, which men deliver to one that is learned, saying, Read this, I pray thee: and he saith, I cannot; for it is sealed: and the book is delivered to him that is not learned, saying, Read this, I pray thee: and he saith, I am not learned!' What thinkest thou, Lazarus ? Is not Jerusalem even so ? Are we not all in heaviness and asleep ? Rulers and poor alike ? Yet I feel that in us everything is possible. Think of the great strength of a man the great understanding, the great

wisdom of men such as Solomon and David. How
the heart doth leap with joy, and then doth faint
with grief! To what end is all this? For death
alone? Nay, I cannot think so, Lazarus."

"The Romans say a man's life is given him but
to teach him how to die," said Lazarus. "Think,
too, Nicodemus, how powerless a thing is man when
death approacheth; he is no more than the grass of
the field, green to-day, faded to-morrow. What,
then, of all his heart-beatings?"

"Aye, truly death, death of this fleshly body;
but there is another life within. I know it, I feel it,
Lazarus."

Nicodemus seemed carried away by his own argument, as though he had himself been preaching and
were fired by his own reasoning. "Mindest thou
not the words of Job? 'The Spirit of God hath
made me and the breath of the Almighty hath given
me life.' Surely the breath of God can never die,
but will return to Him laden with the praise and worship of them that love Him."

More moved than he would have it to appear, for
he was not a demonstrative man, Lazarus walked on
in silence till they reached the gates of his house at
Bethany. Here they were met by the ever anxious
Martha, who feared some accident to her beloved
brother.

"What fearest thou ever?" said Lazarus, smiling
at her anxiety.

"I know not; but the night is dark, and ever since
Barabbas did waylay the Pharisee, I fear me for thee
on the lonely road, lest maybe some robber, such as
he, should fall upon thee and take thy jewels."

" Surely 't were better far to be the sister of some poor man," said Nicodemus, smiling, " than to be so troubled."

Then, when they entered the house, Mary advanced to meet them.

" We heard a wondrous story to-day from Cana," she said to the two men. " We cannot credit it, but our kinsman, Nathaniel of Arimathæa, the cousin of Joseph the Counsellor, doth write how that they were all at the wedding of a friend, and Mary was there with her amazing son, this strange Man of whom all speak; and, when they entered, Mary did say to the servants, ' Whatever He saith unto ye, do it.' And there were set there six water-pots of stone, containing water; and this Jesus said unto them, ' Fill the waterpots with water '; and they filled them to the brim; then He said unto them again, ' Draw out now and bear unto the governor of the feast.' And when they did so, behold it was all wine, and of such choice flavour as Nathaniel saith he never before did taste, for he too was there; and all were full of wonder at this thing, which they do term a miracle. What think ye, noble rulers, can this thing be true ? "

But the two men, full of new, strange thoughts, half formed and wholly inexpressible, looked at each other in surprise, and Nicodemus answered: " If 't is true, 't is surely a God who hath come among us."

And, all that evening, they talked much of the Nazarene, and of the strange acts of Annas, and of the new High Priest Caiaphas.

CHAPTER II.

THE Jewish Passover was at hand, and the Nazarene was in Jerusalem.

A few evenings after His arrival, Nicodemus, full of excitement, sought out Lazarus once more.

" Hast thou heard the strange news, Lazarus ? "

" Nay, I was weary and went not into Jerusalem this morn," replied his friend.

·" Surely the thing was strange indeed that happened. This Nazarene, who, since His arrival, doth seem to drive mad all Jerusalem, did make a scourge of cords, and chased from the Temple all those that sold oxen and sheep and doves, and poured out the changers' money and overthrew the tables; and His face, they say, did glow with wrath that kindled as if with fire; yet none withstood Him, and none durst speak. Thou wouldst have laughed, Lazarus, to see the frightened little usurers, sprawling on the floor to grasp the coins that fell hither and thither, and how they quarrelled when one took the other's money, or several darted at the same coin. Oh, their oaths were awful to hear; yet, for all, they durst not stay, so mightily He scourged them. ' Take these hence, take these things hence,' He cried. ' Make not My Father's house an house of merchandise.' Then He said again: ' It is written, My house shall be called the house of prayer; but ye have made it a den of thieves.' And mindest thou, Lazarus, how the prophets Jeremiah and Isaiah do so say?"

Like one awaking from a dream, Lazarus gazed at Nicodemus. "Surely I mind it, Nicodemus; 't is truly a wonderful thing. And what said the people?"

"The children cried out: 'Hosanna to the Son of David'; and some even say the elders raised their voices saying: 'Verily He is the Son of God!' But the chief priests and scribes who were in the Temple were very wroth, and they came round this Jesus and protested: 'Hearest Thou what these say? They call Thee Christ and Lord and the Son of God, and Thou contradictest them not? Verily Thou blasphemest by Thy silence.' But He looked with wondrous mien upon them and answered only: 'Have ye never read, "Out of the mouth of babes and sucklings Thou hast perfected praise"?' Which, if thou callest to memory, is so written in the Psalms; for the marvel of this Man is that He speaketh never a word but that which is written already in the Scriptures. And while they would have answered Him, yet could not, and sought for words to say, there came round Him such crowds of lame and blind and sick, that surely there was no room any longer for priest or scribe; and when he healed one after the other, and they left the Temple whole and with sight restored, the dumb singing aloud in praise to God, the priests did fly forth from the Temple with fear and fury, and hasted to tell Caiaphas the marvels they had seen and heard. And they say that Caiaphas is so wroth that he can neither eat nor drink; nor can he write, but sendeth message after message to Pilate to give order that they lay hands on Jesus; but Pilate, it seemeth, doth but laugh and say: 'Let this madman alone. He doeth no harm, but rather good, seeing that ye high priests can neither give eyes to the blind nor make the lame to walk.' "

Softly as they spoke, Mary came across the springy grass, and stood close listening; then, when Nicodemus had finished speaking, she exclaimed with fervour: " 'T is indeed the Messiah who hath come. Nathaniel wrote truly of the miracle in Cana. It is the Lord."

" How knowest thou, sister ?" answered Lazarus, amazed at the earnestness of her words, which yet seemed an echo of his own thoughts.

" An inward voice doth speak to me day and night, day and night, saying: ' This is the Lord, hear Him, hear Him '; and when I look upon His face in the Temple, and then around on this vast crowd, methinks that only He who made the flowers and birds and sunshine could have made a man so fair, for His look is like a sunbeam lying over a peaceful lake; and the thought within me doth grow and grow and grow; and, with the Magdalene, I have read and re-read the Scriptures, and every word doth testify how this Christ would come; and it grieveth me now that ever we spoke slightingly of His mother, or could dream it possible that she had sinned, for the prophet Isaiah saith: ' Therefore the Lord Himself shall give you a sign, Behold a virgin shall conceive and bear a son.' Had I but minded me of these words, I had first cut out my tongue ere I had breathed a word against her purity."

" Surely thou speakest strangely," answered Lazarus, " and we must beware of blasphemy. I, too,
would see this Man, yet I fear me greatly; for, if He
have such power, maybe I, too, would think Him the
Son of God and fall in worship at His feet; and then
if 't were not after all the Messiah that shall come ? "

" If thou wouldst but see Him," urged Mary,
" thou couldst ask Him, and thou wouldst not
doubt."

Then Martha's voice was heard calling them to
the evening meal, which, in the ardour of their conversation, they had forgotten. Darkness was falling
quickly; only over Jerusalem still hung a lurid glow,
that made the houses stand out vividly against the
background of the darkening trees, and lighted up
with steely gleamings the rivulet of Kedron, that lay
like some great serpent waiting to seize upon the
heart of Jerusalem. Then, suddenly, a distant
sound of voices rose.

" Hosanna, Hosanna! " cried children's voices
on the stilly air, and they seemed to pierce the darkness and fall like notes of holy music into the hearts
of the little group.

" Martha," said Nicodemus, leaning over the low
wall of the terrace, " hearest thou how they salute
the Nazarene ? "

Then Lazarus, too, stood up and listened, and, as
the cry came nearer, something strange and hard
seemed giving way within his heart. He saw, as in
a vision, earth and sea and sky all rolled away, and
crowds falling to the ground in worship and fear and
adoration; and a great, white light that paled the
glory of the sun; and notes, in power and harmony

undreamt of, gave forth, in unearthly cadence of swelling triumph, the news that the Messiah had come indeed, that the kingdom of God was close at hand.

In that one moment, while the voices drew ever nearer, grew ever louder, and, in the darkness, a still darker line of approaching crowds of men was streaked, Lazarus seemed able to measure his own stature, and to grasp its nothingness against the boundless stretches of creation. One man among so many, one tiny atom at the feet of mountains!

And, as the vision faded, the centre piece of its glory approached along the road. Only a strange luminous whiteness, not to be accounted for by dying sun or rising moon, showed that this Man was not as other men.

" 'T is the Lord, let us go forth to meet Him," murmured Mary, with nervous awe and adoration in her tone; and, regardless of Martha's voice, rising querulous now from the house door, regardless of the opinion of the Jewish world, regardless of all inward doubt; as if compelled by some magnetic, supernatural power, the three sallied forth from the gate and, meeting the Christ when He reached the summit of the hill, fell down in worship at His feet. While Lazarus, hardly knowing what he did or said, mindful only that he stood in a majestic presence, from which to win one look he would barter life and power and all his worldly possessions, exclaimed with mingled Jewish courtesy and human awe:

" Enter in, O Lord, enter in; all I have I offer Thee, for all is Thine."

And the great look fell, with love and gratitude and endless blessing, on the head of Lazarus.

CHAPTER III.

IT had been a bold stroke on his part this bringing the Nazarene straight into the house; for Martha's was a ruling, decided spirit, and she had set her face against offering hospitality to this Man, interested though she was in all that she had heard of Him. There was danger in being in His company. Already the Jews had sought to stone Him, and His presence in their house might mean their own death, or at least suspicion of complicity in His condemnation of the ruling powers, and thus cast a slur upon their house forever. Yet, when the Man of Sorrows stood by the gate, when those eyes, overflowing with grief at the sins of nations, fell upon her, she felt herself reduced to nothingness; even the inmost thought of cowardice and treachery seemed revealed, and the consciousness was born in her that she was, if not in the presence of God Himself, in that, indeed, of one of His most powerful prophets.

Pale and doubting and hesitating at His reception, Jesus stood at the gate, wondering how He would be received; as He has stood at the gate of each human heart, pleading piteously for hospitality, for entrance into the affections, for rest in the souls of men; yet pleading, so often, alas! in vain. There was something so pathetic in His glory and in His silent waiting for admission, that Martha felt over-

whelmed. Supposing, after all, that this were indeed
the God ; how terrible every moment that was not
pressed into His service; how unforgivable the sin
of hesitation; yet how impossible to receive Him as
befitted Him! Bewildered and flustered, she made
obeisance to Him, then led the way to the inner
hall. It was of tesselated marble, roofed overhead,
its walls pierced all round with apertures, that let in
light and air. A side door, supported by columns
of porphyry, and opening on stairs of Shittim wood,
gave access to the garden; for Lazarus was wealthy,
and Simon his father, when he had fallen ill with
leprosy, had given up to his children almost all that
he possessed. The lovely house in Bethany and all
his gold and silver and jewels were theirs, and they
gloried in them.

As those holy feet stepped noiselessly across the
chamber, Martha now was convinced that it was no
ordinary man who had entered their dwelling. All
the beautiful things she and Lazarus had amassed or
inherited seemed shadowy and unreal in the presence
of the lowly carpenter. Yet, for all that, she could
not sever her mind from the conventional hospitali-
ties of life. She hurried away, while Mary came
and cast herself at Jesus' feet, and, far away in inner
halls and passages, she could be heard summoning
her maidens to bring forth their best, to set before
the Lord. But Lazarus and Mary remained by His
side, realising how precious was every moment in
which their Christ was with them; conscious that
He, who could command that the stones be made
bread, required no serving, no preparations; only
the worship and living passion of adoring hearts.

Presently, Martha, wearied with the task of gathering her maidens together and of hastily preparing what seemed fitting for such a guest, returned; and, finding Mary sitting in silent worship at His feet, cried almost querulously: " Lord, dost Thou not care that my sister hath left me to serve alone ? bid her therefore that she help me."

Oh, how the sensitive Mary winced at her sister's words; to speak thus to Jesus, the Christ! How all Martha's want of spirituality, of enthusiasm, of religious fire, echoed in those words! The world, the world and its silly self-imposed routine, its futile, paltry laws built up by the narrow brains of men to appease their limited demands; the self-seeking satisfactions required by man, who deems himself the ruler of this world, whose little span of life seems to himself a nation's. To those who believed, as Lazarus and Mary now did, what mattered wine or garment or surroundings ? One thing only was needful, the Bread of Life such as fell from the lips of Jesus; and to Jesus, what must Martha's words have seemed ? To Him, to whom worlds and time and space and life and death were as nothing to the " I am " of Eternity!

How must her words have sounded to such an One ? Yet the Christ, in His deep sympathy, pitied the fretfulness her cry disclosed. This woman's eyes were not yet opened. How then could she fathom the depth and length and breadth —the majesty of the personality that stood before her ? But He saw in all its fulness what we fail to see, the weary anxiety of the woman, the doubting of His justice, if He could see one woman toil thus while another idled. With gentleness and love He answered: "Thou art careful and troubled about many things: but one thing is needful: and Mary hath chosen that good part, which shall not be taken away from her."

And Mary, in adoring wonder, kissed His feet once more and murmured: "One thing have I desired of the Lord, that will I seek after, that I may dwell in the house of the Lord all the days of my life, to behold the beauty of the Lord and to inquire in His Temple. Thou hast redeemed me, O Lord God of Truth."

CHAPTER IV.

THE light came in in streaks through the curtained windows of the highest, most gorgeous apartment in the house of Caiaphas, lighting up the costly silks which hung above the couches, and the amber-coloured robe of his handsome daughter, the dark-eyed Rebekah. After the Magdalene, with whom, of course, she was never mentioned in the same breath, she was the loveliest woman in Judæa. The Jewish nose had halted midway down the face in Grecian fashion, and the olive skin, protected from almost every ray of sun, had grown of an opaque creamy whiteness, faintly stained as though by some sweet pink flower; and the eyes—no one had ever quite known what was their colour; for, though they looked almost black and were fringed with the long, curling Jewish lash, still some declared that, if she looked upwards, they were blue as sapphire, yet that, when she was angry, they flashed ruby red. The beautiful face, the rounded chin of youth, the sweet, smiling mouth, like early barley in a coral pod, betrayed not yet the heritage of soul, for all the pride of a long line of priests, the subtlety of the Pharisees and Sadducees, and the crafty cunning of Annas mingled in the stream that coursed through those blue veins.

Of an intriguing spirit and brought up amongst

the politicians and great rulers of the day, she had
become a personage of some importance in Jerusalem, and young lawyers and rulers, anxious to
ingratiate themselves with Caiaphas, and young
Romans, and even Greeks, were included in the no
small group of her admirers.

Her mother, Annas's daughter, was an invalid, a
poor weak woman, whom dread of Caiaphas's outbursts of bad temper had reduced almost to im-
becility.

Rebekah was no mean linguist, too; she could
converse in Greek and Latin, and was often of great
assistance to her father; but this was more from the
pleasure of the importance she derived from it than
from any wish to help, for Rebekah loved no one
like herself.

To-day she lay across her couch, gazing moodily
from the window, while her maidens played to her
on the cithern, an instrument the Greeks had lately
introduced.   But its notes seemed but to irritate her.

"Stop, stop, stop!" she cried.   "Ye do play
such mournful tunes, 't is like the wailing at a burial.
Come tell me, when ye passed the market place, were
there great multitudes listening to this—this carpenter.   Saw ye any rulers there?" she asked, with
scathing irony; "or did only the foul, the blind, the
beggars, and the leprous assemble?   For I hear this
Man doth, above all, love sinners, and the beautiful
Magdalene they say hath become a saint.   Oh, the
world must be upside down when the Magdalene
doth become a penitent."   And while she spoke and
laughed there was something fraught with scorn
and malice that reminded one of Caiaphas.   "But

tell me, maidens, saw ye any comely young men in the crowd ?"

" Verily we saw Lazarus and Nicodemus and several wealthy rulers, listening so intently that they saw us not when we passed by."

" Oh, Nicodemus," she said scornfully, " that causeth me no surprise; but Lazarus!" She rose from the couch and went to the window and looked out, while she conjured up the beautiful, stern face of Lazarus. That was the man she had singled out in all Judæa to be the idol of her heart. On the few occasions of her seeing him, he had done no more than give her courteous recognition. Once, at the bidding of Caiaphas, Lazarus had come to the house, but he had barely addressed her. How well the young ruler remembered, when he had left her presence, how she had barred the doorway, and looking him in the eyes had said: " Why hatest thou me, Lazarus ?" And how well she remembered the scorn in his eyes at her unmaidenly assurance, and yet the gentle courtesy of his voice, while he had answered: " Lady, I hate no one." And with a proud gesture she had moved aside and let him pass.

Then in that dark heart had sprung up a love that was so jealous and so fierce that it was almost hate. " He shall love me, or he shall die," she had often murmured to herself.

But Lazarus came no more; and if, perchance, she saw him at some public gathering, he greeted her but distantly.

No alliance would have been more agreeable to Caiaphas than would this. Lazarus was wealthy, Lazarus was clever, and his life was such an one as

Caiaphas would have desired for his daughter, though
he himself could not have lived it.

Besides, he recognised in Lazarus a spirit of meekness that he fancied might make the mouldings of a
creature in his hands; and Lazarus, by the side of
Rebekah, with ambition and craft, would be a
powerful colleague in the council chamber.

" He is spoilt by his own goodness," Caiaphas
would tell himself.

Long did Rebekah muse.   Then, turning to her
maidens, said: " Thinkest thou that Lazarus doth
believe in this Nazarene ? "

" 'T is so said," one of them made reply, not
wholly without malice.   It was a satisfaction to
see one who made others suffer suffer a little in
return.   " They say that Mary and Martha and
Lazarus do receive the Nazarene in their house at
Bethany, and that they believe He is the Christ."

A scowl came over Rebekah's handsome face.
" Tush! 'T is foolishness! He would not be so
great a fool," she retorted scathingly.   " He knoweth that, at most, 't is but a prophet.   Yet I hear
that this Nazarene hath so much persuasion that
even wiser men than Lazarus are bewitched.   Even
my father doth say so much," she added with the
vehemence that, with her, always ended argument.
Then, changing suddenly her tone, she said softly,
so as barely to be heard, and coming to where the
maidens were still seated on their cushions: " Come,
listen, I have somewhat to tell ye."

Then, when they rose, she came close and whispered so that both could hear: " Methinks I, too,
would like to hear this Man.   How can this be

brought about ? It could but be at night," she went on slowly, like one making a plan while speaking—" could but be at night, when my father writeth and my mother hath gone to sleep. We will robe ourselves like poor women, and carry baskets on our heads, and mingle with the crowd."

The two girls' faces expressed such horror that Rebekah burst out laughing.

" Oh, ye two poor frightened things! Can ye not go where the High Priest's daughter can ? Then stay at home, and I will go alone."

" Nay, but it is thou, lády," they exclaimed in one voice. " How canst thou, the daughter of Caiaphas, go out at night to mingle with the crowd ? If Caiaphas hear ? "

" If Caiaphas hear, if Caiaphas hear, well, Caiaphas will laugh," she answered mischievously.

" Nay, he might laugh with thee, but with us he would be very wroth," said one.

" Well then, Caiaphas shall not know. This very night shall we go. Find out where he preacheth, and leave to me the rest."

Half anxious, yet enjoying the prospect of this escapade, the two girls vanished at her order, while she paced the room, the long, orange-tinted robe, which reached her feet, looking now green, now golden, according as it passed through the sun's rays or through the shadow. Nervously she played with the beads of a girdle of amber she wore round her waist.

" Indeed," she muttered, " 't is not the Nazarene that I would seek; but, if to get sight of Lazarus I must needs find the Nazarene, then go I must."

Proud Rebekah, what hath come to thee, that

thou, whom, hitherto, all men have sought, dost follow now one man ? What is love, that strange, subtle fire that eateth out the heart and bringeth the mighty low ? " Oh, I would that Lazarus did feel for me as I for him! That stern, sweet face, how beauteous must it look when melting into love! O Lazarus, Lazarus! "

The afternoon wore on. The streets grew silent, and day slid back, as it were, from the gaze of men. Yet still dreamed on the maiden of the man who cared not for her, pondering, the while, how she could bring him to her feet.

" He shall be mine. He shall," she said at last. " Women are stronger far than men, and I am beautiful." She held a mirror to her face. " Oh, I am very beautiful," she murmured.

" Yet, if this Nazarene should bewitch him ? If he should take the vows of a Nazarite and follow ever after good! Oh, that would be dreadful! No, no, it shall not be that the Nazarene shall come between Lazarus and me. I will not suffer it, I will not suffer it." Then she clapped her hands, that the attendants might bring lights, and left the room to begin her preparations for the night's adventure.

It was almost dark when the three girls issued from the house. They had arranged to go first into the garden at the back, and thence to pass on to the Jericho road, which led to Bethany.

Rebekah looked anxious, and every now and then she bit her lips. Her maidens had learned that the Nazarene would preach that evening from the top of a mountain. The multitude would probably be very great, because, as yet, the novelty of His presence had not worn off. Miracles had only just begun to strike the people with awe and wonder, and, so far, the authorities had feared to check enthusiasm, lest thus to fan the embers of sedition. It would be easy enough to mingle with the listening crowd, but would it be so easy to meet or single out Lazarus ? Would the object of this night sortie be attained ? Their sole chance was that, by walking on the road to Bethany, they would meet the crowd coming to- wards the town and perchance fall in with Lazarus and Mary.

Few suspected in the darkly attired women, with veiled faces, who walked up the hill to Bethany, the proud daughter of Caiaphas and her attendants. Here and there some woman greeted them, or some man called out, but the girls were silent and strolled along.

The maidens guessed easily whom she sought, for it had long been common talk that Rebekah loved Lazarus, but that the proud, stern young ruler would have naught to say to any woman.

Fortune favoured her; she had got not far when a dancing, shrieking, clamouring crowd proclaimed that the Nazarene was coming that way. Rebekah stood against the wall to let them pass, and motioned to her women to do the same; then her eyes searched anxiously in the crowd for the face which to her meant day or night—life or death. But, as yet, she saw it not.

The centre piece of that seething mass of human- ity was the Nazarene. The Messiah walked along the dreary, dirty road, talking little, but, by a strange set earnestness, led men on to follow Him.

What was it that riveted her gaze and made her tremble ? This Man, who knew her not, seemed to unearth the secrets of her soul, and as He passed, for an instant, she saw herself as she was, a brazen, flaunting hypocrite, joining with a believing, enthusiastic crowd, not to worship or to learn, but to seek out a man who cared not for her, and who, in moral worth, was as far removed from her as were the stars. Then, while she looked, she saw the face she sought, pure, pale, and passionless, gazing either at his Master or at heaven, but thinking not of her.

" Lazarus! " The voice that called was full of tenderness and piteous appeal, but it had a sensuous, luring tone which filled him to whom it was addressed with terror. He fell from his grand musings on things of heaven, as one who catches his foot upon a stone falls down a mountain side. An impatient: " Woman, what have I to do with thee ? " was on his lips; but, as he turned, his gaze met two deep, unfathomable eyes that searched his in the darkness. His heart beat quickly. 'T was as though an enemy had caught hold of him and would not let him follow Christ.

" Lazarus, 't is I, the daughter of Caiaphas, the High Priest."

" What wouldst thou ? " he asked impatiently. " What seekest thou ? "

" 'T is thee I seek," rose all but to her lips, in her mad frenzy to be wooed and loved by the young ruler; but something in his face, something solemn in the surroundings, a purified, restraining atmosphere, something she could not account for, checked the words that were on her lips, and rapidly, as an empty basin refills itself with water at a fountain, so wily, crafty thoughts poured in.

"I would hear the Nazarene," she said. "Wilt take me with thee?"

Her voice was soft and low, and he could not detect the false ring in it. What new wonder was this? What if the proud Rebekah should believe, and, by believing, bring her father also to the feet of Jesus? It seemed incredible, but stranger things than that had come to pass; and so poor Lazarus was duped, as so many sympathetic souls are duped who do not recognise the livery of Satan when his servants wear it.

"I will take thee, noble maiden," he said, with gentle voice; "and as thou hearest, so mayst thou believe." The sermon was over, a sermon such as no man on earth had ever heard before, or would ever hear again. Interested, despite herself, carried away by the persuasive power of the voice, the divine beauty of the Nazarene; clever enough to grasp the purport and to interpret the subtle meanings of each allusion; surprised at the fluent speech of one reputed to be an humble and illiterate man; amazed at doctrines, that were the complement rather than the upheaval of the Mosaic Law, Rebekah almost forgot the subject of her errand, the enslavement of the affections of the man she loved. It could not be, with the words ringing in her ears, "Seek ye first the kingdom of God and His righteousness," and "Blessed are the pure in heart," that she should broach the question of earthly love. Lazarus's face, the faces of Martha and Mary in the distance, the silence of the adoring multitude, all struck her with a sudden, paralysing shock, as if an ice wind had blown across her cunning heart. An overpowering terror seized her. Was this indeed the Christ, or was He a devil? What spirit of folly had led her forth that night to listen to such things? Truly 't was a moral earthquake to hear this Man speak.

From very terror, she seized Lazarus's arm and gasped: " Who is this Man? Who is this Man?"

" Surely 't is the Son of God," said Lazarus. For one instant both hearts were locked in a common interest, while he, believing in her, breathed a prayer to God to open the heart of Rebekah, and, through her, that harder one of Caiaphas.

But the Christ was moving on and the multitude was following Him. The pale moon floated gently above the blue-grey olive trees, giving a weird, subdued colouring to the scene; while on in front the white robe of the Nazarene seemed to glow with a supernatural luminosity that guided the crowd along the mountain path.

Then, in dismay, Rebekah looked round for her attendant maidens; but they were nowhere to be found. They, too, were seeking her, but, in such a crowd, 't would be no easy task to find her in her disguise.

" I know not what I shall do!" she cried. " I cannot see my maidens!"

Unnerved by the words of the Nazarene, and filled with terror at her loneliness and at the growing darkness, her voice trembled with no feigned concern.

" Doubtless we shall find them," answered Lazarus consolingly; " but if we find them not, I will accompany thee to thine house."

Then, while she thanked him, Satan, with a sardonic grin, closed up once more and followed in their wake.

With the comfort of Lazarus's presence came a sense of safety, and terror flew away. Gradually the words of the Saviour lost their hold on the sandy soil on which they had fallen. Love and the presence of the loved one, two forces stronger than life or death, even than eternity to some, regained their sway, and the beautiful Rebekah's good angel fled forever. And Lazarus? Lazarus began to feel the magnetic influence of her presence. The power of evil he knew was close, appealing to him in the form of a lovely woman, whose soul he longed to save. Chained to his post by the claims of courtesy and chivalry, he could still cry out to the white-robed figure descending the hill, " Lord, save me, Lord, save me." Words that Rebekah's lips had never learned. " Take no thought for the morrow, take no thought for the morrow."

Surely 't was Satan who thus misused the injunctions of the Messiah. Why did they ring thus ? Why, why should he, a ruler of the Synagogue, in the vigour of his manhood, surrounded by wealth, sighed after by the most beautiful woman in Judæa —why should he wander footsore and tired, hurrying hither and thither after a man who preached impossible doctrines, surrounded by a vociferating crowd of illiterate, uneducated fanatics ? and for what ? To attain a crown, of whose value he knew nothing, to enter a kingdom, of whose existence, even, he was not sure. Earthly life, what joyous, moving excitements it presented to one young and influential as himself! A leader of the people, surely that were better than to follow in such a crowd, seeking after—what?

For one instant, this horrible temptation seized him, or, rather, it was photographed on his brain, for there was no wavering in the man himself. He was like a man betwixt two flashes of lightning, each one of which lights up a different piece of scenery. They had walked quickly, they were almost alongside the Christ.

" Lazarus!" He knew not whether the name had been breathed to him or not, but he met the yearning look of infinite pity, infinite love. In that look he saw the great height attainable by the soul; and indistinctly he could discern the rungs of a ladder that went ever upwards to an altitude of infinite variety and limitless possibility. His soul, his will, his very being, grasped once for all Eternal Life, and he lost it never again.

And Jesus and the multitude passed on.

Two eyes in the crowd followed with sadness the figures of Lazarus and Rebekah; those of the Magdalene. There was no jealousy in that look; on the contrary, there was gentle resignation. It was part of the Crucifixion of Joy that she knew had been allotted as the expiation of her former sins. Oh, how vividly the past rushed back, paying her out, as is ever the case with sinners even in this world. She was reaping now, reaping bitterly, wearily, in the noonday sun, the fruits of her own sowing; but, as she had told the mother of Jesus, the very grief seemed to give birth to a new joy; the joy of suffering for her dear Lord's sake. As her eyes followed the two dark figures that now barely emerged from the gloom around, her heart seemed to die within her, and, by its death-throes, to give birth to a new ambition of her soul.

Love, human love, companionship, friendship, were passing away. Humanly speaking, she was alone. Dark shadows seemed to be rising up, a great wall shutting her out from all the brightness of this world. The conviction of man's solitude here on earth was forced upon her, and with it came the remembrance that there was One who never failed in His companionship and solace.

Yet what right had she to be pained if Lazarus cared for some other woman ? What claim had she, the harlot,* on the heart of any man ? The wealthy ruler's least of all. It was all right and as it should be; yet, at her heart, lay a dull thickening of grief.

Lazarus was certainly not prepared for the scene that awaited him on his arrival at the house of Caiaphas. He was about to conduct Rebekah to the presence of the High Priest; but she, laying her hand on his arm when they reached the wall of the garden, bade him be silent.

" My father knoweth not that I went to hear the Nazarene," she whispered. " Come into our garden, and I will tell thee."

What could he do but follow ? He could not leave her at that hour in the street, yet he much disliked the situation.

* The author has adopted the popular view of Mary Magdalene's mode of life before she had repented and been forgiven by the Messiah.

The moon was high in the heavens now, lighting up almost with brilliancy the walls of Caiaphas's house and the grass around their feet. The garden was laid out in Roman fashion, with paths and labyrinths and stiffly cut yews; the leaves of the dark fig trees glistened in the moonlight, while the cedars rose like ghosts from the dark corners, their weird branches spreading out from them like great curtains of velvet; and everywhere was that deep night silence that raises thoughts of death—except far away in the town quarters of the city, where distant music floated upwards and wild dogs barked.

The hour, the strange silence, the moonlight, the weird beauty of the haughty woman in her new appealing meekness, all these were not without effect on Lazarus's mystic temperament. The man who loved things beautiful around him could not but appreciate the artistic poetry of the situation, or fail to admire the unusual beauty of the daughter of Caiaphas.

As he pushed open the iron gate of the garden let into the wall, she turned her head towards him.

" I would speak with thee, Lazarus," she said, a faint touch of the domineering, despotic spirit returning; it was the voice of one who brooked no opposition.

" The hour is late, and my sisters will be waiting for me; maybe too, the Lord hath returned with them. If thou art safe within these walls, noble lady, I would return."

Rebekah winced at his words, but, in her frenzied love, there was no room for pride. *Now* Lazarus must be caught, if caught he could be by deepest

wiles of feigned meekness, by despair, by appealing
love. To him the daughter of Caiaphas was at present naught, and this she knew; to be loved by Lazarus one must be lovable, true, pure. Oh, she knew
well, this wily daughter of the wiliest of Jews—of
whom no nation is more wily—that she was none of
the things she would appear to be, yet that she must
needs seem all to win him. She felt, too, that now
was her final chance. If Lazarus—Lazarus, enchained so far and kept in her presence by the claims
of courtesy, should leave her now, never again would
she have such a chance in such a place at such an
hour. Her lips paused only to give her brain time
to revolve the best means of winning him to stay.
For one moment, whose madness later made her
shiver, she thought of using the weapons that with
others would have been so powerful. Could he resist, she wondered, the softness of her arms entwining
round his neck, the sweet intensity of her soft lips,
the clinging appeal in her silvery voice, the crystal
tears in those speaking eyes ? No, though she knew
full well that Rebekah brought low in meek subjec-
tion to love, the haughty daughter of Caiaphas telling her tale of seductive passion in that secluded
garden on a summer's night, would have driven most
hearts in Jerusalem mad, from very love and wonderment, still to Lazarus it would be no temptation;
the very boldness of it would disgust him. " Yet
he must have a heart," she murmured to herself;
then added, " Whereof I have not the key." Then
aloud, fearful lest he should suddenly depart, she
said: " I would talk to thee one moment and ask
thee more of this Nazarene."

Oh, lowest wile of woman, to take the World's Salvation as her bait to gain so base an end!

"Perchance this woman seeketh to believe," he said to himself, and suffered her to lead him across the dewy grass to a marble seat beneath a palm that waved gently hither and thither in the evening breeze.

Then, with one hand on the back of the marble seat and the other resting on her knee, she turned towards him. "Thinkest thou, noble Lazarus, that this is indeed the Christ? For if thou dost, methinks I must needs think so too, for thou art learned and well versed in His sayings."

"Oh, if thou wouldst but believe!" said Lazarus, in his intense wish to instil into her some of his own faith turning and looking straight at her, his face burning with heavenly fire.

"Look not at me thus, Lazarus," she said.

"Forgive me, I thought of naught but of how deeply I would that thou didst believe," he answered somewhat brusquely.

"What matters it to thee whether I believe or not?" she retorted bitterly.

"It mattereth to Him," he answered, "for without His knowledge not one sparrow falleth to the ground. It mattereth to me, because I would win all souls to Him for their own sakes."

"And to win my soul what wouldst thou do, most noble Lazarus?" And she looked searchingly into his face with her great eyes.

Her deep voice stirred Lazarus strangely, her words seemed to cut the clear air and throb there, as if with expectation.

" What wouldst thou do ? What then is my soul worth, thinkest thou, Lazarus ?"

" What is thy soul worth to thyself ?" he answered. " What thinkest thou of Eternity ?"

" Methinks," replied Rebekah, " that Eternity with thee were well spent, whether in Heaven or Hell."

He turned and fixed his eyes upon her sternly.

" Dost know that which thou sayest, noble maiden ?" he asked her solemnly.

" Yea, I know well that I do love thee, Lazarus, and that, if thou wouldst but love me in return, I, too, for thy dear sake, would love the Nazarene; but if so be that thou dost spurn my love, then care I not whether Satan have me or not, or whether, as the Sadducees say, there be resurrection or another world at all; for where Lazarus is not I would not live."

" Thou art mad," said Lazarus, rising from the seat and pacing up and down the path in front of her. Then he came and stood in front of her. " Thy words have moved me strangely, maiden," he resumed hoarsely, " and I would ask thee to let me go, for this conversation becometh neither thee nor me. The hour hath bewitched thee, and thy mind is overwrought with listening to the Christ's words, and the long journey hath wearied thee. To-morrow thou wilt have forgotten thy words, and so shall I."

Then Rebekah rose, and, with a despairing gesture, wailed bitterly: " Thou mayst forget, but I shall not, for night and day I think of thee, and long but for thy heart only in all Judæa. If thou

3

hadst loved me, I would have tried to believe in this mad carpenter, for what thou believest I could not do otherwise than believe; and, if He promised thee Eternal Life, I too must needs have that Eternal Life; thus should I not leave thee either in life or death."

But here her voice grew shrill and angry, reminding Lazarus of those extraordinary fits of rage to which Caiaphas occasionally gave way.

" But if thou wilt not of me, then will I curse and curse and curse the Nazarene, because He and His strange doctrines have taken thy heart away from me; and my soul shall be upon thee, and, maybe, my life, for I cannot live without thee."

Kind-hearted as Lazarus was, his heart ached for this impetuous girl.

" Thou talkest foolishness," he said to her, trying even to smile away her excitement. " There are many noble rulers who are more worthy of the hand of Caiaphas's daughter than am I, who am so wrapt up in this one great conception of salvation."

" And what are great rulers to me, if they be not Lazarus ? " she went on impatiently.

" Nay but, maiden, listen; Lazarus would be but a sorry husband for thee, with his heart given to the Christ. Maybe, one day the Christ will be condemned to death; for it is written that for the sins of the world He must yield His life; then they too will be condemned who loved Him, and thou and I, Rebekah, perchance would die a terrible death."

" What matter that, if I were with thee and thou wert with me ? " she asked passionately, her glow-

ing face upturned to heaven, the while she spoke,
a faint hope illuminating her brow.

For one moment Lazarus paused for words that
might repulse and yet not wound.

" Noble lady," he said, " farewell; thou art not
thyself to-night, and to listen to thee were wrong;
for thou thyself wouldst weep if thou didst know the
words which thou hast said. I thank thee for the
love thou offerest, but 't would be but sorry love I
gave thee, for my heart and soul are given to the
Nazarene; henceforth in life and death I belong to
Him, and of naught else can I think; and if I cause
thee pain, sweet lady, forgive me, for I would not;
but, if thou hast a sorrow for a while, turn thee to
the Nazarene who doth assuage all sorrow. So shall
we be united, thee and I, in one common heavenly
love, that will wipe out all earthly yearning."

But his words fell upon unresponsive ears. A
dull rage curdled in her heart that she, the proud
daughter of Caiaphas, should thus have lowered herself to sue for love, and sue in vain. Far-reaching
plans of hate and vengeance were begotten in her
raging soul. If Lazarus would have none of her,
then she would scheme and plot against the Nazarene, until her father should condemn Him to the
death He merited. She would brook no opposition.
No man or woman should live who should come between her love and her. Her heart had grievously
been wrung by Lazarus; she would wring the heart
of Lazarus in return, and let him feel the full weight
of her hand, the full strength of her hate.

" Farewell," she said coldly; then passionately,
" Go, heartless mummy, and may thy ill-spent love

come back to thee with usury. May eternal life not
fail thee, after all; and mayst thou yet reap all the
joys that thou hast spurned; but if, perchance, thy
dust shall fail to rise again in all the glory that thou
covetest, and if the delusive promises of the Nazarene
leave thee but one atom of remembering heart and
brain, recall to thyself that Rebekah offered thee one
certain thing for all this doubtful wealth, the love
and passion of the proudest, loveliest woman in all
Judæa.''

" Nay, but it is not doubtful," answered Lazarus;
" nor will I wait till I be risen to think of thee, for
every day my prayer shall rise for thee, that thou
too mayst love the Nazarene, and believe that He is
sent of God.''

" 'T will be a thankless, weary task," she retorted
scornfully, as he raised her white hand to his lips.
" Farewell, thou heartless, thou bewitched, misguided ruler.''

With head erect, she stood motionless in the
moonlight; and the heart within her seemed to die
when Lazarus swung open the gate and passed out
into the street. Like one in a dream she listened to
his departing footsteps till they died away. This
was the end, the bitter, bitter end; Lazarus would
never belong to her. That one short hour in the
fragrant, silent garden had brought him closer than
ever he would be again. On that sweet memory she
must feed till ages should have rolled away, while
swathed in grave clothes of finest embroidered linen,
the High Priest's daughter would be lying in her
granite sepulchre.

Who would bring ointments and rare spices ?

Would Lazarus sometimes come and see her grave and think of her?

But between now and then there was life, life; long years of life, with all its possibilities of happiness, with all its whisperings of love; there were thousands of days to dawn, and thousands of silent nights to come and go, and they must be lived—and lived without Lazarus. And Rebekah, the proud Rebekah, sank to the ground and bowed her head, and swayed backwards and forwards in her grief, till the cry of the watchman at the corner of the street reminded her of the hour. Then with a step weary as if with sudden age, and weeping passionately, she crept into the house; while the watchman cried out again to the sleeping world:

" Babylon is fallen, Babylon is fallen, and all the graven images of her gods He hath broken unto the ground. Babylon is fallen, Babylon is fallen! Fall-en."

CHAPTER V.

FOR a long while, almost from the moment when the Messiah had first entered his door, Lazarus had been ailing. His illness seemed to baffle his physician; for it yielded to none of the simple remedies he prescribed. Gradually, almost imperceptibly, Lazarus grew weaker, but, as day by day his body became more feeble, his faith seemed to strengthen. Never was man tended with more devotion, Martha seeing to his bodily wants, while Mary sat and read to him, or prayed with him in his moments of despondency. Moreover, during the first stages of his illness he had been daily cheered by the presence of the Nazarene; but this was before the Jews had grown so virulent in their persecutions. Who can imagine a more peaceful family circle than that little one assembled around Lazarus's sick-bed—the two devoted women, refreshed at intervals by the presence of the Saviour? Who can describe the purity of the spiritual and moral atmosphere the Christ diffused around Him? And Lazarus, lying on his couch by the window and gazing on the setting sun sinking behind the mountains and tinging the olive grove and fig trees of Bethany, would wonder why death held no horrors for him beyond the pain of separation; for that he would die of his illness he felt certain. It could not but be that the little band of believers should sometimes ask the question of their heart, why Jesus, who had snatched so many who were strangers to Him from the jaws of death, should daily see this man he loved convulsed with pain, saddened by the prospect of separation, and yet doing nothing to relieve him.

" He hath but to say the word," Martha would sometimes say; " yet He speaketh it not." Once, even, she cast herself at the feet of Jesus and en- treated Him to save her brother. But the words of the Lord were but scant comfort at such a moment:

" Thy brother shall rise again."

" I know," said Martha, with that querulous im- patience, that common-sense which so many good people, who are devoid of charm and gentleness of character, possess—" I know that he shall rise again in the resurrection at the last day."

Then, floating on the waves of unbelief, pardon- able perhaps at such a moment, rose the words: "I am the resurrection, and the life he that believeth on Me, though he were dead, yet shall he live." And at the words the sick man's face would light up with a trusting confidence and joy that made the by- standers to wonder. It was as if a little glory had alighted from the Christ on to the man who loved Him so.

Then, when Lazarus was alone with Martha, he would say: " Entreat not the Lord, for who know- eth what glory will yet be revealed ? His will be done on earth."

Thus the loving faith and trust of Lazarus never wavered.

Perhaps one of the hardest trials of all was the

scoffing and mocking of the Jews; for Joanna, the
wife of Chuza, who often came to see Lazarus and
to bring gifts of fruit, never failed, with the garrulity
of her class, to recount the gossip gathered in the
market-place, if not to the family of Lazarus, at least
to Rachel their handmaiden.

"What say the Jews of our master Lazarus?"
the latter inquired one day. "Do they say that the
Lord will restore him or that he shall die?"

"They say, ' Could not this Man, which opened
the eyes of the blind, have caused that even this man
should not have died?'"

"Yet he is not dead. Methinks the Lord doth it
to try the heart of my dear mistresses," said Rachel,
who shared her master's belief in the Messiah.

Once more it was evening, and Mary had escaped
from the heart-rending surroundings of the sick-
chamber while Lazarus slept; he was looking paler
and more wan than he had ever looked before. It
was about the hour that the Nazarene was wont to
return, for, while preaching to the multitudes He
seemed to find relief in the solitudes of the country,
and to like to shun the noise and tumult of great
cities. Sadly she stood on the terrace that looked
down upon that valley, in which she had once striven
to comfort her poor brother. How doubly pathetic
was that memory now! Loving and trusting as she
was, she could not help joining in the strange wonder of those days. Death, with its attendant terror,
had seemed so far while Christ was near. To be
sure, in the far distance, death was looming on them
all, for they knew the Lord must die; and it seemed
a certain thing that, after His death, the Jews would

seek to destroy all those who had believed in Him
and followed Him, or who testified of Him by word
or pen. Indeed, it had been common talk amongst
the disciples and the followers of Christ that they
were ready to die with Him, if needs be. Thomas,
who was ever wont to see the darker side of things,
had even stated openly that to be a follower of Jesus
meant certain death; and certainly the terrible end
of John the Baptist justified this assertion. Then,
out of these very thoughts, that rose from the
gloomy mists, not so much of doubt as of amazement, there came to Mary an illumined fancy, big
with consoling possibilities, glorious in its awakening
of faith. What if this approaching death were one
of mercy ? What if Lazarus were being taken from
the wrath to come—from terrible temptation, from
loss of faith, or from a violent and awful death ?

"The ways of the Lord are past finding out," she
murmured to herself, "but who shall gainsay
them ?"

Then, as the darkness began to fall, she fell to
speculating, as we have so often speculated in gazing
on the lifeless features of those we love—"What
then is death ? This strange, brief moment when
all is over ?"

"I will ask the Lord," she murmured to herself;
but even while she spoke she heard the gate of the
garden being shaken, and a voice calling her. A
quick pain shot through her heart. "The Lord
cometh not," she said to herself; for the Holy One
of Israel needed no opening of gates, and was wont
to appear to them suddenly and unexpectedly. But
it was night now, and, for fear of the Jews, it was

not the Christ's custom to journey after dark.   Her
heart, prone now to constant shocks and dreads, beat
violently; yet with no physical fear she approached
the gate.

"Who is without?"

"'T is I, Mary Magdalene.   I come with a message."

Mary unfastened the gate quickly.

"Welcome, all they that come in the name of the
Lord," she said.

"I will not detain thee but for a few moments,
for Martha doth not willingly see me here," said the
Magdalene sadly.

"This grief about our brother Lazarus hath softened much the heart of Martha," answered Mary
gently, taking the Magdalene's hand in hers; "but
why comest thou?"

The two women walked along the path together
till they reached the marble seat on which Lazarus
had given way to despair so dire.   It was so dark
now that neither could see the other's face.

"'T was James and John that bid me come, Mary,
to tell thee that Caiaphas sought this day to lay
hands upon the Lord."

A cry rose from the lips of Mary, but the Magdalene interrupted her.

"Nay, fear not, Mary; His hour hath not yet
come.   They have not taken Him."   Then she
went on: "'T was a wondrous sight, the brethren
told me.   The Lord stood in the porch of Solomon,
and great multitudes were assembled.   And on the
terrace of his dwelling stood Caiaphas, the High
Priest himself, and listened; and Nicodemus with

him; and all the Jews believed that Nicodemus (who, it is known, loveth the Lord) had persuaded him to hear His words.   He had just finished the words: ' Though ye believe not Me, believe the works; that ye may know and believe that the Father is in Me and I in Him.'   Then, as He spoke these words, the multitude raised a mighty voice; 't was, some said, as if it thundered: ' Works—what works ?   Heal Lazarus, and we will believe.' "

" 'T is verily a marvel," murmured Mary.

But the Magdalene went on: " Then, when the crowd grew even more angry and came nearer, as though to strike the Christ, the wily Caiaphas did choose that moment to send forth soldiers; and a centurion rushed into their midst followed by ten soldiers. ' Seize ye Him,' he cried; and all the multitude with one voice shouted, 'Seize Him, crucify Him, for He blasphemeth '; and every now and then a voice cried out, ' Show us Lazarus whole,' and all the time Caiaphas stood and watched to see them seize the Lord.   The soldiers were upon Him. James doth tell me that the Roman centurion's brown hand did rest upon the white garments of the Nazarene, when suddenly he fell back as one that had seen a vision, and, while he stood with gaping mouth and wide-open eyes, the Nazarene did disappear."

" And now where is he ? " asked Mary, after a brief pause.

" He hath gone again to Jordan, and will tarry many days," rejoined the Magdalene.

" Then Lazarus my brother will die," wailed Mary, and, giving way at last to the human grief,

which, in the absence of the Lord, had gained the
mastery, laid her head on the Magdalene's shoulder,
while every now and then she moaned: "Lazarus
will die and my Lord is away."

And the Magdalene, whose deep grief none but
the mother of Jesus had divined, joined her tears
with those of the other Mary, and cried as though
her heart would break; yet, to give courage to herself, she sobbed: "He will live again, he will live
again."

At that moment the door of the house was opened,
and a woman came out of the porch and looked
around; then a querulous voice exclaimed: "Mary,
Mary, where art thou?"

Mary rose to answer her sister's call, but the
Magdalene made as if she would depart.

"Nay, stay; thou wouldst see Lazarus," said the
kindly Mary, "and thou hast walked many miles;
thou must rest and be refreshed."

But the Magdalene answered: "Nay, nay; anger
not Martha, for she hath much to trouble her."

They turned their footsteps towards the house,
and Martha came to meet them.

"This is a fitting time, forsooth, when thy brother
lieth sick, to wander in the garden. Thinkest thou
I have naught to do that thou leavest me to serve
alone?"

Mary had scarce murmured a meek, "Forgive me,
sister," when the eyes of Martha fell on the Magdalene.

"What dost thou here?" she asked sternly; for
she had been brought up in the sternest principles
of morality, and with all the Pharisaical hatred of

acknowledged sinners. She could not overcome her dislike of the Magdalene, although she had tried to modify it of late.

Ever striving to keep peace, Mary said gently to her sister: " She hath brought a message from James and John, to bid us not tarry for the Lord, for that He cometh not; and she is weary and footsore with the long journey."

The Jewish hospitality filled the gap of loving friendliness in Martha's heart, and she bid her welcome.

" Woe is me, that the Lord still tarrieth," she said, " for our brother is very weak, and but now he sent me forth to see whether the Master cometh. ' I cannot die without the Lord,' he said."

" Methought I would take the Magdalene to him, if so be he is awake," said Mary presently, glancing nervously at her sister, as though fearing she would not allow this visit. " Peradventure the night will seem shorter if the Magdalene tell him what hath happened to our Lord."

Martha's face hardened, but she said neither yea nor nay. " The night is far spent, the day is at hand," she murmured enigmatically as she re-entered the house. Mary conducted the Magdalene across the tesselated pavement to the gorgeous room, in which was a couch hung with costly silks. With his face turned in patient watchfulness towards the door lay the dying Lazarus, longing for his Lord.

But the sight of his poor thin face, the eager expectation in his eyes, that died out when the two women entered, was too much for the Magdalene, who had loved him so truly and so long; ever since,

as a proud young ruler (proud in the rectitude of his
immaculate life), he had passed her with disdain as
she sat at the Virgin's Well and chatted with the
passer-by. Wounded and stung by his indifference
as she had been, it had yet been the first means of
leading her to more serious thoughts. Since then her
heart had filled with admiration and respect for this
rich young ruler, who could resist the charms of—
what she knew herself to be—the most beautiful
woman in Jerusalem, and one who for several years
had been courted by all the greatest men. Then,
from that admiration, had grown an adoring, wor-
shipping, respectful love, the shadow, as it were, of
the purified love she now felt for the Saviour; and
when, united by the common bond of devotion, they
had met at the Lord's feet, she had been content to
think that in religious thought, at least, they were
as one. But Lazarus had known nothing of what
she thought.

It was as if suddenly, with approaching death, a
far-seeing second sight had come to him; as if scales
had fallen from his eyes, and it were given to him to
read the hidden thoughts of men. He said pityingly
to the Magdalene, who had thrown herself on her
knees beside his couch, and was shedding silent tears
behind her hands: " Weep not for me, Mary, weep
not for me." Then, while her frame shook with
suppressed sobs, he laid his wasted fingers with reverence on her golden tresses, and stroking them tenderly, murmured: " Who knoweth yet what the
Lord will do ? " Then, when human strength gave
way, spiritual weakness seemed to strengthen.
" Would I could see the Lord ! Would I could see

the Lord! My God, my God, hast Thou forsaken me ?"

This was indeed a bitter time of trial and temptation to these poor women and to the dying Lazarus. To the dying man it seemed as if demons of despair were dancing around his bed, as if Satan himself grinned at him and hissed: "Where is now thy God ? Where is now thy God ?"

Once he shrieked out, as though in answer to their gibings: "Yet I will still believe, I will believe. Depart from me in the name of Jesus. Yea, though I die, I know that my Redeemer liveth and that He will take me unto Himself."

And angels unseen and unheard, except of Lazarus, echoed in glorious cadence of softest heavenly music: " I know that my Redeemer liveth."

But the two poor women were torn with grief. They felt now that the Lord durst not appear in person; but they knew that, if He were to speak the word, their brother would live. It needed all their teaching of many months to believe still, in the face of this seeming desertion by the Christ. They had sent messenger after messenger on horseback to Him, to where He sojourned near the river Jordan; but all He had answered them had been: " This sickness is not unto death, but for the glory of God, that the Son of God might be glorified thereby."

His words had given them a little hope, but when day succeeded day and Lazarus grew weaker, each hour seeming to make his breath more laboured, it seemed as if the very words of the Lord Himself for once lacked truth. The " If " of life entered the soul of Martha.

If, after all, this man were an Antichrist, a deluder of souls, a fanatic who but fancied Himself the
Son of God; a semi-illuminated prophet who understood the Truth, who knew the worth of righteousness but who had no power from above ?   Then
again, if this doubting were but a temptation of the
Evil One ?   Or again, what if God were trying and
wringing the heart of Christ, as when He had allowed
Him to be tempted by the devil on the Mount?   What
if Christ's prayers to His Father were unanswered ?
What if He too were enveloped in gloom and
loneliness ?   Oh, what a mystery was life and death!
And into the core of Martha's soul there crept once
more the question, Why had this world been created?
Why had each creature been born into a world of
mystery and darkness ?   But, all the time, the two
Marys clasped the hands of Lazarus, as if by pressing they could instil their courage into his deaden-
ing veins.   What if, at the last moment, he were
wrested from them eternally by a flickering out of
faith ?

No, to the end, be the future what it might, if the
sisters were to live on to face disillusion and a crushing out of all their hopes till the fatal knock of
death should be heard against the window, the flame
of faith must be kept alive.

The silent chamber, dimly lighted by the Roman
lamp, such as had now become the fashion in Judæa,
grew even stiller and more gloomy, the three women's figures more immobile, the expectant eyes of
Lazarus more dim; his breath came and went more
painfully, and his body seemed torn by a spirit that
was struggling to escape.   Only the faint sound of

croaking frogs and the far-off barking of dogs disturbed the silence.

Presently Lazarus murmured faintly: " Sing to me, Mary." It was as if he had bridged over years of suffering and trial and gone back to the time when he was a little child and Mary had sung him off to sleep.

Steadying her voice and wiping away her tears, Mary raised her voice on the silent night, singing to a lovely Hebrew chant the words of the Psalmist David—words that seemed written in answer to their doubtings: " The Lord is righteous in all His ways, and holy in all His works. The Lord is nigh unto all them that call upon Him. He will fulfil the desire of them that fear Him: He also will bear them up and will save them. The Lord preserveth all them that love Him: Refuge failed me; I cried unto Thee, O Lord; I said Thou art my refuge and my portion in the land of the living. Attend unto my cry, for I am brought very low. Bring my soul out of prison, that I may praise Thy name."

Then, when her voice faltered, the Magdalene took up the strain and sang: "Yea, though I walk through the valley of the shadow of death, I will fear no evil, for Thou art with me; Thy rod and Thy staff, they comfort me."

As the words died away on her quivering lips, the expiring eyes of Lazarus met hers with a smile of deepest love and gratitude. Then the jaw relaxed, the hand that lay in Mary's twitched convulsively, and the last hope of those trusting women died when Lazarus fell back dead. And into their souls there crept a dull stagnation; something seemed to die within them, or to flee away with the spirit of their brother. The living flame of faith flickered lower and lower, and over the prostrate body of Lazarus bent but soulless images that could only weep and weep and weep.

CHAPTER VI.

THE morning after Lazarus's death, Jerusalem's streets were thronged with people hurrying to and fro. Groups of Pharisees, looking joyous and triumphant, formed themselves in the market place and outside the Temple and the principal buildings, and occasionally a Sadducee would stop and make some derisive observation, to which the others would respond with shouts of laughter.

Nor were the higher authorities less preoccupied; now and then, pressing his horse forward till it pranced almost on to the heads of the crowd, rode a centurion with a message from Pontius Pilate or from Caiaphas, summoning a chief ruler or a leading priest, as the case might be. Occasionally some great rabbi would arrest his course to ask news of him; and the soldier would either shake his head, or laughingly make some such answer as the following: " His own friend hath done for him. Lazarus is dead; if the Nazarene could have saved any one He would have saved His beloved Lazarus. But Lazarus is dead, and though the two women, Martha and Mary, sent to Him many times, He would not go."

" I hear," said another, " that He even said to their messengers that Lazarus would not die: ' This sickness is not unto death, but for the glory of God,

that the Son of God might be glorified thereby.'
How is He glorified ?"

"No, Jesus hath failed," joined in another. "I
own that, for a time, I almost believed in Him myself; His presence is certainly a most majestic one,
and He is some great prophet without a doubt.
But Lazarus's death proveth that He is not the Son
of God; still, we cannot forget His miracles, for
already twenty-eight have been recorded of Him.
We cannot, because one man hath died, ignore the
marvellous feeding of the five thousand, the restoring
of the withered hand, and the healing of the lunatic
child."

"Ah," answered another, "thou, Nicodemus,
wert ever a believer in the supernatural; I hear that
thou hast even visited this Jesus by night, thereby
putting thy life in danger, for, if Caiaphas should
suspect treachery in thee, a ruler of the Synagogue,
before nightfall thou wouldst be in Barabbas's place,
or chained beside him. Or, wouldst thou escape by
saying that thou wast in love with Martha or with
Mary ?"

Said another voice, scornfully: "If so, Nicodemus, thou hast but a sorry chance, for both
women have, I hear, devoted themselves to the
service of this Jesus; and naught but a marriage
such as, it is rumoured, was his mother's, will com-
mend itself to them. I fancy thou wouldst not care
to be a second Joseph."

But Nicodemus made no answer. His eyes, uplifted towards the hills above Jerusalem, shone with a
light of rapture and devotion, as though he strove to
pierce the skies and gain enlightenment in its deep

blue expanse. He heeded not the mocking words around him. He was lost, as one in a dream. He had just come from the presence of the Nazarene. There still rang in his ears the words: " I am the light of the world. He that followeth Me shall not walk in darkness, but shall have the light of life."

Oh, for light, more light, to understand! It had all seemed so clear to Nicodemus. He had followed, disguised, it is true, Jesus of Nazareth, ever since the first miracle of the turning of water into wine. He had sought Him out at night, either in the dark silence of the shore of Galilee or in the house of Lazarus at Bethany. He had tried, oh, so hard, to believe. In bewildered wonder he had crept to Jesus' feet and had poured out his doubts, his endless questionings and earthly arguments, that yet had taught him nothing.

" Rabbi," he had said, " we know that Thou art a teacher come from God, for no man can do these miracles that Thou doest, except God be with him; yet, if Thou art the Son of God, why art Thou here in the guise of a poor carpenter ? Why doth not the very earth quake beneath Thy feet in obeisance to its Creator ? Why is it not filled with angels ministering to Thee ? Why, oh, why, cannot I, who have read much and studied deeply, understand ? "

Oh, how well he remembered those words, uttered in reply, in solemn, tender pity, for man's want of faith, for his inability of accepting that which he cannot prove by human argument, or by nature's law. It was as though the voice that had answered were full of tears.

" Verily, I say unto thee, except a man be born
again, he cannot see the kingdom of God." And,
despairing at his impotence to understand, Nicodemus, wrathful at himself, at his own helplessness,
impatient almost with the Saviour for speaking to
him in parables; bitterly, cynically, yet half grasp-
ing Jesus' meaning, had exclaimed: " How can a
man be born when he is old; can he enter the second
time into his mother's womb and be born ? "

Then the Divine voice had rung out in explana-
tion of His marvellous saying; had shown him that
it was no natural birth that He had meant; for all
that, a birth not less miraculous, a birth of water and
of the spirit, without which no man could enter into
the kingdom of God.

Then, wondering and despairing still, mad with
his own blindness, as a blinded animal would dash
its head against the wall in its impotence and want
of comprehension at what had happened to it, so
Nicodemus had wailed: " Lord, Lord, how can
these things be ? I cannot grasp them; they are
too wonderful for me."

At which, with a touch almost of irony, the appealing voice had answered: " Art thou a master of
Israel and knowest not these things ? "

" A master of Israel "; yes, he, Nicodemus, had
set himself up as a teacher and ruler of Israel, he
who could not even understand the teaching of this
carpenter. How poor, how mean he had felt in the
presence of this Man, clad in coarse attire and standing barefoot on the shore of the lake ! No moon
had illumined the dark night around, and the gloom
had seemed to Nicodemus an apt setting to the

blindness of his brain and soul. Yet around the
Lord there had seemed to hover a faint shimmer as
of glory emanating from His presence. With infinite tenderness and pity He had gazed on the Jewish
rabbi, so mortified and abased; then, sadly and with
deep persuasiveness, the voice had risen once more
out of the darkness and rolled in waves across the
still water of the lake, like strains of floating music:

" If I have told you earthly things and ye believed
not, how shall ye believe if I tell you of heavenly
things ? "

Then, gazing full at Nicodemus, Jesus had pronounced words which neither he nor any other man,
having once heard them, could forget: " God so
loved the world, that He gave His only begotten
Son, that whosoever believeth in Him should not
perish, but have everlasting life. God sent not his
Son into the world to condemn the world; but that
the world through Him might be saved. He
that believeth not is condemned already, because
he hath not believed in the name of the only begotten Son of God. And this is the condemnation,
that light is come into the world, and men loved
darkness rather than light, because their deeds were
evil. For every one that doeth evil hateth the light,
neither cometh to the light, lest his deeds should be
reproved. But he that doeth truth cometh to the
light, that his deeds may be made manifest, that
they are wrought in God."

Each word had stung Nicodemus's soul as with a
lash; he, too, had loved darkness. Fear, physical
fear of derision first and of death afterwards had kept
him from openly confessing his belief in Jesus as the

Son of God. He, too, was one of those who had feared the light, who had stolen stealthily by night to glean salvation from the teachings of the Nazarene. What a coward he had felt himself, how he had despised himself, and yet he had muttered to himself, when he had left the Lord: " If, after all, His teachings are but the outpourings of a madman or a wilful deluder—if, after all, He is a blasphemer, calling Himself the Son of God, and being but a poor human being like myself, where, then, would the honoured Nicodemus, the mighty ruler, be, if he believed Him? Deprived of power in this world, scoffed at and derided, perchance doomed even to a shameful death. That would be his portion in this world; in the next to be condemned by the real God for having believed and acted on the ravings of a blasphemer."

So, in the darkness, stumbling at every step of the homeward way, sorrowful and puzzled at the words of salvation that still rang in his ears, Nicodemus, the great ruler, had taken the road outside Jerusalem and reached his home by one of the terraces that lay beyond the walls, lest his attendants should hear him enter at that hour of the night. Then, once within his own walls, he had cast himself on his bed, seeking in vain for sleep, and starting up at almost every watch of the night, to call out in mental agony, " Truly, truly, this is the Son of God."

And now just when the germs of belief seemed about to start into being in his heart, just when miracle after miracle was striking terror to his soul, in the intensity of its wonder, and just when the words of the Nazarene, with their sad persuasiveness

and their clear, truthful intonations, were beginning
to unfold to his heart what can only be realised
through revelation, but never evolved from man's
philosophy; just when his flitting thoughts and
wavering heart seemed to be catching hold of truths
that had seemed impossibilities before; just at this
moment Jesus appeared to have lost the power of
working miracles.   How easy it would have been,
argued this human brain, to prove to the world that
He was all that He professed Himself!   One little
word, even from a distance, if all was true that the
disciples said, would have sufficed.   The Jews themselves were looking for this miracle, the chief priests
dreading it.   With the death of Lazarus seemed
buried the hopes of all the believing world.   His
resurrection would be the death warrant of Jesus
of Nazareth.   How often already had Caiaphas
foretold His death, either through the gift of prophecy, or because, as High Priest, he knew that he
himself would bring about the doom of Him who
drew so many to Him!   There was no room for
Caiaphas, no room for any High Priest, either if
Jesus were the Son of God, or, if not being so, the
people believed in and followed Him as such.

Already the attitude of the Jewish people was becoming dangerous.   They were divided into many
parties, some calling Jesus a prophet, others persuaded that He was the Christ indeed, and selling
all they had to follow Him.   Already some of the
leading rabbis had issued orders that He was to be
captured and brought before them; but the order
had been but a half-hearted one, and the soldiers
who were sent to execute it knew the spirit of the

populace so well, that they feared them more, if they should lay hands on Christ, than the rulers, if they should fail to take Him. Indeed, although they did not dare speak openly about it, yet it was a matter of great wonder that the preaching of Jesus was allowed.

" So He speaketh boldly, and they say nothing to Him. Do the rulers know indeed that this is the very Christ ? " It was rumoured in Jerusalem that both Caiaphas and Pontius Pilate believed in the Nazarene, both as the Son of God and as the King of the Jews; or, at all events, that they did not dare deny it. It became a matter of superstition amongst the poorer people that he who should first lay hands on Him would die a terrible death. This fear communicated itself to the very soldiers who were sent out to fetch Him. To the question: " Why have ye not brought Him ? " they would answer: " Never man spake like this Man." Yet all the Pharisees durst answer was: " Are ye also deceived ? Have any of the rulers of the Pharisees believed on Him ? but this people, who knoweth not the law, are cursed, and they alone believe."

CHAPTER VII.

NO wonder, then, that a party shrinking beneath the terror lest power and affluence should depart from them for ever, should rejoice at the turn events had taken. The expected miracle of Lazarus's resurrection had not occurred. The Nazarene's want of sympathy, or, perhaps, His fear of the threats to take His life, which was believed to be the cause of His not returning to the house of the sorrowing sisters, had changed for the moment the current of popular favour. Several lukewarm believers fell back into the ranks of the sceptical, while others, like Nicodemus, struggled hard to believe that there was some good reason for Jesus' apparent indifference to the grief of those He was known to have loved so well. Of course, the base attributed it to the most cowardly of all motives, fear. It seemed clear enough to Caiaphas that Jesus, knowing that the miracle was expected, would be conscious that the home of Mary and Martha would be a likely place for His capture. This was what Caiaphas tried to persuade himself to believe; yet it did not coincide with the fearless attitude of the Christ till then, nor with the fearlessness of His words. In any case, this was an opportunity which, as a politician and a ruler of men, he must take advantage of. It was such an one as, perhaps, he would never

have again. Now the Nazarene must be put an end
to; His seditious preaching hushed for ever; His
bold denouncing of the Pharisees and the scribes
avenged. But it would be a difficult task, he knew.
Pontius Pilate was under the influence of his wife,
who, it was known, favoured the belief in the Nazarene, if not as the Son of God, at least as a great
prophet and a good man come from God. Pilate
was difficult to approach upon the subject. Then
about Nicodemus, one of the most powerful rulers
of the Synagogue, there were strange rumours.
How could he, Caiaphas, get at him by stealth?
To make use of Nicodemus himself, nay more, to
approach the Nazarene, unseen, and to hear His
blasphemous words, and out of His own mouth con-
vict Him, making Nicodemus a party to the destruction of this Man who dared to set Himself up in
defiance of the High Priest; oh, it would be a mas-
ter-stroke, one that his base, intriguing soul would
glory in. It whetted his thirst for vengeance, while,
at the same time, it intoxicated him to foresee that
proud soul abased, that majestic presence on the
cross, blood flowing from the fair side, and all the
humiliations of an ignominious death heaped on the
shoulders of the Man whom even Caiaphas, deep
down in his heart, admired, at the same time that he
feared Him as a supernatural being. For had He
not held His own, unsupported either by wealth or
position, by party or by followers? How could
Caiaphas have played that part? No, the wily High
Priest knew full well that his own position was main-
tained only by his arrogance, and that it was by the
fear of himself he had built up his successes on the

ignorance of a down-trodden race; that, were he but
a lowly carpenter, with all the world's powers and
dignitaries against him; did he but loosen the reins
of despotism for one moment, or, by preaching what
he knew to be the truth, open out the path of liberty
—that of the spirit, as opposed to the letter of the
law,—he, Caiaphas, before whom all men now bowed,
would be hurled both morally and physically from
his high place and become of no account.   He knew
he would be powerless to emulate the Nazarene he
affected to despise, the carpenter who conquered
souls by His sublime meekness, His unshrinking
truth, and His awful purity.

Yes, side by side with his dread lest the Jewish
people should escape him; side by side with his
hatred of the Nazarene, and fear of the possible
overthrow of his power and place, were a sullen jealousy and an envious rage, that one by birth so meek
and lowly, should be so much the greater man than
was he, Caiaphas.   How he hated, Pontius Pilate,
too, and Claudia, his proud, domineering wife!
How, of late, she had set him at defiance!   What a
slap in the face it would be to Pontius Pilate should
he be forced to condemn the Nazarene to death!

Alone in his chamber, this priest, who had been
ordained to bring true religion and peace to the
Jewish people, revolved in his mind how he should
destroy this Man who stood, in the grandeur of His
simplicity, between him and power.   To acknowledge Him as the Son of God were to destroy
the power, not only of Caiaphas, but of all the high
priests and Pharisees forever.   For one moment
(for Caiaphas was not without intelligence enough to

look at both sides of the question), he had asked
himself what would be the result should he himself
recognise the power of the Christ and join the ranks
of the believers.   No man versed in the prophets,
as Caiaphas was, could well disbelieve that, even if
the Nazarene were not the Christ Himself, He was
an emissary from heaven whose coming had been
predicted.   Absently, as if to persuade himself for
one moment, Caiaphas turned the pages of the book
of the prophets that lay close to his elbow.   He
almost started at the words that seemed to give the
answer to his unuttered question, for he was a superstitious man: " Who hath believed our report ? and
to whom is the arm of the Lord revealed ?   He is
despised and rejected of men: a man of sorrows and
acquainted with grief: and we hid as it were our
faces from Him ; He was despised, and we esteemed
Him not."

Caiaphas with breathless interest re-read the words
He had so often read before.   The stillness outside,
the gloom within, the strange similitude of the picture drawn by Isaiah to the person of the Nazarene;
for one brief moment all this impressed the man,
who was shrewd enough to understand the prophecy,
yet not to recognise the Saviour it foretold.   Chapter after chapter he devoured in the hope that he
would, at last, light on some passage that would
justify the condemnation of the Man who called
Himself the Christ, and was not; but the prophet
was against him.   Again his eyes fell on the book,
and they lighted on the words: " Seek ye the Lord,
while He may be found, call ye upon Him while He
is near."

Caiaphas pushed the book impatiently away from him, and paced the room with rapid strides. The long sleeves of his robe waved backwards and for- wards in the air, and now and then he clutched at them impatiently, as if their very stirring added to his irritation. What if, after all, this Nazarene were the Christ, and he, Caiaphas, should condemn Him to a felon's death? Surely no eternal punishment would be great enough for such an one; and for an instant the great Caiaphas trembled. Then he crossed the room and leaned on the window-sill, and looked out on the silent night. All was dark and still; a few stars only gave just sufficient light to bring out in vague relief the outline of the white walls of the houses of Jerusalem.

Presently he started at steps he heard that passed beneath the window. He leaned forward, and in clear tones called out: "Watchman, what of the night?" but his voice had not carried far enough, and instead of making answer, the watchman, mind- ful, perhaps, that he was outside the house of Caia- phas the High Priest, sang out in a clear, deep voice: "Break forth into joy, sing together, ye waste places of Jerusalem, for the Lord hath comforted His people, He hath redeemed Jerusalem."

Caiaphas drew back. "He too," he muttered to himself. "Surely the world hath gone mad about this one Man; but it shall not be said that Caiaphas was thus led hither and thither, swayed by the voice of an ignorant people, lashed into fanaticism by the words of an impostor, who tries to cajole them by honeyed words and feigned humility. No, Caiaphas the High Priest shall still retain his power, and if this

Man is after all the Christ "—here he broke off into a horrible, unmirthful laugh—" if Caiaphas is wrong then let His blood be upon me and upon my house, and let me be damned for ever and ever. Yes, I would barter even my soul, rather than let that proud Claudia and that self-sufficient, prating Roman fool, the Procurator, triumph over me. I have borne enough; the Nazarene shall die, and that speedily."

And, even ere these words had passed his lips, a flash of summer lightning illumed the room, and, to the overwrought brain of Caiaphas, it seemed as if, within that light, the figure of the Nazarene, in dazzling white, appeared to him; and the sad, speaking eyes were turned on him reproachfully, and a voice, whose music haunted him till his dying day, in gentle accents murmured: " Why go ye about to kill Me ?"

CHAPTER VIII.

PALE dawn stole in at the window of Rebekah's chamber and found her sleeping still a restless, feverish sleep that had overtaken her towards early morn. The beautiful white arms lay motionless outside the coverlet. The long lashes touched lovingly her pale sad cheeks, as though they would caress them.

Silently her maidens entered and, with noiseless footsteps, moved about the room. Then one sat by her side and watched her while day crept nearer and nearer, big with the tidings that would so distress her.

" 'T will be a sorrowful awakening," said one to her companion.

" Methinks I have no strength to tell her the sad news," rejoined the other. But even their light whispering had stirred the girl, whose whole being was indeed awake and alive with uncertainty and with dread.

She started up from her couch into a sitting posture.

" What news have ye of Lazarus ? " she cried, her voice framing the words her brain, as yet, had scarce conceived.

The maidens looked from one to the other and answered not; so, with a furious look and a voice of thunder, Rebekah burst out with: " Speak, I command ye. Have ye then not sent a messenger to Bethany ? "

" Lazarus is dead," said one.

" He died ere dawn," the other added.

" Oh, oh ! " 'T was a groan and shriek and bitter, bitter cry that rent her very heart; and the proud Rebekah buried her face in the pillow and moaned and sobbed continuously, " Lazarus, Lazarus ! "

So this was the end; the end of her fond delusion that, while Lazarus lived, by the power of her strong will he might still be hers. The end of life, the end of vengeance. All her plotting and scheming had come to naught. Death had baffled her. Lazarus had escaped her. Oh, 't was the Nazarene who had wrenched him from her by some trickery.

" For hatred of my father hath He done this thing," she cried. " But, perchance he is not dead, and they have stolen him away, that they might seem to bring him back to life. He is not dead, he is not dead," she moaned in frenzied accents.

" Yea, the messenger did see him on his couch, and many stood around and wept," said one; " but thou shouldst not mourn, for this man loved thee not; he was altogether gone mad after this Nazarene."

" He loved me not, but I loved him," replied Rebekah; "and now I need do naught but die, for wherefore shall I live."

" There are other rulers, fairer still," the maidens answered her, " and wealthier, and who do love thee."

" I tell thee I cannot live if Lazarus be dead," she cried, and beat her silken cushions in her despair.

" They say the Nazarene will yet bring him back to life," said one maiden, at her wits' ends how to comfort the impetuous Rebekah in her grief.

Rebekah raised her head and gazed at them with eyes all red and swollen beyond recognition.

" What say ye ? "

" They say the Nazarene hath the power even to raise the dead," replied the maiden ; " and that He will raise up Lazarus, for He greatly loved him."

" Thinkest thou this ? " said Rebekah, sitting up, for the moment oblivious of her grief.

" We cannot tell, but 't is so rumoured among the multitude."

" If Lazarus be raised, then I, too, will believe," she muttered ; "but I fear me it is not to be. No, death hath been stronger than Caiaphas's daughter. There are yet some things I understand not, though for a woman I have learned overmuch ; one is, why Lazarus loved me not, the other, what is death ? If the Nazarene doth conquer death, then surely is He, as 't is said He claimeth to be, the Son of God. But I must know for sure that Lazarus is dead ; for in these days none speaketh the truth, and ye do but give me rumours, that themselves were gossip retailed from mouth to mouth by gabbling servants ; I would see, therefore, for myself whether Lazarus is dead. Bring hither my cloak, and habit me, that I may go to Bethany ; order my mule to be in readiness at once."

It was indeed an unexpected guest that forced her way through the gates into the very room where Lazarus lay, oblivious of the presence of the inquiring crowd. Various nationalities and creeds were represented there, haters of the Pharisees and open enemies of her father. She cast herself on her knees beside the bed and seized his hand in hers.

"Dead! dead!" she wailed, "verily and truly dead. 'T is no jugglery nor fooling. He is dead indeed." Then excitedly she turned to the assembled crowd. "Where, then, is this wonder-working Nazarene, this performer of miracles?" she asked scornfully, trying to disguise by haughty and disdainful tone the burning excitement she felt within. "Why is He not here? Where is the friendship that hath been spoken of so much, if He cometh not to the sick-bed of His friend? Go fetch Him, one of you. Tell Him that Caiaphas's daughter doth command His presence, and would witness a miracle." She talked excitedly, almost madly; but none stirred, only looked at her in wonder. "Can ye not move?" she shrieked. "Will none obey my bidding? Or do ye know that He, too, cannot conquer death? That He is no Christ, but only some poor, juggling carpenter, that doth bewitch the people?" Then Martha, fearing a disturbance, went up to the girl and drew her gently away.

"Noble maiden," she said softly, "didst thou then love Lazarus, that his death doth grieve thee so?"

All Rebekah's haughtiness returned at the directness of this question.

"Who art thou, woman, that dost presume to question me? What is it to thee whether I loved Lazarus or not?"

"To me 't is very much," said Martha, with a gentle impressiveness that was not without effect upon Rebekah; "for all who loved Lazarus I love."

For one instant, the proud daughter of Caiaphas felt constrained to open her heart to this gentle woman, who spoke and looked like Lazarus.

" Yea, I did love Lazarus, yet he loved not me," she answered scornfully; " but I would have him live, because I cannot live if he be dead."

" He will rise again," said Martha.

" What meanest thou ? " inquired Rebekah; " that he will rise now, or in the Judgment Day ? If thou sayest now, I could understand thee; but hereafter—that is too far off a thing for my vain mind to grasp."

" Methinks the Lord will raise him yet," said Martha, musingly; " but whether now, or at the Resurrection Day, my brother will rise again."

" But canst not send for this Nazarene ? Ye speak of all His power and love, and yet, when death doth carry off your brother, ye do stand gaping and wailing and doing nothing."

She stamped her foot impatiently. " Will none stir ? " she cried again.

" Peace, hush thee, maiden," answered Martha, in a tone half gentle, half authoritative. " We have sent many times, and He cometh not. We sent when he was sick, and now we have sent to tell Him he is dead, and, if He cometh not, 't is that He hath good reason or His hour is not yet come."

A look of mingled frenzy and despair stole over the features of Rebekah.

" He is afraid to come," she said with scorn; " for He knoweth that He cannot raise the dead."

Then, overcome with excitement and fatigue, the proud soul unbent, and casting herself by the bed,

whereon lay Lazarus, she sobbed as though her heart
would break.

" We will leave her to weep awhile," said Martha,
making a sign to all in the room to leave. Then the
girl, whose prayers till now had been but empty
words, poured out her aching heart to the dead
body of the man she loved.

" O Lazarus, wherefore didst thou leave me
thus ? Where is now thy scorn and pride ? Wilt
thou still have none of me, even in death ? for in
the silent tomb I would lie near thee, if thou wouldst,
so I might be with thee.   O Lazarus, speak; tell me
where I shall meet with thee again; whether there is
Eternal Life, and what it is; and how to find thy
God, if God there is."

Long the maiden mourned and wept.   At last, a
gentle voice behind her murmured: " He will surely
rise again."

Rebekah lifted her head.   " Ye do all cry that he
will rise again.   Yet He cometh not who, ye say,
can cause it.   What manner of friend is this who
hasteneth not to raise, if raise He can ? "

Then, drawing her cloak around her and casting
one long, despairing look at the dead body of Lazarus, she strode from the house, her maidens following; and as she passed between the throng they all
fell back and did obeisance to the daughter of the
dreaded Caiaphas.

CHAPTER IX.

THE dawning of a Syrian day was stealing over Jerusalem; dark clouds hung in thick, woolly masses across the sky. The corn, still green by daylight, stood colourless and grey, awaiting the glorious revivifying ardour of the sun. Only a pale golden haze over the hills beyond—approaching like the feet of swift messengers of glad tidings, or of angels who have been present in the night—gave promise of day; as yet, it was but a watch-signal of the coming morning. The air was still cool, the birds had not yet begun to twitter in their nests; there was a hush, as though nature were listening to the farewell of night, or, awe-struck, to the commands of God, ere this day dawned that was teeming with such import to individuals, to nations, to the whole world, though it knew it not. It was as if the word of God were being uttered behind the dark veil of those massive clouds: " Arise, shine, for thy Light is come and the glory of the Lord is risen upon thee."

But as yet all was darkness still, and the city of Jerusalem slept, wrapt in that stagnation of soul and body, that apathy in which it had been enveloped for so many years; that folding of the hands to sleep, that paralysis of the brain, that had shut out from the world (as the blindness of the eye shutteth out God's light) the many revelations that had been made to it, and kept back the knowledge of the extraordinary events that from time to time had there occurred.

If a God were to be born to us to-day, and to live and die amongst us, how many would know Him for a God ? So the earth slept while Jesus trod it, as it slept before His advent, as it has slept often since, forgetful that salvation was walking along the highway, powerless to cry out, " Lord, save me." And all the while, tear-worn, dusty, and travel-stained, the Eternal One was passing by and on, through the gates of death, and back within the portals of eternity.

But day was now stealing across the sky, ripping up right and left, backwards and forwards, the dark clouds, seaming the heavens with shafts of light, slashing each cloud with radiancy, unfolding one by one the glories of morning; till at last the sun, like a golden ball hurled on earth by a boisterous god, or leaping like a giant upon the world, burst forth with light and warmth, a messenger, though that world knew it not.

" Lift up thine eyes, look round about and see," it said; but the world slept, and Jerusalem slept, oblivious that that day the God of Eternity would weep.

While flushing day crept quickly across the sky, a woman left the house of Lazarus to take the road from Bethany to Jerusalem. Weary as she was with a night of watching, the cool air seemed to revive her scorching eyelids, yet she hesitated. Outside her house she cast her eyes across the glorious horizon, half doubtful; while from within could be heard the faint murmur of wailing from many voices.

" The harvest is past, the summer is ended, and we are not saved. Woe is me for my hurt! My wound is grievous: but I said, Truly this is a grief, and I must bear it. There is none to stretch forth my tent any more, and to set up my curtains."

The voices wailed alternately; then suddenly a woman's tuneful voice sang out: " Righteous art Thou, O Lord, when I plead with Thee. How long shall we mourn ? Yea, blessed is the man that trusteth in the Lord and whose hope the Lord is."

" Mary, Mary!" The voice was low but stern. The song ceased and a beautiful woman with long, flowing hair, which, in the sun, had a reddish tinge turned suddenly; then rose from her knees and came in meek obedience to her sister.

" Wilt thou not then come with me to entreat the Lord ? Yet thou sayest that He can restore him even now. If we wait till they have laid him in the grave it will be too late." The tone of the elder woman was almost hasty.

" My sister, I need not to leave his side to entreat my Lord. Hath not Nicodemus taken Him the news of our brother's sickness ? Had He wished to restore him, He could have done so from Jerusalem. The city is but fifteen furlongs off. He would have sent over one of the twelve with the message of life, or He would have willed him to live from a distance and he would have lived. Lazarus is dead, but were he living, he would not wish to live if his Lord did not so will it; and, except to our mortal eyes, he is not dead, for thou knowest that our Lord hath said

that those who believe on Him shall never die. Oh,
Martha, trouble not thyself, but kneel with us and
pray.''

'' What should I pray for now, seeing that he is
dead ?'' replied Martha almost impatiently.   Then,
with a sudden resolve, she raised her head, and,
drawing her cloak around her, stepped out into the
cool morning air, and hurried down the road to
Jerusalem.

Many were the thoughts revolving in her brain
when she walked forth, a brave, strong-minded woman, to entreat the Lord, whom she failed to understand.   Of an energetic, indomitable spirit, full of
self-reliance, she had a horror alike of mystification
and of sentiment, with a full belief in the power of
coercing events.   To sit down and wait for the workings of God to take effect would have been beyond
her.   She was always fretting lest she had left some
machinating stone unturned.   She was imbued with
the idea that there was power in a multitude of
prayers, and that one moment's inaction would reap
its reward of infruition.   She had been a careful
housewife, and much responsibility had devolved on
her, for the three had been left without a mother at
an early age.   She, Martha, had had to be mother and
father to the two younger ones, Lazarus and Mary.
This had given her an irritability of temperament
and a certain domineering manner which, to her
credit be it said, she strove hard to master.

For a long time she had shut ears and heart
against the strange rumours that were bruited
abroad respecting Jesus of Nazareth; she had dis-
believed the reports about His birth and had even

spoken disparagingly of His mother. She had looked upon Joseph of Nazareth with scorn. Caiaphas, too, who was a relative of theirs and now High Priest, would never definitely speak of Jesus.

But they were strange times in which the Jews lived then. John the Baptist had greatly stirred the Jewish world, and indeed the Roman and the Syrian world as well, by preaching a gospel of repentance and baptism, and many of the Pharisees and Sadducees had gone over to his doctrines; and yet when He had been baptised by John, it seemed difficult to believe that Jesus could be greater than he, though the Baptist had himself averred it.

" Thinkest thou, Lazarus, that the Son of God would be baptised of a wild fanatic such as John ? For that John is mad is common knowledge, and that he hath bewitched the people."

Thus Martha spoke. But this had been before the family at Bethany had been honoured by the presence of the Messiah under their own roof. Since then, Lazarus had followed the Lord, followed as a hungry man wanders till he finds bread. By the Sea of Galilee, into the mountains where Christ prayed and preached, Lazarus had followed; followed, thirsting for the stream of truth that flowed on to life. What strange new doctrines were these to one who had been brought up in the old Hebrew law, fed on the vengeful tenets of the Psalms! "An eye for an eye, a tooth for a tooth," had been the old religion. " Resist not evil, but whosoever shall smite thee on thy right cheek, turn to him the other also," was the new. And, " Give to him that asketh thee, and from him that would borrow of thee turn thou not away!" Love, blessing, forgiveness, what strange new doctrine was this? It never before had been so seen in Israel. No wonder that a keen observer, a studious, spiritual-minded man, like Lazarus, should feel mystified and puzzled, yet inspired by doctrines at once so pathetic and so powerful. With Mary he could talk of all these things; she had always been of a gentle, sympathetic spirit, ardent and enthusiastic in her worship and affections, deeply religious, and yet with a strain of mysticism that permitted the seemingly impossible to find a place in her too willing heart.

She, too, to Martha's dismay, had often joined the crowds that followed Jesus of Nazareth along the roadside, listening to His incomparable sermons, witnessing miracle after miracle; wonders that filled the priests with dismay and doubt, and awed the Tetrarch, yet failed to persuade the multitude that He was the living God.

Often and often she had tried to get Martha to accompany them.

" If thou wouldst but listen once to Him, Martha, thou wouldst feel all the troubles of this world removed from off thy shoulders, and perfect peace would fill thy soul. His words are like the softest music, and yet they sound deep like the waters of the sea, and they are so true, so real, thou canst not but believe them. They are indeed the words of a God, for never man spake like this Man. It is the Messiah who is here; I know it, I feel it, Martha. If thou wouldst but once accompany me and follow Him, for most times He speaketh to the multitude!"

But Martha had made answer: " Thinkest thou, Mary, that the Messiah would come as a poor carpenter and in poorest attire, with naught else but a chiton and a tunic ? Thinkest thou not that the heavens would rend themselves, and the very thunder-clouds be in waiting on the Lord ? Thou art easily carried away, Mary, for thou dreamest much, and Mary Magdalene hath filled thee with these foolish fancies."

" Ah! poor Magdalene. Would I could indeed instil into her life a little joy, and stay the sorrow at her heart! Yet see, even to her He hath been full of pity and love; to her who was aforetime jeered at by the multitude, despised by men and women, who wept daily in the wilderness, conscious of her sins, yet not knowing whence to learn the way to a better life. He hath spoken to her words of sympathy and heavenly love, and now she is a devout, pious woman, having naught to do with any, save only the praying to this Jesus, whom she calls her Lord."

" He can be no God who speaketh to harlots and goeth about with sinners," Martha had replied; for the very mention of Magdalene, the harlot, closed her heart. " The Messiah is not yet come, for, when He cometh, the world will be overwhelmed with the glory and the shame. He will walk through the sea with His horses and scatter the sinners as a whirlwind. Mountains will quake and the valleys be laid low, and every man will know that He is the Lord. There will be no doubting, and all shall know that the Lord He is the God. We must not be blinded by false prophets."

Then, in despair, Mary had exclaimed: " When

Christ cometh, will He do more miracles than those which this Man hath done?"

But Martha had hardened her heart, for she had seen no miracles, and would believe in nothing that she had heard.

"He is a prophet," she had replied, "but He is not a God."

CHAPTER X.

THE Temple had been all day the scene of thronging crowds. The people in and round about Jerusalem had gathered there to hear the Nazarene preach; some from curiosity and some to scoff, but the greater part to listen to those wondrous words, which, while upsetting all past teaching, brought peace and comfort to the heart, and visions of unending happiness in the future. How simple was that teaching! No burnt-offerings, no more sacrifices, only water to the thirsty and food to the hungry; forgiveness and salvation offered to all who would accept it. The tone of the Nazarene that day had been almost broken-hearted; His appeals to the hearts of men more pathetic and more powerful than usual in their pleading earnestness. Who on earth can ever fathom the grief of the Man of Sorrows at the hardness of heart of people who daily saw His miracles and heard His words, yet would not believe?

" Why do ye not understand My speech ? Because I tell ye the truth, ye believe Me not."

Incensed, the crowd had hurled invectives and abuse against the meek testifier of the truth.

" Now we know that Thou hast a devil," cried some.

" Who art Thou ? " cried others.

" Where is Thy Father ? " cried others derisively.

And, in meek solemnity, with eyes that turned to Heaven in mute appeal for forgiveness for those around Him, the voice, that had so often kept the Jewish crowd in check, replied: " Ye neither know Me nor My Father; if ye had known Me, ye would have known My Father also."

Goaded on by the Pharisees, the crowd had yelled and roared and taunted, till, at last, grown furious at the continued meekness of the Preacher, they had even taken up stones and cast them at Him. A terrible cry arose when the Nazarene's fair flesh was struck again and again by the stones hurled at Him. It was the voice of a woman who stood in the crowd:

" My son, my Lord, they have hurt Him. Oh, are they mad that they know Him not ? Oh, foolish generation, who hath bewitched you ? "

But, even while she had cried, the tender eyes of the Nazarene had fallen upon the mother whom He loved. Perhaps to spare her pain or to prevent further sin, or because His hour was not yet come, He had ceased speaking, and walked without shrinking towards the crowd. Terrified by His temerity, perhaps, or cowed by some invisible power that held them spell-bound, the crowd had stopped molesting Him and had fallen back to let Him pass; and, turning to each other, had murmured, in strange contrast to their late behaviour, " This is the Christ," while others had said, "Or, of a truth, the Prophet."

And so Jesus had passed out of the Temple in safety. But now evening had come, and with it the faint chilliness that in Southern climates takes the place of frost at the approach of the cold season.

The cloudless sky had turned from deepest blue to palest green, and the dying sun had, as it were, spilt its blood across the west, leaving a gold-red haze behind the waving palm trees that stood against the skies in dark defined relief, showing the pattern of each leaf. Here and there a star opened a twinkling eye and glimmered faintly, and the roads that looked so white in the midday sun grew greyer every moment. Olive and cypress trees, leafless vineyards, houses and walls and hills were every moment shrouded more and more in the mantle of darkness that was falling silently over the earth. Every now and then a bat, whirring out from a neighbouring tree, or a pariah dog howling outside the walls, was the only sound that broke the stillness. Along the road to Bethany a woman was hastening with cloak tightly drawn around her. At that very moment Martha was also speeding her way from Bethany to Bethsaida to beseech the Lord.

It was Mary Magdalene, who was hastening to Bethany to join her tears to those of the other Mary. No darkness frightened her, no journey seemed too long for her to hasten where she knew her Lord would be.

While she hurried along the road her thoughts turned to Jesus, as they were now ever wont to turn; the loving, penitent heart, broken with disillusions, sickened with the nausea of unholiness, emptied of all earthly love, but restored and comforted by the divine, had room for naught else now but the Nazarene. Every now and then a strange misgiving overcame her. How was it that Jesus had allowed Lazarus, whom He so loved, to die? Was it

6

that He had been captured and imprisoned ; or,
worse, put to death ?   For all those who really believed in Him were imbued with the foreboding of
His approaching death.   The Nazarene Himself had
prepared them for it, and, as each day dawned, each
one of His true followers in turn rejoiced that He
was still with them, but dreaded what might befall
before the night.

"I go My way and ye shall seek Me; whither I
go, ye cannot come."

Poor Magdalene!   How she trembled, thinking of
the moment when He who had brought salvation
and forgiveness to her poor worn-out soul would depart, leaving her desolate in the world, that world
which had been cruel alike in its adulation and its
judgment!   Would she have the strength, despised
and scoffed at by women, persecuted on account of
her great beauty by the worst type of men, would
she be able to weather the storm alone ?   Poor,
weak, loving creature, would she have the strength?
She had no more faith in herself, no courage left;
only a growing remorse that had kindled into a de-
vouring flame, and then been quenched by the love
of the Saviour, who had brought words of consolation to the sinner:

"Neither do I condemn thee; go, and sin no
more."

How well He had understood, this pure and spotless Jesus, the terrible lurings of sin, the horrible
temptations of a loving, clinging soul; and how
poor, erring sinners were goaded to further sin by
the harshness of the world's judgment; plunged into
still lower depths by the powerful and the hypo-

crites, who pointed the finger of scorn at others in the hope of blinding their fellows to their own far greater sins.

Yes, it had been new life, a new, strange comfort, this theory of faith, repentance, and forgiveness; this wiping out of the past her soul had longed for. She—who had seen the worst of human nature, who had learned to look with loathing upon man and all his selfishness; tortured with remorse; trembling over loss of self-respect; weeping at her forfeited good fame; longing for relief, like the thirsty flower for the refreshing rain, and dying bird for the rays of the glowing sun—had fallen down in worship at the feet of the perfect Man, who brought salvation to trusting women instead of ruin; who crowned all manhood by His pure humanity, and conferred undying honour on all womanhood by the manner of His birth.

But she had grown humble and diffident, this poor, worn woman.

Away from Jesus, she dreaded life. If her Lord should die, she prayed that she might also die. Then, in the grey twilight of that Eastern night, thoughts stirred her deeply, as oft they do when we are alone, and, most of all, alone with nature, and the words of the Nazarene came back to her, when He had likened Himself to a good shepherd, and all that that implied.

Oh, how wonderful it was, this change in her! How her heart glowed with gratitude and love! Then midway in her journey and in the silent darkness, the Magdalene fell down on the soft grass by the roadside in deep humility, and bowed her head and prayed to God to grant her once more to see the face of Jesus and to keep her from again falling into sin.

So absorbed was she in her prayer, that she failed, at first, to hear footsteps coming along the road. For a moment she was overcome with womanly fear at being alone on the highroad at such an hour. She, least of all, should thus be seen; for, since her awakening, she had remained almost nightly within doors, or in the company of the mother of her Lord, who had been all sympathy and love to her. Of late her only pleasure in life had been in following the crowds to hear the preaching of the Nazarene, either in the Temple courts or in the open air.

The night was dark, so rising quickly from her knees she slid behind an olive tree. The two men approached, talking in tones that in the night air sounded loud and clear.

The Magdalene started. She knew one voice well; she had heard it many times speaking to crowds, and also in the Temple cursing and denouncing sinners like herself. Surely it was the voice of Caiaphas. Those harsh, dictatorial accents, full of self-assurance, could belong to no other man. What brought Caiaphas along this road so late? A sharp pain struck her heart, as though she had been stabbed. If it were Caiaphas hastening to the house of Martha, it must surely be to lay hands on Jesus. Perchance He was already taken. Oh that she were there to throw herself between the captor and the captured, to tear the former limb from limb! Surely God would give her strength to save His glorified Son. Then she whispered softly to herself, "But

He would not let me. If His hour had come He would bid me be silent and watch for the workings of the Lord."

Then there came a great longing over her to hurry on and warn them of their danger, for where Caiaphas went there mischief must for sure be brewing. She knew a short cut through the olive groves, if only it was not too dark. But who was the other man? She strained her ears to listen. They were close to her now. They halted and seemed engaged on some hot argument, for they paused to catch their breath. Truly to marvels there was no end. The man with Caiaphas was Nicodemus. For one instant there floated through her mind the thought that Nicodemus had persuaded Caiaphas to go and witness the expected miracle, the bringing back of Lazarus to life. For one moment her heart beat with joy. Oh, if Caiaphas also should believe!

The kingdom of God would be established, and Jesus would reign for ever. Then her sudden joy expired; it was not to be; she knew it well from Jesus' lips that He must die. Then mischief must be abroad; either Nicodemus was a traitor, or Caiaphas had laid a plot. They were on their way to Martha's house, but with no good intent, and her heart ached for the poor women left alone at such a moment. She must hasten to warn them; but how? The only road by which she could reach Bethany sooner than Caiaphas and Nicodemus was one beset with dangers; through dark olive groves, that often at night were infested with evil-doers. To the forgiven Magdalene, the newly awakened, purified Magdalene, fear came in a new form. Her former

ill-fame created terrors for her she had never felt before; but, full of new-bidden strength and faith, she
raised her heart in prayer, and drawing her veil
around her face, she started at a running pace across
the soft herbage of the by-path.

"Mary, Mary Magdalene, whither goest thou?"
a soft voice called after her. She half paused to listen; then, with redoubled energy, began to run
again. Then she became conscious of a presence
near her; she durst not turn her head, but her heart
breathed a prayer for help.

A sudden light brought her movements to a full
stop; a flashing light that diffused a strange, inexplicable glow, illumining the grey-green olive trees
and enveloping the path and bushes with a curious,
iridescent halo, that, while giving light, showed
neither flame nor fire. It was like a fairy web of
gold hanging on tree and bush.

A great terror seized upon the Magdalene. It
was not physical fear, but the dread of being
brought face to face with the supernatural. While
she gazed, with dilated eyes and parted lips, the
glory seemed blurred by a shadow. It was as
though the centre of the glowing light were forming
itself into a little cloud. Her heart beat so violently
that in its throbbing it seemed to make to vibrate
every nerve and fibre of her body. With one hand
she held tightly across her bosom the blue veil which
was worn by all the women of Jerusalem in that day.
With the other she smoothed back her lovely golden tresses, straining her eyes to bursting to pierce
the glory that hung from tree to tree. Then, with
a sudden thought, she fell on her knees, and bowing

her head to the ground, in words of deepest humility and a voice weak with agony, she murmured: " Oh, my Lord, my Lord, they have slain Thee! Jesus, Thou Saviour, in pity Thou hast visited me!" and faint with gratitude and adoration, and torn with anguish, she almost swooned away.

Then a voice she knew, but which was not that of the Christ (whose voice was like to none on earth), called out again: " Mary, Mary Magdalene, bow not thyself before me, for I am the least of all men. Rise up and listen. I am not the Christ, but Lazarus."

Kneeling still, and struggling with emotion, the Magdalene raised her beautiful face, half dazed still from the agony she had undergone; and some of the glory that shone around her touched her lips and hair; and, while she looked, the shadows seemed to grow more and more distinct; till, finally, the form and features of Lazarus seemed to stand in very life before her, but with a strange spiritual light upon them, such as she had seen occasionally on the face of the Nazarene.

" Thou, Lazarus?" she murmured inquiringly in awe-struck tones. " Thou here? But I saw thee die, and, even now, I was hastening to Mary to warn her that Caiaphas and Nicodemus are on their way to Bethany; and they will have gained upon me on the highroad."

" Fear not," replied Lazarus. " I have come to tell thee that our Lord is not yet come to Bethany, nor will He be for three days more. Thou hast naught to fear, even if Caiaphas and Nicodemus go to Martha's house. They will find only Mary, for Martha hath gone to entreat the Lord, and He cometh not yet to restore to me my life."

" And art thou, in truth, dead, Lazarus ? How then speakest thou to me ?" asked Mary Magdalene.

" Whosoever believeth on the Christ shall never die," Lazarus replied solemnly.

" Yet thou art dead, Lazarus, thy grave clothes are yet about thee; thou sayest that thy body lieth in the grave. Tell me, then, what is it to die ?"

" To die, Magdalene, is but to begin to live; to begin to understand, to begin to know how great God is, how small we are."

" Truly this is strange, that thou shouldst be dead but speaking still to me," replied the Magdalene.

" They that sleep in the Lord are ever near those they love," said Lazarus. " If thou couldst but see with purified eyes, as I now do, thou wouldst perceive that the world is peopled with the spirits of those who have died, as they of this world call it, but who, in verity, have but begun to live. They are about me while I speak to thee."

Mary paused, as if to give herself courage to reply.

" Dost thou know all things ?" presently she asked. " Dost thou know wherefore was the world created and why death came into it, why it was permitted by our Lord Jesus that thou shouldst die, if in truth God be His Father and He hath power to save ?"

" Be silent, woman," replied Lazarus severely. " None of these things do I know yet. All that has come to me in death is the certainty that all this is for right; but I understand it not. I know only that to understand it fully is impossible. I would fain explain away what to me becometh daily more inexplicable, yet more certain. Oh, Magdalene, if thou couldst but travel in the spirit world, as I am doing, thou couldst not but believe. I have seen Jesus, and He hath charged me to bid thee tell His mother that three days hence she come to the house of Martha to see Him raise my body from the grave, where it now lieth; for the glory of the living God will this thing be done."

But, argumentative still, as women are, longing to convince herself by further questioning of the reality of what she saw and heard, she murmured : " Hast thou, then, been to heaven ? "

" Nay," he answered, " not to the heaven where God doth reign, for no man can see His glory till the Messiah be ascended; but it is heaven to me to know that eternity existeth, and that from such glories and wonders, as neither thou nor I can understand, Jesus hath come down to save mortals, such as we. Oh, if the world could but understand or, not understanding, be content to believe and pray!"

The first faint streaks of dawn were trembling in the sky, a blue, cold light began to play lightly on the olive branches, and already the golden haze of glory seemed to be melting almost imperceptibly. Lazarus's face was growing indistinct. The air seemed filled with the rustling of wings; a noise, as a flight of birds, sounded in Mary's ears, mingled with the music of strings of countless harps in unison; and then a chorus of voices burst forth in such a chant of exultant praise and harmony, as it had never yet been given to man or woman to hear.

Entranced, and faint with wonder and emotion, the Magdalene watched the fading of the beloved form; then, as the voices grew more distant and the face more indistinct, a regret that pierced came over her, in that she had failed to ask for guidance how to gain eternal life.

" Lazarus, Lazarus, rabbi," she exclaimed, " tell me before thou goest how must I die that I may die in Christ ? " But he made no answer. Then faintly, from the distance came the voices chanting: " Truth and love. Truth and love."

And, overcome with all she had gone through, full of penitence, remorse, and wonder and devotion, the Magdalene fell upon her face, caring nothing that her beautiful hair caught in the roots and branches and tanglewood beneath her; conscious only that Jesus loved her, and that for her sins His life was to be yielded up, that to wash away her stains, His blood, the blood of the Innocent, the Perfect One, must flow.

CHAPTER XI.

THE news that Lazarus was dead spread with the rapidity of lightning. His illness, and the probability or the improbability of his being saved from death, or restored to life, had for so many weeks been a common topic that it was no wonder that his death filled the believers with dismay, and the Pharisees, and, still more, the Sadducees, with joy.

Joanna's tongue had not been silent, nor yet had Rachel's, and when some messenger had come from Jerusalem with some delicacy ordered by Martha, in the hope of tempting the slender appetite of the invalid, he had found himself surrounded, on re-entering the outskirts of the town, by a vociferating, clamouring crowd of inquiring gossips.

There was still greater significance in this death for the chief priests; it renewed their power over the Jews, while it also renewed the controversy between Caiaphas and Pilate as to the expediency of laying hands on the Messiah.

The apparent failure of the expected miracle rendered the Nazarene a less dangerous opponent.

Some anxiety was felt by Caiaphas when he heard of the continued absence of the Nazarene from the house of Martha and Mary. It seemed to him, in his insensate craving for revenge, that his Victim was escaping him; while Pontius Pilate was secretly glad, both at the disappearance of the Christ and the discomfiture of the wily Caiaphas.

"Where is now the courage of thy Nazarene?" Caiaphas had asked the Procurator at the Sanhedrim; and, in the same taunting tone, Pilate had answered:

"Where is now thy Victim?"

The hours were few in which Mary and Martha were allowed to sit and mourn their dead in peace. Of a noble and respected family, as the wealthy ruler had been, it was impossible that his death should not cause some stir, for all that his recent leaning towards the tenets of the Nazarene had caused him to be looked upon of late with some suspicion. Accordingly great interest was taken in the promised presence at the funeral of several representatives of the different sects who suspected or dreaded that Lazarus might not be really dead; and Caiaphas had prevailed on the jackal Annas to be present.

"We can trust none," he had said, "and this Nazarene may so bewitch the people that they may fear to tell us the truth. It must be thou or I, for I would trust to no man's eyes or ears or tongue in this affair; and it would look better that he that was High Priest were there than that he that is; for thou wouldst be deserting no office and wasting no time if, peradventure, thou wert walking in the olive groves by Bethany at eventide, when the funeral procession was approaching."

Caiaphas had not seen fit to tell his father-in-law of his midnight journey to Bethany with Nicodemus, when he had hoped, if not to lay hands on Jesus, to get tidings of His movements; when he had also seen the body of Lazarus.

An endless multitude of people thronged all day the road from Jericho; great rabbis, followed by their retinue, mules laden with spices and myrrh, ointment and spikenard. The room in which Lazarus lay, now bound in grave clothes by the tender hands of Martha and Mary, was like an ever-moving panorama. According to Jewish custom, all the friends and relatives came to bid farewell to the corpse and to mourn with the sisters; and the ever-active Martha forgot some of the poignancy of her grief in the dispensing of hospitality and in attending to the comfort of the thronging crowd. Nicodemus was there, in attendance on Annas, glad to have so good an excuse for coming to the house at Bethany, without appearing to be attracted by curiosity or devotion. The two men were allowed the first access to the corpse; and, while Annas let his eyes wander curiously around him, as if he dreaded some juggling or chicanery, Nicodemus looked across the corpse at him and said: " Methinks he is dead in very truth."

But the wily father-in-law of Caiaphas would risk no answer, lest, perchance—for all words of Nicodemus seemed borne out by facts—he still might be the dupe of circumstances.

Then others thrust themselves within the room, some curious, some interested, but all, with ready Eastern sympathy, eager to comfort the bereaved women. Those belonging to the nobler grades of Jewish social life were doubtless struck with the incongruities of the surroundings: the superb hangings and costly adornments of the house, and the humble, mean attire of many of the mourners. Last, but not least, their dignity was offended by the presence of the Magdalene.

" What doth this sinner here ? " said one or two, albeit with bated breath, not to wound the susceptibilities of the owners of the house.

" She loved Lazarus," said one.

" Methinks the ruler had good taste," put in another with a jeering laugh, suppressed at the remembrance that a corpse lay in the adjacent chamber; " for she is the comeliest woman in Judæa."

" Methought the righteous Lazarus took no heed to any woman," said a third.

" Tush," said Nicodemus. " 'T is not as ye do think, ye foul-hearted, foul-mouthed generation. This woman was purified by the Nazarene. He cast forth seven devils from her, and Mary, the sister of Lazarus, who is ever kind, doth help her much to lead a better life."

This statement was met with a shrugging of the shoulders and an upraising of the eyebrows; and one bolder than the rest remarked: " Perchance, if Lazarus had lived, he would have taken her to wife. The followers of the Nazarene do strange things, I 'm told."

But the conversation was interrupted by the voice of a servant crying out: " Make way, make way. Simon the Leper doth come this way."

As though one smitten with the plague came in their midst, the whole crowd dispersed, jostling and pushing each other this way and that, in their hurry to avoid contact with the afflicted one; and soon, as if by magic, the chambers were emptied of their human throng, to let the wasted vision of diseased mortality pass in.

One or two beckoned to Mary and Martha, but they shook their heads, and Mary whispered softly: " We fear nothing; he is our father."

However strict the Jewish laws, none could at such a moment refuse the father access to the body of his son. Simon, like his daughters, had retained a lingering hope that the Nazarene would save Lazarus from death, and so had put off his visit from day to day, till he had been too late to bid his son farewell. Great tears coursed down the cheeks of the poor old man. It was the overflowing of a sorrowful cup, filled to the brim with life's bitterness. Though he was compelled by the Jewish law to live apart from the rest of the world, his son had been the hope of his old age; he had watched his career with all the love and pride of a father, who feels that, but for some untoward accident, he might have been great himself.

Lazarus had been his second self—a second self, but free from his affliction. The rectitude of his son's life had been his joy; his high position, his pride; his kindness to his sisters, a burden lifted from his own shoulders. It was through his son that he had learned to know the Nazarene; yea, who knew what hopes of recovery Simon had fostered in the presence of the Christ? Yet both father and son had been disappointed in their hope of being healed of their disorders by the Nazarene. For all that, it was characteristic of the members of this family, plucked, as it were, like brands from the burning, that they never wavered in their faith. Perhaps it was the intensity and unity of their trust that compelled the miracle that followed.

Hideous in his horrible disease, the poor old man stood gazing at the lifeless features of his son.

Then he looked at Mary, who was still kneeling by the bedside, and shaking his head sadly, he repeated: " He is, in truth, dead. He is, in truth, dead."

Then, fearing the return of the mourning friends, or perhaps that by his presence he was keeping them away, the old man, unattended and lonely, as he had come, tottered away, leaning a little more heavily than his wont upon his staff of olive wood.

" Thou and I, thou and I," he muttered. Then, as if to keep his faith alive by the sound of his voice, he cried out as he passed as rapidly as he could across the garden, where the crowds had taken refuge during his visit to the body of his son: " Bless the Lord, O my soul, and all that is within me bless His holy name." And here and there a voice, pitying or scoffing, according to the nature of the heart from which it emanated, cried out: "Who healeth all thy diseases! Why then hath He not healed thine ?" Again: "Thou art grateful for little, poor Simon." Then, as if given a sudden inspiration of conviction, Simon turned round on the scoffing crowd, and, with a mighty voice, cried out: "My son will yet rise again."

And while the Jews questioned among themselves "What meaneth he ? Now or at the resurrection?" the poor old man took his solitary way down the road that led on to Jerusalem, a sharp pang seizing his heart as, every now and then, a child or an older passer-by darted across the road, lest they should touch him, exclaiming in horror ill-suppressed: " 'T is Simon the Leper."

" Who knoweth what trickery they have contrived in yonder chamber ? " said the ever-suspicious Annas to a bystander, dreading even now a miracle at the last moment, and neglecting no opportunity of instilling disbelief in its reality, should it apparently take place.

The sad day was over, with its bereavement and its disillusions, its horrible disappointments, its fruitless yearning for the glorious Presence which would have so revived their drooping spirits. Lazarus had been laid in his grave amid the chants and wailing of nearly all Jerusalem. The air around the grave was heavy with the perfumes that had been brought as gifts. One by one the mourners had departed, leaving a little group of intimates behind. Yet still Annas lingered, half in awe and half suspicious. Then, while the women continued to kneel beside the grave, he approached Martha and addressed her courteously enough.

" Lady," he said, " wouldst permit that these, my soldiers, roll a stone upon the grave ? "

" Wherefore ? " asked Martha, eying the wily Jew with some distrust.

With shifting glance, he yet tried to look her steadfastly in the face. " I fear some trickery," he said ; and the accent of truth rang out in the greasy voice.

" Art not ashamed to say such things?" asked Martha testily. Then, drawing herself up to her full

7

height, she added proudly: "Yea, if thou fearest aught." With unutterable scorn the word "fearest" was pronounced. "If thou fearest aught from heaven or earth, do what thou wilt. Set thy soldiers to roll a stone before his grave."

Then the scheming Annas realised that he had taken a false step, for, if miracle there were, then it would assuredly be said, "Yet Annas placed a stone against the door"; giving double strength to what might otherwise have been passed off as a trick. Accordingly, hastily he replied: "Still, if thou will it not, 't is all one; for there will be no miracle."

But Martha, justly angered, raised her head proudly and made answer: "Nay, but I will now that thou have this stone rolled on my brother's grave; and, if thou wilt but bid thy soldiers do it in the presence of these who linger still and can bear witness to it, I will myself send message to my kinsman Caiaphas, or, if needs be, go to Pontius Pilate to tell him of thy words."

Annas started, stung by her tone and words; then laughed an angry laugh. "Methinks that He who can raise one so dead as Lazarus can also roll away the stone."

"Thou speakest well, thou treacherous Annas," replied Martha, with some heat; "for, if my brother rise, it will be at the bidding of Jesus, the Son of God, with whom all things are possible."

With these words she signed to the soldiers to roll a stone against the tomb, stifling the wish to cast one last long look at her brother, lest Annas should make it an excuse for delaying to fulfil her wish.

Then the soldiers, partly to annoy Annas, whom

they hated for a crafty Jew, and partly from Roman courtesy to the two sorrowing women, rolled a huge stone against the mouth of the tomb. But Annas had already proceeded down the hill, as though refusing to be witness to the act that he himself had first suggested.

Nicodemus lingered for one moment to bid farewell to the two he knew and loved so well, and to ask the question he had already longed to put: "Thinkest thou still the Lord will come ?"

"He will come, He will come," wailed Martha; "but my brother is dead; my brother will rise no more."

"But at the resurrection," chimed in Mary softly. And then, while Nicodemus hurried on to catch up with Annas, the two women, with arms entwined, wandered back to their solitary home, bereft for the future of all its joy and sunlight and the chief interest of their lives. Behind them walked a little band of old and trusted friends, wailing and bemoaning according to Jewish custom. On the clear evening air their voices sounded like a celestial chorus.

"I will weep bitterly. Labour not to comfort me. For it is a day of trouble, and of treading down, and of perplexity by the Lord God of Hosts in the valley of vision. Look away from me, look away from me: I will weep bitterly."

Then a woman's voice alone took up the verse from the Song of Solomon.

"Where is thy beloved gone ? Whither is thy beloved turned aside ? that we may seek him with thee."

Then they all joined in once more: "Look away

from me, look away from me, for I will weep
bitterly."

Mary heard the words, that rose in tearful strains
behind her, and, turning, saw the Magdalene's white,
sorrowing face close to her own, trying to frame the
words of wailing, while the great tear-drops fell from
those lustrous eyes that had driven men mad aforetime.

" Who knoweth how thy aching heart doth suffer,
my poor Magdalene ? " she murmured soothingly,
and stretching out her hand to her.

Then once more the mournful voices chanted : "I
said, O my God, take me not away in the midst of
my days. As for man, his days are as grass : as a
flower of the field, so he flourisheth. For the wind
passeth over it, and it is gone ; and the place thereof
shall know it no more. Look away from me, look
away from me, for I will weep bitterly—I will weep
bit—ter—ly."

The voices rose and fell and there seemed no comfort anywhere. Now that the cherished body was
no longer there, the house seemed more desolate
than ever, and a great night was in their hearts ;
deeper even than the gloom now falling silently,
though the moon was veiled and the stars shone not
out. And, as the last lamp flickered out in the
house of Bethany, all hope in the hearts of those
who were bereaved died with it, for there was no
message from the Lord. Brother and friend and
God, all had gone from them at once. But there
was no wavering of their faith.

" For the glory of God is this thing done," said
Mary. " We must tread the winepress alone."

But Martha, in the petulance of her fatigue and grief, exclaimed: " If the Lord had been here, our brother had not died "; and in her revolting heart, she cursed the Jews and all unbelievers and them who sought His life and thus had kept Him away. Great as was her faith, it was not so great that she could believe that, if He had so willed it, He could have raised Lazarus from afar.

Then, wearied out with physical fatigue and the effort of brain and heart that tried in vain to pierce the veil of the incomprehensible and remain steadfast, despite assailing doubts, the two women sought repose and fell asleep from sheer exhaustion. But in the chamber below, as outside in the garden, the mourners still wailed: " Look away from me, look away from me, for I will weep bitterly, I will weep bitterly."

And so that saddest of all nights rolled away into the tide of eternity, till at the Judgment Day the Almighty should bid its waves leap upwards to the steps of His throne and unfold on its swelling crests the innermost secrets of its annals.

CHAPTER XII.

IT was winter and a little group of disciples clustered round a fire of wood. These were wondrous times, when none who believed sought rest, or, if compelled to, allowed themselves but little sleep.

Believing Jerusalem was convulsed, disbelieving Jerusalem triumphant, that the expected miracle—the raising of Lazarus—had not taken place. During the absence of the Lord the disciples themselves were debating it with wonder. One gave as a reason that " He feared the publicity," another that He durst not do this miracle on account of His friendship with Mary and Martha.

" If they have not believed hitherto, will they believe because He raise up Lazarus ? " asked Peter.

" Nevertheless, for very love, methinks He will yet do it."

" What said He unto thee when thou didst give Him the message of Simon the Leper ? "

" He said, ' Let us go unto Judæa again.' "

" And I," said John, " brought to His remembrance that the Jews sought to stone Him, and 't were not wise to go thither again."

" And what answered the Lord ? " inquired another.

" He answered, 'Are there not twelve hours in the

day ? If any man walketh in the day, he stumbleth
not, because he seeth the light of the world; but if
a man walk in the night, he stumbleth, because
there is no light in him.' "

" And how interpreted thou this saying ? " asked
another.

Then John, leaning forward, said: " Who can
fathom the words and doing of our Lord ? Yet, it
seemeth to me that He spake that the time was not
yet fitting; that, when the hour should come, then
the Jews would seek Him out, for He hath told us
further—'Our friend Lazarus sleepeth; but I go that
I may awake him out of sleep.' "

" If he sleep, he shall do well," said one.

" Yet one hath been from Bethany to-day saying
that they have laid him in his grave. Have the
physicians so far erred that they take sleep for
death ? Luke, thou art a doctor, tell us, can such
things be ? "

" It hath been known that those in a trance have
been laid in their grave, and, after many days, have
been raised again. But my heart telleth me it is
not so in this case. For the glory of God hath it
been that our Master was not there; else they that
seek to slay Him, or to entangle Him in His talk,
would speak of some bedazzlement or trickery. So
much the Lord doth love Lazarus that, had He seen
him sick, for very love He would have restored him,
but now that he hath lain in the grave three days,
surely the world will believe, if He do bring him
back to life."

" 'T is difficult to believe," said Thomas; " for
study hath given to each argument an answer."

" Study hath given no answer for bringing back the dead," said Peter, cynically; " yet I would my Lord did not return to Bethany, for I fear the Jews: This death of Lazarus the ruler doth make them bold, and Nicodemus was ever an unstable reed, drawn hither and thither by divers doctrines."

At that moment one of the disciples threw another log on the fire, and a flame leapt up, making visible the dark foliage of the fig trees, and lighting with a thousand glancings the damp rocks behind.

There, in the midst of them, illumined by other lights than earthly ones, stood motionless the Nazarene; and, as if in answer to their wonderments, He murmured, in His sweet, sad voice: " Lazarus is dead."

" He hath seen Martha," said one, " for I was told that she was near here this eve."

" Tut, the Lord needeth none to tell Him," said another.

Then the sweet, murmuring voice went on: "And I am glad for your sakes that I was not there, to the intent ye may believe. Nevertheless, let us go to him."

All sprang to their feet at the Lord's command. Doubtless He would start on His way at night, in order to reach Bethany before daybreak ; and Thomas, believing in His power to restore, but not in His power to save them, yet full of undying love, turned to his fellow-disciples and addressed them.

" Let us also go, that we may die with Him," he counselled.

Then, falling down at Jesus' feet, they murmured: "We will follow Thee wheresoever Thou goest, and we will die with Thee."

And the earnest, loving voice made answer:
"Greater love hath no man than this, that a man
lay down his life for his friends."

It had been happy, that home at Bethany, on
which such grief had fallen. Separated from their
father, Simon, by the laws of the country, by reason
of his leprosy, they yet nurtured great affection for
him, and often visited him.

Martha and Mary, united by the common grief of
widowhood, had agreed to share the house in Bethany, and to make a home for their younger brother,
Lazarus, a man whose learning and integrity had
earned for him the place of youngest ruler of the
Synagogue. They represented in the Jewish people
a type of persons that, before and since, has been
found in every place, in every country—namely, a
quiet, God-fearing family, who, from the very dis-
cretion of their acts, brought no comment and no
interference on themselves.

From their earliest youth they had been trained
to follow, not so much the laws of the High Priest
as the ancient commandments of Moses; and, till
their father had been struck with sudden leprosy for
having, in a fit of drunkenness, blasphemed, they had
merely led moral, orthodox lives according to the
Jewish tenets, without concerning themselves with
any special sect or doctrine. It was only when this
swift visitation came upon them, with its awful certainty and rapid judgment, followed by the com-
pulsory alienation from the home, and later, when
the sorrow of widowhood was added, that their
thoughts, pressed back into the purifying furnaces of

grief and solitude, began to turn to things divine.
Rigidly brought up in strict morality, devoted to
their parents, they had to witness the death of their
mother, through grief at the disgrace wrought in the
family by the plight of Simon. A horror of sin, if
such were its results, had terrified them into submission to the divine will; but to Mary alone had been
vouchsafed the revelation of the possibility of an inner life of love and devotion that depended neither
on necessity nor fear—that true philosophy that
comes of faith, that choosing of a good part which
should not be taken away from her. Who can tell
when her heart first burned within her ? Perhaps
abuses of the Jewish law had excited in her revolt at
all that was not true. Perhaps the narrow-minded-
ness of Martha's views, or the love of luxury in which
Lazarus had indulged; or, perhaps, the favour of
the Lord. Who can tell what gave to Mary the
loving heart of a little child who seeks but to be with
the object loved, that trustfulness which Jesus had
so often upheld in contrast to the self-righteousness
of the self-seeking Pharisees ? Doubtless it was in
great measure due to the chastening influence of the
griefs that she, in common with her brother and her
sister, had endured; sorrow had drawn them to the
Man of Sorrows. Who can apportion the quota of
humanity in the Christ, or say how far He was constrained by cords of human sympathy and bands of
human love ? Sure, if the best emotions of humanity
did not move Him as powerfully as they move mankind—yea, far more so—this Godhead were of none
avail; for the will to love, to comfort, to redeem,
could only come with absolute knowledge of man's

feebleness. A Man of Sorrow and acquainted with grief—surely in that lies our greatest comfort,—who felt more keenly than all others and had more often to suffer the bitterness of desertion.

" Couldst thou not watch with Me one hour ? " and the bursting soul, thirsting for human sympathy, not for the sake of comfort—for none but the Divine could comfort Him,—yearning for loving converse and companionship; longing to win souls to God; turned for refreshment to a family who, if still ignorant, desired to learn the truth. Little wonder if, in that time of superstition and disbelief among a priest-ridden populace, a family that sought to understand, and welcomed the Saviour of mankind, should find favour in the eyes of God and be honoured with the greatest miracle the world has ever known. Little wonder, too, that if they shared the privilege of His friendship, the participation of His mysteries, the comfort of His divine assurances, the manifestation of His power, they should also, later, share His humiliations, His scorn—nay, the threats of death, the persecutions that He had undergone. For when our Lord should have died and risen; when the thirst of vengeance of the priests and Pharisees should still remain unsatisfied, whetted, rather, by the lingerings of belief in the breasts of the Jews, who than Lazarus could be better fitted to carry on the witness of tradition; who be a better buffet for the faults of others; who more feared or more detested by the lovers of power than he who, by his very presence and his experience of death, could transmit to the world living proof of the power of the crucified Messiah ?

For his fleshly body to rise again would not be un-
mixed happiness. It would mean to have suffered
the pains of death without entering into rest or peace
or joy. It would mean the being made the witness
of Christ's work on earth. It would mean a repetition of his sufferings, and, later, a second dissolution
of the body; perhaps, also, a prolonging of existence
beyond the ordinary span of life, and, therefore,
extra suffering. It would mean, further, life made
more intolerable by the knowledge of eternity and
the impossibility of persuading men of what he
knew. Above all, it would mean a greater responsibility as regards the daily actions of life—to him
that seeth is the greater sin.

There must have been something infinitely sweet
in the appearance of Lazarus; for when the Lord
looked on him He loved him. The Nazarene, weary
with infidelity, worn out by disbelief, distressed, perhaps (who knows ?), that most of His followers were
of the lower class, uneducated, and therefore the
more obstinate in their superstitions, in their understanding the more obtuse; overwrought with the in-
tricate controversies that the Pharisees had forced upon Him, hoping to entangle Him, had turned in very
weariness towards the little children who stood about
as though inspired with added hope by the fresh
eagerness of their faces; as if to illustrate, by their
meek trustingness, the only possible means of peace.

" Suffer the little children to come unto Me, and
forbid them not: for of such is the kingdom of
Heaven." Who can tell the weariness of trying to
force by controversy and argument the acceptance
of a proposition that was so simple ? "Verily I say

unto you, whosoever shall not receive the kingdom of God as a little child, he shall not enter therein."

And He had taken them up in His arms and laid His hands upon them and blessed them.

Lazarus had stood near when the preceding words left the Saviour's lips. For months he had been following the Nazarene from place to place, thirsting for knowledge; yet for all he was a lawyer and a ruler of the Synagogue, unable to recognise the teaching of the Christ, unable to grasp the startling doctrines, to reconcile them with the teachings of his childhood and the surroundings of his daily life. He had heard the Nazarene pray, and he had prayed, but there had seemed a pall of unbelief upon his heart. Arguments, such as he had learnt in his legal profession (for almost every man that made any claim to position in those days was a lawyer), seemed ever to crop up. If this Man could save to the uttermost why did He not do so ? If He really was all-powerful, what need to suffer and to toil and to preach ? All the quibbles of unbelief, the torment of uncertainty, which is the world's greatest curse, which, since the world began, has raised its beguiling voice, like the voice of a siren, to lure men from the path of life; all the demons of despair, had torn at the heart of Lazarus ever since he had heard the preaching of the Nazarene; but the answer to his prayer had been coming, though he knew it not, coming, as it always does, by inward revelation, not as the result of argument. He had heard the chirping voices of the Jewish boys and girls as they clustered round the Christ, and he had approached to learn how Jesus spoke to the young.

With the suddenness of a flash of lightning from above, and with infinite peace and infinite gratitude, his eyes had been opened; for the first time he had seen. For the first time in his life's dark gropings there had shone a little light.

" Whosoever shall not receive the kingdom of God as a little child, he shall not enter therein."

Children, who argue not, who understand not, and yet who believe. At that moment he had realised the wondrous truth.

Christ's kingdom is not the creature of inductive reasoning; its being cannot be proved by argument.

Much that we see and hear is cruel, unjust, untrue. Nature alone is the witness of God, revelation alone that of the power of Christ. Miracles, prophecies, the law, the letter—what were these to unquestioning obedience, to devoted love, to trust in Christ? The one had nothing to do with the other. Theology was but a science built up on contradictions. If there was an all-powerful God, why were sin and misery and illness and injustice? Why were suffering millions only, after a short span, to die? Why did animals groan with the burdens of men? Why did He not reveal Himself in such a way as to exclude all unbelief and make eternity of damnation impossible? That is, that will be, to the world's end, the constant question, and only nature can give the answer. Since there is a world, and there are trees and flowers and times and seasons, for which thou canst not account—for canst thou bind the sweet influence of Pleiades or loose the bands of Orion ?—since thou thyself art but helpless organism, albeit a being with a brain and a throbbing heart, that hath

not love, nor mercy, nor understanding, stand un-
doubting and contemplate the works of a Creator.
Thou canst but acknowledge Him; and if, in His
mercy, He reveal to thee eternity, instead of leaving
thee for endless years in gloom, in doubt, in trouble
for thy future, welcome that revelation, and believe,
as thou canst not but believe, for all thou canst not
understand, and fall down and worship with thy soul
and body that Being thou wilt never comprehend.
For only God can comprehend God's nature.   To
grasp eternity thou must be eternal; to plumb the
depth of sin thou must be spotless; to fathom love
thou must be Christ; and since thou canst be none
of these, be content to trust, to worship, to love that
human God who hath placed Himself within thy
grasp.

Such thoughts had come to Lazarus, and salvation
had seemed, as it often seems to us, for a few moments a simple thing.   But as the voices of the children had grown more faint and the Lord's image less
distinct along the road, only a white gleam in the
growing dusk of evening seeming to speak of the
glory that was going by, it had seemed to him as if
a spirit walked beside him muttering, the while,
words of mistrust and doubt: " What if it should
not be true ?   What if it is all a lie ? "

The voice had sounded so distinct that Lazarus
had turned quickly to see whether any one was
there.   Then, in his troubled vision, it had seemed
as if two black wings had rustled away; but it might
have been but the effect of clouds, or quivering
evening shadows; yet, in very fear of losing the new
faith, the young ruler of the Synagogue had mur-

mured: " Satan, Satan, trouble me not, for I seek
the Lord."

Then, filled with the terrors of the vision, if vision it
were, and lest the Lord should disappear, he had cried
out appealingly: " Lord, help me! Lord, help me!"

That is a cry that hath ever reached the Holy
One. Full of His own meditations, sad and troubled
as they were, the Lord had checked His steps. In
the glowing gloom His white garments had seemed
to gleam and His eyes to blaze like two burning
coals; and as the glow in the western skies had illumined his features with its dying rays, Lazarus had
thought he had never seen anything so radiantly
glorious yet so solemn. Then, as the Lord had
stretched out His arms towards him, His shadow
had made a faint cross on the red sand behind.
Then, as human sympathy springs into being one
knows not how, Jesus, in whom it was as strong as
His divinity, deigned to be drawn to the young ruler
who thirsted so for knowledge, and who was so near
to the truth; who, by his own effort, had thus prepared himself for revelation.

Seeing the young ruler approach, the disciples,
who from respect to their Lord were walking apart
from Him, lest they should raise the dust upon their
Master, had moved on, as though to leave the two
alone.

Then, kneeling down before that glorious image
of a perfect Man who, without the added glory of
angels or pomps or kingdoms, could, by the power
of His own purity, force men into obeisance, Lazarus had cried out: " Good Master, what shall I do
that I may inherit eternal life?"

And, floating on the evening air, interwoven with the scent of flowers and cedar wood, had come the question: " Why callest thou Me good? there is none good but one, that is, God."

It was as if the voice had said, " Thou givest Me the attribute of God, yet believest not that I am He."

Then, knowing that He spoke to one well versed in the Mosaic Law, the Nazarene had gone on in a tone of pity, mingled with a little scorn—as though implying, "Hast thou not enough in thy religion to save thee that thou comest to Me?"—" Thou knowest the commandments, Do not commit adultery, Do not kill, Do not steal, Do not bear false witness, Defraud not, Honour thy father and thy mother."

And then Lazarus, with tears almost in his voice, as though he feared the guidance to eternal life were not forthcoming, had replied: " Master, all these things have I observed from my youth."

Then Jesus had perceived that in this man there lacked one thing only. The love of Christ was in him. The wish to know the religion He came to preach, the sighing and longing after righteousness, the yearning for salvation, all these were his, but he was hampered by the luxury that incites to indolence, the love of comfort that fetters action. He was a philosophic dreamer only, and as so many are, believing, trusting, hoping, but hanging back, for fear of what he might lose of temporal wealth and earthly pleasures, perhaps of social position. And Jesus had known all this, and in His heart there had come a longing that this yearning soul should be one of

those who followed Him.   Beholding him, He had
loved him, and with infinite pity and tenderness
had made answer: " One thing thou lackest: go thy
way, sell whatsoever thou hast, and give to the poor,
and thou shalt have treasure in heaven: and come,
take up the cross, and follow Me."

A look of disappointment had come over the face
of Lazarus.   This was not what he had expected.
He had expected some mystic word that would
direct him straight to the eternal throne.   He had
known that he had led such a life, in regard to purity
and uprightness, as the Nazarene preached; but this,
to give up his possessions—for Lazarus was a rich
man—this would mean ceasing to be a ruler of the
Synagogue, a lawyer, and a great man in Bethany
and Jerusalem.   Was this then the spirit of a little
child, to be the possessor of nothing, to look to the
Father for everything ?

Surely this thing was not so easy.   A life of believing and uprightness, yes; but poverty ? pitiful
poverty, to a man who had worn purple robes and
been greeted in the market place with the cry of
Rabbi, Rabbi!   Verily they said truly that this Man
was but the God of the poor and of sinners and,
grieving at the Messiah's words, wishing inwardly
that the test of love had not been so severe, he had
gone on his way, followed by the sad, sweet eyes of
the Nazarene, yet with the words of Jesus deeply
rooted in his mind.   In the garden of the house, the
garden in which his soul delighted, and which the
Lord would have him to give up, he had seen Martha
and Mary walking with arms entwined, watching the
beauty of the dying day, while they waited for their

brother's return before partaking of the evening
meal. He had called out to them, and there had
been that in his weary, anxious tone which had
struck sadly on Mary's sympathetic ear.

Martha, at sight of her brother, had hurried into
the house to see that all was in readiness for him,
for she prided herself on naught so much as the well
ordering of her household. But Mary had come to
greet him, and, kissing him, had bade him come and
be seated on the terrace. Although it was winter,
the air was warm enough, the very slight chilliness
only making it the clearer and adding ruddy gor-
geousness to the flame-washed sky. From the terrace, which hung high above Jerusalem, was a lovely
view of the city, and beneath lay the valley of the
Jordan with the tall cypresses and cedar trees of the
Wood of Ephraim filling in the gap. Here and
there a star was beginning to twinkle; opal and
pearly tints, then grey, like the breast of the turtle
dove bathed in sapphire, were stealing slowly over
primrose and carmine ; the pale new moon was
rising steadily, looking almost white, then turning
golden with departing day. " Verily it is like
twilight and dawn meeting together," had said
Mary. Then, linking her arm in his, she had murmured gently : " Hast thou seen the Lord to-day ? "
Then, at sight of the pained look on his face, she
had murmured softly : " Art tired, Lazarus ? Rest
thee and speak not."

Surely this woman was beloved by the Lord, for
she represented the very essence of sympathy, which,
only in that house, He had found in its veriest per-
fection. And Lazarus had answered wearily : " I

have seen Him, Mary, I have entreated Him this day, but He hath asked too much of me. Mary, I cannot do as He would have me."

And overwrought with weariness of soul and body, already attacked by the fever which was soon to bring about his death, Lazarus had laid his head on the marble supports of the seat and sobbed like a little child. And Mary, wondering truly, but loath to ask, had clasped him to her bosom and let him sob out his heart there in the solitude and darkness of the garden he was so soon to leave. Then, in the growing darkness, she had raised her eyes inquiringly to the pale lamps of heaven and, with tears pouring down her cheeks, had sought for words with which to calm the troubled soul of the dear brother; and softly, like one who soothes an ailing child, she had murmured the words that had come uppermost: " Seek the Lord, and ye shall find Him. Knock, and it shall be opened unto you." And, as if in answer to her words and to the unuttered prayers that struggled in the heart of each, a voice had called with yearning, " Lazarus, Lazarus! "

And from the deepening shadows, standing with feet that gleamed brightly on the dew-bathed turf, had appeared the form divine of the Nazarene.

CHAPTER XIII.

N O wonder that when dawn began to steal across the sky and to struggle through the curtained windows of the High Priest's dwelling, it should find him still awake, perturbed and irritable, and pacing his room, as was his wont when greatly moved. It was a terrible face, this face of Caiaphas, when freed from the look of unctuous pomposity he strove to make impressive to the crowd. He, Caiaphas, had taken a false step; nay, more, he had exposed himself to Nicodemus, a powerful colleague. For once the great deliverer of the law had erred; erred in his assumption, erred in the plot he had concocted, and in the means he had resorted to for its achievement. What now, if Nicodemus should expose him to Pontius Pilate ? Worse still, if Cæsar should hear of the midnight flitting of the great High Priest to the house of Martha ? Had his plan succeeded, he would have turned towards Nicodemus and twitted him with having been his tool. He had intended to try to entangle the Christ in His talk, to lead Him to speak of Himself; nay, more, to ask Him again the question that the Majestic God-Man had already so often meekly answered, yet with a power and emphasis none could fail to recognise as something more than human; the " Who art Thou ?" which had echoed from every lip during

the ministry of Christ on earth. He had felt sure
that Jesus would be with those He loved at the
news that sorrow and death had overtaken them;
and down in his heart he felt that the answer to his
question would be bold and true: " I am the Son of
God." Oh, then, what delight to condemn the
Nazarene out of His own mouth, and what a refine-
ment of revenge to make Nicodemus a party to the
condemnation!

Perhaps far down in his own breast had lain a
doubt whether, after all, the Christ could restore
Lazarus to life. If He did, it would be useless to
resist the populace or to try to persuade them either
that the Nazarene was but a man like other men, or
that He had a devil. But nothing had turned out
as he had expected. Caiaphas the great lawgiver
had made a mistake, as even the greatest do sometimes. Why had he not, he asked himself, sent
messengers first to Bethany to find out whether the
Nazarene was there?

" The wily Galilean, some spirit doth assist Him
surely. It seemeth as if He had known that I would
come." He went to his window, musing while
murmuring these words, and looked out on to the
white walls of Jerusalem, just beginning to glow in
the light of morning.

He had found Mary alone, praying by the body
of Lazarus. Martha even was not there. She had
barely raised herself at the great priest's entrance.

" Hast thou come to bless him ere he die ? It is
too late," she had said.

Her question had seemed for one moment to show
Caiaphas the vileness of his own intent; but, quick

to seize on an advantage, he had replied: " I came, as kinsman, to condole with thee and Martha."

Mary had looked up at Caiaphas for one moment. Something in the tone of Caiaphas had filled her with surprise. It was not like Caiaphas to recognise the kinship, or to do aught from kindness; nay, more, for many months they had been under a curse from him for harbouring the Nazarene.

As if to dispel her wonder, Nicodemus had taken the opportunity, while Caiaphas had walked towards the body of Lazarus, to whisper to her: " Methinks he came expecting to see Jesus raise Lazarus from the dead."

Mary had shaken her head sadly. " We too had hoped so much," she had answered. " We sent to tell the Lord, and the Lord did make reply that this sickness was not unto death, but for the glory of God. Yet now the physicians all declare that this is no trance, but that our brother is dead indeed, and to-night we bury him."

Breathless, Nicodemus had asked: " Dost thou still believe, Mary, that Jesus is the Son of God, and hath power to raise the dead ?"

Slowly, but with proud head and trustful eyes upraised to heaven, she had replied: " I believe that Jesus is the Son of God."

At her words, Caiaphas had turned round suddenly; then, shrugging his shoulders, he had replied: " Ye are all gone mad together. If thy Christ had raised thy brother Lazarus, I too would have believed; but now——"

" He will raise him in the resurrection," she had replied with gentle sadness, fretting, as those do who cannot prove their words. "Yet He is the Lord," she had added with simple trust.

Signing to Nicodemus to follow, Caiaphas had turned to go.

"Thou blasphemest without knowing it. God forgive thee," he had said. And, with uplifted head and pompous step, he had left the house, stopping at the threshold to shake the dust from off his feet.

One gleam of satisfaction alone had relieved the gloom of his nocturnal visit. If he had missed the Christ, he had satisfied himself that Lazarus was really dead. No trickery could bring him back to life. The sunken eyes and protruding brow, the white fingers, the cold, cold feet; all had been taken in by Caiaphas's eagle glance. If he had betrayed himself to Nicodemus, it mattered little, for no man henceforth would follow the Christ. All Judæa had expected the resurrection of Lazarus. All Judæa had been disappointed, and a disappointed people would be facile to gather back into the fold of the great High Priest. The triumph was to be short-lived, though he knew it not—but it was a triumph, nevertheless. The absence of the Nazarene, the two poor women alone and sorrowing, Lazarus, the friend of the Galilean, dead like any ordinary Jew dog, as Caiaphas expressed it,—all these failures lent themselves to the accomplishment of the High Priest's prophecy that Jesus would die that year. With spies and soldiers everywhere, Caiaphas expected soon to learn where Jesus was, and what kept Him away from the house of Martha.

"'T is fear, fear lest amongst the multitudes, or

amidst the uproar, I or Annas should lay hands on Him." So thought Caiaphas aloud; so, later, he expressed himself; but, deep down in his heart, he knew that the Man who boldly in the Temple had denounced the scribes and Pharisees, even the very ruler of Israel himself, and called them hypocrites and whitened sepulchres, could have no fear. Yes, he had noted in the eyes of the Messiah, the only time he had seen Him in the multitude, a look that could goad a man only to untempered penitence, or to deepest hellish hate. That look had pierced Caiaphas to his inmost being. It had seemed to read the secret of his heart, with pity and with scorn that one so learned could be so ignorant, or that, knowing, could so wilfully withhold his knowledge from the nation, and try to cheat his God. That look had ranked Caiaphas with the devils, and surely the sin of Caiaphas was one with that of Satan, who pitted his strength against his God, and tried, poor puny atom of evil, to strive with the Creator and Director of the Universe.

Wearied with his ceaseless pacings to and fro, Caiaphas threw himself upon his couch. His triumph, the triumph of the law, was close at hand. With the failure of Jesus (for what could it be but failure, if Jesus was afraid to save His friend for fear of the multitude ?) would begin again the power of the Pharisees, only it would be a thousand times more strong and more despotic. Like wayward children, the people would return. Like one repulsed, they would fall back beneath the sway of Caiaphas. He could hear himself denouncing from the altar their temporary infidelity.

" Did I not tell ye from the beginning that it
would be so ? " he thought he heard himself saying.
" Did I not tell ye so ? Ye would not believe. But
ye have set at naught all my counsel and would
none of my reproof. I also will laugh at your
calamity. I will mock when your fear cometh."
Oh, how delicious would be the return of that fawn-
ing, cringing people !   What sacrifices and oblations
he would exact; what tyrannies he would enact to
punish them for daring to oppose their will to that
of Caiaphas !   It was a consoling dream of vengeance
and triumph and requital.   The great priest leaned
his head against the wall and smiled to himself a
cold, triumphant smile that had a diabolical imprint
upon it.

The door was flung open and a servant announced
Nicodemus.

" Methinks he takes too much upon himself in
seeking me thus early, and all because last night I
walked some paces with him," said Caiaphas to himself; but, when Nicodemus entered, his face assumed
a pleasanter expression.

" Welcome, Nicodemus.   Hast thou forgiven
me ?"

" Forgiven thee ? "   The simple Nicodemus regarded the High Priest with wonder.

With that fascinating Jewish familiarity that had
bewitched so many, Caiaphas rose from his couch
and placed his hand on Nicodemus's shoulder.

" Now, friend Nicodemus, I will tell thee the
truth, but thou must not be angry.   Last night I
fooled thee; I hoped to catch the Messiah, as ye call
Him.   Ha ! ha !   The Messiah indeed !   And I

feared me that, if I had thee not with me, thou wouldst warn Him, and so I should lose my prey. Therefore I behaved to thee as if I too were a believer in this blasphemer."

But Nicodemus answered nothing, and Caiaphas with a little less certainty in his manner went on: "But He fooled us, this Nazarene; for where I, Caiaphas, expected to find Him, He was not; so our night errand was a wasted one, and thou mayst mock Caiaphas and point thy finger at him for a fool. What sayest thou now, Nicodemus? Did I not feign well?"

"Not better than could be expected of the High Priest," replied Nicodemus in a tone of asperity and cynicism, of which Caiaphas had not thought him capable, and which might hide meaning he would not relish.

Yet he continued: "I knew thou wouldst be angry, for no man likes to be fooled by another; but, last night, we were both fools, for thou fooledst me and the blasphemous Nazarene fooled us both." Here he laughed harshly. "But at any rate we have done with Him; He hath disappointed the people. His power, 't is evident, cannot always be put forth, or He would have spared His friend Lazarus the pains of death." Then, reseating himself, Caiaphas continued unctuously: "So it is that all that is not true cometh to an end. At one time it seemed truly, from what the people said, that this Galilean did participate in some way of the divine; but praise be to God (here Caiaphas rolled his eyes upward toward the ceiling), who doth not let the wicked flourish for ever. This wavering of the people hath been cut short. The bewitchment is over, and their souls will return unto the law of Moses. They will have learned much that is true and noble from this fanatic; they will return in strengthened faith to their own rulers, and Judæa will be more quiet than before."

Nicodemus, bewildered, yet half doubting, was about to reply; but, even while he opened his lips, there was a great noise below as of tramping feet, and presently cries and shrieks rose on the air with bewildering clamour and confusion. The voices of men and women and children were joined in a song of praise, and cry after cry went up, "Hosanna! Hosanna!" Then a chorus of young voices broke out spontaneously in the beautiful words of the Psalmist, chanted to the tune of a melodious Hebrew hymn:—"Surely His salvation is nigh them that fear Him; that glory may dwell in our land. Mercy and truth are met together: and righteousness shall look down from heaven. O Lord, how great are Thy works! Make a joyful noise to the Lord, all ye lands. Know ye that the Lord He is God. Make a joyful noise unto the Lord, all the earth: make a loud noise, and rejoice, and sing praise. Praise ye the Lord. Praise ye the Lord."

As the noise approached the house of Caiaphas the High Priest could hear, during an occasional lull, hisses and groans. Then, now and then, a voice shrieked out: "Where is Lazarus? Give us Lazarus."

Caiaphas sat silent, clasping the sides of his cedar-wood chair, and bit his lips, affecting to have no curiosity. Nicodemus, however, had rushed to the window-seat with spontaneous eagerness to see what the clamour might portend.

But it could not be that Caiaphas, the restless, arrogant, wrath-eaten Caiaphas, would long be silent.

With a deep, harsh, derisive laugh he called out to Nicodemus impatiently: "What seest thou? Is it, perchance, Lazarus restored by the Son of God?"

Nicodemus turned his head for one moment in answer. "I see naught but a vociferating crowd assembled round a beggar man." Then, stretching farther out of the window, he called to one of the soldiers who always stood at the entrance of Caiaphas's door: "Wherefore all this tumult?"

"It is the beggar Rabneh, who hath returned from the Pool of Siloam," replied the soldier. "They say it is he that was blind and whose sight was restored by the Nazarene."

"Is it in truth so? Is it he?" asked Nicodemus, as softly as the distance would permit, lest Caiaphas should hear; but no whisper escaped the alert ears of the suspicious High Priest.

"Peace, thou fool!" he roared. "How can it be he?"

But Nicodemus paid no heed. The crowd had assembled beneath the window, gabbling furiously, quarrelling, vociferating, howling with praise, or shrieking in derision, and thronging around a poorly clad man, some shouting: "How were thine eyes opened?" others crying out: "It is not he, it is another like him, it is not he."

"Where, then, is the beggar we have often seen on the wayside, begging, and ofttimes entreating the Christ; where is he, if this be not the man?"

" Go and fetch him ! " cried a voice.   But, even whilst the voice was lost in the tumult of disputings, two old people of the poorest class, leaning on sticks, approached, and the Jewish crowd, courteous in all its laws and ways, fell back to let age pass by un-molested.

" Here are his parents; mayhap they will know if he be their son," cried a scornful voice.

" Give ear, give ear," cried the people; and then a dead silence ensued, while one of the Pharisees stepped up to the old couple.

" Speak," said he, with a tone of authority.   " Is this your son who, ye say, was born blind ?   How, then, doth he now see ? "

The crowd seemed electrified into silence, and a great hush fell on all while they waited for the an-swer.   So sudden was the silence that Caiaphas could contain his curiosity no longer, but strode to the window and, laying a powerful hand on Nicodemus's shoulder, drew him back to make room for his own portly figure.

Too excited to resent this insult, Nicodemus ex-plained the situation to the High Priest.

" See, there are the parents of the blind man, but they are so old and full of fear that they are slow to answer."

Then, in a voice he strove hard to make steady, the old man answered: " We know that this is our son, and that he was born blind, but by what means he seeth, we know not; he is of age; ask him; he shall speak for himself."

Then, turning to the man again, the crowd shouted as with one voice: " How were thine eyes opened ?

Tell us, or we will kill thee as a blasphemer and a liar."

Then the beggar spoke: " A man that is called Jesus made clay, and anointed mine eyes, and said unto me, 'Go to the Pool of Siloam, and wash '; and I went and washed, and I received sight."

" Dost thou say, then, that He is the Christ ? " asked one of the Pharisees again; for he knew that if the man would but say that Jesus was the Christ they would cast him out of the Synagogue. For the unbelieving Jews had already agreed that this was to be the penalty of those who acknowledged the Nazarene to be the Christ.

But the beggar, fearing entanglement, was silent.

Then the Pharisee spoke again : " Give God the praise. We know that this man is a sinner."

Fearing the multitude, the man did not cry out, "He is the Christ, He is the Son of God "; but, full of gratitude for his new-found sight, he could not let the Pharisee's words remain unanswered.

" Whether he be a sinner or no, I know not," he replied; "but one thing I know, that, whereas I was blind, now I see."

Then said they to him again, hoping to confound him out of his own mouth: " What did He to thee ? How opened He thine eyes ? "

Then, still fearing the crowd, but growing stronger in faith and loyalty, the beggar answered: "I have told ye already, and ye did not hear; wherefore would ye hear it again ? will ye also be His disciples ? "

Then they reviled him, and said: "Thou art His disciple; but we are Moses' disciples."

" Well spoken, well spoken," muttered Caiaphas, and the voices went on speaking: " We know that God spake unto Moses; as for this fellow, we know not from whence He is."

Then, oblivious of all danger, and conscious only of a great love and gratitude to the compassionate Jesus who had opened his eyes, the beggar spoke again: " Why, herein is a marvellous thing, that ye know not from whence He is, and yet He hath opened mine eyes. Now we know that God heareth not sinners, but, if any man be a worshipper of God, and doeth His will, him He heareth."

" He argueth well, this beggar," muttered Caiaphas, carried away against his will by the man's words.

The beggar continued: " Since the world began was it not heard that any man opened the eyes of one that was born blind. If this Man were not of God, He could do nothing."

Then the multitude divided amongst themselves, some believing, and some reviling; yet, united in wonder and curiosity, they shouted: "What sayest thou of Him that hath opened thine eyes ? "

And the beggar, fearing the while that he would be torn to pieces, replied, with faltering faith: " He is a prophet."

" Thou sayest so now, but thou almost said but a moment ago that He is of God; where is He then, that He may witness of thy sayings ? "

" I know not," replied the beggar.

"No, thou knowest not for thine own ends. He, too, hideth Himself for fear of the people," cried some of the crowd. " He feared even to be at His friend's death-bed, lest the sister should revile Him, or the Jews take Him."

And the crowd began to lay hands on the beggar to smite him, and push him about, gibing him the while and taunting him with coarse speech; while Caiaphas, standing back from the window, lest he should be noticed by the crowd, muttered ominously: " Well done, well done, my people."

9

CHAPTER XIV.

SUDDENLY, like a mist or cloud formed from the sun's effulgence into a mass of golden atoms held together by their own glory, a figure clad in white, that seemed to irradiate its own shimmering purity with dazzling lustre, and to set at naught the brilliancy of the sun itself—the figure of the Nazarene—stood in the midst of them. The crowd fell back in awe, and all looked upwards, as though they thought He had descended from the heavens; for none had noticed His approach, or could tell whence He had come. Caiaphas started backward with a curse. "How long shall this man trouble us?" he muttered. Then, turning to a messenger—for one stood always at the entrance to his chamber—he commanded: "Go, tell the soldiers that stand below to hold themselves in readiness to lay hands upon this Jesus, and to bring Him hither when I give the word. Dost hear, fool?" he exclaimed sharply, when the man seemed to hesitate.

" 'T will be no easy task," replied the soldier; " for though the people revile those who say He is the Christ, yet, when they see Him they fall down and worship Him, and easily would tear to pieces those who seek to slay Him or lay hands on Him."

With cynicism and contempt, the High Priest replied: " It will perhaps make thy task the easier,

coward, if thou tellest the soldiers that, unless my
word be obeyed and the Nazarene brought here at
my bidding, they shall forthwith be cast into prison
and, maybe, crucified. Though they be Romans,
Pontius Pilate hath agreed that, in all things, those
who are in my service shall be tried by Jewish law.
Speed thee now, or thou, too, shalt fear the power
of the law."

Caiaphas could have put forward no two stronger
incentives to action than the calling of a Roman subject a coward and threatening him with the humilia-
tion of a Jewish punishment.

"This man is beyond forbearance," muttered
the man, as he hurried down the stairs to obey Caiaphas's behest.

Then, with cruel delight, seeing that Nicodemus
quivered and winced at his words, Caiaphas turned
to him and said: "What thinkest thou, Nicodemus?
Have I not done well? Is it not time this mum-
mery had an end?"

Distraught with rage and impotence, yet not
courageous enough to throw himself upon Caiaphas,
Nicodemus answered: "Doth our law judge any
man before it hear him and know what he hath
done?"

Caiaphas laughed. "Thou, too, art gone mad,
Nicodemus. Art thou also of Galilee? Search and
look, for out of Galilee doth arise no prophet."

But Nicodemus answered: "Methinks it was of
Galilee the prophet Isaiah spoke in the words: 'The
people that walked in darkness have seen a great
light: they that dwell in the land of the shadow of
death, upon them hath the light shined.' Now I re-

call that thou thyself didst once preach in the Synagogue that this people was by way of the sea beyond
Jordan in Galilee of the nations."

Caiaphas scowled. " Verily thou hast good mem-
ory, Nicodemus. 'T will be well that Cæsar and
Herod learn that Nicodemus, the great ruler of the
Synagogue, believeth that this Jesus is the Son of
God."

Then, fearing lest he had said too much, he resumed the playful, half-patronising, half-deprecating,
persuasiveness with which he had won over so many
enemies. " Nay, heed me not, good Nicodemus,"
he went on; " thou hast a right to thine own
thoughts; but thou art wrong, this Man is not the
Christ. Nevertheless, let us step out on to the roof
and listen, for He hath good flow of language, this
Nazarene, and He interesteth me greatly."

Half sullenly, and half incredulously, yet wondering at the sudden change of mood of the cunning
priest, Nicodemus followed him on to the flat roof.

As they stepped out, they heard the voice of the
Nazarene speaking to the beggar; and Caiaphas
leaned forward to listen.

" Dost thou believe in the Son of God ? " asked
the gently entreating voice; and the words thrilled
Caiaphas against his will.

" Who is He, Lord ? " replied the beggar, looking
with doubting wonder, yet with love and gratitude,
at the Perfect Man before him, His face marred only
by the lines of suffering and pity drawn on it.

Breathless, the two rulers listened for the answer
that Caiaphas had gone to Bethany to hear. It
seemed as if, in answer to the questionings of their

hearts, the Nazarene raised His eyes towards them, rather than to the beggar; as if, also, the message concerned both the individual and the world collectively, a vital truth addressed to every soul throughout the universe: " Thou hast both seen Him, and it is He that talketh with thee."

Caiaphas rose excitedly. " Dost hear this blasphemy, Nicodemus?" he almost shouted; but his voice was drowned in the uproar of the people; some crying: "It is the Lord, hear ye Him. The Messiah hath indeed come down." Others crying out: "He hath a devil."

But the beggar, as if struck suddenly with a revelation of the truth, cried out, in a voice that seemed to rend the skies: "Lord, I believe, Lord, I believe."

A smile, so heavenly as to be beyond the power of man's description, illumined the Messiah's face. His eyes were raised to heaven, as if in prayer and thankfulness for giving Him this one soul, at least, in all that multitude.

Caiaphas, meanwhile, was marching up and down the terrace, oblivious of the crowd, which, if it had not been so absorbed by the presence of the Nazarene would have espied him.

" This time I tell thee, Nicodemus, I will not delay. Even now will I give the order to arrest Him. This man bewitcheth the people with a devil."

" Nay, forbear," cried Nicodemus hastily. " Listen yet awhile. He goeth to Solomon's porch to preach to the multitude. If thou wilt slay Him it will be the last speech He maketh, and I would hear Him yet this once."

" As thou wilt; but it is the last time; my mind is made up," answered Caiaphas. And, while he spoke, he clenched his fists, and his features hardened into an expression that was diabolical.

" Yea, 't will surely be the last time," said Nicodemus to himself. But already the divine voice had begun to speak, and the crowd was silent, sitting, standing, kneeling around, while the little children clustered around the knees of the Nazarene, and looked boldly up into the face they loved and feared not.

His subject was that on which He had enlarged aforetime; that of the shepherd, the hireling, and the sheep.

When He paused, the cry went up, " What meanest Thou ? Thou speakest in parables. Who is the shepherd, who are the sheep ? Thinkest Thou that we are blind also, or fools like sheep, that these parables for children are for such as we ? We are not beggars, we are not blind."

Caiaphas heard, and murmured in approval: "The Nazarene hath overreached Himself. The Jewish people love plain-speaking."

Then, in answer to the crowd, the voice of the Messiah rose again: " If ye were blind, ye should have no sin; but now ye say, we see; therefore your sin remaineth."

Then He proceeded to unfold the meaning of His parable.

When He ceased speaking, the Jews began discussing among themselves. Here and there a voice was heard crying out: " Show us Lazarus, and we will believe."

" They are no fools, the Jewish people," muttered Caiaphas; " they are a fair and reasonable
people."

When the name of Lazarus was repeated by the
crowd, a great sadness overspread the face of Jesus;
this the people misread for trouble at His impotence,
or at their detection of it.   Fiercely and half mad
with excitement, they gathered round the Nazarene.

" How long dost Thou make us to doubt ? " said
one.   " Tell us plainly if Thou be the Christ."

Then once more Jesus answered them : "I told ye
and ye believed not; the works that I do in My
Father's name, they bear witness of Me.   But ye
believe not, because ye are not of My sheep.   My
sheep hear My voice, and I know them, and they
follow Me.   And I give unto them eternal life, and
they shall never perish, neither shall any man pluck
them out of My hand."

A scoffing voice called out: " Nevetheless they
have plucked Lazarus from out Thy hand."   A
mocking laugh went up from the crowd, and Caiaphas joined in it.   Then the voice of Jesus rose
once more :

"My Father, which gave them Me is greater than
all, and no man is able to pluck them out of My
Father's hand."

" He maketh out that Lazarus is with the
Father," cried one.

" I and My Father are one," went on the calm,
impressive voice.

Then some of the Jews took stones and hurled
them at Him; but fearlessly, and with an indifference that brought a shout of admiration from the

Roman soldiers standing round in waiting for Caiaphas's message to arrest Him, the Nazarene continued :

" Many good works have I showed ye from My
Father; for which of these good works do ye now
stone Me ? "

Then the Jews cried out: " For a good work we
stone Thee not, but for blasphemy, and because that
Thou, being a man, makest Thyself God."

Once more the stones flew round the golden head
of the Messiah. One of the disciples stepped forward, as if to shelter Him, but the Messiah raised
His hand and went on:

" If I do not the works of My Father, believe Me
not; but if I do, though ye believe not Me, believe
the works, that ye may know and believe that the
Father is in Me and I in Him."

Then, exasperated by His calmness, the Jews rose
up and approached Him menacingly. Luke, who
was standing just behind Jesus, stepped forward and
took two of the children by the hand; then, raising
them in his arms, handed them to their mothers,
who stretched forward to receive them over the
heads of the multitude.

Then, like a lion who has awaited his prey only to
make its seizure more assured, Caiaphas thundered
forth these words: " Quick, Gilner, hie thee to the
soldiers. Bid them bring this Jesus to me here a
captive." Then, with an after-thought, he added:
" But no violence, mind ye."

The messenger, mindful of the High Priest's former threats, precipitated himself into the street, and
Nicodemus, fearing the scene that was about to en-

sue, and yet not brave enough to try to defend the Nazarene; fearing also that he would at last be goaded into giving vent to the rage that seemed to suffocate him, bade a hasty farewell to Caiaphas, and took his leave.

Caiaphas remained alone, his head so bent that his chin rested on his breast. It all depended upon him now, the death or the life of the Nazarene. It all lay in his hands, the hands of Caiaphas. If—but it was too ridiculous to speculate upon—if this was the Son of God, even then Caiaphas would try to oppose, rather than descend from his place of power— for what was a high priest, after all, but a foreshadow of the future, ordained to keep alive in the hearts of men the promise of God to send the world a Saviour? When the Saviour should come, priest and ordinance would cease to be; this he knew well. Alone Caiaphas reasoned with himself. Shortly they would bring Jesus before him; surely, if He were the Son of God, He would give convincing proof of it. Either the great High Priest would be forced into obeisance and submission, or, if the Nazarene were but a fanatical prophet, a defier of the law, a blasphemer, a devil let loose to betray the people, Caiaphas, the great Caiaphas, would find it out. But deep, deep down in his heart that was gradually closing every door to faith, hardening each plastic fibre with ambition, lust, and greed, echoed still the words, " I am the good shepherd."

Yes, if he would but own it to himself, Caiaphas knew that there was something in the words of the Nazarene that had in it the ring of truth; that, like true coin, could never pass for false.

Too clever, too learned, was Caiaphas not to know
the fast hold the Pharisees had on the people, not to
be conscious that this enthralling power of lawyer,
scribe, and Pharisee musts needs be broken through
before the people could be set free to worship the
living God.

Oh, he knew it well, this great High Priest; but a
certainty of power in this world was more to him
than a shadowy, uncertain place in God's eternity.
Ambition, the love of power, the greatest temptations that can assail a man, were too strong for
Caiaphas.

The day wore on, and, so absorbed was Caiaphas
in his dreams, that he forgot his midday meal and
his usual visit to the Synagogue.

The men were long in returning. Hour succeeded
hour, and Caiaphas sat wondering why the soldiers
came not with the Nazarene. He waited before
sending other messengers, for he had given injunctions that no violence was to be used; maybe the
Jews, or, at least, the followers of the Nazarene, the
twelve who had declared themselves forever on His
side, had offered some resistance. Yet it was
strange that none came with a message, that there
was no uproar, no tumult in the streets. Once he
stepped out on to the terrace, and sheltering with
his hands his eyes, he scanned Jerusalem, its roofs,
its winding streets, the distant groves of palms; but
nowhere were crowds, or even groups in sight.

" Perhaps they have killed Him in their zeal," he
murmured to himself. As the afternoon wore on,
and the glowing Eastern twilight fell almost suddenly, he began to marvel that none had come to

him, and the thought oppressed him.   It was
strange indeed for Caiaphas to be thus unvisited
and   unattended.   Now   and   then   a   waterman
walked down the road with his goat skin slung
across him, crying out mournfully, " Ho, any one
that thirsteth."

Here and there a woman came out from her door
with a pitcher to be filled ; but the gloom of evening
gathered quickly, for winter was beginning, and the
Feast of Dedication was then at hand.   He could
see the priests closing the doors of the Temple, and
on distant roofs a few praying with their faces towards the East.   The night stretched across the sky
like a veil of crape, and still the Nazarene came not,
nor did the Roman soldiers return ; and Caiaphas
had to own himself defeated.   Deeper and deeper
fell the darkness on Jerusalem, and at last the city
slept, as she will sleep " until the day break and the
shadows flee away."

CHAPTER XV.

THE same night that Caiaphas was pacing his terrace—raging madly, like a wild beast deprived of its prey; baffled in his ambitious schemes, cheated of his dreams of vengeance, growing each moment more infuriated, more malevolent, more determined—a middle-aged woman was kneeling on the stone floor of a poor cottage at Nazareth. The whole room was dimly lighted by a candle standing on a stone shelf built into the wall.

The face was beautiful, more from expression than from feature. The brow, especially, impressed one by its whiteness, but the eyes turned up towards heaven were full of tears, and the corners of the lips, that prayed so fervently and met each moment in such reverence but to form words of piety and devotion, were drawn downwards, as if in agony. Yet there was no despair, no passionate vehemence on the face or in the prayer, only a meek, submissive pleading for resignation; and as, every now and then, a salt tear rolled down the gentle, fragile cheeks, it was swallowed meekly, as though such tears were symbols of a revolt to be subdued.

A soft footfall moved close up to the door; then a light hand rapped gently on it. Mary rose like one returning from a trance. She held her hand to her heart one moment, not in physical fear, but with a foreboding of some dread news, to bear which would tax all her fortitude. Then she listened; it could not be Jesus, her Son-God, for He needed no opening of doors to appear to her. No, it must be a messenger, or, perchance, Joseph returned from Bethany; but the step was light for Joseph, who was no longer young.

Then, when the rapping came again, she stepped to the door and opened it.

The moon was high in the heavens and its rays entered the cottage in a long streak of bluish white. The virgin mother's golden hair looked silver beneath its radiance, and the pale face grew paler still. A woman stood without, but, with her back to the moon's glory, her features were undistinguishable.

" 'T is I, Mary Magdalene, the sinner," said a voice faint with penitence and meekness.

" No longer a sinner, since thou art forgiven," said the elder woman, drawing her in lovingly. " But what dost thou here at night ? ' T is not safe for thee, Magdalene, with thy beauty, to come thus late at night; for, till men's eyes be opened to understand, they do not honour women as one day they will."

" Yet, for thy sake, all women henceforth will be honoured," exclaimed the emotional, loving Magdalene; and kneeling at the elder woman's feet, she raised the hem of her garment and kissed it reverently.

" Nay, do not do so," said the other hastily; " worship me not, for I am only human like thyself. 'T is of God's mercy that He has chosen me to be the mother of our Lord."

" In the far future many will worship thee, in that thou wast so chosen," replied the Magdalene. " But I must not tarry with my news that will soothe thy aching heart: I have seen Lazarus."

" Is it even so ? " said the virgin mother calmly.

She had seen too many miracles, been too closely bound to the Messiah to be surprised at the news that Lazarus had risen; or, indeed, at any miracle performed by the God-Man. Then she went on: " What said Martha and Mary at the miracle ? Did many believe ? "

" Nay, but it is no miracle, mother of the Christ," replied the Magdalene. " It was his spirit only that I saw in the olive groves, and he bade me tell thee that thy Lord was not at Bethany yet, but safe with the brethren."

Over the sweet face there came a quieter, more peaceful look, as of one who had received a respite from some dreadful danger.

" Will He not then restore him ? " asked the gentle voice.

" I know not," answered Mary Magdalene sadly, lifting her veil from her face and seating herself on a stool.

" Poor Magdalene! Thou dost love Lazarus," said the mother of Christ, " and they who love must suffer."

The eyes of the Magdalene filled with tears; then, laying her hands timidly on the Virgin's knees, as though to touch so lovely a woman were to defile her, she replied: " Lazarus I have ever loved. But how should a ruler of Israel call a harlot wife ? Yet, in his very scorn of me I love him; and, now that I know Jesus, the joy that I can feel so deep a grief for my great sins is as strong as is my love; and so my grief hath become a joy, in like manner as my joy is the offspring of my grief. 'T is a strange mystery, this love of Christ, that maketh all things bearable; but, mother of Jesus, is it not a wondrous thing that Lazarus, who in life was wont to pass me on the other side and forbid his sisters to have speech with me, should after death appear to me a sinner?"

The virgin mother, borne down with grief, yet ever quick to sympathise, smiled her sweet, pathetic smile.

" Perchance, Magdalene, the dead know all," she answered; " he knoweth that thy heart is right with the Lord. Dost but remember His words : ' To her much is forgiven, for she loved much ' ?"

" Those words are written forever on my heart, O mother of the Lord. For when the Lord spake them they were life to me. Oh, it is marvellous, this new life of love, and yet of mystery, for we know nothing, do we ? Yet, when He speaketh, one's heart burneth within one and one knoweth that every word He saith is true. Methinks it is not a thing that comes by learning," went on the Magdalene.

" It is a gift of God that Jesus hath brought on earth," replied the mother. " It is a problem none can solve. The wind bloweth where it listeth, and thou hearest the sound thereof, but canst not tell whence it cometh nor whither it goeth. So are they who are born of God."

" May I bide with thee this night ?" asked the

Magdalene presently. " It is late to return to my dwelling; and thou, thou canst not sleep for thinking of thy Son. We will talk and pray together till the morning. Methinks that, when near to thee, I am closer to the Lord."

Then, in tones of deepest reverence, and stroking the thin, fair hands of the mother of Jesus down to the pointed finger tips, she murmured : " His mother, His mother, the mother of the Lord. The living witness of the greatness of the Lord, who hath visited His handmaiden to bring glory and salvation into the world."

As she spoke, the Virgin raised her face instinctively towards heaven.

" When thou dost gaze upwards thus, thou dost bring to my remembrance a lily looking towards the dying sun, expectant of the dews of heaven," said the Magdalene, and once more, with deep devotion, she kissed the Virgin's hands. Then, taking a clean napkin from the table, she proceeded to pour water into a basin.

" Be seated," she said in tenderest voice, " and I will wash thy feet, thou holy one! It will rest and refresh thee during the night watch." The virgin mother raised a hand in deprecation.

" Call me not holy, Mary; none is holy, save God alone. Who am I that thou shouldst wash my feet ? Even a poor sinner, like thyself."

" Thou hast no sin," replied the Magdalene; " and to wash each other's feet, in deep humility, is the commandment of our Lord."

At her words, meekly and modestly, with deprecating gesture, as if not desiring such attention, **the**

Virgin allowed Mary to wash first one foot and then the other.

With tender reverence, Mary laved each slender foot, kissing it when she had finished. Then she cast from her the cloth that she had bound around her waist.

" Nay, naught wrought with human hands shall touch thee, mother of my Lord "; and, catching hold of her own luxuriant golden tresses, she wiped the Virgin's feet till they were dry. Then, touched by strong emotion, she fell to the ground at Mary's feet and cried out : " Oh, would that I were pure and holy as thou, thou queen amongst women. Woe is me that I have sinned. Would that I were pure, would that I were pure!" And, with face bent down, she wept as though her heart would break. At sight of her abandonment, the Virgin lifted her heart heavenwards and prayed silently that comfort might be sent to the poor patient soul.

Then, as if in answer to her prayer (for whose prayer would be answered, if that of Mary were not?) a moonbeam shot straight through the window, lighting up the opposite wall; and, in dark relief, the shadow of the window frames stood out, its form a cross; and a voice of sweetest music murmured: " Let not your heart be troubled, neither let it be afraid."

At that moment, the clatter of horses' hoofs rang on the silent night, sounding hollow and resonant on the stony street.

The Magdalene sat up, and pushing her hair from her eyes with one hand, held out the other to clasp the Virgin's.

In constant apprehension of the death of their dear Lord, the followers of Christ were ever ready to scent danger, ever steeling themselves for the dreadful moment when their Saviour would be taken from them. He had warned them, in His tenderness, that the support and comfort of His presence, the sweet companionship, would not last forever. Yes, all this they knew, but the agony of separation had yet to come. The sight of the suffering of their Beloved One was soon to wring their hearts, and, as love grew stronger, their coming grief became more sure. Each unwonted sound brought terror to their hearts.

The two listened.

" 'T is some message from Caiaphas or Pontius Pilate; or, perchance a fire hath broken out in some ruler's house," the Magdalene suggested to reassure the Virgin's heart.

" Peace! cheat me not," replied the Virgin sternly; " they halt at this very door. They think to find Him here, but His hour is not yet come."

The horses drew up at the door, and one could hear them pawing the ground, and a man's voice giving orders. Farther down the street some dogs began to bark.

The Virgin rose and stood with mild dignity in the chamber, hard by the door. Half fearful, yet half eager, the Magdalene pressed behind her, her long tresses falling almost to the ground.

A loud, hasty knock, and the door was opened. At sight of the Virgin, standing ethereal and lovely in her beautiful simplicity, faintly outlined by the streaks of early dawn, now striving to get the better of the waning moon, the soldier started.

" Surely this is some angel," he muttered to himself; then, making his gruff voice as gentle as he could, he said: " Good woman, the High Priest, Caiaphas, hath commanded me to search this cottage, lest the Nazarene be hidden here, and, if I find Him, to bring Him to him."

" Sir, do as thou wilt," replied the Virgin. " The Lord is not here, but, if He were, ye could do nothing unless it were given ye from on high. Seek ye Him."

The men searched, but without much ardour. They were not anxious to find the Nazarene, nor had they imagined that He would be there, for it was well known that He dwelt not now at Nazareth.

" Mother of the Nazarene," said the soldier, after he and his men had searched the house, " I have yet an ugly message to convey to thee. Caiaphas hath commanded that, if we found not the Nazarene, we should bring to him all within this house." While he was speaking his eyes fell on the Magdalene.

" Thou here ?" he exclaimed. Then his lips parted with a coarse, rude smile, ready to speak some prurient jest. A look from the mother of the Christ arrested him, but the Magdalene had seen and understood the look, and bent her head humbly to the ground. That henceforward would be the cross she would have to bear. The moral crucifixion of the world's opinion had begun. No nails could pierce more sharply, no spear strike more deeply, no burden be bitterer or harder to bear than would the judgment of the world on sins that she had done with. For God forgives more quickly than does man. It would never be wiped out, that past of Mary Magdalene's; daily, hourly, the familiarity of men, the taunts and coldness of women, no better, nay, worse than herself, would remind the Magdalene of that thoughtless past of wantonness and passion. Years of endless writhing torture lay before her, a weary battling against man's proffered love and woman's jealousy and hardness, till welcome death should come to free the hunted being.

"This is the Magdalene, my friend," said the Virgin's gentle voice; a voice that came from one who knew that the Magdalene's fame could not be damaged by the friendship of one whose love partook of the divine, and, like that of Jesus clung to the one loved alike through good report and evil.

With rough courtesy, the soldier bowed before the majestic form of purity incarnate.

"One to whom the immaculate Mary of Nazareth hath given shelter is safe from all men."

With infinite sweetness the Virgin answered the rough soldier: "I thank thee, proud Roman, for thy kindly words; may it be so done unto thee and more." Then wrapping her cloak around her, so as almost to cover her face, she again addressed him: "If thy orders are to convey us to Caiaphas we must obey."

Then, in the cold, grey light of dawn, the two women were conveyed outside. But, when the soldier was about to assist the Virgin to mount the horse that was to convey her, the Magdalene stepped forward.

"Forgive me, brave soldier," she interprosed, "but no man hath ever laid hands on this woman of all women. Wilt permit me to help her on the horse?"

" Methinks 'twixt thee and me there is not much
to choose," the soldier muttered; " but as thou
wilt."

At his word, the Magdalene lifted the frail figure
of the Virgin, with almost a man's vigour, yet with
all a woman's tenderness, on to the horse.

" Thou art not so fearful for thyself," the Roman
went on coarsely, as he placed the Magdalene on the
horse and shook her fallen tresses around her.

The Magdalene blushed; then, with the appealing, trustful manner that had been her charm and
her perdition in days gone by, " Friend," she said,
" speak no more to me in words of jest. Magdalene,
the sinner, is no more. We are two lone, sorrowful
women who look to thy manliness for protection."

Her sweet seriousness touched the Roman soldier,
and, beckoning to his comrade to lead on the horse,
he took the reins and led his own behind. For
nearly an hour the strange cavalcade proceeded thus
in the lightening darkness through the streets of
Jerusalem, and the sun was up and the shadows
were sharp and well defined when they halted at the
house of Caiaphas.

As to Caiaphas, he hardly knew himself why he
had commanded the soldiers to bring the mother of
the Nazarene to him. Furious at having been foiled
in capturing the Christ, and with a growing conviction that he was being treacherously dealt with by
those in his employ; full of suspicion—as those are
who are themselves unworthy—and enraged at any
obstruction to his arrogance, any crossing of his will,
he had been prompted in his action partly by the
wish to lay hands on all or any connected with the

Nazarene he could; and partly by curiosity to see
this woman so many talked of, and to hear her ver-
sion of the circumstances of her Son's birth. These
times were too uncommon, too unsettled, by the
teachings of the lowly carpenter, for even Caiaphas
to be able to close his eyes to the fact that the Nazarene was no ordinary man. To justify himself,
nay, more, to enjoy the full flavour of his vengeance,
he must know all concerning Him that he could
glean from those who had conversed with Him.
From the first he had feigned ignorance of the
preachings in the Temple, the assemblies by the
seashore, the miracles, the strange doings and sayings
of this young madman, as he had named the Christ;
but the day had come when, if Caiaphas had made
up his mind to crucify the Man, he must know
enough to give good reasons for His condemnation
to Herod and to Pontius Pilate; even to Cæsar,
should he demand it; nay, more, he must have an
excuse to give himself.

Two rulers of the Synagogue, Nicodemus and
Lazarus, had gone over to this Man. Lazarus, indeed, was now dead, but Pontius Pilate himself,
urged on by his wife, this Claudia Procula whom
Caiaphas hated, was beginning to speak in tones of
no disfavour, even of admiration, of the Nazarene.
Surely, therefore, it was time to tremble and to act.
But he was not prepared for the presence of the
Magdalene. Her beauty troubled him, for he was
as licentious as he was hypocritical; nay, more, he
owed her a grudge, in that she, a sinner, had repulsed his advances when, disguised as a peasant, he
had mingled more than once in the crowd that

chatted with the maidens at eventide by the well of Samaria.

" Thou art too ugly," she had ofttimes cried to him before them all, "and thou hast a priestly face." And the maidens would shriek with laughter, for they knew full well that he was Caiaphas. But that was in the days gone by, before the Magdalene had become a follower of Christ. She had almost hoped that they would not bring her before Caiaphas, and, but for her affection for the Virgin, she would have asked to remain in the outer chamber.

While they were being ushered into the presence of the High Priest she drew her veil closer over her face; but Caiaphas, fearful always of treachery, bade her lower it. When she did so, her long, golden tresses fell about her, and, changed though her face was with grief and weeping, he knew that there was but one woman in Jerusalem with tresses such as those.

" Thou art in questionable company, Mary of Nazareth," said Caiaphas, laughing coarsely. "Methinks that, for one reported so immaculate, thou choosest strange associates."

Both women were silent.

" Hast naught to say, woman ? Dost thou fully understand that the life or death of this Nazarene doth lie with me ? "

Then, raising her pure eyes steadily to Caiaphas, the Virgin answered: " Thou couldst do naught at all were it not that power were given thee from above. He hath escaped thee many times, for His hour was not yet come; but He knoweth that He must die to save the world from sin."

Uneasy at her words, Caiaphas turned to another subject: " It seemeth thy Son did not raise Lazarus ?"

" He will be raised up," replied the Virgin.

" At the resurrection, forsooth," said Caiaphas, shrugging his shoulders.

Then the Magdalene, who had been silent, burst forth with a gleam of triumphant daring: " Yet I spake with Lazarus yesterday."

The brows of Caiaphas flushed crimson, and he clenched his fists. Terrified almost, he leaned forward, and forgetful of all else, he gasped: " Thou hast talked with Lazarus ?" Then, shaking his head and rising from his chair: "Thou art mad, woman. Thy penitence hath turned thy brain. But now they brought me tidings that he hath lain in his grave two days." With strange agitation he rose and paced the room. " The soldiers, too, must be bewitched, since they fear to tell me what hath happened."

Then the voice of the Virgin rose distinct and clear: " 'T was but his spirit Mary saw."

" Ha! thou shouldst not speak in parables, Magdalene, for they ill become thy lips, which are made rather for man's kisses than for the telling of grave matters. His spirit forsooth! Thou lovest Lazarus, and in thy dreams he visited thee. Poor fond, foolish woman, he is no more on earth." Then, turning from her, he addressed the Virgin: " There are strange things spoken of thy Son's birth. Is He in truth not the Son of thine husband ? Then whose Son is He ? These incredible reports work harm; they but unsettle the minds of men and entangle the thoughts of the populace.   No virgin yet hath borne a son, yet methinks, with eyes like thine, thou couldst not tell a lie.   Whose Son is He ?

Proudly, and with head thrown back, the Virgin answered: " He is the Son of God." And, even while she spoke, there gathered round her head a filmy radiance of glory, that even Caiaphas could see.

He staggered back; then, pointing with a finger towards the Virgin, cried: " What is that light ? " And Magdalene, conscious that the glory of the Lord was nigh, fell down in solemn worship at the Virgin's knee.

Then, for a moment terrified, Caiaphas cried out, " Woman of Nazareth, who art thou ?   What art thou ?   Speak, for on thy word dependeth the salvation of the world.   Speak, and tell us plainly who is thy Son ?   Whence is He ?   Is He but a poor carpenter, or is He the Son of God ? "

" He is Very God and Very Man," replied the Virgin; "but the mystery I cannot tell thee, for I know it not.   All the learning of the scribes and Pharisees, all the philosophy of this earth cannot explain why I should have been chosen to be the mother of my Lord, nor how He did enter the womb; but I declare unto thee that this Jesus, whom they call my Son, is the Son of God, descended from heaven and made man; but how I know not.   Only I know that the Lord hath so revealed it to me.   But this I say truly, that he who believeth on Him shall be saved from eternal damnation."

" It was never so known," said Caiaphas.   " Why

should the Son of God come thus to judge the world ?''

"He cometh not for judgment, but to save the world," replied the Virgin, her face still illumined by the wondrous light. "He came to call sinners to repentance. 'T is God that judgeth, and He will come again to judge the world."

"Why, then, do I not believe?" asked Caiaphas.''

"Because thou wilt not, Caiaphas," replied the Virgin fearlessly.

A long silence followed, while Caiaphas mused. Then, as if suddenly remembering that these two women stood still before him, he looked up.

"Leave me, I pray you, to consider of this thing, for it hath never so been known in Israel."

Then came to pass a thing which never yet had been. Caiaphas, the great High Priest, escorted the two women through the ante-chambers and past the soldiers to the street.

CHAPTER XVI.

IT was about four o'clock in the morning when Martha was awaked from her sleep by Mary, who stood by her. Weary with the shortness of her rest, she stretched herself heavily; then, with the recollection of the sorrows of the preceding day, that came back to her with a rush, she sat up and, with a bewildered look, brushed back the dark tresses, now streaked with grey, from her forehead.

" I would not wake thee earlier, Martha," Mary said: " but this night I had a dream that Lazarus our brother was risen and stood by me, and thus spake to me: ' I am risen for the glory of God and to show forth His handiwork.' "

" Dost waken me for a dream, Mary ? " asked Martha, somewhat fretfully. " Thou art tired and thy thoughts were full of our brother and of the longing for the miracle of his healing."

Nay, but I woke thee not for that alone," said Mary; " but because two messengers from the Lord wait below. The Lord cometh nigh to the city."

Martha stood up at last. This was indeed news calculated to stir her active mind and soothe the anxious craving of her restless heart.

" I will go forth and meet Him," she said, beginning to attire herself in haste. " I will go forth and entreat Him once more, for He can yet raise our brother."

"Nay, our brother did say, ' Entreat Him not,'" said Mary.

"Nevertheless, I will go and meet Him," retorted Martha, averse, as always, to anything that savoured of dictation.   "Wilt not come too?"

"Nay, I will sit and wait here for the Lord," said Mary, "or, maybe, I will carry flowers and spices to our brother's grave."

Then Martha rose, and with pale face, and eyes darkened and hollowed with weeping, stepped out amidst the grey shadows of early dawn to meet the Lord. She found Him surrounded by His little band of disciples, as ever the central figure, and on His face there was a look that Martha had never seen before. It expressed anguish, and, at the same time, a measure of exultation. His visage shone with a radiancy not wholly to be accounted for by the reflection of the rising sun, that was struggling feebly through the olive groves. With deepest sympathy and love He turned to Martha, and she, at sight of her Lord, strengthened and revived in faith, and realising all she had suffered by His absence, sank weary and humble and abased (as Martha seldom was) at His feet, and cried out in bitterness of soul: "Lord, if Thou hadst been here, my brother had not died."

Peter, incensed at her reproach, exclaimed: "Who art thou, woman, that thy brother should live when all men die?"

But she, heedless of the warning words of Mary, heedless of the angry looks of the disciples, and with a return of faith and hope in the presence of the Saviour, went on: " But I know that, even now, whatsoever thou wilt ask of God, God will give it Thee."

A look of joy came into the eyes of the Nazarene. In the midst of all the unbelief and scoffing and persecution of the world, the faith of this woman seemed a slight refreshment, a little solace, a little return for all the sacrifice; and, as if with sudden power from above, in prompt answer to her quickened faith, the voice of Jesus rose with inspiring force on the cool, unbreathed morning air: " Thy brother shall rise again."

Then, falling at His feet, fighting with herself to force submission to His will, Martha cried out: " I know, I know that he shall rise again in the resurrection at the last day."

Surely she believed and trusted to the fullest extent of the Jewish law and her Pharisaical upbringing; but the vision that was hidden from her was Jesus the Nazarene as God, and resurrection on earth. It was too simple to believe. Then, once more, as if to test the faith of this true daughter of the Jews, the Nazarene spoke words which not only fell on those around, but seemed shed, like the fragrance of flowers, on the waves of the air placed in their keeping, to be wafted hither and thither throughout all space, forming into sweetest music, heralding like silver trumpets to the ages and generations yet to come, shaking the hills and making the valleys tremble, crying out through all the centuries of time, echoing and re-echoing from snow-bound mountain peaks, thundering forth across the storm-clouds,

murmuring like summer zephyrs, and tossing from
star to star, weeping like rain, bubbling forth in
mountain torrent, burning in glowing nuclei of fire
in the hearts of men—the message of life and peace
and love eternal: " I am the resurrection and the
life; he that believeth on Me, though he were dead,
yet shall he live; and whosoever liveth and believeth
in Me shall never die. Believest thou this ? "

And in deepest love, the battle with mistrust and
doubting over, the longing for the restoration of her
brother merged into meek submission to His will,
she murmured : " Yea, Lord." Then, not knowing
whether she really understood His words, went on :
" I believe that Thou art the Christ, the Son of
God."

Then, she still kneeling in oblivious devotion at
Jesus' feet, one of the disciples stepped forward,
and touching her on the shoulder, said : " Hearest
thou not ? The Lord hath need of Mary. Bring
her here."

At these words she rose and retraced her steps
quickly along the road. The cool air, laden with
the breath of awakening flowers, echoing with the
music of the birds, rejoicing in the sun's promise of
a glorious day, had given her physical support and
courage, as the word of the Lord had soothed the
agony of her heart and brought faith and resignation
to soothe the torture of bereavement. It was with
lightened step and smoother brow, with a smile of
restored calm and hope, that she entered the garden
Lazarus had loved. Already it and the porch and
lower chambers were filled with Jews of all sects and
classes, who had assembled once more to mourn

with the late ruler's sisters. Some, too, had come from curiosity, to see whether the Nazarene had sent any message; others, in answer to offered bribes from Caiaphas.

To-day the wailing and chanting had a less mournful tone, as if to bring comfort to the bereaved ones: "I have eaten ashes like bread, and mingled my drink with weeping. Thou hast lifted me up, and cast me down. My days are like a shadow that declineth; and I am withered like grass. But thou, O Lord, shalt endure for ever; and Thy remembrance unto all generations. Thou shalt arise, and have mercy upon Zion: for the time to favour her, yea, the set time, is come."

"Thou shalt arise, Thou shalt arise." What blessed prophetic message was that which greeted Martha on her return, and why did her heart leap within her and burn with strange excitement?

She paused at the entrance to the garden. It would not do to arouse the suspicious curiosity of the Jews by telling them that Jesus was waiting outside the little town. Drawing her veil over her face, and mingling with the crowd, she wended her way through the porch and across the tesselated court, where, out of deference to the dead, the small bubbling fountains had been stopped. She sought out her sister in her own private chamber. There, in sackcloth and ashes, with bowed head, praying lest her faith should die a moral death, sat Mary.

She started at Martha's voice calling in subdued hoarse tones: "Mary, Mary, the Master is come and calleth for thee."

Mary arose with feverish haste. She had expected

this, so the message brought comfort but no wonder.

"He waiteth for thee just without the gates of the village," resumed Martha. "I know not why He calleth for thee, but there is that in His words and look that is like prophecy. I know not what hath come to me, but this day doth seem full of import, and I feel strangely comforted for the death of our dear brother."

"It is surely because thou hast been with the Lord, and He hath comforted thy soul," said Mary. Then, perceiving that the court was crowded with mourners, she whispered to Martha, nervously: "How shall we keep this crowd from following us?"

Then, with Eastern disregard for any privacy, with that gloating over horrors which is the characteristic of all the lowly classes throughout the world, the crowd of mourners, seeing the two women pass out silently and with veiled faces, murmured: "They go unto the grave to weep there." And, as if the sisters' grief was theirs, and the necessity of sustaining them with sympathy amounted to a religious law, they followed them.

Then, when the sisters took the opposite road to that which led to Lazarus's grave, they fell a-murmuring. Some said: "Their grief hath made them mad." Others, "Whither go they?" And one derisive voice said scoffingly: "Maybe that Lazarus is risen and they go forth to meet him." And so, murmuring, quarrelling, and wailing, the Jewish people followed the two women; till, O wonder unexpected and to be marvelled at indeed, they led them to the presence of the glorious Jesus! Impetuous as ever, fearing revenge or treachery, Peter sprang forward, as though to stay the crowd.

" Are ye mad, ye women ? " he said impulsively, " to bring this crowd of unbelieving fools to the presence of our Lord ? Do ye, too, now seek to slay Him because your brother Lazarus is dead ? "

But Mary, conscious only that her Lord, the Messiah whom she loved, was there, near her once more, after these weeks of watching and waiting, fell down in adoration at His feet, echoing, but not in reproach, only in tender faith and love, the words of her sister: " Lord, if Thou hadst been here, my brother had not died."

And, at sight of her great grief and faith, the Jews who stood around wept too, and once more through the olive groves resounded the wail of bitterness: " Look away from me, look away from me, for I will weep bitterly."

Then, in their half belief, reproaching Him, the Jews cried out: "If Thou hadst raised Lazarus we had believed."

No earthly pen would dare describe, no human heart can realise the sympathy and mingled grief of the Messiah. Surely never was the union of the Godhead and the Manhood in the person of the Christ more strongly manifested than at the death of Lazarus and the sorrow of his sisters. The grief of separation, the agony at having been absent, the sorrow of the two women He loved; all this was no less acute because as God He might have avoided it. But to do so would have been to set aside His manhood, to shirk the responsibilities of earthly life. It

was as if the power of God had been for a brief moment laid aside, to let the griefs of manhood have
their sway; nay, more, it was as if Satan had been
allowed in these last hours to tempt the Messiah
with a temptation that assailed alike His Godhead
and His Manhood.   What greater temptation to the
Man than to use His God-given energy for the sake
of human friendship ?   What to the God than to as-
sert His power by one transcendent act ?   What
more heartrending task than to wait in meek submission to God's will amidst the taunts of scoffing enemies and the tears of those beloved ?

Jesus wept.   Surely all earthly grief and desolation, the disillusion of friendship that has failed, the
inability of expressing one's tenderness to those one
loves, the general impotence of humanity, are forever comforted by those divine tears wrung forth
from the aching heart of the sorrowing Saviour.
Slowly they rolled down those troubled features on
to the white garment, crystal drops of mingled
purity and love; but they were not allowed to fall
to earth.

Ever foremost in his devotion, John pressed forward and stayed them in their course, as though he
would fain be washed in those pure waters.   Yet
one fell to earth, and, as it fell, a snow-white starry
flower with seven points united by a tiny corona
sprang into life.

But while the disciples were exclaiming at this
wonder and trying to attract the attention of the bystanders to it, the cry went up: " Behold how He
loved him."   And others cried again, as so many
had cried before: " Could not this Man, which

opened the eyes of the blind, have caused that even this man should not have died ?"

The hour of temptation was fast passing away, the patient submission to God's will was near to its reward. The answer to the prayer of the Messiah was close at hand, His groanings and His trouble were about to have their fruit.

Gently, in a voice that reached only the two women, the Nazarene murmured: "Where have ye laid him ?"

And the crowd, hoping and half believing that, at last, it was to see the miracle the nation had been expecting, howled and shrieked: "Show us Lazarus and we will believe."

Mary, in much humility, entreated the Lord to come and see the tomb where they had laid him.

Then, when the cry grew ever louder, "Show us Lazarus and it sufficeth us," Thomas approached the crowd and, raising his hand to still the tumult: "Men of Israel," he said, "wherefore call ye for Lazarus ? Do ye not remember how our Lord spake in parables? How the rich man did call to Abraham from hell, and cried and prayed that Lazarus be sent unto his brothers from the dead, and how Abraham gave answer: "If they hear not Moses and the prophets, neither will they be persuaded though one rose from the dead ' ?"

But they cried only the more: "Show us Lazarus, show us Lazarus," though the shouts were now less boisterous.

Then Thomas perceived that Jesus was already following the two women towards the tomb of Lazarus, and that half the crowd were already beginning to go after Him.   Many faces he recognised amongst them, among others that of Nicodemus, eager and anxious.   Presently he came up to Thomas.

" Why asketh He where they have laid Lazarus ? " he inquired of the disciple.   " Surely He knoweth all things ? "

" Methinks it is lest the Jews should imagine that we have agreed upon some trickery, for they seek daily to destroy the Lord."

" Thinkest thou that He will raise Lazarus ? " he continued.

" I know not; it seemeth like it; but who can tell ? "   And so, discussing, arguing, inquiring, bickering, the little band of Jews, that was growing every moment thicker as one passer-by after the other swelled its ranks, followed the two bereaved sisters, who showed the way to the Nazarene.

Who can tell what thoughts filled the soul of the God-Man ?   Thoughts of God, thoughts of friendship, thoughts of loving sympathy at the joy He was going to restore to the house at Bethany.   Thoughts, perhaps, of His own death, which was soon to follow the resurrection of Lazarus.

They stood opposite to the grave now.   It was a cave hewn from one single piece of rock, and at the entrance, hiding the ghastly sight, the corpse, hateful to the Jewish eyes as a thing defiled and unclean, stood the stone that Martha had insisted on having rolled in front of it at the words of Annas.   From between the apertures came forth the sickly odour of frankincense and myrrh and other spices, with which the body had been embalmed.

In silent awe, the crowd ceased the cries that were

some of taunt and some of praise, and the two women raised their eyes in sorrowing anxiety; while the Lord, groaning and weeping, stood by the grave, with eyes upturned to heaven. Meanwhile the multitude kept increasing, till half Jerusalem was there to witness the glory of the Lord.

Closed round the Lord, to keep Him from harm's way, stood the twelve, the traitor, Iscariot, on the outside. A little to the right were Mary and Martha, Mary just in front of Judas; behind them throngs of Jews, attired in many-coloured garbs of red and blue and white and purple, according to their rank or station.

The sun beat fiercely on their heads, for the glorious miracle of the world was to be enacted in the full light of day.

Presently Mary felt a clutching at her sleeve, and starting, half in terror, half in bewilderment at being thus roused from her reflections, she almost touched the hideous face of the traitor Judas, that was peering into hers.

" Dost not fear that, because of this, the Lord will die ? "

Mystified by his words and still more at the look of mingled greed and craft and despair upon his face, Mary stepped forward to bring herself away from him. But he thrust out his head and hissed: " If Lazarus doth live again, then surely will Jesus die. His blood be upon thee and Martha, and upon thy children and thy children's children."

Terrified and amazed at this uncalled-for curse, Mary was about to make reply, when, brief and terse, the voice of the Messiah gave command:

"Take ye away the stone." And He pointed with his finger to the grave.

The hour was come. But a few moments longer would the veil be stretched between the power of God and the belief of man. The air seemed freighted with portentous marvels, each heart palpitating with suspense.

The disciples sprang forward to obey; yet, even now, the voice of unbelieving common-sense, of faithlessness, of law-bound argument, sounded from Martha's lips. In horror and no simulated terror, she shrank from the dread sight she feared would meet her eyes.

"Lord, by this time he stinketh, for he hath been dead four days."

With a gleam almost of indignation at her want of belief, her worldly clinging to the social rites and conventionalities of Jewish custom, yet able still to tolerate the iron-bound limits of man's narrowness, the Nazarene fixed His full gaze upon her.

"Said I not unto thee, that, if thou wouldst believe, thou shouldst see the glory of God?"

Then, as the breeze chases a faint ripple from wavelet to wavelet, there rose a murmur through the multitude: "Verily He will raise him."

Then the disciples rolled away the stone, and the restlessness of the crowd increased; they were ready to burst into shouts of praise or fall in adoring worship; but the impulse was restrained by gestures from the disciples entreating peace.

In the glorious splendour of that Eastern sun, that glowed with an added brilliancy, as if in expectation of the stupendous miracle that was to be performed,

the Saviour stood. Unabashed, unflinching, beneath its scorching rays, with eyes that seemed to
pierce, like eagles, through the circles of blazing
light beyond, even to the very throne of truth itself,
to the feet of the Eternal *I Am*, the Christ uplifted
His fair head to heaven; and at that moment forked
tongues of fire, silvery and golden, like the sun
dancing on waves, or a shower of gold, played round
about His head. Then the Saviour of the world
upraised His voice in prayer to Heaven, in accents
of such certainty of answer, such oneness of com-
munion with the Father, as could leave no doubt
within the hearts of men!

" Father, I thank Thee that Thou hast heard Me.
And I knew that Thou hearest Me always: but because of the people which stand by I said it, that
they may believe that Thou hast sent Me."

There was a momentary silence, while the crowd,
believing now, without a doubt, that this was indeed
the Christ, stood also with eyes upturned to heaven,
waiting, expecting, for they knew not what; each
weaving in his own fancy the next act of this
colossal drama. Then, in a voice that thundered,
as though calling across endless æons of years and
days, and floating across the waves of time and of
eternity, beyond the bounds of heaven and hell,
Jesus gave forth those words that ranked Him God:
" Lazarus, come forth! "

CHAPTER XVII.

AND Lazarus came forth. A faint twitching of the members, a sort of convulsive tremor running from the head to foot, was all the multitude could see, as they pressed forward, a seething mass of tightly packed humanity, to witness this final and gigantic miracle.

In the doorway of the cave stood Lazarus, scarce able to move for the tight swathing of his grave clothes. His hands were tied close to his sides, and his face was bound about with a napkin. Standing there, he looked like some earth-sodden mummy, taken out of a sarcophagus and stood on end, or like a statue hewn in stone. No features, no colouring of life were visible. Immovable he stood and waited, while thousands of hearts seemed almost to cease to beat, checked, as it were, by some magic awe-inspiring wand. There are moments when no cry of ecstasy, no shouts of applause, no clamour of approbation, can express the quiverings of admiration, wrung from a fanatical crowd, like a hushed silence that dares not utter sound. And so it was on this unmatched occasion. A terrible quiet, as if a destroying angel had struck the bystanders dumb, had fallen on all; an awful thrill that seemed to lock together by magnetic force in one great manacle the soul of each onlooker; a terrible faintness as of death; a blinding of the eyes, as though the sun's too-scorching rays had struck the eyeballs; and, here and there, a dumb opening of the mouth as if to speak, though utterance could not come. A sickening dread, as if heaven and hell would open wide their gates to them. This, and far more than this, fell on the Jews, and the crowd, that had denied the Christ and clamoured to see Lazarus alive, were satisfied, each doubt laid still, each question answered. The power of the Eternal had been shown.

What could they do but fall down in adoration and belief? This would come, but meantime the multitude, from sheer excitement, wept.

One voice alone was raised in doubt.

" Is it indeed he ? "

It came from one well known to the Nazarene. It was a voice He loved, as often it is the voice one loves the best that wounds the most.

It was Thomas the unbeliever who had spoken— Thomas, to whom faith came ever hardly, yet who loved the Lord. But the words had lashed the seeming feverishness of silence into a living cry.

" Is it he ? Is it he, or is it another ? Show us thy face! Art thou indeed Lazarus ? "

" Loose him and let him go," commanded the Messiah, for all answer; but the voice that had spoken with such force to raise the dead man from the grave was weary now, and tired and disappointed. Even now, when the great miracle was over, when God Himself had seemed to bow to earth to fashion the triumph of His Son; when heaven and hell, at His command, had thrown back their

portals to let the spirit enchained of God return to
earth; when the great fulfilment of a nation's
yearning had come to pass; still they believed not
fully.   Would they believe when, mounted high on
a tree of shame, should hang the Son of God, in
proof of boundless love ?   Would they believe when
He should be seated on a cloud weighted with God's
own glory to be worthy to bear the Conqueror of
sin to heaven ?   No.   The answer to His agonised
prayer had been accorded; the great experiment,
the precursor of the greater love to come, had been
completed; science, suspicion, philosophy, conven-
tionality, the laws of this world and the next, all
had been overruled; yet from the voice of His own
follower had come the cry of doubt, sprung up again,
like some posionous weed that will not be denied its
growth.

The tears of Christ had been shed in vain; Lazarus returned but to tread in the same pastures, on
the same piercing thorns, to battle once more with
the same enemy who had lived in the hearts of men
while Lazarus died.

None at first durst approach the motionless body;
then John, the beloved of the Lord, stepped forward
at his Lord's behest.

One by one John cut with the dagger that hung
by his side the cords that bound the hands and feet,
leaving to the last the face; but whether he feared to
look on Lazarus, or wished to keep them in suspense, not one could tell.   Meanwhile the crowd
continued silent, almost breathless.   At last the
napkin fell, and Lazarus stood there in all the beauty
of his countenance.

Then rose such an uproar as could be heard almost at Jerusalem. 'T was as if a million lions roared by the shores of a stormy sea. Some prostrated themselves, women shrieked, some even dropped down dead with wonder; while little children, paralysed with fear, hid their sweet faces in their mothers' robes and howled.

Soldiers forgot to keep order. In the tumult no voice was granted precedence. All was confusion and astonishment and fear, except where here and there some fell in adoring worship at the Messiah's feet; others tore down the hill towards Jerusalem to tell the first news to the Pharisees of what the Nazarene had done.

CHAPTER XVIII.

" THE Magdalene standeth without and asketh audience of thee." These were the words that greeted Pontius Pilate immediately on entering the audience chamber.

" 'T is a strange request," the Procurator murmured; " yet methinks it may have somewhat to do with the rumour that hath reached my ears, that Caiaphas did see her yesterday and also the mother of the Nazarene. I was about to look into this, for, even if he go so far in his hate of the Nazarene as to persecute Him, and even slay Him, this frightening of women doth ill become a high priest, and I will have none of it."

Then, turning to the soldier, he said: " Bid her pass in."

Weary with her night of watching, pale, yet ever beautiful, the Magdalene came into the presence of the Roman Governor.

" What wouldst thou, Mary?" asked Pontius Pilate, with that tone of temperate kindliness that showed his wish to give justice and consideration to all. " Thy request must be made short, for I have much to do this day. By midday I must meet Caiaphas at the Tribunal, where the question of the releasing of a captive to the people will be finally decided. Doubtless 't is touching this that thou art come, and to plead for the Nazarene; for I hear that thou art altogether gone over to His teaching. 'T is true that He is not yet arrested; but, doubtless, thou hast heard that He is being sought for by the soldiers."

" Nay, most noble Roman, I come not to beg the life of the Christ. For the good of the nation it must needs be that He die. He Himself doth hourly prepare for that great day of grief. I have a message for thee from Nicodemus."

Then, glancing round at the two soldiers, who stood one on each side of the doorway, she continued meekly: " But what I have to say is for the ear of Pontius Pilate only."

Pilate waved his hand to the soldiers to leave the room; also to the scribe who, with feigned diligence, was writing in a corner of the room, shooting salacious glances at the Magdalene, and hopeful that Pontius Pilate would forget his presence.

" And thou too, thou eavesdropper," said Pontius Pilate with a laugh, noting the direction of the Magdalene's eyes. " Thou too canst go, and, if thou wilt listen, listen without the door."

Then the Magdalene stepped nearer to the table at which the Governor was seated.

" Will Pontius Pilate pledge his honour to a poor woman," said the Magdalene, " that the words which I shall speak to thee this day no ears but thine shall ever hear ? "

" I promise thee on my honour as a Roman. I swear to thee on the life of my wife, whom I hold most dear of all that I possess, that no one shall ever hear again the words thou shalt say to me this day."

"I believe thee, most noble Pontius," said the
Magdalene simply.   Then, in an awe-struck voice,
that had in it a strange impressiveness, she said:
"To-morrow Lazarus will be raised from the dead."

Pilate started.   "Woman, what sayest thou?
How knowest thou?"

"Verily 't is true, most noble Pilate.   Lazarus
hath visited me this morn and told me so."

"Then, if Lazarus came to thee, he is not dead,"
said Pontius musingly.

"'T was but his spirit, noble Roman.   His body
hath lain in the grave three days.   If thou wilt send
to see, thou wilt find that he is still there.   Indeed,
a Roman soldier guardeth it."

Pilate rose and walked to the window; then, after
a few minutes' silence, he turned to the Magdalene:
"Almost I believe thee, woman, for thou speakest
in tones of truth.   Yet how can I help thee in this
matter?   Why comest thou to me?"   The last
words were uttered almost impatiently, as though he
disputed the responsibility she would fasten upon
him.

"Ah, noble Pilate, it is well known throughout
all Jewry that thou and thy wife Claudia do love the
Nazarene."

"Love is a strong word, woman," answered Pontius Pilate; "I do much admire this Nazarene for
His power and for His courage, in that He feareth
not death, and also doth try to redress the wrongs
of the afflicted; for a redresser of wrong is at all
times deemed a madman.   My wife, too, hath filled
my thoughts with talk of Him of late, for she, like
all women, hath a weakness for them who defy the

law. Withal I reckon Him not the Christ." Then, with more earnestness he asked: " Dost thou ?"

" Yea, I know it, noble Pilate. He is the Lord, and I am here to implore thee to come and see Him raise Lazarus, for then thou, too, wilt believe." As she said these words, she fell down at the feet of Pilate. " I beseech thee, oh, I beseech thee, O Pilate, come and believe!"

Pilate frowned, and a great melancholy and a look of doubt came over his face.

" Thou temptest me sore," he said, " and to refuse so fair a woman doth go against my wish; but what would all Judæa say; nay, more, what would Cæsar say, if he should hear that I had assembled myself with the believers in this Nazarene to see His miracles ?"

" What matter what they say ?" pleaded the Magdalene. " Surely if to follow the Nazarene bring even death, 't were better far to die in Christ than to live denying Him."

More moved than he durst show, Pontius Pilate answered: " Thou speakest but lightly of death, fair woman. Surely this Nazarene hath wondrous power, for even I, a Roman, quail when I think of death."

" 'T is no death to die in Christ," rejoined the Magdalene. " 'T is but to live again forever."

" That is His creed, I know, but I cannot accept it. I dare not come." Then, fearing that she would press him further, he murmured something about the hour.

Rising to go, the Magdalene shot yet a wistful glance towards him. But his eyes were gazing at

the deep blue sky or the waving palm that stood
against it.   The very air seemed heavy with importance.   Presently, with a swift impulse, Pilate came
close to her, and looking at her lovely face, now purified and refined by her new life, he said: " Farewell, woman, and I thank thee that thou hast
thought to save my soul.   Pontius Pilate hath many
troubles, and the greatest is, that he cannot understand.   Carry a message to thy brethren that, if I can,
I will save the Nazarene; for, be He the Christ or
be He man, He doth deserve to live."

Sadly the Magdalene turned to go.

" Mary, one word more," called Pilate after her.
" If thou shouldst have speech with the Nazarene,
tell Him I fain would save Him if I could."

" The Lord knoweth what is in the hearts of all
men," said the Magdalene.   " We will pray that
thou mayst believe."   And so, sad at the failure of
her mission, she departed.

When the door had closed behind her, Pilate rang
a bell that was on his table.   When the centurion
appeared—he had been wondering at the long interview with the Magdalene—he said : " Bid a man ride
at once to Bethany and bring me word where the
body of Lazarus lies.   But mind, not a word to any
else, or it will be chains instead of women's arms
around his neck this night.   Bid him ride quickly."

But Pilate sat gazing out into space, with a sort of
vague surprise that the world still looked as it had
looked the day before, and musing on the imper-
fection of man's understanding.   Surely, if this
were the God, we should all know it.

At the Sanhedrim he met Caiaphas.   The meeting between the two was not a friendly one. It was impossible for a fearless, straightforward man like Pilate to have much in common with the wily Jew whose intriguing seemed to be how to intrigue still more. The attitude, till now, of Pontius Pilate towards him had been that of a man who stands on his own unquestioned power, and yet acknowledges what another has attained by cunning. Surely these Jews were highly gifted. Yes, it pleased Pilate to draw out the High Priest, to appeal to his pride, to his learning, his high position—and then to mock him. There was nothing noble in the soul of Caiaphas. He would have descended to any depth of cringing, provided he were certain of his company. With Pilate, whom he feared, he did not cringe, but put on an assumed indifference he was far from feeling. Pilate had once said with curious truth that the beginning and ending of Caiaphas was himself.

To-day both were troubled by the same cause. The humble Carpenter, the Nazarene, the despised and rejected of men, had yet had power to wring the withers of the two chief governors of Israel; but the difference of the two men was this—Pilate longed to believe. If he could have believed, power and wealth would have been laid aside. Caiaphas did believe, but as the devils, we are told, believe and tremble. He was closing up each corner of his heart, stopping, like the deaf adder, his ears, for fear that true belief should come and force submission, and thus wrest from him power and temporal glory. Better the substance than the shadow. Better Caiaphas worshipped by the populace, bowed down to, besought and feared, than a humble doorkeeper, perhaps, in the house of the Lord.

In these days Caiaphas rarely read the prophets, lest some text of his own choosing should confound him. The man he least desired to see was Pilate. The man Pilate most desired to see was Caiaphas. No Roman could fail to know that Judæa was ruled by the letter of the law. A legal education was considered the most important in the schools, a strict adherence to the Mosaic ordinances enforced by severest penalty at the earliest age. As enlightenment brought wider range of ideas, so the law of the Sabbath grew more rigid, the noose of the Mosaic Law was drawn the tighter round the people's necks. No one coming from an outside world, and an independent one, like that of Rome, could fail to see that the law of Moses was but wielded as a sceptre of despotism over a lawyer-ridden country. The day would come when Rome itself would take some hints and terrify its own people by the tyranny of an enforced religion that brooked no resistance, that made even argument a sin, that made absolute the dominion of the law.

It was easy to see, thought Pilate, why the chief priests feared the Nazarene, for by His miracles He completed prophecy, and by His actions enforced the commandments of the Mosaic Law; thus confounding the tyranny of perverted argument exercised by the Pharisees and priests for their own ends and crushing out by such fulfilments the slanderous assertions disseminated by His enemies that His doctrines were opposed to the teaching of the Scriptures or the ordinances of the Jewish law.

When Pilate descended the steps of the Tribunal, where, half from absence of mind and half from a great half-formed uncertainty, he had tempered justice with no unsparing hand, he saw Caiaphas hurrying on in front.

" Art loath to meet me, Caiaphas ? " he said to himself. Then, turning to a centurion, he bid him follow the High Priest and ask him whether he could have speech with him in the ante-chamber or at his dwelling. " 'T is one to me," he said, " so I have speech with him."

More feelings than one made Caiaphas avoid a meeting with the Procurator. Anger and fear contended in his heart, and the two are ill-matched companions. He was angry with Pilate for letting go free the two Roman soldiers whom he had sent up for trial for not obeying his orders to lay hands on the Nazarene. Indeed, they had played a double game, for, instead of returning to own themselves defeated, they had appealed to Pilate, and thus forestalled Caiaphas's complaint of them.

" Everything leadeth me to believe that this man thinketh the Nazarene to be the Christ," he muttered to himself. Then he feared a little what Pilate would say at his having dared to attempt to lay hands on the Nazarene, without first asking his permission. Further, if it had come to Pilate's ears that he had visited Bethany in the company of Nicodemus and sent for the two Marys to inquire of them, then indeed Pilate could scoff with reason.

" Tell the illustrious Governor that I have much to write this morning," was the message he returned to Pilate, hoping that his insolence might so offend him that he would stay away; but the proud Roman would brook no such messages.

" Tell the High Priest that his writing must needs wait until to-morrow, for that I must have speech with him, and that I am even now upon my road. Ye Jewish people have yet to learn courtesy of speech," he muttered to himself; but, on the road, his strange musings returned to him, and, weary with the searchings of his heart, he forgot his anger and impatience.

For one moment there was an awkward silence, the two men reclining on couches drawn close together, a custom the Romans had introduced.

Caiaphas was puzzled to know what had brought Pilate there; and Pilate was debating how to begin his questionings without exhibiting too great an interest in the Nazarene.

" I have much to discuss with thee, Caiaphas," he began. " The Feast of the Passover is at hand, and the question of whom we shall release is not to be lightly settled. The people do expect that one shall be delivered unto them. Who sayest thou, then, should be released ? "

The wily Jew joined his finger-tips and appeared to muse awhile; though, in reality, he was watching Pilate's face from the corner of his eye. Pilate, too, looked away to hide the anxiety that was gnawing at his heart, lest another name than the Nazarene's should cross the lips of the priest he had begun to hate. For he knew that Caiaphas would lay hands on Jesus; and, in such case, Pilate desired to set Him free. Both men were silent, while each tried to cheat the other. Brain against brain was pitted,

each anxious to use his ingenuity for his own ends,
each reluctant to breathe, either in favour or disfavour, the name that lay nearest to the lips of both.

"Methinks Barabbas hath a great claim," said
Caiaphas presently. "He hath lain long in prison,
and for not so grievous a fault; for, though he slew
the Pharisee, methinks he slew him but in self-
defence."

"Thou growest merciful," said Pilate scornfully,
irritated, he scarce knew why.

"'T is ever a priest's place to be merciful, inas-
much as he expecteth mercy," replied Caiaphas, in
his dissembling unctuousness.

A flush of anger came over Pilate's face, and the
words of the Nazarene recurred to him: "Woe unto
ye, Pharisees, hypocrites." Then, pushing into the
thickness of his own mental conflict, he went on:
"What saith Annas? Doth he, too, recommend
Barabbas?" He knew full well he had given Caiaphas the opening he desired, and had speeded the
conversation in the turn he would fain have it take.

"Well, since thou askest me, noble Pilate," replied the priest, striving to make his voice indifferent
as well as temperate, "Annas is not content only
with the releasing of Barabbas; he would have further the Nazarene condemned at the Feast of the
Passover."

"Does he, too, fear Him?" asked Pilate with
increasing scorn.

"None fear Him," replied Caiaphas, pretending
to ignore the caustic remark. "None fear Him;
but it is a law of the Jews that, if one call himself
the Son of God, he shall die the death."

Then, with strange passion, and a vehemence too powerful to be repressed, Pilate shot out the words: " And if He be the Son of God, what then, most noble Caiaphas ? "

This was a question too wide for Caiaphas to deal with unconsidered, too unexpected to be readily replied to; but, ever an adept at cunning, Caiaphas rejoined with subtlety: " Dost think He is ? "

Then Pilate remembered all the risks he would run, should he side openly with the Nazarene; nor was he assured enough in his own mind to answer with full confidence.

" I ask thee a question, and thou answerest me with another," he said impatiently. " Give me thy answer, for thou art great in argument and in the knowledge of the law, and I would argue with thee, as we do in the Tribunal; for argument hath that good about it that oft two lies do form a truth; and, when one doth controvert the other, he that contradicteth contradicteth what he himself doth think to make the other in his turn contradict again; thus, much is learned, and the truth is often come at; for both sides are openly discussed, and the judge hath means thereby to form his judgment.

" Say, if this were the Son of God and we should condemn Him, how would it be in the Judgment Day ? What say the prophets will be done of him that destroyeth the Son of God ? "

" If He were the Son of God," rejoined Caiaphas, guarded in his answer, yet interested in the argument, " He could not be destroyed by human hands."

" Then I will ask thee yet another question, Caia-

phas, for I am in the mood to prove thy learning and
my own.   Dost believe that a Messiah will come ?"

" Most assuredly," said Caiaphas.   " All the
prophets say so."

" I accept thy answer," rejoined Pilate, with an
elated look.   " Then, if the Messiah hath yet to
come, how thinkest thou that He will come, and
whence, and when ? "

" Such momentous problems, noble Procurator,
take much time and thought to solve.   Methinks it
would be better to choose an occasion when business
presseth less."

" Nay, nay, my friend," replied Pontius Pilate
hastily; " where a man's life is in the balance matters surely press; and, if this man be a Messiah, for
sure there is no more urgent matter to you and to
me and to the whole world; but answer me, Caiaphas: How thinkest thou the real Messiah will come?
How is it written ? "

Caiaphas hesitated, from no ignorance, but that
he was revolving in his mind how far he would be
compromised if he should quote the prophets; and,
betwixt fear of seeming ignorant and dread of com-
promising himself, he was sorely troubled.   Then
he replied: " Zechariah hath said, ' Behold, thy
King cometh unto thee: He is just, and having salvation; lowly, and riding upon an ass, and upon a
colt the foal of an ass.' "

The words seemed to come reluctantly from his
lips, as though he were the unwilling mouthpiece of
the prophecy.   Then, as if to conceal their full significance, he added: " But there are many other
things that hath not yet come to pass.   It saith

again: ' And it shall come to pass in that day that light shall not be clear nor dark.   But it shall be one day which shall be known to the Lord, not day, nor night: but it shall come to pass, at evening time it shall be light.'   Then again it saith (here the High Priest raised his voice to an even, monotonous pitch, as though prophesying in the Synagogue) in another place that ' the mountains shall be removed.'   But all these signs are not yet come."

Then, with curling lip, Pontius Pilate asked in a tone of assumed indifference: " Dost remember a passage (for I too at times do read the prophets) in the prophet Malachi ?   ' And now, O priests, this commandment is for you.   If ye will not hear, and if ye will not lay it to heart, to give glory unto My name, saith the Lord of Hosts, I will even send a curse upon you, and I will curse your blessings: yea, I have cursed them already, because ye do not lay it to heart.   For the priests' lips should keep know-ledge, and they should seek the law at His mouth: for He is the messenger of the Lord of Hosts.' "

Caiaphas flushed a deep crimson, and his lips grew white at the words of Pilate.

In a bitter tone he answered: " Thou speakest in parables, noble Procurator; I understand thee not."

" My meaning was," said Pilate, smiling to him-self, " to ask thee whether thou hast no fear, sup-posing that, after all, this were the Christ, that thou thyself mayst meet with eternal death, if so be thou hast wrongly understood the message of the Lord."

" Eternal life, eternal death, who knoweth of these things ?" asked Caiaphas impatiently, yet with a troubled look.

" Thou art, then, verily a Sadducee, like Annas thy father-in-law, and thy wife his daughter. Verily women have great power in this our day."

And his thoughts went back to his own wife, Claudia, who had stated her belief in Jesus and who dreamed so strangely.

" Yet I would ask thee further, noble Caiaphas, for of all our speech no certain thing hath come; neither whether this be the Christ, nor whom we shall release at the Feast of Passover. Answer me; if, as ye Sadducees believe, there be no resurrection, what profiteth a man to do good or evil? And why, then, fast ye? Surely 't is loss of time to be sad, if there be no ensuing good. If 't is true, let us waste no time; let us make merry, Caiaphas, let us eat and drink, for to-morrow we die."

Pilate laughed at his own words, in which there was a scornful ring. Then, lowering his voice, went on: " In truth, Caiaphas, hath it not a little truth, this saying of the Nazarene that hath upset thee so —That ye shut up the kingdom of Heaven against men, and ye neither go in yourselves nor suffer them that are entering to go in ?"

" I am no Pharisee," said the High Priest angrily.

" How then art thou a ruler of Israel ?" asked Pontius Pilate laughing; " for they were mostly chosen of the Pharisees; but methinks the world is upside down, for Judæa hath strange intruders that yet do rule her. We have the Idumæan Antipas and Philo and other Alexandrian Jews, and even Greeks; yet the Greeks and their influence are hated of the Jews. Thou art here to preach salvation to the people, and thou believest not in that salvation. Surely, 't is a strange assemblage, and every man's hand is against another's. Each hath a creed of his own, and he that ruleth the larger portion is but he that is the strongest. It seemeth to me that this Nazarene doth restore the right, for He declaimeth against what is evil, and showeth the whole nation the way to God. I know not whether He be the Christ or even a prophet; but this I know, that if we would observe His teaching good only would ensue. He wisheth neither to rob nor to destroy, nor to take the place of any man. He preacheth such a doctrine that, I feel sure, were Moses here, he would himself pronounce it better than his own. Listen what sweet philosophy is this: ' I will have mercy and not sacrifice, for I came not to call the righteous, but sinners to repentance '; and again, that philosophy of forgiveness—was ever philosophy so great ? ' Resist not evil; but whosoever shall smite thee on thy right cheek, turn to him the other also. Love your enemies; bless them that curse you.' '' Then, when Caiaphas would have interrupted him, he went on: "Listen yet to this strange argument: ' If ye salute your brethren, what do ye more than others ? Do not even the publicans so ? ' ''

'' He is a dreamer '' rejoined Caiaphas, shrugging his shoulders; '' such things cannot be.''

'' True,'' said Pilate, '' if such things were, you and I would no more be needed, for there would be no tribunal and no law.''

And he laughed lightly.

Caiaphas, pleased at the turn of the conversation, laughed too.

"Methinks that thou wouldst make this man King of the Jews and then come and conquer Him," he rejoined, half jokingly, yet glancing furtively at the Procurator.

"Nay, Caiaphas, I swear to thee it is not so; I know not whence He cometh, nor what or who He is; but this I do maintain, that I see no sin in Him deserving death."

"He hath said that He is God; therefore He is a blasphemer, and, according to our law, He ought to die," said Caiaphas.

"Your law, your law," retorted Pilate pettishly; "it is with thee the beginning and the end of all things; yet ye know it can be upset at will. What sayest thou about that robber whom thou forgavest all his sins, because he brought thee a basket of orto-lans overladen with fat and buried in vine leaves as sacrifice?"

"He that dwelleth about the altar must feed by the altar," said the High Priest unctuously.

"Mayhap, Caiaphas," answered Pontius Pilate, roaring with merriment; "but 't was in fasting time, 't was in fasting time. Thou seest, Caiaphas, that I hear overmuch. Oh, Tiberius did laugh when I did narrate the tale!"

"Didst thou tell Tiberius?" The words were rushed out almost with dismay.

"No harm is done, I assure thee, my good Caiaphas. Tiberius laughed a long space; then he said, ' Had I known, I would have sent him a bottle of Falernian to wash them down.'"

"'T is some vile falsehood invented in the market place," said Caiaphas angrily. "I wonder, great

Pilate, that a man in so high a position as thyself should listen thus to servants' tattling."

"Trouble not thyself, good Caiaphas," laughed Pilate. "Thou shouldst have bidden me to share it with thee. But, to return to this question of the Passover, what sayest thou? Shall we execute Barabbas, if needs be that one must die to satisfy the people?"

Caiaphas was silent; then, diplomatically, he answered: "Shall I consult with Annas, and send thee word?"

"Nay, nay," said the outspoken Roman, laughing, "we want not the opinion of deposed high priests, nor of the fathers of our wives! I shall consult no father-in-law, nor shalt thou. Speak, whom shall we release unto the people?"

Then, looking shiftily at Pilate, Caiaphas answered: "Myself, I would release Barabbas, for he hath lain long in prison."

A spasm, as of pain or grief, shot across the face of Pilate, and there was a moment's silence, in which the two men seemed to be measuring their moral strength, like two duellists with their swords. The Roman was the weaker, for, in a disappointed voice, already feeling the battle partly lost, yet still resolved to make a fight of it before he yielded, Pilate said: "And whom wouldst thou sacrifice for the people?"

And Caiaphas, knowing that he was the stronger, with devilish intention, answered: "The Nazarene."

Oh, what a multitude of reflections coursed through the brain of Pontius Pilate, as he once more looked forth from the window on to the shining roofs and turrets of Jerusalem, rather than meet the gaze of the man who, he knew, hated him even as he hated the Nazarene, and even now took pleasure in the grief he was inflicting. Even while he gazed upwards toward the sky, he wondered why it did not open and give a sign that this was the Son of God, if such He was. Then, feeling that the question must be settled, he turned to Caiaphas.

" Tell me again, Caiaphas, on what charge shall we then try Him and condemn Him. Hath He indeed guilt at all, or is it but to satisfy the proud Caiaphas, to make his words of prophecy come true ? "

" He hath blasphemed, I tell thee," answered Caiaphas sharply, beginning to lose his temper, " in that He hath called Himself the Son of God."

" To call Himself the Son of God is not a sin," retorted Pilate, fighting yet, though he felt the weakness of his argument; " for we are all the children of God. Thou thyself in thy prophecy dost say that ' Jesus should die for this nation, and not for this nation only, but that also He should gather together all the children of God which were scattered abroad.' Who, then, meanest thou by the children of God ? "

Doubtless, in his subtlety, the High Priest could have found some pungent answer with which to explain away his words, but, at that moment, a noise of many voices raised in excited talk, and the tramping of many feet outside, drowned the last words of Pilate; and ere Caiaphas could reply a centurion entered hurriedly.

" Pardon, rabbis," he began, " but it seemed to

me my message justified my speedy entrance. Lazarus is raised from the dead. I have it from one who saw him leave the grave. He waiteth outside to give thee further news, if thou wilt see him.''

While the man was speaking, Pilate rose and held on with one hand to the couch, while he turned his head with terror-stricken look over his shoulder towards the soldier.

'' Dost believe 't is true ? '' he asked.

'' True, how can it be true ? What fool's folly is this ? '' interrupted Caiaphas, stamping his feet, and with one arm clasping his elbow while he bowed his chin upon his hand. '' 'T is some foul trick, some chicanery of this Nazarene and His company. Maybe they have taken away the body of Lazarus, and this is some other man.'' Then, turning to Pilate, he continued: ''With all thy arguments and unwillingness, we are too late to stop the people now. They will altogether go after this juggling Nazarene. Hadst thou but heard me, the quieting of Judæa had been an easy task. Now who will say how it will end, for this unlearned people will believe that this is a miracle from God. All Jewry hath waited for this day and wondered why it came not. Four days had this schemer left the people to grow heated with endless uproar; and now He bringeth His pretended miracles to a frenzied people, who know not whether they dream or not.''

But Pilate answered nothing to his recriminations.

'' Bring us hither thy messenger,'' said he, turning to the soldier.

'' It is Chuza who hath come.''

''And who is Chuza ? '' asked Caiaphas, with

scathing scorn, " that his word is to have weight with the two rulers of Judæa ? "

" Peace, Caiaphas; I would but hear the rumour from his lips," said Pilate, and he signed to the soldier to bring the man.

A moment later there was announced a little man whose black ringlets and piercing eyes proclaimed him a Jew, while his dress was that worn by the house stewards of the time.

He came in, making low obeisance, but with a troubled look, as if recent events had overwhelmed him.

" Who art thou ? " asked Caiaphas with scorn.

" May it please thee, High Caiaphas, I am now the steward of Antipas; but I was the steward of Herod, and so well did I rule his household for him, that Antipas did bid me stay."

Caiaphas became less cynical.

The steward in the house of the Tetrarch was a man at least deserving of consideration.

" And dost thou know the Nazarene ? "

" May it please thee, High Caiaphas, I have a wife Joanna, who for many years suffered from the disease of madness; and, at the seasons of the moon, she would throw herself into the fire or tear her clothing. She had seen many physicians, but they had availed her nothing, and much money had been spent, which I could ill afford."

" Albeit thou robbest the Tetrarch not a little," put in Caiaphas, with a sneering laugh.

" Let him tell his tale," said Pontius Pilate with impatience. " Proceed, Chuza."

Then the man went on : " But when my wife did

hear through her sister, Susanna, who is married to a tanner near to Bethany, that this Man did work such miracles, she too went and besought Him. And He turned to her in the crowd and said to her: ' Woman, thy sins are forgiven thee '; and straightway she was cured, and returned unto me whole.''

" What said Antipas to this miracle ?" asked Caiaphas, with the same self-satisfied, scornful smile. " Is he not wroth that thy wife doth thus run after the Nazarene ?"

" He said only, ' 'T was a pity that she had been cured, for else, perchance, she had not returned,'" said Chuza, simply, at which both Caiaphas and Pilate laughed.

" But touching Lazarus ? 'T is of him that we would hear," said Pilate. Then, remembering that he would be on dangerous ground should any remark of his be carried back to Antipas, he went on with assumed indifference, that Caiaphas did not fail to note, and, later, profit by. " What tales are told ?"

" Nay, they are no tales, my lords," replied the Jew, his whole face changing when his thoughts reverted to the strange phenomenon of that night. " 'T is even so. When Joanna, my wife, heard that Lazarus was dead, she entreated me to accompany her to the house of Martha of Bethany, but my master Antipas hath had two great feasts at his house, and I could not take her thither for four days. But late last night we travelled the fifteen furlongs' journey to comfort Mary and Martha, and to carry spices to anoint Lazarus. Then when we reached the dwelling a great multitude stood around, and we feared lest something had happened to the Nazarene.

But Mary came out to us and whispered that, if we would follow the multitude to the tomb, we would see the glory of the Lord. So we followed to the tomb of Lazarus, and there the Nazarene called out in a loud voice: ' Lazarus, come forth!' ''

" Well, well," Pilate broke in impatiently, when the man stopped for breath.

He went on: "And immediately he that was dead came forth, bound hand and foot with grave clothes, and his face was bound about with a napkin. And Jesus said unto them, ' Loose him, and let him go.' ''

Then when Pilate said nothing, but remained wrapped in silence, musing over Chuza's words, Caiaphas broke in impatiently: "And the people, what said the people ?"

Somewhat maliciously, eying the High Priest narrowly while he spoke, Chuza answered: "Many of the Jews believed when they saw the things which Jesus did; others went their way to tell the Pharisees the things which they had seen."

" Enough, thou mayst go," said Pilate, handing the man a few coins. " Thou hast well told thy tale."

" Indeed 't is no tale," protested Chuza.

" Silence, and begone, fool!" thundered Caiaphas.

The man hastened away, and at first no word was spoken by the two remaining in the chamber. The hour was late, and the time for Pilate's midday meal had passed. But he recked not of food, this hardy Roman. Since their discussion had begun, this sudden news had weighed the balance on his side. He knew that the fact that Lazarus had not been raised

had been the strong point of the Pharisees and Sadducees; but, now that the miracle had been accomplished, his arguments had been greatly strengthened, while those of the disbelieving Jews and of
the scribes and Pharisees had been proportionately
weakened.

Caiaphas was now eager to be rid of his guest,
that he might think over this event in silence, and
form alone his schemes of tyranny and vengeance.
He could not but be conscious that this raising of
Lazarus, whether a real miracle, or some trickery,
had changed the aspect of affairs, and would lessen
his hold upon the people. He started, for in his
musings he had forgotten Pilate's presence.

" What thinkest thou now ? " asked Pilate.

" Now, now; why should I think differently ? "
answered Caiaphas. " I think the people are gone
mad, and that the Nazarene hath a devil." His
voice and tone were sore and irritable.

Pilate rose to go. " Thou wilt not be persuaded,
Caiaphas. Yet I hold Him free from all sin. I will
go farther into this affair and, mayhap, will see
privily the Nazarene," said Pilate; " and if I find
no guile in Him I will let Him go, shouldst thou lay
hands on Him, and will condemn Barabbas."

The tone was defiant and abrupt, and he left with
a blunt farewell, to return to the Palace of Herod,
where the Roman Procurators were wont to stay at
the time of feasts, in order to keep order in Jerusalem. In his heart he wondered what Claudia would
say at this fresh news.

Caiaphas shrugged his shoulders. Then, when
Pilate's departing footsteps were no longer audible,

he muttered: " We shall see, Pilate, who is the stronger, thou or I. We shall see." And over his face there gathered such a glance of hellish hate and malice, mingled with scorn and craft, that surely no such face would ever shine with virtue more.

CHAPTER XIX.

THE Sanhedrim had been called together; and more, it was not without disquietude that Caiaphas had appeared in the midst of the assembly. Jerusalem was convulsed by the events of the preceding day. Lazarus was alive again to swell the ranks of Christ's supporters and the High Priest's opponents.

" Our enemies are multiplied," Caiaphas had said unctuously to Nicodemus, and the latter had answered with significance: " Yea, methinks they are too strong for us."

In the privacy of his own chamber, with none but Annas to hear his asseverations of what he meant to do, the infuriated accents of his oaths, the mingled scorn and terror of his remarks, Caiaphas gave up all pretence of being actuated by religious fervour or noble impulses.

" Yes, if I be eternally damned, if Satan claim me for his own, if this be the Christ, the very Son of God, yet He shall perish, for that He hath striven to contend with me, to pervert the nation, to insult the teachers of the law, of whom I am chief. Dost not fear, Annas, thou who art the father of many priests, that if this Man once gain the mastery all priesthood shall be ended ? What need of priests, if a common carpenter can come and teach in our synagogues and flout us ? Thou and I, Annas, may go and live in some mean cottage in Nazareth, for it seemeth that out of that village cometh greatness. Thinkest with me, Annas ? "

" I think," said Annas, talking for once without prevarication and without affectation, but with the experience of age and many years in a position of responsibility, " that, in thy hate of the Nazarene thou dost make too much of this thing."

" Hate ? Thou hast well said hate, Annas," retorted Caiaphas, in his anger forgetting all but his own malevolence. " I hate Him for His presumptuous teachings, for His scheming and pretended simple ways that do entangle this foolish Jewish people. Doth He think, because He cajoleth fools and beggars with His quackeries, that I, great Caiaphas, can be deceived ? Ah! He shall see yet who is the stronger. He shall yet learn that those who cross the path of the High Priest are but brushed aside."

And Caiaphas made a gesture as though he raised and tossed aside some obstacle from his path. No offended elephant waiting to tusk his enemy, then seize him in his trunk and hurl him into the air, could have presented a more terrible aspect of rage and fury. Annas's heart recoiled within him at the remembrance that this man was the husband of his daughter.

" Poor Rebekah, methinks she too must suffer," he murmured.

Then, while the two men were preparing to leave the room, gathering up parchments, placing others aside, there rose on the air once more the cries of :

"Lazarus is risen, Lazarus is risen!" which all through the night had whipped Caiaphas's blood into foaming waves of fury.

"It seemeth to me that if thou dost murder one the other will still remain," said Annas, shrugging his shoulders; "for, whether Lazarus was really dead or not, I know not; but now he liveth. Of that there is no doubt."

"Call it not murder," answered Caiaphas, "because a blasphemer shall meet His just reward. Wouldst thou, too, be a believer?" he added scoffingly.

"I believe not that He is the Christ," replied Annas seriously; "but I do believe that 't is a man of hidden power. We know not how or whence; perhaps of Satan, or—who knoweth? And I think that we must use caution, lest some hidden danger spring upon us."

Caiaphas looked at him for one moment, as if debating whether he had gone mad; for the voice of Annas was the only one he ever listened to, the advice of Annas the sole advice he ever followed. Perhaps no man in Jerusalem was so much the counterpart of his own vileness.

"What thinkest thou then, Annas?" he said impatiently.

"I hardly know," replied the older man. "If thou wouldst have me tell thee what I would have done had I still remained High Priest, and such strange event befallen in my reign,"—here he lowered his voice,—"I would have had Him caught by stealth and murdered, for to make a sacrifice of a man is ever to make him a martyr. To make a pub-

lic function of an execution is ever to run danger of
division amongst the people; and with one who
could raise Lazarus, be it by chicanery or not—I
know not, and whether Lazarus were dead or not, I
know not, nor will know—yet, methinks the man
must needs have power who can do this thing,
whether by God's assistance or Satan's magic; and,
since there is such stir about the death of Lazarus,
a lesser ruler of the Synagogue, surely there will be
threefold over the death of one who calleth Himself
the Son of God."

Caiaphas was silent. It seemed as though these
wise words of Annas carried conviction to him, but
that ambition forbade such secret dismissal of the
man he hated. The people had believed in Him.
The people should see who was the more powerful.
The man who had publicly denounced the law should
perish by the law. A public example should be
made, and Judæa should for ever be rid of the possibility of a reappearance of such fanatics. The world
must be freed from all such mischief-makers.

" Thou wouldst have them say that I, Caiaphas,
am afraid?" he asked, shrugging his shoulders.
" No, it is the people's voice, the voice of them who
seemed to follow Him, that shall condemn," he went
on, growing fiercer and more sullen. "If He be the
Son of God, let His God save Him!" Then suddenly clutching the old man by the arm and placing
his coarse lips close to his slowly deafening ears,
he said: " I will not be dictated to by Pontius
Pilate."

Here indeed he struck home, for it was through
Pontius Pilate that Annas had been bereft of his

High Priestship. " His mumbling words reach not the people's ears," Pilate had said in rough jocoseness to Tiberius; and so Annas had been deposed, and, to blunt the edge of his disappointment, his kinsman appointed in his place.

The two hurried along the street to the council chamber, already packed with all the rulers of the Synagogue, and all the chief priests and high officials.

While the two were walking through the crowd, the people pointed and hooted at them, and hoarse cries of: " Lazarus, Lazarus!" continually reached their ears.

Pontius Pilate, contrary, to his usual custom, was not present, a fact that gave great satisfaction to Caiaphas. A heated discussion at once began. It was evident that, in the face of such a miracle, two courses alone were open. One, the impossible one to the law-eaten, power-seeking Pharisees, that of acknowledging the God-given power of a good man, if not the divinity of the Son of God; the other, to lose no further time in putting Him to death. Nay, more, the Sadducees went so far as to say that Lazarus must also be destroyed.

" He is a living witness of this thing," said one; and Caiaphas shrugged his shoulders in impatience.

" Ye do speak as if this were indeed a miracle and Lazarus had been dead," he said.

" Nevertheless, this Man doeth many miracles."

" What shall we do ? " said another.

Then Nicodemus, resolving to make one last attempt to use his high position for the service of the Lord, rose up and said: " Surely ye would not slay

Lazarus. Yet, if the Nazarene be slain, will not all the people and Lazarus tell still of His great deeds?"

Caiaphas shot a glance of wrath at him.

But Nicodemus continued speaking: "What harm doeth He? Let us leave Him alone. Surely the State hath nations that do war against her, and many enemies; she needeth not to war against one man. Let Him alone."

Then, while no one uttered aught, as though his words were taking effect, the voice of Annas rose on the silence, for there must needs be silence to hear the old man's voice.

"If we let Him thus alone, all men will believe in Him, and the Romans shall come and take away both our place and nation."

Caiaphas shot a look of approval and gratitude at Annas. He recognised the diplomacy of the remark. Annas had profited by Pontius Pilate's absence to cast a slur on the intentions of the governing race. Yet, if Pontius Pilate should come to hear of this, it could not be said that Caiaphas the High Priest had pronounced the words. Annas had spoken well and tersely, and Caiaphas's countenance beamed with sated craft.

But Pontius Pilate was, in a sense, popular, and there were many in the building who owed place and power to him, and resented the covert attack on the good faith of the Procurator. His absence, too, had filled their minds with uneasiness. Perhaps an open rupture was to come between Caiaphas and the Roman Governor; then woe betide those who had sided against Cæsar's viceroy! These and many other reflections crossed the minds of the more temperate of the Pharisaical party, many of whom were friends of Lazarus and Nicodemus.

Here and there a voice rose, crying out: "He is not worthy of death."

Then Caiaphas, with that arrogant impatience which, from its very daring, so often carried the day, exclaimed roughly, insultingly: "Ye know nothing at all. Who are ye to set yourselves against the prophecy of one who is of the lineage of Aaron? Have I not prophesied to you that it is expedient for one man to die for the people, and that the whole nation perish not? If this man live, the nations of God will run hither and thither to seek after vain preachers; but, if He die, they will gather themselves together in one fold henceforward, in patient obedience to the laws of Moses. To save one man's life will ye sacrifice a nation? Will ye not rather by one man's death deliver all the children of God?"

Silence, that unwilling silence that might yet be intrepreted as consent, reigned in the building for some moments, while one after another those who were against the condemnation of the Nazarene, yet felt themselves powerless to oppose the will of Caiaphas, rose and left the council, hoping thereby to show their disapproval. Caiaphas followed each with eyes that gleamed with satisfaction.

"Cowards!" he muttered from his place. "Cowards!" despising the very characteristic that yet caused his satisfaction. " They dare not gainsay me."

The exit of these people was followed by a sudden buzzing of voices, murmuring, arguing, expostulating.

Yet all who remained felt that, by doing so, they owned themselves convinced; many indeed were partisans of Caiaphas.

Then, seeing the moment of his victory come, Caiaphas rose and addressed the council: " Men of Israel, Rulers, Chief Priests, Sadducees; I see that ye are ready to quit you like men and not allow this agitator to provoke the people. Is it, then, agreed that an order go forth to capture this wily Man and to bring Him before Pilate for examination ? "

Purposely the cunning Caiaphas omitted the word condemnation. To bring the Nazarene before Pontius Pilate did not necessarily mean to condemn Him to death; albeit that Caiaphas knew that the one would lead to the other; but the artful ignoring of the words that would imply the Saviour's sentence carried the day with those he was addressing.

" Yes, we are agreed," they shouted. "Let Him have fair hearing before Pilate." And hastily, lest fresh objections should be raised or conditions made, to give no time for the tide of political assent to turn, Caiaphas descended the steps of the Tribunal and hurried away, leaving Annas to conclude the business of the day.

And that day an order was published throughout Jerusalem and all Judæa, including Galilee, that if any one set eyes on the Nazarene, He should be brought before Pilate.

CHAPTER XX.

IN the cool of the garden the reunited family at Bethany sat once more at evening, watching the sunset over Jerusalem. The strangeness of the situation, the great marvel of the resurrection of Lazarus, formed the subject of every conversation.

" Is it indeed thou, Lazarus ? " Martha would say in smiling wonder; and he, smiling in return, would turn his face towards the light and answer: " Dost not know thy brother ? "

But Mary sat in silent adoration at the wonder of the thing, barely daring to look at her brother, asking no questions, in silent gratitude at this great happiness. All signs of mourning had disappeared. Instead, all through the day, little groups of people gathered outside the gates, clamouring to be allowed to see the risen Lazarus, who, only too glad to be the living witness of the Messiah's power, never wearied in seeing and speaking to the multitude.

The first to come had been Kishish, the physician. None better than he knew that Lazarus had indeed been dead. All that human skill could do he had done to save the life of this favourite, wealthy patient. Nay, more, he had striven with a purpose, for he knew full well what influence his death would have upon the Jews, and how important it was for the peace of Judæa that things should remain as they

then were.   He had been absent by the bedside of
a sick person at the time of the miracle, and had
treated the announcement of Lazarus's resurrection
with a scorn and derision not unnatural in the circumstances.   Yet, when he saw his patient reclining
as usual on his couch, a great amazement seized him.

" Who, then, is this Man ? " he asked Lazarus
breathlessly.

" A Physician of the Soul," replied Lazarus.
" One who for healing needeth no medicine and no
herb."

" Verily 't is a wondrous thing," said Kishish.
But he too was powerless to believe the simplicity
of the act.   Rather would he believe that he had
been wrong in pronouncing that life had fled; would
confess that he had erred, rather than believe.   Faltering, failing, presumptuous humanity that can explain nothing, yet fails to believe what it cannot
understand !   Truly had the Lord pronounced words
of verity when He had said: " If they believe not
Moses and the prophets, neither will they believe
though one came from the dead."

Yes, the great miracle was over, Lazarus alive, the
signs of mourning were wiped away.   The wailing
had ceased, once more peace and gladness reigned
in the home at Bethany, and already it seemed as
though all that had happened had been a dream.
The brain and heart of man lack the capacity to hold
so great a miracle; and humanity is so prone to ob-
stinacy that, even when its right course is pointed
out, it soon glides back into its old grooves, its old
understandings, its old stagnation, and the divine
fire in it smoulders dully or goes out.   Occasionally,

for a space, the flame of faith springs up. At such
times the soul is lit up by its flashes. Dark things
stand out defined and clear; comfort and warmth
and rest are there. But the flame needs feeding.
And, alas! the watcher tires, there is no heaping on
of fuel, no stirring of the dead embers, so the light
dies out.

But, in the heart of Lazarus, faith was awake for
evermore; faith strengthened by the evidence of
things, not unseen, but seen; to him who had longed
to believe had been vouchsafed the greatest blessing
of all—to know.

For many days the sisters left him quiet, for there
was that in his expression which silenced questioning. Great deputations came from far and wide to
question him. Lawyers, scribes, Pharisees, all
flocked to ask him what his sensations had been at
the moment of his death and what on his return to
life. Had he been to heaven and seen the Living
God ? Had he been to Hades and seen the spirits
that await the Judgment Day, or had he been to
hell and spoken there with Satan ? Each, according
to his belief or sect, asked for more knowledge; but
to all Lazarus only shook his head and answered:
" If I told you, ye would not believe. Ye would
say I had dreamed a dream."

Then, one evening, Martha exclaimed fretfully:
" Methinks there was little gain in thy death and
resurrection, if thou hast naught to tell us."

Naught to show the world ? Lazarus took on a
look of unutterable grief at Martha's words.

" Thou knowest not what thou sayest," he answered her; and, while he spoke, his gaze was raised

to the vaulted heavens, and rested there in patient musing.

Yes, so it would be always. No miracles, no words would ever strike home where revelation had not penetrated. No human power, no earthly preaching, no laws, could ever produce that spark of living fire that came from God direct.

Yes, all know, all understand, where salvation is to be found; 't is a Pool of Siloam awaiting all. And all mean one day to wash in it—when they find the time convenient. All intend to be saved, all believe; but there is ample time; and, meanwhile, there is much to be done, buying and selling, laughing and making merry, decking and feasting, striving for power and place; and, when we reach the pool at last, the angel is not there to stir the waters.

So mused Lazarus, yet it seemed to him that Martha was partly right. Not to tell of his experiences during those four days was to keep back much helpful knowledge—perhaps, even to oppose God's purpose. Yet he had received no word to tell the world. Those four days seemed to him so sacred, so utterly unconnected with this world, that he had not dared reveal what he had seen. For some days he had been dazed with the marvel of it, and there had been no Christ to help or guide him; for immediately the miracle was over the Nazarene had departed to Ephraim, both to escape the multitude and to prepare for His death, which could not be far distant now. Already Jerusalem was filling fast with the inhabitants of the outskirts and the country round, who gathered there to eat the Passover and to purify themselves beforehand.

Many wondered whether the Nazarene, in defiance of the command for His arrest, would come to Jerusalem for the Passover. The Temple was thronged daily in the hope that either He would appear, or that Lazarus would take His place and preach on the subject of his own resurrection. But a great silence reigned as to the whereabouts and actions of Jesus, some going even so far as to believe that the Messiah had taken the place of Lazarus in the tomb, misapplying the words: " Greater love hath no man than this, that a man lay down his life for his friend."

Who can enter into the sadness of His days at Ephraim, with only the society of His rough, untutored disciples. He had restored Lazarus, but even the companionship of the family at Bethany was denied to Him; it would have been dangerous to visit them, for the Jews, who congregated daily to see the restored Lazarus, would doubtless have followed Him, and told Caiaphas of His whereabouts. Those were days of terrible anxiety to the three at Bethany. Filled with undying gratitude and longing to cast themselves in adoring worship at His feet, they yet durst not move from Bethany, or even send a word of love and reverence.

Once more Martha raised her inquiring, half-doubting voice to Lazarus.

" If He be the Son of God, why must He die ? Since He could bring thee to life, cannot He save Himself ? "

The cry was doubtless prompted more by agony at the thought of the Messiah's death than by disbelief; and in that light Lazarus replied to it.

" 'T is because He is the Son of God that He must die."

" Oh, I would see Him yet again," moaned the loving Mary. " My Saviour, my God, my Christ, my Life, would I could die for Thee!"

And, now and then, it seemed as though across the night there stole the tender words: " I have loved thee with an everlasting love."

Oh, to know that the Son of God was there, and that they were powerless! At these times, Lazarus would go into quiet places and pray, as if his heart would break; and all was gloom and grief within their souls, not for themselves, but for what the Saviour was to endure.

" To think that I, I, Lazarus, a sinner, should live, and that He should die. Oh, gladly would I give each one of my possessions, that once it would have grieved me to resign, that I might die for Him, or, by following Him, spare Him one brief hour of pain."

At Jerusalem the commotion of the people kept increasing. Messengers arrived almost daily at the doors of Caiaphas with the news that they could gain no tidings of Him, and the prisons were becoming thronged with men punished by Caiaphas for not bringing Him.

Strange were the tales that gained report as, one after another, the messengers returned. Some said that Pilate had forbidden his capture, others that many times they had laid hold on Him, but that He had slipped through their hands and seemed to vanish into air. Caiaphas could not fail to see that the latest miracle had weakened his position; and, later, he even meditated the death of Lazarus. He had said truly that all who crossed the path of Caiaphas should be brushed aside. Nicodemus had gone over openly to the Lord. Pilate came no more to the council chamber. Annas was hooted in the streets and pelted with stones. Even threats against the life of Caiaphas had been reported. Several of the Pharisees and rulers of the Synagogue believed in Jesus secretly, while not daring to confess it. Strange stir, forsooth, this Man had made, this carpenter's Son.

And so the days went by, and Lazarus's death and Lazarus's resurrection became matters of the past, swamped by disturbing doubts and fears about the future.

Once more the watchman passed by the house of Caiaphas, but the High Priest closed his ears. The time for repentance, for hesitation, for remorse was over. Satan had claimed this man, and he had been given over to him, as if unworthy of a contest.

" Let the heathen be awakened, let the heathen be awakened," cried the watchman, " for the day of the Lord is near, in the valley of decision, the valley of decision! "

CHAPTER XXI.

BETHANY was wrapped in night and silence; through the olive groves, grown dark and desolate with approaching winter, not a breath of wind stirred a silver leaf. In their chambers the household of Martha slept. The three alone slept not, but prayed and talked alternately, and all seemed restless.

"The pain deepeneth at my heart," said Mary.

"A great fear cometh over me," chimed in Martha. "If we could but have news of Him, that He liveth."

"Were He dead, we should have tidings of it," said Lazarus; but they knew not whether he meant from hearsay, or through supernatural means.

"Surely He knoweth that we love Him and fain would die with Him," said the loving Mary. "Be still! I hear a knocking at the gate!" she added quickly, ever the alert one, and she raised her hand. All stood up, with looks alternately of hope and dread. "Perchance, 't is He," said Mary.

"Or soldiers come to seek Him," added Martha, about to clap her hands to call together the attendants.

"Nay, silence," ordered Lazarus. "If 't is the Lord, wake no man, and, if 't is He, let Him not wait."

"He is not wont to knock," said Mary, "but doth come in some God-like way we wot not of."

Then they proceeded to the gate.

A woman's figure stood there. When she saw them approaching, carrying a swinging Roman lamp, she called out: "'T is I, the Magdalene."

"Thou, the Magdalene? And at this hour? What brings thee, Mary?" The voice of Lazarus had a strange vibration while he spoke, and his hand trembled while he tried to undo the bolt. The Magdalene's voice had been the last he had heard ere he had died, its echo had seemed to die and live again with him. Even now the peace her words had given him, the loving but despairing look, the glistening tears of love and agony; all had come back at the sound of the Magdalene's voice.

"I come once more with a message," she began, looking round tremblingly while she spoke, to see whether she was being followed. "I would come into the house and speak with you, for the enemies of the Lord are abroad to-night; 't was therefore that I came so late. Forgive me, Martha, that I disturb thy rest."

But Martha laid her hand gently on the Magdalene's shoulder, with unwonted tenderness.

"Rest, Mary?" she said. "We cannot rest while the fear of the Lord's death is ever before us."

By this time they reached the house.

"I have news that will rejoice your hearts," continued Mary Magdalene. "The Lord cometh to Bethany to-morrow."

"We will make ready for Him," broke in Martha, and already her housewifely mind flew to a dozen

details. Could she get this or that to set before her
Lord ? The finest table linen must be brought
out, the oldest wine made ready. Jacob, the old
servant, must be sent early to the market, to see
whether ortolans were to be got; yet, in her heart,
she knew that the Lord would partake only of the
simplest fare.

" He cometh not here," said Magdalene, " lest
His enemies should search for Him, but will lodge
in the house of Simon, thy father." And, all the
while, Magdalene looked not towards Lazarus—
although she longed to gaze on those much-loved
features, to see whether death had changed them—
lest her gaze should betray the wild joy that filled
her heart.

" Wilt not speak to me ?" said Lazarus to her
gently. " Hast forgotten how thou didst see me die
and comfort me ?"

Mary's pale face flushed to the very temples, to
where the fair tresses rose in crested wave around
her head; but she answered not.

Then, half reproachfully and half inquiringly,
Lazarus went on: " Thou didst not see me rise
again ? Where didst thou hide ?"

Magdalene blushed again, but, in the dim light of
the lamp, the blush was not observed. None knew
better than herself how she had longed to rush and
see him, but she had feared two things: to betray
her joy, and to leave the Virgin Mary.

" I did not like to leave the mother of our Lord,"
she answered; "for she is in daily torment lest the
Jews do kill the Christ, and every night she mourn-
eth, and every morning dreadeth that that day be
come."

" And thou dost minister to her ? " asked Lazarus
with gentle tenderness.

" How could I otherwise ?   She hath no one but
this Son, and Him she dares not claim as hers, in
that He is the Son of God.   Methinks her state is
more piteous than the poor woman's who can hold
her children to her breast and know they are her
own."

" Nay, but she is blessed above all women," answered Lazarus reverently.   " Nations shall worship
her and think that, through her, they shall obtain
salvation."

" Is she then as a saint ? " asked Mary innocently.

" Nay, she is naught but woman like thyself; but
she was chosen for her pure simplicity."

" Like me! " exclaimed the Magdalene.   " Like
me!   Would I were indeed like her, pure and sin-
less.   To be with her is like sitting in the Temple
when they sing psalms."

" But thou art forgiven; and a sinner forgiven is
no more a sinner."

The Magdalene looked at him with gratitude and
joy.   " Dost know all things now, Lazarus ?   Why
this earth was made, and why that God did let sin
enter, and why the Christ must die; and didst thou
go to heaven and to hell ?   And when will the end
of all things come ? "

Woman-like, she asked one question after another
without waiting for an answer.   Woman-like, she
thought that the knowledge of these things was
death's requital; the end to be attained by it.

In breathless silence, as though yet hoping that
their brother would tell the secrets that their hearts

longed to know, would grant the Magdalene's request, though theirs he had refused, the sisters waited, leaning against the wall.

" I know nothing at all, nor ever left this earth. Dost not remember, Mary, how I met thee in the olive groves ? "

" And was it really thou ? Methought after that, perhaps, it was but a vision or a dream. Thou didst give me a message which I took faithfully."

But Lazarus made no answer; his eyes were raised to heaven, and his lips moved as if in prayer. " I have asked whether I may tell thee what befell me," he said at last, " and methinks I may for the glory of God. Surely if I die, who will testify of these things, if I speak not ? And do thou Magdalene write. Thy father was a scribe, and thou too hast the art. Bring hither thy pen and write what I shall say, that future generations may know what befell Lazarus for God's glory."

In the stillness of the night, with the dim lamp throwing giant shadows on the wall, and barely lighting up their features, the three women half sat, half reclined, upon the carpets that covered the wide Roman hall, their eyes wide open with expectant wonder, listening while the Magdalene wrote a scroll that, later, would be destroyed; so that tradition only would echo on the wonders told that night by Lazarus.

" There was but one moment—when thy song ceased, Magdalene—when my faint heart did fail me. It was but the failing of the flesh, the sudden suffocation when the heart doth cease to beat. Then I awoke, as it seemed, from sleep, feeling light

and well, as if a burden had been cast from me; and
then I saw that I was even in this garden, and a
multitude of people, whom I knew well, were assembled to see the burial of some great man. I spoke
to some, but none did answer me nor looked my way,
and methought I was struck dumb. Then I heard
one say to the other: ' 'T is the burial of Lazarus.'

" Then I bethought me I would go back to see
whether my body still lay there, for I said, ' If Lazarus doth still lie here, then indeed the spirit and the
body are not one, even as the Lord hath spoken.'

" Then I entered my room and I saw my own
body stretched out on the bed, and all ye good
women and Joanna and Rachel too did tend me and
embalm me. And, while I looked, methought,
' How much of foul greed is in that face, how much
of weary thought; yet how little hath that body
understood the burden that it carried.'

" I looked at the costly curtains of my room. I
smelt the fragrant scents that rose on the air; I
noticed the costly cedar-wood carvings and the
Ethiopian ivories, and I said: ' Thou fool; and
didst thou think all this beautiful and rare, and thyself great, because thou hadst these things, and
versed in love and wisdom because thou hadst read
the sayings and doings of other fools as great as
thy own self ? '

" And then it seemed as though the body mocked
me, and while ye were striving to bind one arm in
grave clothes, it did rise and seem to point at me
with blue, dead fingers, and a voice like mine did
seem to say: ' Truly now thou hast escaped me, but
in life we were not divided. Who was the stronger,

thou or I ?   When thou wouldst pray, thine eyes did
fall with sleep, and when the Spirit bade thee go and
seek the poor, thy feet refused their office, and thou
didst leave it for a more convenient day; and so, all
through thy life, 't is comfort and ambition that
have been thy creed and thy pursuit, and they are
Satan's, and so am I, and so also is all flesh and
lust.   'T is all from Satan.'

"And while he spake I wept to see my body
thus, that might have been much otherwise had I
but known the Spirit's power; and to myself I said,
' If I could but live again I would live differently,
for now I know.'

"And the voice near me whispered: ' Trouble
not thyself, for thou art forgiven, in that thou
believest in the Christ.'   ' Nevertheless,' I thought,
' because I do believe, I wish that it had been even
so, and that this earthly temple had been kept more
beautiful.'

"Then they raised my body and bore it forth
'midst wailing cries, and I would fain have wiped
the tears from off your faces, but I could not; and
I followed by the side of mine own body to see
where they would lay it, and all that night I wandered by the house and sought ye and called ye by
your names, but ye could not see me.   Then at
midnight came another spirit to me, that of an old
man, and he took me by the hand and said: ' What
doest thou here, Lazarus ?   Why dost thou still
stay near thy home and thy riches and thy vessels
of silver and gold ?   Thou hast much to see and
hear, for that thou art dead for the glory of God and
shalt live again.'

" ' And shall I see Him yet again; Him whom my soul delighteth in ? ' I asked of the old man. ' Shall I see the Christ ? '

" ' Yea, thou shalt see Him again even on earth, for thou shalt rise again; but go now, appear to thine whom thou lovest best, and repeat the message that shall be spoken to thee; for, during the first twelve hours that follow death, 't is given to thee to comfort those that thou hast loved, if so be thy love be pure and good, and that they need thee.'

" And then, sweet Magdalene, I saw in memory thy sad eyes, as they had been at my death-bed, and methought, ' Surely 't is she that needeth me the most.' Yet when I came to thee, I bethought me of what the Lord would have me do, and it came strong upon me to give thee the message of which thou dost wot."

Here Lazarus looked lovingly at the Magdalene, and her eyes began to fill with tears of mingled joy and wonder.

" And didst feel that thou wert dead ? " asked Martha.

" Nay, I felt only a great rest and lightness and that evil thoughts no more oppressed me; but, for all else, I seemed to be yet myself, and to be yet in the same place. And I said to the old man: ' If this be death, where then are heaven and hell, and where is God and where is Satan ? '

" ' Be still,' he said. ' Dost thou that hath but lately left thy fleshly case, with all thy evil thoughts and wrongful understandings, and thy cavilings, and hankerings after thine own goods, dost think that thou art fit to come before the God Eternal ?

Thou art still in this world's surroundings. Thou art in Hades, and Hades is the air and space around the earth. See, thou art quite close, so far only art thou risen, as high as yonder tree.'

" Then I seized him by the white sleeve of his robe, and in my hands it felt soft like the downy clouds, like wool, yet without substance, and in deepest agony I cried: ' How then can I know whether I be saved ? ' ' Dost believe in Jesus, the Christ ? ' the Spirit asked. ' Verily and indeed I do,' I answered. ' Then the same hope that brought thee here will help thee still.'

" Then a great joy filled mine heart, a joy to which no earthly joy can be compared. The joy of certainty and rest, which no man hath on earth. ' Why, then, do men fear death ? ' I asked again. ' They fear what they know not. They believe in a life and a death of their own thinking. They live in dreams of their own making and waken but to die.' ' And who art thou ? ' I asked. ' I am the Spirit of Truth. In the world I cannot live, for Satan seeketh to destroy me, and he is the father of lies. Some I visit may seek for me, but there is no Truth on earth. Here I abide, and, when all dreaming and scheming and lying and cheating are at an end for any man, I meet the soul that hath loved Truth and I leave it not again. But thou must go back to the earth, and I cannot come with thee. See that thou speak the Truth and love the Truth and live it.'

" Then I asked him: ' What is Truth ? ' And the old man answered: ' Truth is that which a man heareth in his heart, and observeth not. 'T is the voice of the I AM. And all know what is Truth, but they love it not. Yet the greatest gift of all is Truth, for he who hath it not causeth his brother to err, which is the greatest sin of all. Truth is like a pointed sword held heavenwards so that the light flasheth on both sides. 'T is like a ball of crystal, so suspended in the air that it leaveth no shadow, and all men can see its purity. Truth is like the eyes of the new-born babe that cannot speak. Truth is like white sails on a sea, a light set on a hill; it is fearless as a hero in a battle; a head with an iron neck that none can sever. Like a rock that no earthquake can make tremble, so is Truth. Truth echoeth through ages and will not be stilled, and it shineth forth to the generations still to come; but all in vain.'

" Then he took me across the air, over the trees and valleys, and first he pointed out to me Jerusalem, and while I looked I saw an angel with black wings flying hither and thither over the heads of the multitudes. I remembered the black wings that had seemed so near me on the road to Jericho, and I bade the old man pause awhile and tell me who was the angel with the sombre wings. ' 'T is Satan,' he made answer, and even while he spoke the angel raised his face, and on it was such a look of blank despair as I have never seen on that of any man. ' What doeth he here ? ' I asked. ' He feareth that the glory of God is nigh at hand. He goeth about making lies; he striveth yet to harden the hearts of the Pharisees and the scribes against the Christ. Caiaphas and Judas and many others have been given over to him, but he will have more. He fighteth hard for Nicodemus and for Pontius Pilate. He thinketh yet that the divine spark he hath in him of God can fight with God.' ' Will he, then, die ? ' I asked. ' The spirit that God hath made can never die,' replied the Spirit of Truth; ' but, one day, Satan will be given to good works, and that will be his hell; to preach the gospel of Him he hateth, and tend the sick and suffering, for the Spirit of the Almighty will prevail. ' Beware, Lazarus, for he will sift thee as one sifteth wheat, and tenfold more when thou dost return to life. Here he cannot touch thee; but now that thou hast learned the way to live 't will be harder for thee. But thou art forever the testimony of the power and love of Christ, and the Spirit of Truth will be with thee.'

" I felt greatly troubled and I said: ' Shall I fail ? Shall I fail ? ' And, like sweet music wafted over great waters that rolled with hollow sound beneath, methought I heard the words: ' Fear not. My grace is sufficient for thee, for My strength is made perfect in weakness.'

" Then I saw that other spirits came and went about us, and all looked peaceful and quiet, as though no longer troubled about aught below. And I knew no one face, but all seemed those of friends that I had loved, and, as they flitted past me, they cried out, ' Welcome, welcome.' Then I saw that where I was there was no night nor day, only a strange glow of light; and of hours, of time, of sleep —they were not. Then I said to the Spirit of Truth: ' Is there naught that I can do for the Christ in these four days ? Can I go and comfort the hearts of the desolate or watch beside the sick ? ' ' Thou hadst

all life for that,' the Spirit of Truth replied reproachfully. ' Now it is too late. Thou canst not do it
till thou goest back to earth.' Then, thinking of
the years I had misspent, how the Lord had bid me
leave all and follow Him, I wept. But the Spirit of
Truth consoled me. ' Weep not,' he said, ' for
thou canst pray. This is denied to no one but
Satan; he may not pray; oft great troubles, great
adversities, and terrors come upon him and he fain
would cry out to the Lord; but he knoweth that
God heareth him not, and that prayer from him
availeth nothing.'

" So then I knelt like a little child and prayed
there where I stood, and, while I prayed, others too
came round me and prayed also; and the sound of
our voices rose like music on the air, and it was as
if angels' voices, too, joined in with us and sang:
' Tell it to the Lord, tell it to the Lord! '

" And the Spirit of Truth prayed too; and, when
we had all risen, he said to me: ' Prayer is the key
to heaven, for with prayer there cometh faith, and
faith leadeth on to heaven. Remember that when
thou comest again on earth, and cease not to pray.'

" And I bowed my head, for I seemed not as a
ruler; but the spirit of a little child had come upon
me."

CHAPTER XXII.

" THEN the Spirit of Truth took me by the hand and said: ' Come now and I will show thee the earth as it really is; not as it seemeth to thee. Thou shalt see into the hearts of men.'

" And, hand in hand, we flew over the houses of Jerusalem, and over the golden canopy of the Temple, and, as we passed, it was as if the roofs of the houses were removed, and we saw into the houses, and then it seemed as though a veil were torn from the hearts of them that dwelt therein, and we could read their thoughts. First the Spirit took me to the house of Pontius Pilate. His room was dark, but, while we stood at the window, our own radiance seemed to light it up and show us where he lay, tossing on his couch; and we heard him say: ' This Man hath done no evil by the Roman law. He shall not die.' Then he rose from his couch and paced the room, his fists clenched, and his voice rang out with a bitter cry: ' If I could but know whether He be the Christ! Is it, oh, is it indeed He?'

" Then I said to the Spirit of Truth: ' This man would fain believe; why, then, hath he not the power?' And the Spirit of Truth made answer: ' He will not let himself believe, for fear of Caiaphas. He knoweth the Roman law, and the Christ hath

done naught against the Roman law, but he feareth
Caiaphas; for once Caiaphas did send wo~d to the
Emperor about the pictures of his gods he had set
up, and, again, about the Corban. Twice hath
Pontius Pilate erred, and twice did Caiaphas obtain
hearing of the Emperor, so now Pilate feareth to
offend him. Thus in this world do men barter great
things for little, and eternal salvation for the good
opinion of men like unto themselves. Yet the heart
of Pilate is such an one as God doth love. 'T is a
noble heart that would do right, a kind heart and
one that hateth to do injustice. Yet he hath so
mystified himself that he knoweth no longer what
Truth is.'

" Then he took me to the house of Caiaphas, the
High Priest, and the heart I witnessed there in all
its nakedness made my own heart faint, for on it I
could see no white spot at all, only craft, and malice,
and vengeance, and defiance. It was as if the spark
of the Holy Spirit had been quenched. Greed and
hate and suspicion were in that heart. Love could
not lodge therein, nor Truth; it was like a garden
choked with weeds. ' This man,' said the Spirit,
' is a devil, for he knoweth by the spirit of prophecy
that is given to him through Aaron that Jesus of
Nazareth is the Christ; but he hath sold his soul to
Satan, rather than have it said that a greater than
he is on earth. He knoweth that He whom he
persecuteth hath power given Him from above. He
knoweth that the vengeance of God will come upon
him, and, though he knoweth not for a surety that
there is a future life, yet he feareth it, and that he
will be eternally consumed. All this he knoweth,

and therefore doth he sin wilfully; and wilful sin is
the worst of all, and cometh rarely.   For most men
sin because they think not, or are too busy, or too
careless, or are choked with the cares of this world;
nearly all would fain believe, but cannot; but this
man doth believe and will not.'

"Then Truth held a mirror before my eyes, and
in that mirror I saw a vision.   I saw Caiaphas struggling with a man in armour, and the man's armour
flashed forth blue lights like tongues of dying fire,
and he upheld his sword.   Then he thrust his sword
into the side of Caiaphas, and the blood spurted forth
in jet-black streams, as if the heart of him had been
corrupt.   And, hovering over the High Priest's
body, I saw once more the black-winged angel
whom the Spirit of Truth did call Satan, and he
cried exultingly: 'Thou art mine, Caiaphas, thou
art mine forever!'

"And while he spoke, the look of despair I had
seen on Satan's face o'erspread the countenance of
Caiaphas, filling me with such horror and such dread
that I longed to see somewhere a pure heart, or a
ray of sunlight to relieve my soul of this darkness
and desolation.   Then turned I to the Spirit and I
said: 'I can look no longer at this vision, for the
despair doth penetrate my heart.'

"Then he took the mirror from me.   'Look now
at no vision, but the Truth,' he said.   And, even
while he spoke, I saw that Caiaphas paced the room
impatiently, and looked ever towards the door.
And presently I saw it opened and a man enter
crouching and ashamed, like one who thinketh himself too vile to live; and, as he approached Caiaphas,

15

I could see his face upturned, and lo, it was the face of him that is called Iscariot, and I started when I saw him, for methought he had been the follower of Christ."

Here Lazarus paused, as though fearing to impart a secret that was not his own; but Martha, looking at him, said: " I have ever had a strange mistrust of Judas."

" Yet we must not speak of this," said Lazarus, " for 't was but as the vision of a dream."

But the women's eager faces seemed to impel him to proceed. Another day was dawning, and now, one by one, the members of the household came in silently to the hall, marvelling to find their master there at this early hour. They ranged themselves in rapt attention to hear the words that fell from him.

" And when I looked on Judas," continued Lazarus, " I saw he had the same despairing look that I had noted in the face of Caiaphas. Withal there was not that hatred in him, and I pitied him, for I saw that his was a weak, timid heart, and that he feared this Caiaphas. When Judas entered, Caiaphas looked sternly at him and his voice came angrily. ' What wouldst thou with me, Judas ? Have I not done with thee ? Didst thou not covenant for thirty pieces of silver to sell the Nazarene ? Wherefore troublest thou me ? '—' I come to crave thy pardon, noble Caiaphas, and to beg thee to release me from my promise, for I wot not what I said. Methinks I was drunk with wine to say I would betray the Lord for thirty pieces of silver.' ' Dost want more ?' asked Caiaphas, eying him with doubt. ' Nay, I

want none at all,' said Judas, 'only to be freed from
this my promise. I cannot betray the Lord.'
'Fool!' roared Caiaphas, beyond himself with rage.
Then, seizing Iscariot by the sleeve, he took him to
the window and pointed to the pale mists of dawn
that hovered in tenuous masses above the earth.
'Seest thou that sun just showing above yon mountain?' he asked the wretched man, whose despairing
eyes were barely lifted and whose head was bent
painfully beneath the iron grasp of Caiaphas. 'Before that sun shall rise again thou wilt be lying with
thy eyes glazed in death, unless thou keep thy
promise to betray this Jesus.'"

"Oh, poor Judas!" exclaimed the tender-hearted
Mary. "Could we not help him to escape this
man?"

"He hath the Lord," said Martha sternly.

But Lazarus continued: "And even while Caiaphas was speaking, methought I saw the frame of
Judas shrink into an image half its own size; yet
still I hoped that he would say: 'I will die, I will
die gladly rather than betray my Lord.' But instead, as though greatly fearing Caiaphas, he turned
and fled; and as he fled, Caiaphas laughed a laugh
so full of scorn and hate that 't would have more
fitly issued from the lips of devils. 'Ha, ha,' he
scoffed, 'thou who wouldst betray thy friend for
thirty pieces of silver, dost think to cozen Caiaphas?
Like all traitors, thou fearest death, and 't is death
I will hold over thee, thou red-haired poltroon!'
And I wept to think that I could not go to Jesus
and warn Him of His foe; but the Spirit of Truth
had read my thoughts. He smiled and said: 'Poor

fool, and who art thou to think thou canst inform thy Lord of aught ? All that thou hast but now perceived hath been known to Him since Time began—aye, before Time was.' Then, sick at heart at the sight of all this treachery, I turned me to the Spirit of Truth and said : ' Canst thou not show me some pure hearts to raise my drooping spirits ? Are there no good upon the earth ? ' And Truth answered : ' There are few ; none are wholly good, but some have trust.'

" Then he took me through palaces of the Jews and of the Romans and into the houses of great merchants ; but nowhere saw I one heart that thirsted for knowledge of the Christ. The women were content to deck themselves with jewels and to scold their serving-maids, and each spake ill of another's beauty or her virtue. Here and there I saw little children who looked to heaven and asked their parents : ' Who liveth beyond the clouds ? ' But their parents only answered : ' Torment me not with questionings ' ; or, ' When thou art a grown man thou wilt know.' And therewith the child must needs be satisfied. It is thus that ignorance and darkness are continued from one generation to another.

" Then the Spirit took me into the houses of the rulers of the Synagogue, the governors of the people and the lawyers, and, looking into their hearts, I saw that there was but little knowledge in them, only such as was required to cozen other men. They cared not for their country's good, nor for the glory of the Lord. In their hearts was only love of money and great power, and they craved strength but to crush the lowly, not to oppose the foe. They laid tithes and taxes on the people, to fill their own coffers, not for the grandeur of the land; and of all there scarce one spoke the truth, and of the lawyers none; but all they strove for was to entangle men in their talk and to make them bear false witness. And all I saw were hypocrites and liars, and it seemed to me that no man could be saved on the face of the whole earth, and I marvelled that God consumed them not with fire.

" Then the Spirit of Truth spake yet again and said: ' Now will I show to thee the sweetest, greatest spirit of all women that are upon the earth.' And he took me far across fields and villages and hills till he came to a house in Nazareth, and I said: ' This I know is where dwelleth the mother of the Lord.' And the Spirit of Truth said: ' She is blessed above all women, and many nations will worship her. Nevertheless, she is not divine, for all she hath been chosen to give earthly life to the Son of God. But priests of many countries will seek to make her so, in that they may catch the souls of women; for 't is ever women whom Satan first entangleth.'

" Then said I: ' Who then is Satan ? and if God hath so great power, why doth He leave this man to buffet and seduce the world ? '

" Then the Spirit of Truth spoke sternly to me: ' Be silent, and inquire not into the things of God! I, too, know not whence is Satan, nor wherefore. He was before the world was made. Of that knoweth only God. Canst tell how the lights do hang in heaven and how the seas do rise and fall, yet go no

farther ?   Dost know how the leaf of the flower un-
foldeth, or the child is gendered in the womb ?
These things first find out, and when thou hast in-
formed thyself of all earthly things—what whiteneth
the snow, and whence the rivers rush to reach the
sea; when thou hast learned how forms the fish
within the shell, and why the mountains quake—
then thou canst ask of God, if thou art bold enough,
wherefore He did create thee, and whence is Satan.
Wouldst be a scholar, wouldst learn philosophy, ere
thou canst read; wouldst fight a battle ere thou
canst buckle on the sword ?   Be content, and ask
not, but for the spirit of a little child, and to be born
again in faith and love.'

" And, thus rebuked, my eyes fell in confusion,
and once more they sought the earth, and I saw the
virgin mother kneeling on her floor.   Never shall I
forget the purity of that enraptured gaze, that
seemed mutely to appeal to Heaven to ask the
meaning of this grief that had befallen her; why she,
who had preserved ever her virginity, and married
Joseph of Nazareth but for a companion and protection, should have had a child, and further should
have suffered the scorn of the world and the suspicion of her husband for so many months.   She was
dressed in a simple woollen gown that fell from
neck to feet, and her hair, yellow as wheat that doth
await the reaper, did shimmer in the sun, contrast-
ing strangely with her dark pencilled eyebrows, but
harmonising with the liquid lustre of her deep blue
eyes.   And, looking at this small, frail woman, I
marvelled how she could endure so much and live;
and I inquired of the Spirit of Truth: ' Doth this
woman pray always ?'

" And he answered: ' Always; and with prayer she hath achieved many things. When Joseph found that she was with child, he would have given her a bill of divorcement, and all her friends did scoff at her. " Wherefore didst thou marry Joseph?" inquired they of her. " To be the father of thy child ? "

" ' And, greatly troubled, Joseph did entreat her to advertise him whence was this child; and, loath to hold her up to public scorn, he said: " I will put thee privily away, if thou wilt tell me; I will neither stone thee, nor give thee a writing of divorcement; I will be as though I were the father of the child."

" 'But she could do naught but cry: "I know not." And none would credit her, and all her kindred came about her murmuring and saying: " Why hath this reproach of the enemy come upon us in this day, and on the lineage of the House of David, that a virgin should be found with child ?"

" ' But Mary could only weep and say, " I know not, I know not "; and she shut herself up and denied herself to all, for the reviling of her enemies overwhelmed her. But, in her heart, she knew that the child was of the Lord; for the angel Gabriel had appeared to her, the same who had appeared also to Elisabeth her cousin before the birth of John the Baptist; and the two women talked much together of these things and were filled with the Holy Spirit, which is from the beginning given to all whose hearts are gentle and as little children's. But none could understand this thing, or believe that it was the doing of the Lord. For all that, Mary prayed on in patience that, even if all the world would not believe it, Joseph might receive assurance that she was a pure woman, true and faithful.   And then one night her prayer was answered, for an angel from the Lord appeared to Joseph, and thus he spake: " Joseph, thou son of David, fear not to take unto thee Mary thy wife: for that which is conceived in her is of the Holy Ghost.   And she shall bring forth a Son, and thou shalt call His name Jesus: for He shall save His people from their sins."

" 'And when he woke from sleep, he went to Mary and fell down and worshipped her and said: " Mary, Mary, forgive me ; I have done thee grievous wrong.   Blessed art thou amongst women."

" 'And Mary, who was ever tender and loving and forgiving, looked at him kneeling at her feet, and said: " How wouldst thou know, Joseph, except the Lord did tell thee ?   But forbear to kneel to me, for I am but the Lord's hand-maiden."   And then Mary opened her mouth and sang a beauteous song, a song so sweet that the nations will sing it evermore; and at the Judgment Day shall again be heard the song of this pure, faithful woman.   And, as she sang, I heard a chorus of angels join in and sing, " Praise, praise to God in the highest, and on earth peace." '

" And again Truth handed me the mirror in which to see the vision of the future; and I saw one with a sword pierce the heart of the Virgin through and through.   Again I saw her bowed down with grief and desolate, wandering towards the grave of her slain Son; and, as she walked, great drops fell from her eyes, and, wherever one did fall, a pure white lily did spring up to mark the place. ' See how even the righteous suffer! Why is this?' I asked. And the Spirit of Truth made answer: ' This too shalt thou know, when all things be made manifest; but I tell thee that the present suffering is as naught compared with the glory that shall be revealed.'

" Then he took me to where I longed to be, to Ephraim; but when I would fain have spoken to the Lord, he said: ' Thine hour is not yet come.'

" And I wept to think that I might not go to my Lord. Then the Spirit of Truth went on: ' So weep all in Hades that have loved the Lord. They sigh and long for Him; but 't is worse for those in hell, for they sigh and long in vain.' Then I said to the Spirit of Truth: ' I would see hell.'

" And the Spirit of Truth looked very stern and answered: ' Dost know that by the blood of the Lamb alone thou art saved from hell?' ' Verily,' I answered, ' I know that it is by the mercy of God and the love of Jesus that I too am not in the innermost hell.'

" And even while I spoke the Spirit answered: ' Yea, thou shalt see hell also, for two days are past, and in two days thou shalt see earth once more.' Then I said to the Spirit: ' Must this thing be, that I live again?' ' Yea, thou must live again and also die,' the Spirit answered; and my soul did faint within me at these words.

" Then the Spirit took me hither and thither, and I now saw every man did seek his own, and no other's glory, and how they who believed not sought to fashion their own destiny and straighten their own paths; and then I saw how some great judgment overtook them, such as they had never recked of.

The miser's money was taken from him by his enemy; the lover of the wanton woman found her faithless. The steward of the rich man gave his lord's gains to another, and while the king went forth to conquer other lands an enemy came unawares and took his country. The husbandman who would reap his grain saw not the rain-clouds gathering above, or the thunder thickening behind the mountain; and the sailor who left the harbour in fair weather heard not the distant moaning of the wind that soon would lash the waves into a storm that would engulf him.

" And I saw, as the preacher saith, that the race is not to the swift, nor the battle to the strong; but that victory is only for them who wait patiently for the Lord. And I wept at the remembrance of the years that I had lost, of the houses I had builded, the orchards and the gardens I had planted; and I saw that all the labour of man is for himself, and that yet withal he is never satisfied."

CHAPTER XXIII.

" THEN the Spirit took me by the hand and said:
'Come back to Hades, and thou shalt descend to-night into hell.' And we flew though the
air more swiftly than the birds. Then said I to the
Spirit: ' I feel so strong, like to a young eagle; yet
on earth I was ever weary and footsore.' And he
made answer: ' It was the body chained thee.
When the spirit is delivered from the body, at that
moment it feels lifted up and is capable of all things.
The spirit is of God and therefore perfect. The
will and the flesh belong to man, and war ever with
the spirit. Thy thoughts now are pure, being by
the body undefiled. Thou seest clearly with the
eyes of the spirit; thou hearest keenly with the
spirit's ear. Thine heart can love the Lord because
it hath no fleshy taint, being wholly of the spirit.
So it is that thou feelest perfect joy and rest, for
thou hast no weariness of the flesh.'

" ' Then, if the spirit be of God,' I asked,
' whence are the evil spirits ? ' ' Ask me not,' said
the Spirit of Truth. ' The Spirit of Evil and the
flesh are one. At the Judgment Day all shall stand
reunited to their fleshly bodies, as thou wilt shortly
be; but the righteous join their mortal bodies but
for the hour of the Judgment, and, when they enter

into eternal glory these bodies will return to dust.
But the wicked are reunited to their bodies for evermore.   They can never again be free of them.   And
henceforth they have but the nature of the flesh.
There is nothing spiritual left to them, with which
to lessen the heaviness of their flesh.   All that the
flesh lusteth for, they attain; and then, when the
flesh wearieth of that which it attaineth, their lust is
turned to nausea; and one of hell's chief torments
is to have known the delights of being in the spirit
and then to return to the flesh.'

" ' And the eternal flames,' I asked, ' are they real
flames, that burn and scorch the body ? '—' They
are the inward flames of eternal desire without hope
of satisfaction.'   Then on my head he placed a helmet.   ' This,' he said, ' is the helmet of Salvation,
which I place on thy head, lest the flames should
scorch thee.'

" Then I knew that I was saved by the love of
Jesus, and that I should descend to hell only to see
the woe I had escaped; and I fell to the ground and
thanked the Lord that, of His mercy, He had redeemed me; and I vowed a vow that, when I should
return to the body, I would give all that I possessed,
and follow Jesus, for that naught else availed in this
world.   Then I took his hand, and he led me
through the air, and my heart was filled with a
grievous dread of that which I should see.

" ' Now thou shalt know what is real sin,' said the
Spirit to me.   ' Many indeed already think they
know; but the ways of the Lord are different from
those of man, and many who thought that they were
righteous groan now in hell.'

" And now we no longer flew, but hovered, as if 'twixt heaven and earth; then fell, and fell, and fell; and, while we fell, methought I heard the noise of rocks that crashed and crumbled, and the great light of Hades became ever dimmer, and there came a gloaming as of eventide, and then dusk. Then we came to a dreary field, with no corn, or flowers, or green leaves therein; only a desolate, grey waste. And figures sat about in groups with bent heads supported on their hands, and waiting, yet without hope; and I asked the Spirit: ' Who are these?' And the Spirit answered: ' These are they who in their lives have done neither right nor wrong; who have risen, and slept, and eaten, and drunk, and harmed no man. These are they who, having talents, buried them, and have come to the Lord with empty hands; and, as they lived on earth, so will they live through all eternity, doing nothing, learning nothing, reaping nothing, for there is naught in this field to reap.'

" ' Are they not gladdened even at the sight of us?' I asked. ' They can never any more be glad or sorry,' replied the Spirit. ' They laugh not, neither do they weep.'

" Then we looked across the field to where was a long stone building, and here it was darker still; and the Spirit unlocked the door, and all was silent, and so dark, that I could not perceive whether there were people there or not; yet presently could I hear faint sighing; and soon a little light arose from the open door; then I saw figures groping about and clutching each other, as if to make sure that others were also there; and great blocks of rock lay across the passage, yet so dim it was that they could not see whether it was rock or forms of beasts.

"And, as I wondered, the Spirit said: ' These are they who have been silent when they should have spoken, who shrank from all responsibility, who helped not one another, who witnessed neither for good nor evil, who accused not the wicked nor held up the oppressed, who would be neither hot nor cold. These are they who heed not, neither give, saying, " Perchance this man deserveth it not "; who say to the one who asketh for advice and comfort: " I cannot tell; see thou to that." Of these is Pontius Pilate, and hither will he come; but only for a season, for he will suffer much on earth at the hands of his own country. All these will through eternity continue in this twilight. There will be no night in which to rest, and no day in which to see what is around them, for they would not see the straight path, they would not guide the helpless, nor oppose the evil; so now they know not what lieth close, whether it be danger, friend or foe, wild beast or falling rock; and they sit motionless for fear of what they know not, daring not to go forth and face what is before them, as in life they lacked courage to stand by the righteous and the oppressed. The more part of these are of noble blood, who feared to bring reproach to their name or to soil their garments; who would not sit at meat with sinners, yet who did shut their eyes if their own familiar friend did sin, and reproached him not. These are great sinners, but, seeing that they have not judged others, nor harmed any, but by silence, they go not into the nethermost hell,'

" ' What is the worst sin of all ? ' I asked.—
' There is one sin we may not speak of, that even
the angels wot not of; and we know not whether
any man hath committed it, nor where the hell is.
Of that knoweth only God.   But one of the greatest sinners is he who never forgiveth; for this cause
he too is never forgiven.'

" Then we passed through a long, dark building,
like to a sepulchre; and, as we passed out, I felt a
cold air come against me, as if the north wind blew
over mountains of ice and snow; and figures that
were unclothed ran hither and thither, crying out
for garments and for fire; praying that even scorching fire might come upon them, rather than this
cold.   And the Spirit of Truth said: ' These are
they who have no mercy; who have loved neither
father nor mother, nor husband, nor friend, nor
children; who have not cared if others suffered or
needed help, nor listened to those that loved them,
nor drawn with love the hearts of those that erred.
Here they freeze and freeze, yet die not, and no
warmth cometh to them ever.'

" Then I saw that most of these were women
whose hearts were cold; and, as we passed, one ran
after me and seized me, and she said: ' Give me of
thy warmth, give me of thy warmth.'

" But, even while she spoke, she fainted from
very cold; and I said to the Spirit: ' Who is this
woman, for methinks I have seen her picture when
on earth ? '   And he answered: ' That is Jezebel.'

" Then we hurried on, for the night was well-nigh
spent, and the Spirit of Truth did tell me that I
must needs make speed, for that the next day the

Lord would need me for the glory of His name; and, in deep thankfulness, I thanked God that I, so great a sinner, should have been chosen to testify to His power. And as I hastened along, I looked from side to side, lest, haply, any that I loved was in this hell; but none saw I that I had loved, though many that I had known on earth and had thought righteous, and most were Pharisees; and many that I had thought to have seen were not there.

"Then I said: ' If time be short, show me the nethermost hells, that I may know of the greatest sins.'

"And while I spoke, the ground on which I stood gave way, and we fell still lower; and Truth said: ' Look around and see the confusion of this hell, for in it God hath put no check, and the lack of it hath made them as if mad.'

" And I saw men and women running hither and thither in haste, yet doing nothing, save quarrelling and tearing each other to pieces; yet death would not release them.

" ' Who are these ? ' I said. ' These be schemers and plotters and lawyers,' said the Spirit of Truth. ' They ran to and fro on earth and laid snares for men; and they still do so, but now they fall into their own toils; and to the makers of laws none hearken, for none careth for the law, for he hath naught to gain who keepeth it, nor hath he aught to lose who transgresseth it.'

" And, looking on their faces, I saw such fury as I had thought that no man could wear, for they seemed to place no bounds upon their rage and envyings, for they had lost all power of self-restraint,

and no longer could direct or bind their thoughts.
And their mouths were full of cursing; such words
proceeding from their mouths that, though I could
not understand them, I felt were cries of hellish hate
and foulest loathing, such as were never known on
earth.   Women and men cursed equally, cursed
each other, and God for making them, and Satan
for bringing them hither; yet their revilings brought
them no relief, their foul words no content, and
each tore hither and thither like one possessed.

" Then I said, ' Surely there are none worse than
these.'

" But the Spirit took me past this pit of horror
where men crept in and out like worms beneath a
corpse, and I saw another hell, and at one end of it
an iron gate with spikes.   And in this hell was a
great concourse of men and women.   And one having the appearance of an angel, and bearing a lan-
tern in his hand, did run along between the crowds
of men and women; and, when he reached the gate,
he sprang thereon and cried: ' Behold the gate that
leadeth out of hell.'   And all followed him, but,
when they strove to clamber over it—for none could
open it, it being strongly barred—the spikes did
enter their flesh and tear them.   Then they returned
and told their brethren, to entreat their help; but it
availed nothing.   And every time the angel ran
anew, so ran others; yet all failed to pass beyond
the gate.

" And the Spirit of Truth said to me: ' These be
they who have corrupted youth and childhood, and
the pure-minded among men, and have beguiled
them, so that they have strayed.   Just as in their

16

lives they led believing souls to the gates of knowledge, and then left them to be wounded by their
sin, so now they themselves are led, for they fancy
ever that at last they will escape; but the spikes
do tear them and will in no wise let them pass."

"Then I looked and saw that many of these were
women; at which, marvelling, I said: ' Do women
lead the innocent to their undoing ?' And the Spirit
answered: ' Yea, more ofttimes than men.   It never
satisfieth a woman till she hath caught a young man
in her toils.   Then she leaveth him; and he, taught
by her, betrayeth other women; but for one man
that betrayeth a woman there are twenty women
who betray men, and these are oft the mothers of
children.'

" And I marvelled that women had been created.
Then I looked up, and on a high mountain peak I
saw a woman of exceeding beauty poised.   And her
eyes were turned on hell; and I asked Truth: ' Who
is she ?'   And he answered: ' That same is Eve,
the mother of all mankind.   She sitteth on the highest mountain peak of hell and looketh down and
seeth the grief that she hath brought upon the world
by disobedience; and she weepeth always and pray-
eth without ceasing; and her grief of repentance is
so great that it is to her even as hell; and it shall
be counted to her for righteousness, for she hath
believed and repented and suffered much, and, one
day, she shall be forgiven; but not till she hath seen
the victory over sin, not till she hath seen even the
Holy One in hell.'

" Then I asked the Spirit: ' Will the Christ come
to this hell ?   Wherefore ?'   And the Spirit of

Truth answered: ' That I know not, but methinks that 't is to give hope to them who were not on earth at His appearance; that, when they see Him, they may believe and tremble, and repent.'

" Then I saw a crowd assembled, and high places raised, like thrones, and men in long robes ascending them, as if to preach; and, as each rose in the high place, another came and tore him down and cried: ' Who art thou to call thyself a priest ? ' or, ' Who art thou to call thyself a ruler ? I will be priest, I will be ruler.' And, so soon as the one that did pull the other down did reach the throne, he too was dragged down and buffeted.

" And the Spirit of Truth explained: ' These are they whom ambition hath consumed. They sought high places and some gained them. Then these were puffed up with pride; then others came and took their place, and they were stricken to the dust.'

" Then I heard peals of laughter, the like to which I had never heard before. Methinks Satan must laugh so. And I looked around and saw no man near, save them who rose and fell in the high places; and the Spirit of Truth spake thus concerning them : ' These who hear this laughter are they who scoffed and derided at religion, and at them who tried to act aright; and they who made afraid the timid hearts. Now they hear ever this laughter around them, and seek to find whence it proceedeth; but they seek in vain; and the laugh continueth day and night, and ever it seemeth to them that none standeth near; till at last they go well-nigh mad for very horror, yet the laughter ceaseth not, and will never cease.'

" Then we came to almost the nethermost hell of all, and the smell was foul, as of a putrefying, stagnant pool, heavy with fever-laden mists; and the rocks grew closer, as though they would crush out all light. ' Here dwell the greatest sinners of any thou hast seen,' said the Spirit of Truth; ' the religious hypocrites and the priests who pervert the people. They who make weak women confess their sins, that they may listen to uncleanly tales, and hold the secrets of the fearsome, like daggers, over their heads. Of these Caiaphas will be—and his day is close at hand.'

" And I looked and saw that the place was crowded with long-robed priests with folded hands, which they could not unlock; the women came and cursed them, and their sons and daughters came and cursed them, and cried out: ' Who then was our father ? '

" And, while I looked I saw that they were struck with blindness, and there was none to lead them as they walked; thus they struck their feet against the stones and rocks, and ofttimes fell to the ground.

"And the Spirit of Truth said: 'In life these men knew the truth and hid it from the people, beguiling them with rumours and tradition; and now they themselves are struck with blindness, and ofttimes the crowd doth rend them, and they cannot help themselves.'

" Then remembered I the words of the Nazarene: ' Woe unto ye, ye blind guides, which say, " Whosoever shall swear by the Temple it is nothing, but whosoever shall swear by the gold of the Temple he is a debtor ! " ' '

" Then I saw that this was the greatest punishment of all, to be blind and in hell, and to know that this blindness is forever and ever. Yet could I not pity them as I did the others, for I thought of all the rulers and high priests that I had known, and could call none to mind that spake the truth or taught it; and I considered how the laws of Moses had been perverted by these hypocrites, and that their sayings and writings would remain written for generations; and I wondered not that the worst punishment of eternal blindness should be theirs.

" Then we came to a field which was fair to see, with fruit and flowers that hung in bounteous profusion everywhere; and I said: ' This can be no hell ! '

" But the Spirit shook his head and made reply: 'This is the garden of hell, where the women wander for one hour in every day. This blessing is accorded them because of the mother of the Lord. 'T is only since the birth of the Christ on earth that it hath been planted. For her sake, and for the sake of their suffering on earth, women are given one hour that they may rest them from the torture of hell. But not all women are allowed to enter here. 'T is like unto the Garden of Eden, in which the Lord placed Adam and Eve; for, each evening, an angel with a flaming sword doth chase them from the garden, even as Eve was chased, and crieth out : ''Depart, depart, ye sinful.'' '

" And as I gazed, I saw that many women of exceeding fairness wandered in the cool shade of the garden, and for one hour their eyes did shine and their smile was sweet. And even while I looked, the angel with the flaming sword which turned each way appeared and cried, as Truth had advertised me: ' Depart, depart, ye sinful.' Then, with deep wailing and moaning and tearing of hair, the crowd of women rushed down the alleys, looking neither to the right nor to the left.

" And I asked : ' How have these women sinned ? ' —' These are unfaithful, haters of children, envious, loving luxury, driving men to sin and theft by their desire for sumptuous living, backbiters, liars, bearers of false witness against other women, tattlers; and the worst of all are they who marry without love, and they who force their children to barter themselves for gold.'

" Next we came to a freezing lake, which stank of brimstone and other noisome things. And, as we looked, behold blue lights illumed the lake, and over it was ice. And a vast concourse approached from the farther side, making as though they would cross over; but midway, the ice did break and they fell in; and great blue flames burst forth and scorched them as they plunged into the lake.

" ' This,' said the Spirit of Truth, ' is the Lake of Liars. The blue lights are like their words that have misguided men. The ice is like their promises that they have broken; and now they are plunged into the scorching flames of hell.'

" Then Truth came near the lake, and the spirits cried: 'Approach not, come not near, for we hate thee, Truth.'

" And I looked and saw that the lake did stretch farther than the eye could reach, and in it were countless souls, with the appearance of wriggling eels and serpents fighting, hustling, holding on to each other, trying to lift themselves out of the mire.

" And I said to the Spirit of Truth: ' Why are these so many ? Surely they do outnumber all others in hell.' And the Spirit answered: ' Because all men are liars. Some lie to each other, and some to God, and some to themselves; but all are liars, and none speak the truth. Some indeed know not what truth is.'

" Then I said: ' Tell me what others dwell in hell.' And Truth replied: 'There are the mischief-makers. Their hell is like unto the liars', save that an eternal wind doth blow on their ears; and there are the traitors; they too are in a bottomless pit, and are divided thus: traitors to their country, traitors to their Lord, traitors to their friends, traitors to their kinsmen. These last are worst of all; for, if a man honour not his own flesh and blood, whom then will he honour ? Besides, these are they who weary souls by much reproving, and they who judge. They who judge are weighed in balances; day and night are they weighed, and ever are they found wanting; and the weighing ceaseth never and every evil thought they have had towards others is returned into their own bosom.'

" Then I inquired: ' Wherefore still remaineth so much room in hell ? ' And Truth answered: ' For the generations to come, there are many races and many generations yet to come, and each that cometh after will be judged more hardly, because it hath known the truth and hath suffered lighter persecution. Last of all will come the judgment of them of the West, who make profession of belief in Jesus;

but many of these will not believe, though belief encompass them around, and though all the works of Christ lay open before them.' Then the Spirit added: ' This is thy last night in Hades, and we must return, for thou must pray ere thou rejoin thy body.'

" Then meekly I took him by the hand, and we rose once more straight through the air, like arrows shot upward from a bow; and while we rose thus swiftly, yet could we hear the wailing and the gnashing of teeth and the howling of those beneath; and I said: ' I would the Christ saw not such sights.' But he answered: ' He will spare Himself no suffering, but drink the cup of bitterness to the dregs.'

" And after that the Spirit of Truth bade me depart; and at his words I wept, for a great fear came upon me; I feared to live again after that which I had seen. I clung to the Spirit of Truth and I said: 'Leave me not alone, I pray thee, in the valley of the shadow of death.' And it seemed to me, Mary, that thy voice sang to me the words that thou didst sing when I was at the point of death: ' Yea, though I walk through the valley of the shadow of death, I will fear no evil, for Thou art with me; Thy rod and Thy staff do comfort me.' And a great peace came over me and I fell asleep.

" When I awoke I was once more outside the road of Jericho near to Bethany beneath the olive groves; and I saw the face of Jesus and the disciples, and I saw thee and Martha and the Jews who came to wail and mourn. And at the sight of Jesus' face my strength returned, and I said inwardly: ' If Thou canst die for me, then I can live for Thee.'

" And I saw that Jesus wept for the love He bore
me and the love He bore Jerusalem, and for its unbelief; and I knew that He would I had not died,
and that, having died, I should not live again to die
a second death. Yet would I live and die daily, if
I could serve the Lord forever; for I know that, beyond here and Hades, there are things reserved for
them which love the Lord that pass man's understanding. Then I prayed as I had never prayed
before, for I knew for a very certainty that Jesus
was the Christ, and that men with their vain imagi-
nations are but as worms before the Lord, and are
without understanding. At last, when night was
past, I heard the voice of Jesus calling me, as it
were, across great waters; and my spirit hastened
to the voice of God, and I stood inside the sepulchre ye had prepared for me; and I saw a body lying there, and I shuddered at the thought of that
which was before me, and of the power of the flesh;
and I would indeed that it were not so that I must
live again. Yet I longed to see the face of the Christ
once more, and to show forth His glory to all men,
for I thought that then, indeed, all could not but
believe. So I laid me down once more on the body
that had pained me so in life, and I cried, ' Not my
will, but Thine, be done on earth, O Lord!' Then
I heard the voice of the Christ—that sounded like
silver trumpets on the mountain tops mingling with
summer fountains—cry out: 'Lazarus, come forth!'
And at those words of Jesus I stood once more on
my feet. Yet still the people believed not in
Him."

CHAPTER XXIV.

WHEN Lazarus ceased speaking, morning, striking right and left with her flaming wand of truth, lighting up each secret corner of the world, burst in through the open casement, and forced herself in ardent streams of light beneath the doors and through every crevice of the house in Bethany.

She lit up faces weary with their vigil, worn with the excitement of this wondrous narrative and their eagerness to grasp the full purpose of this revelation.

When the Magdalene had finished writing, she fell upon her knees in prayer. None knew what she prayed for, whether in appeal, or thankfulness, but Lazarus looking at her, his gaze softened and a great resolve showed in his eyes.

Then, one by one, they rose from their posture on the ground, to go and bathe and set about the duties of the day. But Martha was less restless and solicitous.

Lazarus's tale had roused her interest; nay, more, had filled her with a vague dread and wondering that one so great as Jesus could condescend to sup with them that night; and, in a moment, as one sees things in a flash, it came to her how futile must every effort be to make things worthy of such a guest. Then, while her sister marvelled at her quiet spirit, she turned to the Magdalene and said : " Thou wilt go with us, Mary, to serve the Lord at supper."

And the despised Magdalene flushed with pleasure, for Martha's courtesies had the attribute of rarity.

But, although the disciples had striven to preserve the secret of Jesus' return to Bethany, yet, either through servants or by the treachery of Judas, it had been noised about that, not only the Nazarene, but also the risen Lazarus was to be at the feast; and all that day the people thronged outside the door of the leper, fearing to enter on account of the strict Jewish law, yet anxious to see him when he should leave his house. Great trouble filled the heart of the four at Bethany, for, in the midst of their joy at the prospect of seeing the Lord again, there rose the dread of what might follow. Fear for Lazarus was added now to their grief and terror for the Messiah, for he had become to the people the testimony of the Christ's actuality and power.

Beneath the double sway of the high priests and the Romans, the Jewish people were beginning to think more for themselves and to act with greater independence. They would inquire into this matter and learn for themselves the truth.

So it came about that, when Lazarus and the three women, followed by the servants bearing the dishes they had made ready for the Lord, sallied forth from the gates, they found a crowd assembled who, with that daring which even now characterises an Eastern throng, followed them along the road, calling out to them, asking questions, gabbling, quarrelling, gesticulating.

"Art thou indeed Lazarus ?" cried they. " Wert really dead ?"

And with these and like inquiries were mingled ribaldry and jeers; for when the common people congregate, there are always those who think to show their humour with obscene and scoffing oaths.

" Wast so fond of earth thou couldst not stay away ?"

Then, when the crowd continued to vociferate and clamour, Lazarus quickly mounted a little hillock on the roadside, and, facing them, cried out in the deep voice that had been wont to stir men in the Sanhedrim: " Men of Israel, hear ye me; if I tell ye the truth will ye believe me ?"

Cries rose from the multitude: " We will believe, we will believe."

" Nay, I ask yet more; will ye believe that Jesus is the Christ ? for I am here to-day to testify of Him."

Cries rose again: " Art thou indeed Lazarus ?"

" How can I convince ye ?" answered Lazarus in tones despondent at his inability to prove his personality, if his simple presence should not suffice.

" Ye have known me from my childhood upwards. Many are here to-day with whom I went to school. Behold yonder the sons of Zebedee; they will bear witness that I am the same Lazarus. Simon the Leper, to whom I now go, is my father, and these two noble ladies are my sisters. Thou knowest them well, for they have tended many of the sick and poor in Bethany. What more can I tell ye to make ye believe that I am the Lazarus ye have known ? Behold my hands and the features of my countenance. If I be not that same Lazarus, where then is he ?"

Then one, a lawyer, came up to him.

" Noble ruler," he began, " I will speak for this · multitude. We believe verily that thou art Lazarus, but we would hear whether thou wert really dead, and if so be, how thou didst return to life ?"

" How can I persuade ye, my brethren ?" replied Lazarus, tears rising to his eyes in the intensity of his emotion. " I was indeed dead. Ask the physician Kishish; ask them who embalmed me, and them who bore me to the tomb. In truth, I was dead, and if I be alive again, 't is by the power of Jesus the Christ, whom ye call the Nazarene."

Some seemed willing to believe, others shrugged their shoulders, but none molested Lazarus or those with him any more. But some amongst the crowd cried out: " He is bewitched, or he dreameth, and knoweth not what he saith. Maybe he was in a trance."

Their supper in the house of Simon was a happy meeting. Though all were troubled by forebodings of sad events to come, there was in each a spirit of patience and resignation that enabled them to enjoy the present.

Although supper had been laid for all the family of Simon, only one couch had been provided, all having intended to wait on Jesus; but, with gracious condescension, as though what Lazarus had gone through gave him a higher claim to His friendship, Jesus bade him be seated at the same table. With what zeal and tenderness those loving women waited on the two they loved best in the world, though

each with a widely different love; but now even
their love for Lazarus was tinged with the divine
reverence they had for the Nazarene.

Presently, with a burst of that living tenderness
which vainly strove to give full expression to itself,
the Magdalene took a vessel of ointment of spikenard of the most costly kind, that she had brought
with her, and poured it over the Messiah's feet.   To
the careful Jew, such an offering was one for great
occasions only, but to Mary it seemed but a poor
expression of her devotion.   As the rich fragrance
was wafted on the air, filling the chamber with vague
memories of hedgerows and Grecian gardens of roses,
the Nazarene's eyes fell with love and gratitude on
the kneeling figure at His feet.   He saw, beyond
the impulsive gift, the warmth of love and reverence
that had dictated it.   The best of everything must
be her Lord's.   Yet more, He saw a thought distinct.   It might be that the loving Mary feared that
she would not be near Him when He died, to fulfil
the last earthly office, the embalming of His body.
It might be that cruel soldiers would tear away the
body of one she loved so much.   Therefore, to-night,
He should be anointed with the rarest perfumes of
Judæa.   With these thoughts in her mind, her tears
fell in drops like rain on the holy feet; and, as they
fell, she wiped them with her hair, lest they should
defile the members she so reverently handled.

At the feet of the Lord; that had been ever the
favourite posture of the Magdalene!   Would she
ever again be privileged to take it ?   While the disciples whispered among themselves and listened to
the Nazarene, her thoughts flew back with the agony

of remorse—the remembrance of happy intervals in
the midst of pains, than which the poet tells us there
is no greater grief—to those peaceful days before
Lazarus had died. Oh that it could have remained
thus! But the merciless generation was pressing
them on to unsought destinies. They were like
people forced into pathways they wished not to
pursue, with separation, persecution, insult, death
before them; and to support them through all these,
having only that staff of faith, and a vague hope,
whose brightness would be dimmed when the One
who had implanted it should have vanished from
their sight.

Then Judas Iscariot, who was a half-brother of
Lazarus, and had always hated his father's children
and been jealous of the Lord's intimacy with them,
glad of an opportunity of wounding them or of holding them up to blame in the eyes of Jesus, exclaimed:
"What waste is here! Why was not this ointment sold for three hundred pence and given to the
poor?"

Before the Lord could answer, Martha cried hotly,
mindful of what Lazarus had disclosed to them:
"Thou traitor, much thou carest for the poor.
Wouldst put it in the bag with thy thirty pieces of
silver?"

Iscariot's face blanched to the grey whiteness of
an iceberg from which the sun had fled.

Was then his secret known? His eyes sought
those of Jesus shiftingly; while Lazarus raised his
hand in disapproval of Martha's hasty speech. But
the Messiah's gentle voice made answer pleadingly:
"Let her alone; against the day of My burying hath

she kept this. For the poor ye have always with you; but Me ye have not always."

And when He had so spoken, Mary could restrain her tears no longer, and cried out: " My Lord, my Lord, I beseech Thee, leave us not."

Then, leaning towards her in infinite pity for the great sorrow in her heart, the Saviour murmured: " Let not your heart be troubled."

And while He spoke, there were heard outside sounds of voices shouting, " Hosanna! Hosanna!"

A few moments later, the whole house was crowded with a glorifying multitude, who would not be restrained from seeing the great sight of the Son of God on earth, sitting in the house of Simon the Leper, and, by His side, Lazarus, who had been raised from the dead.

And, in the midst of the clamour and confusion, Judas Iscariot made his way out to warn the Pharisees that his secret was known, and that they must needs make haste if they would lay hands on the Nazarene.

CHAPTER XXV.

ONCE more Jerusalem was the scene of wild excitement, and once more Caiaphas and his colleagues were seized with the dread of whether, after all, power was not going to be wrenched from them. If, in truth, this was the Son of God, if really Lazarus had died and been restored to life, what was to prevent more miracles, and might it not be that Caiaphas would ultimately be torn to pieces by the followers of the Nazarene? These were the High Priest's inward thoughts; but, outwardly, he and his supporters admitted only that, if such trickery as the removal of the body of Lazarus could take place, there was no knowing what dupes might yet be made. At a private meeting of the heads of the Synagogue at the house of Caiaphas, a meeting from which all who did not share the High Priest's views had been excluded, they had come to the unanimous conclusion that the execution of the Nazarene, unless accompanied by that of Lazarus, would be useless bloodshed.

" For Lazarus will be, to all intents, a second Galilean," said one, " and who knoweth but that, having been a ruler and one learned in the law of Moses, he will still more pervert the people by his wisdom, so that, perchance, even the rich will follow him? For this Nazarene hath that good in Him that He appealeth but to the sinners and the poor, so that His following is not a powerful one. But, in that He hath raised this Lazarus, it seemeth to me that the danger doth spread higher."

" Yet I know not how we shall take Him," said another; " for the people look upon Him as a God, and He hath ever people around Him."

" "T will be difficult, but not impossible," said Caiaphas with his cruel, self-sufficient laugh. Had I but known last night that both sat in the house of Simon, he that is the leper, I would have caught the two birds with one net; but that dog, Iscariot, did not dare come till dark, and, when I sent to take them, the house and wayside were thronged with the multitude of perverted fools, and the soldiers feared that to capture them might cause disturbance; for naught desire we less than to fan this fanaticism into a civil war. This also know the Romans. Yet sometimes methinks that Pilate doth, for some purpose, assist the Nazarene to escape, that so a sedition may arise and the Romans may take away our country."

An indignant murmur ran through the little gathering of Pharisees.

" And I hear further from Rome," the High Priest continued pompously, anxious to impress his audience with his superior information and his intimacy with Tiberius, " that they are discussing before the Senate whether to add this Nazarene to their twelve gods and thus have thirteen."

A derisive laugh rose from the assembled council; laughter that might have been aimed either at the Nazarene's claim to be regarded as a God, or at the

facile religion of the Romans, who could thus lightly
add to their list of deities.

" Yet methinks," went on another, " that there
must be sedition in the air; else why hath the Nazarene chosen this time of the Passover, when Jerusalem is full of all nations, Greeks and Gentiles, to
come into the city and incite the people ? "

" Thinkest thou that He will come ? " asked the
High Priest doubtfully. " Iscariot brought me word
yesterday that the plot was known; yea, more, that
Martha, the sister of Lazarus, had reviled him about
the thirty pieces of silver. How thinkest thou they
know ? For even Pilate knew not of this thing."

" They have amongst themselves, I am told," said
one, " some spirit of divination or sooth-saying,
such as was used by Saul; for they all seem to
know whatsoever every man doth think, and have
Satan to assist them." Then, to himself, he muttered, " Nay, but He will not come, He dare not
come to Jerusalem."

But, even while he spoke, there rose loud cries on
the clear, cold air; shrieks that seemed to rend the
skies and pierce to the very heart of Caiaphas.

" Hosanna! Hosanna! Blessed is the King of
Israel, that cometh in the name of the Lord."

Like men possessed, drawn by some magnetic
power they were unable to resist, the little gathering
of Pharisees and scribes moved to the open windows
and to the balconies and terraces. But Caiaphas
seemed to shrink up in his seat, with lowered, scowl-
ing brow and clenched fists, which he beat every
now and then against the couch with fury; and his
countenance was filled with menace; while the cry,

"King of Israel! King of Israel!" arose in one grand sound heavy with united voices.

"What meaneth this strange cry?" he asked, alarmed, and he turned his head towards the group of excited Pharisees.

"We can see naught yet," one made answer hurriedly; "only the people, who do cry furiously and throw branches and palms upon the ground."

Like one about to be seized with a fit, or one towards whom a stroke of paralysis is creeping stealthily, Caiaphas sat holding on to his seat, trying to assume indifference; but, all the while, every nerve and muscle was strained to hear whether that cry would come again: "King of Israel! King of Israel!"

Presently, unable to contain himself, he bawled: "Can ye not speak, ye fools? How cometh He?"

There was a moment's silence, while some strained their necks to see farther up the road. Then one turned to Caiaphas again: "He cometh, the Nazarene, and He rideth on an ass, yea, a small ass; it seemeth but a colt."

For a moment, blood seemed to surge into the very eyes of Caiaphas. He felt faint and dizzy; for one instant the roof of his house seemed torn away; for one instant, in the back chambers of his darkened brain and soul, there flashed the image of a cross; for one instant, Caiaphas, the proud High Priest, believed, and almost swooned from the believing.

"Thou liest," he said at last, in a voice thick and charged with the hoarseness caused by his emotions.

In surprise, the group looked back. What then had come to Caiaphas?

One young scribe even ran to him. "Art ill, most noble Caiaphas ? Shall I bring thee water ?"

"Nay, nay, leave me, thou fool," he said impatiently; and then, while the young man drew back terrified, he burst into a peal of horrible laughter, and all looked anxiously one at the other and whispered: "Methinks that Caiaphas hath gone mad from hatred of the Nazarene."

Then they returned to watch the gathering, pressing concourse, all crying, screaming, singing, shouting in honour of the Messiah.

"'T was never so seen in Jerusalem," they murmured.

Then Caiaphas rose and went to the door and called his soldiers, to bid them close the windows and keep out the distracting noise. But in vain; they, too, had fled, and left the ante-chamber empty. But not for long. With loud-sounding, hasty step, the Procurator entered, a scornful smile upon his lips, a strange exultation in his eyes. Without a word, he seized the High Priest by the arm, and with sheer force, dragged him to the balcony.

"Dost remember thine own words ?" he asked rapidly in a voice such as Caiaphas before had never heard. "Thou dost say it is written in Zechariah: 'Rejoice greatly, O daughter of Zion; shout, O daughter of Jerusalem: behold, thy King cometh unto thee: he is just, and having salvation; lowly, and riding upon a colt, the foal of an ass.'"

The rest kept silence while he spoke. Meantime Caiaphas was searching in the dark corners of his retentive brain for some subtle answer to this confounding verse; while they around who were versed in the prophets and the law threw back their memories till they remembered where indeed those words were written, and the circumstance that had inspired the prophet.

And while they all stood silent, the Nazarene passed by on His lowly steed, the embodiment of appealing meekness and submission, yet with a majesty that seemed to enfold in one the Past, the Present, and Eternity; and, as He passed, some strange thrill hushed the crowd, which prostrated itself to the earth in silent ecstasy of adoration. And, almost as if forced to the ground by some unseen compelling power, Pilate and the little group of Pharisees fell down upon their knees. Caiaphas alone remained erect, with lowering glance and folded hands, looking over the heads of that infatuated little gathering of great men, following with steely eyes, that shone with hellish light, the image of the Messiah, who passed by slowly, the colt's hoofs pattering on the cobble stones with short, sharp thuds.

His last chance had come and gone. The memory of his own prophecy had sought to probe his heart, to wrench away the thick coating of pride and unbelief in which it was enveloped. The Messiah had passed by, and Caiaphas had rejected Him; and Satan, scared from the streets of Jerusalem, had yet found shelter in one soul.

Still the populace cried out: " Hosanna! Hosanna! Blessed is the King of Israel."

And the Pharisees who had met that morning to sign the condemnation of the Nazarene and issue an order for Lazarus's capture, rose from their knees and shook their heads, and one to the other said: " Perceive ye how we prevail nothing ? Behold the world is gone after Him."

Then, headed by Pontius Pilate, they filed out one by one, leaving Caiaphas still standing at the window, looking after the people that had deserted him, and turning over within his heart schemes for the achievement of his revenge ; for vengeance would be to him henceforth the sole pursuit of his earthly life, and the basis of his life eternal. The sweetness of life to him now would be when the cry " Hosanna!" should be changed to that of Crucify!"

CHAPTER XXVI.

ONCE more the multitude pressed round the Nazarene, keener than ever to hear the words of one who had performed the great miracle they had all been longing for. All the circumstances too —the fact that the body of Lazarus had lain four days in the grave, and the publicity of his resurrection, had impressed their minds with an assurance in the Messiah's power that seemed unshakable. But to those who believed, each word was fraught with the approaching grief of separation; to His disciples and a few besides, each phrase that fell from Him thus held for them an added tenderness and pathos and would be treasured with the greater care. In a short time they would have to live their lives without the sweet presence that had sustained and guided them. His words would be their only guide through this world and, through death, to life eternal. There were tiny children, too, who were growing up, whom Jesus loved. The message would have to be handed on to them in all its purity and all its hope.

The crowd was waiting. The Nazarene stood ready to deliver once more the message from the Father; never wearying of His mission, ever appealing to them to lay hold of true happiness in this world and their salvation in the next. Then two disciples advanced with reverence, and, plucking at

His sleeve, they murmured something in His ear.
And when the Lord turned round, a group of Greeks
was seen approaching.

" They would have speech with Thee," said
Philip.

He greeted them, as He did every one, with
divine courtesy and love, yet a spasm of pain passed
for a moment across His brow, as He answered His
disciple: " The hour is come that the Son of God
shall be glorified ? "

" What meaneth He ? " asketh one of another;
and Mary, anxious at the look of pain that contracted the Saviour's brow, bent close to Lazarus,
and, in terror-stricken accents, gasped: " Surely
they come to take the Lord ? "

But Lazarus reassured her. " Be not troubled,
sister," he replied assuringly, " they are but Greeks,
who seek to learn the truth."

" God be praised," said Mary; " but why, then,
doth the Master say: ' The hour is come ' ? "

Then, with sadness inexpressible, Lazarus answered: " The hour is indeed near at hand, and the
coming of these Greeks doth signify its nearness;
for all nations shall bow down and worship Him
together. As Caiaphas hath prophesied, so shall it
be; God shall gather together all the children of
God into one place, and all divisions shall be ended.
The middle wall of partition shall be broken down,
and all nations linked together in one common faith.
Surely the coming of these Greeks is the first sign·
that the death of the Master is at hand."

Great tears welled to Mary's eyes. She understood now the grief that rested like a shadow on

His face; and, while she listened to His words, that one after another struck her heart with the certain aim of arrows shot from one who had the cunning of the bow at his finger ends, yet her thoughts dwelt anxiously on the future, with a thousand ponderings.

But suddenly Lazarus ceased to speak, for the thrilling voice of the Nazarene arose in words that were addressed to all multitudes and all nations; words that to those who understood them set forth the great news of His impending death.

Surely the poor, wan face, the lips that never laughed, told their own tale of the secret griefs and temptations of the Man of Sorrows; griefs and temptations more gigantic than could be conceived by mortal man, the temptation to use His power to set aside grief and sorrow, to reject death, while yet accepting them.

At last He cried: "And what shall I say? Father, save Me from this hour. But for this cause came I unto this hour."

Then, as if to defy fate and unbelief, temptation, fear, insult, torment, He raised His face, sublime in its gentle gravity, towards heaven, and, with a voice that breathed with faith and love, He cried: "Father, glorify Thy name."

Then, although the day was fine and bright, and no cloud hung across the heavens, was heard a thunder-clap, then another; yet to some it sounded not wholly like a thunder-clap, so that those standing nearest to Jesus said, "An angel spake to Him; I heard the voice. Methought I heard the word glory." And Lazarus and John and several others affirmed that a voice had called out from heaven, "I have both glorified it, and will glorify it again."

At the words of His Father an expression of radiant gratitude came over the visage of the Nazarene; and, to leave no doubt in their terrified minds as to whether it was thunder or the voice of God that spoke, He said: "The voice came not because of Me, but for your sakes. Now is the judgment of this world: now shall the prince of this world be cast out. And I, if I be lifted up from the earth, will draw all men unto Me."

These words, mystic and ambiguous to many, filled the soul of Lazarus with dismay. How could he live this new life without his Master? His own death and resurrection seemed to have done little towards making people believe. The prospect of his renewed life without the supporting presence of the Christ, to be ended, in all likelihood, by an agonising death, seemed almost more than he could bear.

Then some of the Pharisees and chief rulers, who believed but durst not confess it, lest they should be cast out of the Synagogue, approached Him with the questions that were their endless stumbling-stones; questions of that law which had so wound itself round their hearts and brains that it seemed to stifle spiritual life.

" We have heard out of the law that Christ abideth forever; and how sayest Thou that the Son of man must be lifted up? Who is this Son of man?"

Did the world then mean to spin out its years to the end of time without ever coming any nearer to its God, that the presence of the Son of man was so

difficult to grasp ?   Could they understand a Christ,
but not a perfect man, not a suffering, tempted, sym-
pathising sorrower ?

And Jesus answered almost with a cry, one last
appeal to them to try to believe while yet they lived.

Was it all to be of no avail, this mission upon
earth ?   The wearying thirty years ?   The miracles,
the awful death ?   All wasted, all poured out for
naught ?   Was the sacrifice of the Creator for His
own creation to be in vain ?

" Yet a little while is the light with you.   Walk
while ye have the light, lest the darkness come upon
you : for he that walketh in darkness knoweth not
whither he goeth.   While ye have the light, believe in
the light, that ye may be the children of the light."

Then, wearied and disappointed, His heart heavy
at the future of horror these people were preparing
for themselves, the Nazarene walked through the
crowd, and, as if by magic, disappeared.

" Surely He hath been caught up," said some,
" for, though we look down the road, we cannot see
aught of Him.   Therefore said He, ' If I be lifted
up from the earth.' "

But, notwithstanding this fresh miracle, notwithstanding the voice from heaven, still very few believed in Him as the Christ that should have come.
It was as Esaias the prophet had said, " He hath
blinded their eyes, and hardened their heart; that
they should not see with their eyes, nor understand
with their heart, and be converted, and that I should
heal them."

Then, while the wondering crowd was debating,
squabbling, pondering, scoffing, musing, working

itself up into violent dissensions—such as religious matters ever breed—about the Messiah's disappearance, the voice that so vibrated with truth and suasion, the intensity of whose reality no man could fathom; the voice, that those who had once heard it would never forget, rose in a long and bitter cry, like the dying warning of an eternal farewell:

" He that believeth in Me, believeth not in Me, but in Him that sent Me. I am come a light unto the world, that whosoever believeth in Me should not abide in darkness. And if any man hear My words, and believe not, I judge him not: for I came not to judge the world, but to save the world. He that rejecteth Me, and receiveth not My words, hath one that judgeth him: the word that I have spoken, the same shall judge him in the last day. For I have not spoken of Myself; but the Father which sent Me, He gave Me commandment, what I should say, and what I should speak. And I know that His commandment is life everlasting: whatsoever I speak, therefore, even as the Father said unto Me, even so I speak."

Clear, distinct, like drops of tinkling water fell the words, piercing as nails, leaving no doubt, no want of emphasis behind them, enhanced by all the mystery of an unseen voice; but they fell as water falls on rocks, but to splash up again and glance off. An unmoved nation passed silently along the road, unconscious of the priceless value of the light that was gradually flitting away, and of the darkness that would soon envelop them eternally with a gloomy mantle damp with the sweating of horror of a people re-awakened all too late.

CHAPTER XXVII.

NOTWITHSTANDING all the stirring events and anxieties of that period, notwithstanding the frequent threatenings that were directed at the Nazarene and Lazarus, life in the house at Bethany had resumed its usual aspect, and, to all appearance, ran its ordinary course.

One there was, however, whose whole life had undergone a change. Sins in others, that he had before regarded as intolerable, were spoken of with leniency and made only the subject of prayer by Lazarus. High place, his position in the Sanhedrim and as a ruler, not only ceased to have any value in his eyes, but aroused in him a faint sense of wonder that he should ever have desired them; while, somewhat to Martha's dismay, large sums were daily distributed in secret to the poor.

" Thou wilt have nothing left at last," she said to Lazarus one day.

" He hath said that I should give to the poor all I possessed and follow Him," replied Lazarus simply. " When all shall have been given, the Lord will provide more."

And Martha would go away, shrugging her shoulders, but not arguing, as she would have done in the olden days.

But one there was who watched the face of Lazarus

with an increasing intensity of love that sharpened observation, and who saw upon it a restless expression, as of some inward doubt; and this was his sister Mary.

" Hast any troubles, Lazarus ? " she asked him about two days after the entry into Jerusalem.

" I scarce know whether 't is trouble or not," he answered; " or whether the tempting of some sin to be resisted; and, if it be, whether I should have courage to resist it."

" I know," said Mary half playfully. " I guessed it long ago. Thou dost love the Magdalene."

Lazarus looked at her in wonder at her discernment.

" And she too loveth thee well, I know," went on his sister. " Yet I know not what would be said in Israel if thou didst marry the sinner."

" I care not what they say in Israel," answered Lazarus. " Henceforth I am a free man, held no more in bondage by the letter, but only by the spirit; and if methought I could raise the Magdalene once more in the eyes of those around us, I would do it gladly. Yet there is more in all this than can be readily thought out. I know not whether the Lord would have me do this thing; for when He said, ' Leave all and follow Me,' 't was, perchance, that He requireth all my service, all my heart. Then again, I fear that when our dear Master shall be dead, we too shall be seized and condemned to death, for that we loved Him and can bear witness to His great glory. Thus I know not whether 't were better to link my life with the Magdalene or not."

" What will the proud Rebekah say ? " asked
Mary, leaving her brother's arguments unanswered,
while she followed her own thoughts into other chan-
nels ; " for I hear that, since thy resurrection, she is
like one mad with joy. Thinkest thou she will believe, for she did say, ' If He raiseth Lazarus, I too
will believe ' ? "

" God will it so," said Lazarus, musingly, and
somewhat doubtfully. " I would not judge her ;
but I fear she would believe only if I did love
her ; yet, if I should wed the Magdalene, methinks
she would strain every nerve to get our Master and
ourselves into the power of Caiaphas. Still we know
not."

" Hast spoken to the Magdalene of thy love ? "

" Nay, I will say naught to that loving heart till
I know what the Lord wisheth me to do. This is
no time for marrying or giving in marriage ; yet, if
I could protect the Magdalene from the world's
taunts, I would gladly do it. To-night we sup with
the Master, and my heart is in great heaviness ; for
thereafter He will be betrayed, and then, who knoweth all the grief that will come to pass ? Oh that
Jerusalem would believe," he went on, wearily, his
mind passing to more serious things. " That surely
is the greatest doubt of all, that He doth not make
them to believe."

" Because they will not. Each one hath had his
chance. Aye, a thousand-fold, and they will not,
they will not."

A few hours later, the little band of disciples met
once more. All were sad to-night, for all felt a terrible catastrophe impending. Mary and Martha had

stayed away, for they would have been the only
women present.   All the disciples were to be there,
besides Lazarus, Nicodemus, and others who had
been around Him throughout His ministry.

John had told them that, after this, he feared
there would be no meeting-place, for that the terrible hour was close at hand.   It would be at the
Passover that the fate of the Lord would be decided, for they could not doubt that He would be
arrested the moment He set foot in Jerusalem,
whether He was to be released or condemned; and
all knew that, if Caiaphas's will could turn the
scale, the Messiah would not be released; nay,
more, He had told them that it would be so.   Perhaps they still hoped for some great miracle direct
from God to save their dear Lord; for hope lingers
in the human heart till the very moment at which
death comes and bears away our loved ones.

To-night the Nazarene had prepared a bond of remembrance between them that He would establish
forever; a bond that would last through all the
ages; that would serve for ever to bring back to
them the memory of His ministry and His words
and His stupendous sacrifice.

To-night would be Judas Iscariot's last chance of
redemption.   How would He live on after the Lord
should have shown him that He knew what was in
his heart ?   The tortuous path of that darkened soul
will always remain inscrutable, unknown to mortals,
till heaven and earth shall pass away; perhaps even
throughout the immeasurable æons of eternity.

CHAPTER XXVIII.

IT was the day of the Paschal Feast, and all night
Martha had been busy preparing with her household the lamb and other dishes for the feast, including the thin Passover cakes which it was the custom
to dip into the wine, or any other beverage, and send
round in the cup.

While she worked, the Nazarene, watched by Lazarus, slept or prayed. A great misgiving was in the
hearts of all. Everyone who came from Jerusalem
brought different news, but all based on one great
fact, the wrath of the Pharisees and rulers in general, and of Caiaphas in particular, at the reception
of the Messiah on His late entry into Jerusalem.
It was fear, both physical and moral, that actuated
Caiaphas now. As a frightened dog snaps and flies
at those around him, each in turn, so Caiaphas
tried to hide his own trepidation beneath a sem-
blance of attack.

Yet these rumours filled with dismay the hearts
of those who loved the Lord.

" I fear me; I fear me greatly," Lazarus said.
" He will eat the Passover at Jerusalem, according
to the law of Moses, yet surely they will there surprise Him."

" How can it be," asked Martha, " that Judas,
who doth follow Him day and night, doth compass

to betray Him ? Methinks that even Satan himself would not act thus."

" Nay, Satan doth make others to sin for him," answered Lazarus; " but 't is greed with Judas, the love of money that is the curse of all our nation; that doth even overwhelm the world. Surely the wrath of Caiaphas is not that the Master doth call Himself the Son of God, but that the tables of the money-changers and of the sellers of doves were overturned. The spaces, too, in the Temple court, 't is well known that a Pharisee doth give a high price to Caiaphas to have the right to sell there."

" But to sell the Lord for thirty pieces of silver! the price of the meanest slave!"

" Dost not mind the prophet Zechariah, how he saith, ' So they weighed for my price thirty pieces of silver ' ? "

" But the Lord, the Lord!" said Martha, while tears rose to her eyes.

At that moment Mary entered the room. " The Lord hath need of Peter and John, to send them to Jerusalem."

" Still will He sup with them at Jerusalem ?" asked Lazarus, as he went to do as he had been bid.

Then the Nazarene gave this order to the disciples: " Go ye into the city, and there shall meet ye a man bearing a pitcher of water: follow him. And wheresoever he shall go in, say ye to the goodman of the house, The Master saith, Where is the guest-chamber, where I shall eat the passover with My disciples ? And he will show you a large upper room furnished and prepared: there make ready for us."

" Surely 't is a wonderful thing," said Lazarus to his sisters, " this union of the man and God; for, when He willeth, He can command angels for signs and wonders, and He knoweth all things; yet by His power will He escape none of the troubles of this world; for, methinks, if now He did but command a legion of angels to defend Him from the High Priest, they would descend."

" Verily, verily thou speakest truth," said Mary. " 'T is marvellous that this God, for love of us, should deign to suffer sorrow, as though He were but man."

Evening had come, and Jesus, accompanied by Lazarus and the twelve apostles, started for the Passover Feast. The two women watched them go with tightening hearts.

" Who knoweth," said Martha, " whether they will ever return ? My heart misgiveth me, and Jerusalem doth fill my soul with terror."

But Mary said nothing; only raised an inward prayer that if they should be taken that night they might not suffer long.

And then the two women turned back to their solitary house, from which all sunshine seemed to have departed, as it had when Lazarus had died.

" Mark thee," said Martha to her sister, " there are terrible days in store for us; for if Jerusalem do this wicked thing, to slay the Son of God, surely the curse of God will be upon her, and the nations will trample upon her and slay her people."

" Pray God that our faith fail not," murmured Mary.

Presently, Mary Magdalene, whom they had bid-

den to the Feast of the Passover, and a few other
God-fearing women, came, and in sadness and
prayer the evening passed.

In Jerusalem more stirring events were taking
place. The Feast of the Passover had begun; the
low tables stood ready covered with the dishes prepared by Martha's loving hands, and carried by Peter
and John to the chamber provided for the Nazarene.
The cushions or couches were arranged, the mats
spread out, and one by one they took their seats, the
Messiah taking the chief place, and John reclining
on the couch on the right of Jesus, so that his head
was brought close to the Christ's right arm. They
were dusty with their journey, and when Lazarus
stooped and unfastened the latchets of the Messiah's
sandals, he wished that he could wash those beloved
feet; but there were no slaves present to fetch
water, so in silence he took his seat.

Some instinct made him seat himself next Judas.
If any treason were abroad he would be ready to defend the Christ.

The supper began gloomily. Too many mournful
feelings were wafted hither and thither, anticipations
were too sombre and too terrible.

To Lazarus, who believed that Judas Iscariot was
about to betray the Lord, the presence of the traitor
seemed unbearable. All were paralysed with wonder, expectant of something, yet they knew not
what. How could they tell that evening, that repentance and eternal life would be offered to a soul
so cramped by greed and avarice that it would reject
heaven for hell, and all for thirty pieces of silver?
Surely a sorry price for such a crime!

Then, when Jesus saw that none performed the kindly office of washing of the feet, He rose from the table and sent one of the disciples to fetch water. The lessons would be few that He would teach them now; after to-morrow, the Son of God would be a prisoner. To-night the teachings, that would last through all the ages of the earth, must be set forth; and to the patient, loving Teacher it seemed that no word must be left unsaid that might make the bitter lessons of the future easier.

With amaze they watched Him take off his upper garment and gird a towel round his loins, then pour water into a large copper basin that stood by.

In silence they regarded Him, while He knelt at the feet of one after another of His disciples, and dipped His shapely hands, hands that worked only for the good of many, into the limpid water. None spoke, or offered to relieve Him of the task, lest they should seem to think that He performed only a menial act, when, in truth, they looked upon it as a symbol of some great teaching; yet each was distressed to see his Lord thus meekly kneeling.

" Surely this is the greatest lesson of all," said Lazarus.

When Jesus came to Peter, the apostle could contain himself no longer.

" Thou shalt never wash my feet," he said, standing up, and, with two hands, pressing away the basin.

But, with quiet insistence, the Nazarene replied: " If I wash thee not, thou hast no part with Me."

Then Peter understood that this was some great ceremonial, to complete the bonds of love and ten-

derness between the chosen few and their Messiah;
and, humble as a little child, he answered: " Lord,
not my feet only, but also my hands and my head."

But Jesus proceeded to wash his feet, saying the
while: "He that is washed needeth not but to wash
his feet, and is clean every whit, and ye are clean."
Then, turning His full gaze upon Iscariot, He said,
with a deep yearning in His voice: " But not all."

Then all watched with wonder to see whether
Jesus would wash the feet of Judas too.

But even Judas was not omitted from His loving
hands. There was breathless silence while he
washed the feet of the man whom all suspected now
to be the traitor. And, while He did so, Jesus
raised His mournful eyes to those of Judas and
gazed at him repoachfully.

" Wilt thou too not be clean ?" the look seemed
to say. " There is yet time to draw back; it must
be that I die, but it needs not be through thee.
Thou hast planned thy scheme, they are waiting for
thee without; thou knowest My plans, and art to
tell them whither I go this night; but go not. Let
Me draw thee to Me by the bonds of love. Let Me
cleanse thy soul of all its filth. Return to Me; I am
still here waiting, waiting. Time is passing quickly,
a life's remorse awaits thee in this world, a dreadful
death; in the next an eternity of pain. Draw back."

All that it seemed to say; but Judas shifted un-
easily on his seat, as though the touch of Jesus
scorched his nerves, and he kept his eyes down, as
though searching the water in the copper basin, that
in the light of the lamp shone more ruddily than his
own red hair.

And Lazarus, in grief and wonder, murmured to himself: " His own familiar friend, His own familiar friend."

Then, when Jesus sat down again, a look of pain and grief passed over Him. It was as though He had lost something, or had missed a face from the throng He would one day see again. And, while He explained to them the meaning of His service of humility, a great gloom settled on them all.

" If I, then, your Lord and Master, have washed your feet, ye also ought to wash one another's feet. For I have given you an example that ye should do as I have done unto you."

There was a tone of weariness, almost of despondency, in the tender voice.

He was filled with horror at the duplicity of the man who sat at the table with Him; with sorrow at the greed and hardness of his heart; at the awful future he was preparing for himself. Perhaps, too, in all reverence be it said, there was in the human essence of His Person a shrinking from the trial that lay before Him, and the faintest glimmer of a doubt whether the stupendous sacrifice He contemplated was not in excess of the result to be obtained. Who, in a humbler way, has not felt, after some action of self-sacrifice or self-denial has been performed, " What good has it done after all? I might have spared myself "?

The nerves of the little band were strung to the highest pitch. Encased in bonds of human ignorance and incapacity, they were daily in presence of divine outpourings their understanding failed to hold. The peace and comfort that were to be the parting gifts of the Messiah had not yet come. Their hearts were torn with grief, their brains weary with fruitless speculation, their bodies suffering from the fatigue of many watchings and a long day's walk. Besides all this, was the foreboding of their approaching separation from Him who was the centre-piece of their soul's refreshment, the fountain of revivification. It was as though the demon of despair was sifting them as wheat, as though great dark wings of horror were folding gradually about them. Their emotions held them dumb. Then, in the general silence, the Messiah broke forth with the cry: " Verily, verily, I say unto you, that one of you shall betray Me.' The mask of hypocrisy was to be torn away, the awe-charged atmosphere that hung about them was to explode with a flash of revelation. The unerring, penetrating bolt of Truth was to crash through the outwork of hypocrisy and expose to view the citadel of greed and unbelief and envy. To-night it should be proclaimed that one sat there a traitor to his friend and to his God; the righteous efforts of the little band of believers should no longer be paralysed and polluted by the presence of one who should for evermore be damned. The vile, corrupted thing should be rooted out, as a cancer is plucked out from the body. On this last night of His living, loving ministry the Christ would exert His right to have about Him only those who loved Him. Only to them would that great commission of love and peace be given. No longer should the words of a God fall on the ears of Satan's emissary.

It seemed to the disciples, at His words, as though the wrath of God had been let loose at last. In horror lest, by some mischance, it might be he, mindful that sin was ever near, each one cried out: " Is it I ? Is it I ? "

Had they by any negligence, by any accident, by any careless guarding of their tongues, betrayed the Lord ? God forbid; and a silent prayer went up from all, save Judas: " Lord, save us from this thing."

Then, with a hypocritical smile, trying still, as so many have tried, to brazen out a lie, Judas leaned forward and asked: " Rabbi, is it I ? "

And Jesus, looking at him with deepest pity in His eyes, made answer: " Thou hast said." And, with the words, He dipped a piece of the Passover cake into a cup of wine and handed it to Judas.

Maybe, even now He hoped by this great act of condescension to win him over. It was as though He said: " Although it is thou, yet I still love thee; I still offer thee the salvation that is offered to others. Wilt thou not take it ? "

For one instant, Judas recoiled before his deed; for one instant he hesitated. Then, as if to defy them all, he dipped his fingers in the cup and took the divine offering. A murmur rose from the little body.

One leaned over to the other and said: " Shall we smite him ? Shall we slay him ? "

But Peter, with a voice thick with passion, cried out: " Seest thou the red drops of wine upon thy fingers ? So shall the blood of Jesus be upon thee forever and ever."

Then, when violence seemed imminent, for each rose from his seat and approached Judas menacingly, the Messiah made a sign to him to disappear, before he should be torn to pieces.

" What thou doest, do quickly," He commanded. And the man whom, since the beginning of His ministry, He had loved and counselled, arose and left the room, followed by the sad eyes of the Messiah.

Then, to cheer His sorrowing disciples, the Lord raised His voice almost to a chant, and cried: " Now is the Son of man glorified, and God is glorified in Him."

Then, once more, He poured out wine; but when they pressed Him, too, to drink, He pushed the cup away, with the words: " I will not drink henceforth of this fruit of the vine, until that day when I drink it new with you in My Father's kingdom."

The supper had come to an end, and all stood up and sang a Hebrew hymn. Then, one after another, they followed their Lord out into the moonlight, to make their way with Him to the Mount of Olives and thence to the Garden of Gethsemane; that garden holy for evermore, because watered by the tears of agony of the Son of God.

CHAPTER XXIX.

WHEN Judas rose to go, fearful for his own
life, and obeying a behest he durst not dis-
obey, he did not go immediately to the Pharisees
who awaited him, but made his way by tortuous
pathways to the back of Caiaphas's house. The
door opened at once on his arrival, as if some one
waited, and he was admitted.

" Thou hast been long. What news hast thou ?"
asked Rebekah breathlessly.

" They sit there yet, and if thou wilt follow now,
I can get speech of Him for thee; but thou must
hasten, for they will not tarry long, and I must to
the Pharisees to instruct them of their movements."

" Thou wilt do no such thing, till I command
thee."

" Yet, if I tell them not, I shall lose my money."

" Oh, thou narrow-brained fool, is thirty pieces of
silver such riches to thee that it hath turned thy
brain ? They give thee thirty pieces of silver to betray thy Friend, and I offer thee sixty not to do so;
so thou dost earn double money, and betrayest not
thy Friend."

" Yet, if after all Lazarus will not hearken unto
thee, and thou givest me not the sixty pieces, perchance I shall be too late to warn thy father; thus
will I lose the thirty and the sixty."

" Lead the way," said the haughty Rebekah, scorning to answer such base reasoning, hating to place herself in the hands of so mean a man, yet maddened by her insane desire to obtain speech of Lazarus.

They walked along in silence, Judas full of subtle thoughts, partly remorse, partly hate, but chiefly fear. What if the disciples should turn upon him and slay him ? What if Jesus were indeed the Son of God ?

So swift and silent was their course through the deserted, moonlit streets that less than twenty minutes brought them to the door of the house in which the supper had been held. Here a man from Caiaphas waited for news from Judas. Both drew back into the darkness when the white, majestic form came out, and the pure, impassioned face of the Nazarene was raised sadly to the moon. So serenely beautiful was He that both could but catch their breath at sight of Him. Lazarus was following the little throng by the backways of Jerusalem when a man suddenly plucked him by the sleeve and murmured : "One thou knowest would have speech with thee; follow me."

Lazarus hesitated, swayed by many doubts. He was loath to separate himself from the little band that accompanied the Christ. To lose Him that night was perhaps never again to see Him alive, or perchance, to miss the legacy of some last word of recommendation; for Lazarus knew that, however devoted were His disciples, they were but illiterate fishermen, most of them; and that it would be he himself, as a ruler and a man of position, besides being the living evidence of His greatest miracle, who would bear the brunt of persecution.

Then again, this might be a trap set for his destruction; he felt that at any moment he might be seized and killed or put away, lest his presence should influence the populace. He did not fear death, but it was important that he should live, lest the Nazarene should need him, and also to protect the women who belonged to him. Faintly the image of the Magdalene flitted across his brain.

"Who seeketh me ?" he asked the speaker, doubtfully. But, even while he spoke, a written message was thrust into his hands.

" If thou wouldst save the Nazarene, speak with me at once. Rebekah."

Still he hesitated. " Save the Nazarene!" What did it mean, to save the Nazarene ? Was it possible ? Was He not destined to die and by His death to save ? What new problem was this ? His pure mind had put away, since that day when they had met, all thought of Rebekah's sensual love; he had striven to believe that she was impressed by the preaching of the Nazarene and sought salvation through Him.

He erred, as so many true, good people err, by wilfully ignoring evil when they see it.

Should he go ? Then, even while he hesitated, the little band crossed over the street, and Rebekah sprang forward and seized him by the arm; while Judas, fearful lest his victim should escape him, ran off in the darkness to warn the authorities of the Messiah's movements.

" But capture Him not, till I come again," he said.

" Dost wish speech of me ? " asked Lazarus
sternly. " Then prithee, lady, be brief; for the
Master is already on His way, and I must follow
Him."

" Listen, then," she answered quickly; " I will
strike a bargain with thee. If thou wilt love me and
take me to be thy wife, then will I go to my father
and entreat of him the life of the Nazarene; nay
more, I will see to it that an order be sent throughout the country that any who shall lay hands on Him
or on His followers shall be condemned; but, if thou
shouldst deny me this, ere this bright moon doth
unveil herself again, the Nazarene shall hang upon
the cross on yonder mount; and mayhap thou too
wilt die."

" The cross ? The sign of shame ? " gasped Lazarus, laying his hand on her arm, forgetful of all else
but that the death they planned for his Master was
a shameful and degrading one.

" The cross!" Rebekah said again, " and thy
great Friend, thy Nazarene, thy Christ, will hang
affixed with cruel nails from hour to hour, and all
the multitude will revile and scoff at Him."

" Hold thy peace, woman," cried Lazarus
sharply, shading with his hand his eyes as if to shut
out the dreadful picture from his mind. " Peace,
be still! Hast thou no heart, that thou canst pierce
mine so deeply ? "

" Hast thou not pierced mine ? " returned Rebekah.

" O woman, canst thou not understand that that
short grief of thine, that fancy of thy maddening
brain, is naught, naught compared with this world's
sin, if it should crucify the Lord ? "

" Then if the pain of mine heart be naught, and the sin of crucifying this Man so great, canst thou not give a few years of thy life to save Him ? Am I then so unbeautiful, so despised a thing that thou wouldst rather let die the Nazarene than wed me ? "

Then, turning upon her the full expression of his earnestness, he spoke once more.

" Noble lady, if thou canst save the Nazarene, thou wilt do it for the love of God. Thou couldst not bear to live if thou hadst helped to crucify the Christ."

" Thou dost not know the daughter of Caiaphas," she answered wildly. " There is naught, naught, naught, I will not do if thou dost spurn me. For thy sake have I come here to-night, for thy sake will I endure my father's wrath and the scorn of all the rulers of the Synagogue, for they will say for love of Lazarus the Nazarene was spared."

" And thinkest thou that, if He would be saved, He could not command legions of angels, and even now slay Caiaphas and all the high priests in the world ? "

" Should He do this, perchance we would believe," she answered scoffingly.

" Maiden," said Lazarus impressively, " when I lay dead thou didst come to me and thou saidst: ' If Lazarus do come again to life I will believe.' And every day thou camest to my sepulchre and didst watch to see they stole me not away. And when thou sawest me rise, didst thou believe ? "

" And thou art really that same Lazarus ? " said Rebekah musingly.

" Hast given, then, thine heart to two ? " asked

Lazarus scornfully. " Out of thine heart thou art confounded. Thine own heart doth witness of the Christ, for, if thou lovest me still, I must be Lazarus, and if not, why art thou here to-night ? Nay, maiden, I will not wed thee, nor can I barter my Lord's freedom for all thy promises of love. Farewell! "

" So much dost thou love the Nazarene that, rather than spend thy life with me, thou wouldst see Him die. How thou must hate me! "

But Lazarus had already hurried after the others. For one instant he had hesitated, debating whether it were possible to influence this perverse daughter of Israel, and, by influencing her, to bring about the safety of his Lord. But he knew that it was not to be. The present safety of the Nazarene would mean the holding of Him back from eternal glory, eternal rest; the delaying of His return to the Father who had sent Him, the prolonging of the agony of the earthly ministry.

" What thou doest, do quickly," the Lord had said. It would be best now that all should be quickly over; yes, though his heart fainted within him when he reflected on the Saviour's sufferings, it were better that these sufferings, which had to be, should once for all be undergone, than remain hanging over the head of that gentle Saviour, like thunder clouds about to burst.

It was necessary that He should die; Lazarus, who had been in Hades, knew it better than did all other men.

Besides, he had a question to ask the Lord, if a fitting moment could be found. He must hurry on,

19

and he did so, this time oblivious of courtesy or chivalry to Rebekah, absorbed in the one great fear that he might miss the Lord.

So, in the moonlit night, he tore along the narrow streets—as he had torn along the broad road following the Christ—all the way to the Mount of Olives and into the very Garden of Gethsemane.

When Lazarus gained the side of Jesus, the answer to the question in his mind was given without his seeking it.

" A new commandment I give unto you, that ye love one another." Lazarus started; the eyes of Jesus seemed to fall on him, enveloping him with the tenderness of infinite love, a love wide enough to enfold the world.

Then, in the dark, Iscariot crept up to Rebekah, who was leaning faint and powerless against the porch that stood out from the house, her figure casting a great black shadow on the wall, which was almost white in the moon's silvery light.

" Shall I, then, save the Nazarene ? " he asked.

"Nay, slay Him, slay Him quickly; go earn thy thirty pieces of silver, and, for aught I care," she added furiously, " slay Lazarus too."

And, with a hideous cry, the traitor fled; and the haughty, vengeful maiden wended her way homewards through the silent streets, the hot blood surging to her ears and brow, and oblivious of place and hour and danger and of all, save that Lazarus was gone from her forever and that she hated the Nazarene with an undying hatred.

CHAPTER XXX.

BUT, when Lazarus joined the little band of disciples, the image of Rebekah, yes, even of the Magdalene, forsook his mind. The Lord, the Master, reigned supreme. Everything to-night must be pressed into His service. These last hours were His, and His alone. Knowing the character of the disciples, how, notwistanding their protestations, they were yet ignorant men, whose only strength lay in the fact of their having obeyed the Christ in the spirit of a little child; conscious of the impetuous, changeable, easily panic-stricken character of the dwellers in the East, Lazarus felt that it behoved him specially to follow Jesus. It might be that that night He would be betrayed. All His words tended to make them think so. It might be that all would be cut down with Him. If so, what greater proof of love could he give the Christ than to die with Him ? It might be, though Lazarus would not harbour the thought, that they would flee: some of them, Peter and Thomas, were too impulsive to be relied upon; John and James a shade too presumptuous. He must follow now. " Leave all that thou hast and follow Me," had been the command; he would indeed follow. All he possessed, each rare garment and costly jewel, had been laid aside, and Lazarus even now was clad in the simple white garments worn by the poorer classes. All he possessed? His dearest possession was the heart of the Magdalene. That, too, must be resigned, his love, his sacrifice must be complete; and so, sorrowfully and with head bent, he followed the little band.

The night was heavy with the air of tragedy, the earth alive with anticipation. Their hearts were sick with untold dread as they passed out of the city gates, that in the bright moonlight stood sheer and white, and down the steep ravine of the Kedron, a river here, a brook only where it ran through the Garden of Gethsemane. All was bathed in moonlight, the river, the soft grass, the olive trees. Everywhere were soft, silvery radiance and dark shadow, emblems of the glory and the cross. At every step, in subdued accents lest they should be heard by watching traitors or solitary passers-by, Jesus comforted their souls. "Verily, verily I say unto you, that ye shall weep and lament, but the world shall rejoice: and ye shall be sorrowful, but your sorrow shall be turned into joy. And ye now therefore have sorrow; but I will see you again, and your heart shall rejoice, and your joy no man taketh from you. I go away and come again unto you. If ye love Me ye would rejoice, because I said I go unto My Father." Then, as they wept, He turned and said: "Peace I leave with you, My peace I give unto you. Let not your heart be troubled, neither let it be afraid."

Each word He spoke weighed heavily on Lazarus's soul. The very beauty and unselfishness of the Christ enhanced the horror of not being able to save Him pain—Him, so thoughtful for others, even in this terrible moment. No, it was not life that Lazarus desired for Him; no one having once cast off the flesh could ever wish that again for any whom he loved. It was not, therefore, the Messiah's life that he would save; but he would save Him, if he could, from the insults, the smarting taunts, that lay before Him. Lazarus knew them, these vulgar self-sufficient Orientals, who fawned on those in power, and crushed into the mud those who failed or seemed to fail. Every item of the Jewish character was familiar to him, its extraordinary enthusiasm, its worship of " the rising sun," its brutal, illimitable cruelty to the down-trodden, its contempt of the weak. No depth of horror, no abyss of shame, no stretch of coarse invective, no extremity of pain would be spared the Son of God if He should fall into the hands of Caiaphas. The triumph would drive the Pharisees mad. Already the multitudes were deserting Him. They held aloof for fear of future loss of position, should the Nazarene be condemned. For himself Lazarus thought nothing; how can one live and die and live again, and count life or death as aught ?

The distant murmur of Jerusalem was fading into a faint hum of nightly stirrings. Only the leaves rustled. A great despondency seized their hearts, a horrible foretaste of loneliness at the departure of the Christ. How could they live alone, these men whose rising and down-sitting had been spent with Him ! To go back into the cold, callous, Jewish life, to be taunted with the reproach of failure, and unable to refute it ! To be asked for living truths, and have naught to give in reply but memories that would daily fade, until they should become a dream! What would remain of all this teaching? A tale of some miracles, the story of a shameful death, a few trusting hearts. What sign that salvation had come to the world? Christ would have spoken in vain. How could they hope to persuade the world when He had failed? The very miracles would be jeered at, either as lies, or, if they did occur, as the result of witchcraft. What would survive, or how could they make gift of the inward burnings of their hearts? As if the Christ had heard the searching of their hearts He paused on the greensward and spoke:

" I will pray to the Father, and He shall give you another Comforter, that He may abide with you forever; and He shall bring all things to your remembrance, whatsoever I have said. I will not leave you comfortless: I will come to you."

And, while the disciples wondered amongst themselves, one said to another: " He meaneth Lazarus, He meaneth Lazarus."

But Lazarus denied it vehemently. " Who am I?" he asked. " 'T is the Spirit of Truth that will come, which the world cannot receive."

But the mournful journey was nearly at an end. At each step they would have halted gladly, to hold back the future, to live again but for a few short minutes those precious moments they were conscious now they had too little valued.

A God had come and was passing hence, and they had only now begun to know Him. How doubly treasured would be the memory of those days, now that their tale was almost ended!

Then, with the thought that the grief He was to bring upon them added yet another sorrow to His own, the Nazarene stood still near the entrance to Gethsemane and, turning to them in the shadow of the trees, He said: " All ye shall be offended because of Me this night; for it is written, I will smite the Shepherd, and the sheep of the flock shall be scattered abroad."

" What meaneth this ? " said one.

" He is our Shepherd, and when they take Him prisoner this night, maybe He thinketh we shall flee," said the desponding Thomas.

Then Peter rushed towards Him crying out: " Though all men shall be offended because of Thee, yet will I never be offended."

" Verily I say unto thee, that this night, before the cock crow, thou shalt deny Me thrice," was the sad reply. He believed in no promises, now the end had come.

But Peter cast himself at His feet. " Why sayest Thou this, Lord ? Though I should die with Thee, yet will I not deny Thee."

And all the disciples, raising their hands to heaven, as if to call the moon, the whole creation— nay, more, God the Father, to witness what they promised, cried: " We will die with Thee! We will die with Thee! "

" Be still," said Lazarus. " Raise not your voices, lest the enemy should hear you."

His warning, breathed on the stillness of the night, fell on their ears with startling force. The hour was indeed close at hand. Anxiously they peered between the olive trees, some even dividing the branches of the fig trees and the pomegranates lest a traitor should be lurking there. How awe-inspiring and mysterious were the surroundings, how pregnant with agony was each moment that came and went!

At the gate of Gethsemane Jesus paused for a moment and gave His last command.

" Bear witness because ye have been with Me from the beginning." Then, while they stood round weeping, He added, to leave a little glimmering of comfort in their souls' dark night: " After I am risen, I will go before you into Galilee."

So this was the end, the end of the familiar friendship, the inspiring presence, the miraculous words of teaching and of help. It seemed impossible that one so great could pass away so simply.

Then, when they tried to follow Him, He turned and said : " Sit ye here while I go and pray yonder."

But they made an impetuous movement to follow Him. Then Lazarus said : " We must needs watch, or, maybe, He will not even have time to pray."

Then, when Jesus saw the distress of the warm-hearted Peter and James and John, He bade them come with Him; and, with one human cry for sympathy, He said : " My soul is exceeding sorrowful, even unto death : tarry ye here, and watch with Me."

Who can dare to dwell on that great agony and live. The agony of God brought low. The haunting fear of His humanity that at the last His strength might fail! Oh, ye who scoff at this one moment of weakness and in those two cries—" My God, My God, why hast Thou forsaken Me ?" and, " Father,

if it be possible, let this cup pass from Me "—and
would see in it the proof that He was not the Christ,
have ye ever thought that in this cry was all the
glory ? Very man of very man, a man to hope, a
man to fear, a man to pray, a man weighted with
the sins, not of Himself, but of the world. To die,
not like a warrior on the battle-field, but an ignominious death of abiding torture, a death so unde-
served, that it might well wring out the piteous cry
that seemed to pierce the heavens and penetrate the
radiant hills beyond, and onward to the throne of
God. A prayer that the power of sin might be suspended without this awful sacrifice; that the sword
of Satan might be sheathed before it slew, before
the last foul crime of His death should stamp the
world with infamy for ever.

Then, as though His agony were such that prayer
could no longer pass His lips, He sought His three
disciples.

Asleep, asleep, His own familiar friends. The
one, too, who had promised so much—asleep, dreaming contentedly, in calm unconsciousness of the
anguished soul-throbs of the Christ who knelt in
agony with head bowed to the ground, breathing
entreaties in blood-washed murmurs to the sky.
Who can even picture to himself such solitude—a
man alone—a God deserted!

Yet, at His approach they sprang to their feet,
confused still, knowing not whether it was their
Lord who called, or that an enemy was near.

" Could ye not watch with Me one hour ? "
Strange fortitude this, with which to face the world
hereafter! " Watch and pray, that ye enter not

into temptation: the spirit indeed is willing, but the flesh is weak."

No word of His own agony. What matter who saw or saw not, if it behoved the Christ to die? But for them, how could they withstand with such short-lived ardour?

But His own heart was full of heaviness, and no comfort came. Was this perchance the answer? As they slept, oblivious, callous, so heaven seemed for one moment motionless, unanswering.

Alone, alone, in that great garden of solitude, treading the winepress alone, quaffing the fiery cup to the last scalding drop, the cup that none else would taste, yet that He must drain to the very dregs. No way out, no way out, but through that cross, if men were to be saved, and apparently how little they were worth the saving. The silence and the night only seemed to answer: " Thou must drink it and alone." And, bowing His sacred head once more, He prayed in meek obedience: " If this cup may not pass away from Me, except I drink it, Thy will be done."

And once more He came to see whether any watched with Him; and once more He found them fast asleep.

Still silence only for an answer.

" None will drink it for Thee, none will help. Thou must drink it and alone;" and once more He prayed: " Thy will be done." And as He bowed His head to the ground, His forehead struck a stone and drops of blood fell from His forehead.

Then He came to them again and gazed with pity on their sleeping faces.

" Sleep on now, and take your rest: behold, the hour is at hand, and the Son of man is betrayed into the hands of sinners."

The moment in which humanity had cried out for sympathy had passed, when human sympathy, human gratitude, might have solaced anguish, when united prayer might have brought consolation. The temptation was over; the temptation to escape by the power of His Godhead a degrading death. Their silence had been His answer. Henceforth there would be no hesitation, the flesh was conquered, now 't was His joy to die. The insults and jeers of high priests and publicans alike, the taunts and gibes of a whole nation would never again make manifest that bleeding of the soul. No pain, no thirst, no glaring noon-day sun, no prison chains, or smitings of dirty, sin-stained hands would bring one cry. Like a sheep before its shearers He would be dumb.

The new prayer would be, " Let *not* this cup pass from Me. Fill it to the brim, if so be Thy will, O God, that the salvation of this people be full and free and perfect, wide as the rivers, high as the mountains. The fulness of the sacrifice shall be perfect. Humanity is dead for ever in Me. I live now but to die."

There was no flinching in His next words, no fear, no echo of His awful agony. " He is at hand that doth betray Me."

For some time the disciples at the gate had watched with uneasiness a little line of uneven lights, that twinkled hither and thither on the road, along which they had come but two hours before.

Yet surely so many would not come to seize so
gentle a prisoner. Was it not rather, Lazarus
hoped, the little company of believing Jews, who
came to seek their Lord ?

" Judas ! " The name was more hissed than
spoken by the little band.

Judas,—Judas leading a mixed band of soldiers,
borrowed from the precincts of the Temple, of Jews
and Sadducees, of servants and centurions! The
clanking of swords, the steady tread of men dis-
ciplined to march in unison, lights, suppressed
words of command, and the red glare of Roman
lanterns paling in the blue radiance of the moon ; all
these approached. What, then, did Judas dread
that he should bring so many demons with him ?
Surely a legion of devils ? The moments now were
precipitating themselves one upon another. The
air seemed peopled with spiritual elements, that
warred, yet remained unseen. A strange light,
brighter than the moon, seemed to irradiate from
the Messiah, and to make His figure the centre-piece
of the glorious picture.

Then hurriedly, as though possessed with a demon
of haste that spurred him on to his destruction,
Judas bent forward and kissed on His pure brow the
Friend, the Man, the God.

" Hail, Master ! "

Forgetful of Himself, forgetful of those around
Him, even then the gentle Saviour sought to breathe
into this man, whom He had loved, some remorse
that would bring about repentance.

" Friend," He said, raising His pure eyes in
deepest grief and pity—" Friend, wherefore art thou

come ? Betrayest thou the Son of man with a kiss ? ''

It was as though He said: " Thou wast My friend, thou who comest for a crime, canst thou yet kiss Me ? Of a truth such treachery is past conception. Ah, surely, 't is only the Son of man thou thinkest to deceive. Thou canst not hope thus to cheat thy God.''

But the traitor's work was over, the work that seemed but the spawn of madness now. All that he had undertaken he had accomplished, and he fell back into the darkness; his brain reeled, and his heart seemed to swell within him as though bursting with the sudden revelation of that which he had done.

He had betrayed the Lord, betrayed his Christ, his Friend—for what ? For thirty pieces of silver! But thirty thousand could not bring back for him eternal life! Eternal death, that was all that loomed before him. Oh, why, why had they urged him on to perpetrate this awful deed ? Of a truth they had been keen in intuition who thus had singled out the vilest, weakest heart in all Judæa to do this thing.

Lost, lost, lost, in this world and the next! Through greed and avarice, the leading instinct and the most cursed attribute of the Jews; that love of gain that swamps all noble thoughts, sucking as it were into a whirlpool of fetid water all that is great and good, stifling each exalted aspiration.

Meekly, with that noble gait with which none other could compare, with quiet dignity and with no trace of fear, Jesus stepped forward.

" Whom seek ye ? '' He asked of the commander

of the soldiers, who stood with swords drawn, but turned downwards to the ground.

" Jesus of Nazareth," replied their chief. In truth, he knew not what to call this man whom each named differently, and who called Himself the Son of God.

Far away in their back ranks, the Nazarene could see the face of Judas peering through the gloom.

" I am He," He said, and, as the words of truth unadorned fell on the chilly stillness, a cry rose from the lips of Judas:

" 'T is He, 't is He!" But to the souls of those around him he seemed to say, " 'T is God, 't is God "; and, like one on whom some sudden, blinding light is flashed, the group fell back before the God-like majesty of that fearless presence.

Iscariot, poor fool, had warned them to come with staves and swords and spears and to use force against Him; but this Man made no attempt either to escape or to oppose them, though all knew full well that He had done nothing worthy of death.

Then, when the men fell back, one of the disciples cried out: " Let us flee; they are afraid."

But flight was impossible to the true, brave nature; the cup was being emptied, slowly and surely; the bitterest dregs were yet to come, but He would drain it.

Once more He approached the startled band, and His very presence seemed to strike their souls with terror. Again He asked: " Whom seek ye ?"

And again they answered: " Jesus of Nazareth," and in their hushed voices was a tone that seemed to mean: " We sought a man, we find a God."

Then, lest the fulness of their wrath should fall upon the little band of His disciples, He pleaded for their liberty:

" If therefore ye seek Me, let these go their way."

The great sinewy hands were laid upon His shoulders that had still to bear so much. Fiercely, unnecessarily, they pulled Him hither and thither, shaking and pressing Him who wished but to obey.

He was their prisoner now. The final act of the world's great tragedy was still to be accomplished; the foulest depths of man's iniquity to be plumbed, and the full measure of the blasphemy to be revealed. Their prisoner, He who had been daily amongst them, in the Temple, on the mountains, by the seashore!

Then Peter, unable any longer to bear the strain, impetuous, hasty, longing to wipe out his carelessness and sleep, cried out: " Lord, shall we smite with the sword ?"

And, without waiting for an answer, he seized his sword, and cut off the ear of Malchus, who, besides being in the service of Caiaphas, was his kinsman.

As usual, Peter had committed an act that would suffice only to incense still more the party of Caiaphas against the Christ. A spasm of pain crossed the face of Jesus. This was no time for wrath, or cavilling, or pitting strength against strength. It was a time when only truth and meekness could prevail, if aught could prevail against the prince of this world and those urged on by him. But He could nullify this foolish action. With infinite gentleness He touched the ear and it was healed.

" Suffer me thus far," He said. Then, turning

to Peter, He continued, " Put up again thy sword
into its place: for all they that take the sword shall
perish with the sword. Thinkest thou that I cannot
now pray to My Father, and He shall presently give
Me more than twelve legions of angels ? But how
then shall the Scriptures be fulfilled, that thus it
must be ? "

Poor foolish Peter, where, indeed, was thy faith,
if thou didst think to protect the King of kings with
thy feeble hand ?

But the hour was wearing on. These miracles and
incidents were beginning to influence the little
crowd; the officers must allow no superstitious
fears to animate them; they must perform their
duty. This Man needed no binding and no force,
but the law must be obeyed ; that grinding millstone
that for so many years had pounded and ground
down the brains and hearts of man, till they had
become but a mingled dust of foulness and evil and
severity, a very powder of Satan's own compounding.

So His sacred hands were bound and tied behind
His back, and chains were set round Him who in
one brief moment could have burst them all, if so
He would. What scorn in the words He addressed
to them while their clumsy fingers fumbled with
cord and band! Yet in their fear lest He should
escape what homage to His power!

" Are ye come out as against a thief, with swords
and staves, for to take Me ? "

But to their hearts He seemed to say: " Are ye
too blind to see the difference between an evil-doer,
who would escape death, and one wholly good, who
seeks to die ? "

Then, in the darkness they bore Him away, across the little brook and up the hill that, but a few hours before, He had trodden as a free man indeed, though with a sickening agony in His pure heart. Then a little band of friends had been about Him; now when He gazed round the multitude, He caught no responding look, no friendly glance, for all His loved disciples had forsaken Him and fled. Christ, the Son of God, the Saviour, the Messiah, was alone; bereft of friends; for the stern countenances that the winter moon lit up were those of foes.

Alone! Alone! Yet not quite, for one was there who had himself passed through the agony of death, who loved Him with a reverent, enduring love and would never desert Him. Afraid to come near Him, lest the crowd should fear some miracle, or lest by death He should be separated from Jesus at the supreme moment of His yielding up His life, yet with a heart that yearned to comfort, Lazarus mingled with the crowd. But the spirit of persecution was abroad. The stream of man's evil might run its course to-night at will. Cries rose: " 'T is Lazarus; perchance he followeth to let this Man go. Let him, too, be taken to Annas, for he is a follower of this Man: and, if he hath not fled, 't is that some mischief breweth. Bind him! Bind him! "

" Slay him! Slay him! " cried the multitude, and some of the soldiers crowded round him and tried to take him prisoner. One man even caught hold of his linen robe; but Lazarus, with a twist of his body, slipped downwards out of his garment and fled away in the darkness. Better so, than die while the Lord had need of him. And all the multitude

20

cried out: " 'T is yet another miracle. This man shall never die."

And so they entered the gates of Jerusalem, the band of soldiers swollen to a dense mass of followers, so that it seemed that all the city had assembled to see the Saviour die.

But the divine figure in the midst said never a word, uttered no cry or murmur; and the moon looked on coldly, nor veiled her face. No thunder, no great lights from heaven, no angels ascending and descending, no earthquakes, no falling down of great mountains, no sudden striking of men to death, proclaimed to the world that this Man was different from any other, or that the Son of God would die.

CHAPTER XXXI.

IT could not be supposed that souls such as those of Caiaphas and Annas, souls that Satan's poison had turned dark and foul forever, could achieve so great a triumph as the capture of the Nazarene, without tasting to the full the sweets of conquest. To taunt, to scoff, to jeer at those who are down, was ever the Jewish character; for, as no minds have greater genius than have those belonging to that race, so no hearts can conceive greater bitterness and craft, and wound so cruelly. To Annas first, then to Caiaphas, lastly, before the Sanhedrim, the Saviour would have to go. A threefold agony must surely win a threefold glory. Caiaphas had reasons of his own for not having Him brought straight to him.

" Whither take ye Him ? " asked one after another of the multitude.

" To Annas first, and then to Caiaphas," replied the soldier, in a voice that forbade further questioning.

To Annas, whose link with the Pharisees lay shivered to bits; Annas, who disregarded Sanhedrim and chief priests alike, but who, through machinations and low intrigue, had gained possession of all the secrets of the Jewish world; who, in his old age, cared neither for deposition from nor accession to power, while he held those vital secrets, like swords, over the heads of half the rulers of Judæa. He had promised to counsel Caiaphas how to proceed with this Nazarene. By base jobbery he had succeeded in turning even political events to his account. By playing upon their greed he had pressed into his service all those who could be bribed and otherwise corrupted, and they were not a few. But, to possess this power, a man must needs have money. Accordingly he levied tithes in secret on all Judæa.

Usurers, money-changers, sellers of doves, all these privily sent their contributions, that went to swell the bursting hoards of this ex-High Priest. And it was this Nazarene who had inveighed against these men—" Woe unto you, usurers!"—who had upset the tables of the money-changers, and opened the cages of them that sold doves to let them soar upwards to heaven. Needs must that Annas should see this Man, to find out how much He knew; for if He were to come before Pilate and to divulge these things, the reign of Annas and of his viperous brood would surely come quickly to an end.

The great gates were swung back, while soldiers, holding their lances in front of them, with both hands thrust back the crowd that strove to force itself into the very courts of the High Priest's house. But Peter, only, of the disciples, succeeded in pressing in.

" This is no time, " cried the servants of Annas, " to enter this house; in the morning ye shall see the prisoner at the trial before the Sanhedrim."

" This is no hour for trial," cried the populace.

" The trial will be to-morrow; no man is condemned unheard," rejoined the soldiers, obeying
orders in speaking thus, and fearing a disturbance.
" No man is condemned in Jerusalem unheard,"
they repeated; " and for mercy's sake we brought
Him first to Annas, for perchance he will set Him
free."

" Annas, Annas, 't is indeed the merciful," cried
the crowd derisively, making a play on the meaning
of his name. Then closing doors pressed out the
lingering bystanders, shut out the night and the
free, fresh air, and every living witness of the Nazarene's arrest, for Peter had joined the servants in the
offices of the palace. Alone Jesus appeared before
Annas, but for the guard that attended Him.

Perhaps the old man hovering on the confines of
life and death, with keener memory of prophecy,
with greater crimes upon his head than had any
other ruler, face to face at last with the majestic
presence he had barely seen as it had wandered
through the streets of Jerusalem and up and down
the mountains, proclaiming upon earth its mission,
felt a slight quivering, a fleeting terror lest events
stupendous should befall. The sublime countenance
of the Nazarene, that like a sunbeam had shone on
earth for thirty years, the lateness of the hour, the
silence inside his palace, the dull roar of the voices
of the populace without—all these had their effect
on the old man, who, like all the Jews, was not
without his superstitions and belief in the supernatural. He had long desired to interrogate this
Man, who, for three years had convulsed Jerusalem
with His miracles and teachings; who, till now, had

kept persecutions and condemnation and captivity
at bay; and not by wiles, or power, or interest, but
by the intensity of His earnestness, by the manifestation of His surpassing love.

Like bolts of fire launched from the midday sun,
the glances flashed from the eyes of Jesus on the
little, shrivelled Jew, perished and bent more from
his own iniquities than from age. A charred soul
stunted and consumed by its own inward fires.
What a blissful opportunity was this to spue forth,
toad-like, all his venom upon this diamond purity
that by its very existence condemned!

" Are they all without ? " he asked the guard.

"All save one," replied the man; " and he is kept
in vigilance below, for he did smite the right ear
from Malchus."

" One of Thy disciples did this thing ? " asked
Annas of the Nazarene, glad of an excuse for the
malice that was in his heart.

But Jesus made no answer; yet the patient gaze
He turned on the rough soldier appealed to him with
all the force of a command to tell Annas the truth
of what had happened.

" Yet," he interposed, " this Man did heal the
ear, like as the other, by His touch, while we stood
and laid our hands upon Him."

But the merciful words fell on merciless ears. The
old man made as if he had not heard, and, turning
to the Christ, who stood there weary with the night's
events and agony, he said to Him: " Who art
Thou ? "

But still Jesus answered not a word.

Taking no note of this silence, Annas went on:

" And who are they that follow Thee hither
and thither, yet in Thine hour of need desert
Thee ?"

A spasm of grief overshadowed the face for one
instant, then passed away.

The priest asked again: " What are these doctrines that Thou teachest; these tales of miracles,
this comradeship with poor and sinner ? Where
hast Thou learned them ? Whence art Thou ?"

But still the Nazarene said nothing, gazing upwards, as though in prayer, for strength to drink the
cup.   Of what avail to answer with words of truth
creatures whose only cleverness lay in planning and
detecting lies ? The occasion was too sacred, the
minutes for prayer too precious, the attempt to
argue would but provoke words of greater sin.

" Wilt Thou not speak to me ?" cried Annas,
presently, infuriated.   " Wilt Thou defy me by
Thy silence, or art Thou afraid ?"

And one of the soldiers shook Him roughly and
said: " Speak, answer the priest or 't will be the
worse for Thee."

Then, lifting His great, angelic eyes, pure as a
holy child's, deep with the wisdom and the truth of
ages, the Nazarene prepared to raise that voice
which would ring for evermore in the old man's ears.
With scorn it rang out now, with pity it would return to him on his death-bed; and in the far, dark
distances of hell that voice would ring, in accom-
paniment to his despair, the words, " Too late, too
late !"

" Wilt Thou not speak ?   Then, after all, Thou art
a coward," snarled Annas, some faint glimmering in

his narrow mind teaching him the words to use that most would wound the Man whom all Judæa knew feared nothing.

But no answering, wrathful cry responded to this taunt. Slowly the Nazarene raised His eyes and let them fall upon the little, cringing priest.

" I spake only to the world; I even taught in the Synagogue and in the Temple whither the Jews always resort; and in secret have I said nothing. Why askest thou Me ? Ask them which heard Me what I have said unto them; behold they know what I said."

Each word lashed the ignominious heart of Annas as with whip-cords. Yes, it was late in the day to ask this young rabbi, after three years of ministry, what were His doctrines. Was it not for those very doctrines that He stood there ? His words unearthed, as with a pickaxe, and laid bare the scheming, lying, malicious stirring of the old priest's heart. He shivered, as he might shiver were his body lying exposed and naked beneath the winter's moon.

A blow, a stinging blow, fell on the pale, meek face. Surely it could not be that a man could strike the Lord and live ! The cup was filling quickly, salt and vinegar taking the place of wine. Strength, oh, strength to drink it; but never a cry or a word.

" Answerest Thou the High Priest so ? Thou Galilean, Thou son of ——" His words were checked, he knew not how or why, but it seemed as though his tongue lay paralysed.

Once more the gentle voice was raised: "If I have

spoken evil, bear witness of the evil; but if well, why smitest thou Me?"

It was long past midnight, and Caiaphas was waiting; but Annas was loath to let the Christ depart without having wrung from Him any self-convicting words. This in itself was a defeat to one who knew so well the phases of success.

"'T is useless to sit all night with a dumb, obstinate madman," exclaimed Annas. "Lead Him to Caiaphas and tell him from me that he need fear no more that the lying preaching of this Man shall deceive the nations, for that His tongue doth now refuse its office."

So once more the weary figure was moved away, still bound; and all through the night Annas sat on, wondering strangely; and no man durst come near him to ask him what he thought. And when Jesus passed out into the courtyard to be led to Caiaphas, the people who had remained outside pressed against the gate, and seeing armed men and lanterns and the quiet figure they all knew so well, they cried out with a great cry that reached the ears of Annas in his chamber: "Shall He die? Shall He die?"

CHAPTER XXXII.

ROUND a blazing fire in the big hall leading into the court-yard sat the servants of Annas; for part of the daily scheme of Annas's career of hypocrisy was to be generous to his retainers. There were too many secrets hidden in the dark corners of his house for Annas to be able to neglect or quarrel with his servants.

" The good, the merciful Annas."

Thus spoke the house-servants of the much-hated High Priest. Of his own gold he had built a wall that shone and radiated upon him.

Round this fire the servants, men and women, hewers of wood, fetchers of water, grass-cutters, workmen, and maidens congregated to discuss what now had become almost the only topic of conversation amongst all classes. The excitement was increased by the fact of the propinquity of the subject of their conversation, wonder as to what Annas would do, and what the Nazarene would say.

While they talked and laughed and jested, one figure sat gloomily alone, warming his hands at the fire, colder at heart than outwardly, cursing himself for his impetuosity, bemoaning his temporary absence from his Master, fearing to speak, lest his tongue should betray the Galilean dialect, and fearing still more the vengeance of the man whose ear

he had struck off.   While he sat there his thoughts
could not do otherwise than wander back to all the
words of the Nazarene.

Why twice had the Christ told him He would deny
Him ?   Surely it would only be in the face of some
terrible temptation.   What, then, so awful had yet
to come to pass ?   Or spake He only of the heart
that deceiveth and denieth alway ?   His eyes wandered out into the darkness.   Surely midnight was
long past.   Yet no cock had crowed.   Could it be
that Caiaphas and Annas allowed them not within
the precincts, looking upon them as unclean birds ?
Yet in the Roman quarters, not so far away, there
must be some; and surely they had crowed already.
There must be some parable in his Master's speech.
Would there ever be an opportunity of asking Him ?

A serving-woman paused while she began to place
the early morning meal on the rough table, and eyed
him curiously.

" Surely thou also wast with Jesus of Galilee ? "

A blinding of the senses, a terrible panic, a madness of dark terror.   " I know not what thou meanest."   And he rose and walked to the porch, fearing
that they would recognise him, should they look him
in the face.

Then the maid turned to the others.   " This fellow
also was with Jesus of Nazareth; I myself opened
the gate to him.   Wherefore doth he deny it ? "

" Well, what matter ? " said one.   " Leave him
in peace; the end is near at hand."

" But Annas hath given order that none but this
fisherman, whom he knoweth, should enter," said
the chief steward, referring to John; and all the

little group gathered round the porch and one said:
" Surely thou also art one of them, for thy speech
betrayeth thee ; a curse on thy lying Galilean
tongue."

" I know not what thou sayest," repeated Peter;
and, when all gathered round him curiously, ready
with many questions, he continued angrily: " Cursed
be ye all, ye questioning, prating fools, I tell ye I
know not the Man."

And, on the chilly air, there rose from the Roman
quarter the shrill crow of a cock, announcing the
first hour of morning; and a pang, that was like a
death-blast, shot straight to Peter's heart.

There was a noise of hurried footsteps and clanking swords that jangled on the pavement, and the
Nazarene passed by, and while the words rose on his
lips, " I know not the Man," the Saviour turned
His head and, with the agonised gaze of one who
heareth his best friend betray him, He looked at
Peter.

One more drop of the cup of bitterness was drunk.

And Peter, covering his face with his hands,
rushed out into the night to weep; and again the
cock crew on the stilly night.

CHAPTER XXXIII

"METHINKS at last I hold this Man," said Caiaphas, pacing his audience chamber to calm a strange unrest that filled his soul.

In a corner of the room beside the window, looking out with love-struck eyes, gazed Rebekah, hearing, but scarce heeding, her father's words, for they brought no comfort to her unhinged soul.

" He is before Annas now, the proud Nazarene, and if there be one who can sift a man as wheat "— here Caiaphas made an expressive gesture, turning his hands upwards, as if they were cups in which he sifted flour or grain—" 't is thy grandfather Annas."

" Yet he will find no fault in Him," replied Rebekah absently and perversely. Why she said the words she knew not, except that in her heart a faint loyalty to Lazarus twinkled.

" Why sayest thou this ? " asked Caiaphas excitedly; " dost thou believe that He is sent from God ? "

" I believe nothing; I know nothing," said Rebekah coldly.

Caiaphas eyed her anxiously. Woman has, at all times, been the one enigma no man can solve.

" Then why speakest thou ? "

A sullen silence; then steps across the court-yard below, and muttered voices.

" They come," said Caiaphas; but in his eyes was
no look of expectant triumph, and all his features
seemed contracted with some inexplicable dread.
What if after all He were the Son of God ?   What
if He should strike him dead by some unseen subtle
force ?   Oh, if that daughter of his in the corner
would but break the silence, instead of sitting gazing
in vacancy at the moon !

So versed was he in hunting for the dark spots of
vice in human nature, that the few shining ones of
virtue escaped his view; thus he found himself
suspecting for an instant that even his own daughter
might be plotting to defeat him.

" Jesus of Nazareth."

Wide open were flung the doors, and, between
two soldiers, the Nazarene was ushered in.   One
more drop of anguish to be drunk, one step nearer
to the cross !   The High Priest was face to face, at
last, with the Man he hated, and, at the same time,
dreaded.   It was a grim satisfaction to see Him
bound.   Rebekah, cold-eyed, but curious, looked
on without a word.

Now the chamber was filling; elders, scribes,
Sadducees, a few, very few, Pharisees, all the members of the council, filed in one after another to see
the triumph of their High Priest and the degrada-
tion of the Christ.   Strange men who had been
hired to bear false witness, sycophants, liars, usurers,
lawyers, a strange medley, jostled each other in the
room.   Faint and weary, but unflinching still, the
Nazarene stood with head erect.   But when Caiaphas with loud voice called out, " Ye who do accuse
this Man, come forward," none answered to the call,

and to the question put forth many times, " What hath this Man done ? " no answer came.

Then Caiaphas stamped his feet impatiently, and said: " Do ye mock at me; to bid me condemn this Man, and bring no accusation ? "

Two wretched men of the lowest type, men who had bought their lives of Caiaphas, as the price of their corruption, came forward and averred: " This fellow said, ' I am able to destroy the Temple of God, and to rebuild it in three days.' "

But no words came from the lips of the Nazarene; only He raised His liquid eyes to the two men in silent wonderment and reproach; and, abashed, they shrank back into a dark niche in the wall. Then Caiaphas, terrified, awed, baffled, came one step forward. " Answerest Thou nothing ? " he said. " What is it which these witness against thee ? "

Still silence from the Nazarene and a strange hush throughout the crowded room. Then, overcome with a great terror, fearing lest at any moment the crowd itself should be magnetised into obeisance by this strange meekness, the High Priest cried: " I adjure Thee by the living God, that Thou tell us whether Thou be the Christ, the Son of God."

Adjured by His own self to declare Himself; yielding to an appeal that through all ages will be answered, has been answered by the living God, the living God gave answer: " Thou hast said."

Then, half in fury, half in fear, the High Priest tore the clothes from off him, beginning at the throat, as though he stifled. One, two, three, the ephod lay in ribbons round his body. Never before had the High Priest been seen in such a state of fury, and his frenzy and confusion gave no little pleasure to the assembled crowd of envious priests.

Then, as if to give Caiaphas the one last chance that had been offered Judas—while eternal salvation hovered around the little crowd, and the High Priest quaked with the fear that some might fall in sudden remorse and awakening at the feet of Jesus —He spoke once more : " Hereafter ye shall see the Son of man sitting on the right hand of power, and coming in the clouds of heaven."

It was as if, in His all-embracing mercy, He had said : " Do not think because ye see Me here in bonds, a lonely, weary man, that it will be always thus. Pause, pause and consider that, one day, you will all see Me again in power, and ye will re-member the lowly carpenter who appealed to you in meekness."

But Caiaphas, perturbed beyond endurance, al-most to madness, paced the room, tearing his clothes and exclaiming excitedly, in order to veil his per-turbation : " He hath spoken blasphemy; what further need have ye of witnesses, behold, now ye have heard His blasphemy."

And so the words that Caiaphas had yearned to hear had been pronounced at last, and one drop more of the bitter cup had been drunk.

But something more than the words of the Naza-rene disturbed the equanimity of the High Priest. There was an inexplicable feeling in the air, as though the demons of darkness had been let loose, and the ghosts of supernatural beings came and went; nor could he decide whether it was fancy or sensation. The hours seemed to have halted in their course, and instead of dawn, a cold twilight seemed to have settled on his heart and brain forever. As in a vision, he saw the Son of man descending in the clouds with power. It seemed to him that the voice of the God whom he had pretended to represent on earth, but had mocked and insulted by his actions, called down a curse on him forever. In the twilight he seemed to see his own figure standing in eternal greyness, groping between rocks, seeking, seeking for a light that once had flashed across his eyes and lain for one instant on his soul. A great doubt rose in his heart when he looked round on those upturned faces, exultant in their petty victory, exultant at their High Priest's hesitation. Then over that heart, all riddled with corruption, there stole a sombre pall, like the cloud that settles over the last pale ray of a struggling sun and ends the day; and the decision that ranked him as the foulest murderer on earth was made. But, as moral cowards always do, he needed comrades in his crime.

" What think ye ? " he cried at last to the silent crowd; knowing full well their answer, the only answer they durst give, the only answer his soul craved for. And with one voice rose on the stilly night the words " Ish maveth! Ish maveth! [A man of death.] He is guilty of death."

And, all the time, Rebekah looked on mute, and thought of Lazarus.

21

CHAPTER XXXIV.

SCARCE had the fateful cry died out on the awe-charged air, when a scuffle was heard outside, steps rushing hurriedly by, and cries as of a madman broken loose.

A chill blast struck the heart of Caiaphas. What, if, after all, this Man had followers at His back ready and able to avenge Him ? What if there were a plot abroad, if the little room with its group of rulers and scribes and priests were invaded by the Romans ?

The door was flung open and, unannounced, almost unrecognisable, with eyes that shifted wildly, as though the nerves had lost all power of keeping them in their place, with hair dishevelled and clothes disordered, and with the grin of madness on his features, Judas Iscariot rushed in, holding aloft a bag. At the sight of the figure of the Nazarene he recoiled, as with a sudden memory of horror, but the mind had given way and with difficulty could unfold the one object of his mission.

In and out of the crowd he rushed, holding up his bag and crying out: " Where is the High Priest, where is Caiaphas ? I have sinned, I have sinned, I have betrayed the innocent blood. I would find the High Priest and give him back his money." And he held up his bag piteously to each one of the priests.

" What is that to us ? " said one. " See thou to that."

" Thou hast thy money; go thy way. Thou hast done thy work well and art well paid. Begone! " another said.

Then, with such lightning rapidity that none could stop him, with fingers trembling with excitement, he undid the mouth of the bag, his hands and fingers shaking so that he could hardly do it; and, before any could stop him, he had thrown the silver from the window into the courts of the Temple, where it clinked on the tesselated pavement with a sound that seemed to cry out: " Blood money, blood money."

At that, a number of the priests ran out tumultuously, jostling each other like a herd of blinded cattle, to gather up the money before the people should be admitted to the Temple in the morning. But Caiaphas only shrugged his shoulders and smiled scornfully, as though the thirty pieces of silver and the presence of the madman were no affair of his.

Only the Nazarene turned an eye of pity on the wretched man; and, when that look of love and mercy fell upon the traitor, he bent his head and shuffled from the room.

Then, to end the horrible situation, Caiaphas gave a sign to the soldiers to lead the Christ away to the guard-room, where He would remain till early the next morning, when His trial before Pilate would take place.

Weary with all His drawn-out agony, anguished with the foretaste of a death of torture on the morrow, the Son of God was not yet allowed to rest.

The shapely form was buffeted with the blows of those who guarded Him, the divine face spat upon; those eyes that held in them the rays of eternal sun·· light were blindfolded, for Him to be the sport of the lowest of earth's creatures.

" Prophesy who it was that smote Thee ? "

Blasphemy after blasphemy fell upon ears that quivered in their purity. Taunt and oath and curse echoed round the prison walls; but the Nazarene neither spoke nor moved, nor asked even for a glass of water in His thirst and faintness. The dregs of the cup were thickening, slowly the drops were being swallowed. It would soon be finished now. The grey streaks of His last dawn on earth—before His resurrection,—the few bands of white on the walls of the filthy cell lighted the pale face of the Nazarene. A little more pain, a few more taunts, what mattered they ? A little more strength only needed to go through twelve hours more. Ere that same sun should sink blood-red behind the hills, the agony would be over; the earth be bathed in the blood that would surge for ever over men's sins in a tide of endless patience till the Judgment Day; and the stupendous gift of the world's salvation would be offered, for men to take or leave.

CHAPTER XXXV.

A DARK veil of grief hung over the home of Bethany. Ever since the night before, when Lazarus had returned from the Garden of Gethsemane, they had sat almost paralysed with grief and dread.

The Lord captured, the Master taken! This indeed seemed the beginning of the end; and the attempted capture of Lazarus made them fear that peace had for ever left their dwelling. The life of Jesus on earth would find its lowly echo in that of Lazarus. At any moment he might be seized, as their Lord had been, captured, taunted, condemned. There would be no safety for the future in that home; and yet they regretted nothing. They had put their shoulder to the wheel and never more would they look back, but the vista that stretched before them was dark and drear; trial, fear, trouble, death. At the end a cross, but behind the cross what glory!

Over and over again Lazarus told them of those bitter moments in Gethsemane, and their tears fell at the recital of the agony of their Lord.

Over and over again Martha murmured, with all a woman's tenderness: " To be sleeping, to be sleeping, while the Lord prayed and wept! Oh that we could be with Him!"

Then, before dawn, Lazarus had gone to learn the result of the Saviour's interview with Caiaphas, and where He was.

"Thy face doth tell me, thy face doth tell me," cried Mary, stretching out her hands in deep distress when Lazarus returned. "He is condemned! He is condemned!"

"Condemned by Caiaphas," assented Lazarus; "but to-day He is to be taken before Pilate, and the Romans condemn men not so readily."

"Yet He must surely die," said Mary; "and now, for His dear sake, I would that all were over and He once more with the Father."

"Yea, indeed," said Lazarus, a deep depression in his voice. "God grant it may be soon, for I do hear horrors of this night in the prison, how they did taunt and sneer and strike and—oh! I cannot speak of it." He shuddered, while the two women moaned in sympathy at the sufferings of their Lord.

Then rapidly the three made their plans, which required much thought, for their presence at Jerusalem might excite the populace and effect more harm than good; might result even in the death of Lazarus. Yet they would not stay away. So it was settled that the two sisters should go to the house of the Magdalene, while Lazarus remained in the outskirts of the city, ready to be sent for should they need him, though he knew well that he could do but little, either to give solace to his Lord or to protect his sisters. The last act of the tragedy, that had begun with the creation of the world, was about to be performed. Divine power would not, human could not, bid the actors stay their actions. Each horrible de-

tail of ignominy and suffering, of trial and of condemnation, had been foretold.   Naught else would
avail if man was to be saved.   As man looks round
on man, he wonders where the need to save is
shown, or what is worth in man to save.

In the house of the Magdalene they found the
virgin mother, who had come from Nazareth for one
last look at her God-begotten Son.   One by one,
believing women added themselves to the little knot
of mourners.

Every now and then a disciple, or some friend,
came in with gleanings of news that brought sometimes anguish, sometimes comfort, to their souls.
At one moment it was a fresh incident of that night's
suffering, at another that Pilate would not condemn.

" What sayeth the multitude ? " asked the Magdalene of Nicodemus, who came for one brief instant.

" The multitude ?   What doth the Jewish multitude ever to them who are down-trodden ?   It
treadeth down the more.   Every Jew is born thus,"
replied Nicodemus angrily.   " They do cry, ' Crucify
Him!   Crucify Him! ' and they will that Barabbas
be released."

" Barabbas for the Lord ? " murmured the Magdalene.   " It seemeth past man's understanding! "

Towards midday Lazarus came with the news of
what had passed before Pontius Pilate.   So changed
and weary was his face, that Martha and Mary bade
him be seated, and refreshed him by bathing his
temples in vinegar before they would let him speak ;
albeit their hearts were bursting with anxiety and
eagerness to hear.

" It is all over; they have condemned Him to be crucified," wailed Lazarus; and great, strong man though he was, his voice broke and tears rose to his eyes. " I can scarce tell ye," he added, crying like a woman. " They scourged Him, scourged our Lord; Pontius Pilate with his own hands scourged Him, and Caiaphas did laugh, they say, with joy; but of that I know not ; for I could not stay and not cry out ; and, maybe, for every cry of mine they had scourged Him yet again." At his words the Saviour's mother, with a slight groan and a cry, fell fainting to the ground. " I wot not she was here," said Lazarus. " It seemeth to me that my heart and brain have given way. Hearken unto them."

And in the distance, like the bellowing of furious bulls, or the thunder of a torrent that has broken loose and sweeps everything before it, came the dull roar of men with souls so dead as to be lost to all conception of the majesty, the mercy, or the truth of God.

" Crucify Him! Crucify Him!" rose the cry; and strident laughter, and the gibing voices of men, and the shrill shrieks of women combined to form the delirious clamour that rose beneath the midday sun.

Then Mary Magdalene, no longer able to contain herself, threw herself into the arms of Mary, and cried out bitterly: " And all this for my sins, my sins!" Then, with hearts bursting with such grief as those who live in these later days can scarce conceive—a grief peculiar to those few to whom it was given to know and love the Saviour when on earth —they discussed what should they do.

" We cannot, cannot let Him die," the Magdalene sobbed.

" We cannot leave Him to die alone," said Lazarus. And, all the while, they saw not that the Virgin, in silent grief—for her senses had returned—was searching for a covering for her head and was about to sally forth alone. Her Son, her God to die alone ? Never! not if ten thousand swords should oppose her progress to the cross. The loving heart that had effaced itself for thirty years, to let the course of God's will run on untrammelled, would not rebel against the Lord's decree; but no law, either of Jew or Roman, could deny a mother the exquisite agony of seeing her son die.

Since He had been a little child, He had never wanted her, but the link, however mysterious, had been there; the link between the human mother and the divine Son. As an infant, although God, He had stretched out His arms to her, and hers had been ever ready; they would be ready now, outstretched to Him, that He might know that human tenderness was there, side by side with divine submission. Perchance, He might have a message; or to those tortured limbs she might bring some slight relief; at least,when dead,that beauteous head should find no harder resting-place than the Virgin's knee.

" She goeth to Him; we must go too," said Mary. And, silently, they followed the mother of the Lord, whose grief was greater even than theirs; and, while they walked, the Magdalene spoke in low, sweet tones to Lazarus: " Scourged by the hands of Pontius Pilate! But 't was said he sought to save the Lord."

" Methinks that 't was to save the Lord that he did scourge Him," answered Lazarus. " It seemeth to me that he thought they must needs be satisfied with that, and then would let Him go, for he said, ' I will chastise Him and let Him go.' But 't was the wily Caiaphas and that hell-hound Annas that would not be satisfied, and urged on the people. Oh, had it not been our Lord who stood there, 't would have been a brave sight to see; for all the rulers and their wives and daughters stood round the Judgment Hall to see Him; and to see Pilate and Caiaphas was like watching two cats fighting over one mouse. Like crossed swords were their words, and Caiaphas gnashed his teeth, as if already in hell, at the words of Pilate; for Pilate knoweth full well that there is no fault in Him, and that, from very fear, the High Priest did this thing. Such a populace was there, and men in glittering armour, and priests and elders in costly garments; and, when Pontius Pilate came unto the steps of the Tribunal, he looked as pale as our dear Lord, and his glance did strike across to Caiaphas, and he called out aloud, ' Will ye that I release unto you the King of the Jews ?' Oh, one thought that Caiaphas would die of very wrath at the words of Pilate; for ofttimes Pilate hath taunted him that he feared the Jews would make our Master king. But that ignorant people did only cry, ' Release unto us Barabbas, release unto us Barabbas!' Yet Pontius Pilate spake again to the clamouring crowd—' Behold the Man whom ye would crucify!' And all did turn their gaze upon that face, and His eyes did seem to look far off, and His lips were shut; yet I thought I

heard Him murmur, ' Abba, Father! ' Then there
was silence, and methought, ' Surely one after
another will creep away, for none can look upon
that face and still condemn Him '; and methinks,
forsooth, they would have let Him go, albeit I know
that He needs must die. But Caiaphas, when he
did see that all the multitude did waver, did send
his false accusers to stand before the Governor;
and one said, ' We found this fellow perverting the
nation and forbidding to give tribute to Cæsar, saying that He Himself is Christ and King.' But,
when Pilate heard this, which he well knew was
false, he said again to the chief priests and to the
people, ' People of Israel and all nations, I find no
fault in this Man.' Then Caiaphas grew yet more
fierce, and, fearing lest our Master should escape
him, he sent another false accuser to say, 'He stirreth
up the people, teaching throughout all Jewry, beginning from Galilee to this place. For He is born
a Galilean.' And this he said because he knew that,
by the law, a Galilean must needs go before Herod,
and Herod hateth Pontius Pilate. At this, Pontius
Pilate said with a loud voice, ' I wash my hands of
this Galilean; take ye Him before Herod.' Then
they led Him away, and methought He would have
fainted in the crowd that pressed so sore, so weary
did He look.''

"My Lord, my Lord,'' the Magdalene murmured.

But Lazarus went on: "And Pilate with a loud
voice cried out, ' I am glad that Herod is in Jerusalem at this time, for I see no fault in Him. I
cannot condemn Him by the Roman law.' And
they do say that for many years hath Herod wished

to see the Master. And while Pilate's messenger did go to Herod, the multitude did shout continually, ' He hath blasphemed! Crucify Him! Crucify Him!' Aye, 't was like beasts waiting to lick warm blood. Then, all of a sudden, a silence fell on all; then rose a murmur, and a soldier sent by Herod entered, and soon came forth again walking before the Christ and crying out, ' Make way, make way for the King of the Jews!' And as all looked to see what this might mean, behold the Master, arrayed in gorgeous robes and with a crown of thorns upon His head, came forth, and the eyes of all were blinded with His glory; and Caiaphas did bend his head forward to his breast, and looked upward with his eyes, as is his wont; and into his face there came such fear that methought surely Caiaphas hath been defeated and they have in truth proclaimed Him King; but 't was a sorry jest of Herod to Pontius Pilate. Yet Pilate smiled not when his eyes fell on the Christ, but murmured, ' No man saw I ever so like a king.' ' But the people feared to lose Barabbas, and cried out, ' Crucify Him!' and, the while, Pontius Pilate read the missive from the Tetrarch. Then Pilate stood once more on the steps of the Tribunal, and cried out, ' Chief priests, rulers, and people of Israel, ye have brought this Man unto me as one that perturbeth the people, and, behold, I having examined Him before you, have found no fault in Him, touching those things whereof ye do accuse Him; no, nor yet hath Herod, for I sent Him unto him; and lo, nothing worthy of death is done unto Him nor spoken of by Herod. I will therefore chastise Him and release Him.' But, with one .

voice, they cried out like thunder: ' Away with this
Man, and release unto us Barabbas! '   And again
and again Pilate spoke and said, ' Why, what evil
hath He done ?   I have found no cause of death in
Him; and I will let Him go.'   But they cried more
and more, ' Crucify Him!   Crucify Him! '   At last,
when Pilate saw that there would be an uproar with
the people, and that some even drew their staves
and swords, he cried wearily, ' Take ye Him and
crucify Him.   Do with Him as ye will, but I find
no fault in Him.'   And as they led Him away,
Pilate followed with his eyes until the Master had
left the room; then he sank down in his chair and
covered his face with his hands and would speak to
no man; and Caiaphas did turn to him with such
a look of joy and hate and triumph as never saw I
mingled in one face before.''

By this time they had joined the vociferating
crowd, which, satisfied with its success and weary
with the excitement of the day, had not had time to
notice the added group to the already swelling multitude.

At sight of the weary face of the Nazarene they
could have cried out with anguish.   Never was such
grief and ignominy beheld before.   Thank God,
there never will be again!   Travel-stained, weary,
footsore, bruised and lacerated with the cruel scourge,
almost fainting with the weight of the heavy cross
in the broiling midday sun, with no covering on His
head but the crown of thorns which had torn His
brow in bleeding gashes, but which He could not
even raise from its position with His bound hands,
the world's Saviour staggered on, through taunts

and gibes and mocking words of false obeisance:
" Hail, King of the Jews!" or, " Why dost not un-
bind Thine hands, Thou Maker of Miracles ?"

Suddenly there was a few moments' halt, while
they seized on a Cyrenian going by, to load him
with the cross. Then the women Jesus loved drew
nearer, hoping, if only by some look, to tell Him
how their anguished hearts did throb in sympathy
with His. He turned and gazed on them, His eyes
enfolding first and foremost the mother He loved so
well, and whose whole heart was His.

" Daughters of Jerusalem," said the loving voice,
that had been for so long mute, whose sweet but
searching tones would sound so rarely now on earth,
" weep not for Me, but weep for yourselves, and for
your children."

But 't was for Him they wept, for their powerless-
ness to help Him, and for their sins, that were the
cause of all His agony. And the virgin mother wept
so grievously that it seemed as if her heart must
burst and her eyes shed blood for the greatness of
her grief.

Then all those who loved the Nazarene and believed in Him recalled the prophet's words: "Her
soul shall be pierced with a two-edged sword "; and
again, " I gave my back to the smiters, and my
cheeks to them that plucked off the hair: I hid not
my face from shame and spitting."

Suddenly a horse, with a Roman soldier on its
back, came galloping at full speed through the
crowd, scattering to right and left screaming men,
women, and children, even knocking some down in
his haste.

" Even now will Pilate save Him," the people

murmured.   The horse was flecked with foam, and
the man's brow dripped with sweat.   The clinking
chains of the heavy Roman bridle gleamed in the
sun, yet shone not brighter than the sleek flanks of
the horse or the crest of the soldier's helmet.   But
it was no respite for the condemned God he brought.

He cried out: " Lazarus, Lazarus, find Lazarus.
The Governor hath need of him."

No sign of terror blanched the face of Lazarus,
when, in reverent imitation of his Master, he stepped
forward, saying boldly: " I am he."

" His hour hath come," said Martha, her stern
brow growing even whiter than before, her strong
mouth hardening with dull resignation.

The mute agony in the eyes of the women wrung
his heart.   So soon!   Before the crowd had slaked
their thirst with the blood of one, to demand another's!   The blow had fallen; both in one day
would hang upon the cross.   The last act of the
drama had begun; better almost that it should be
so than this constant scraping of the heart-strings.

Gravely, even solemnly, his sisters kissed him.
The Magdalene, distracted as she was with grief,
could only stretch out her hands and cry: "Lazarus, my love, my life."   And when, with a breaking
heart, Lazarus turned to obey the Governor's command, he saw her borne away by helpful arms, her
golden hair that was almost trailing in the dust,
glowing like a halo of glory round her head.

And, while he walked by the side of the soldier's
horse, the multitude, weary already of witnessing
the agony of the Nazarene, cried out: " He too will
be crucified this day!"

No cheerful cry to end a day of mourning.

CHAPTER XXXVI.

UP and down paced Pilate in his private chamber, while the weary, bleeding figure of the Nazarene was tottering along the road to Golgotha. Never more while a breath remained in his body would peace be in his heart. Each day doubt would strengthen, till from it should be born conviction; when that should come no place on earth could hold him.

On his return to his house he had dreaded to meet his wife, yet the first person he met was she.

She had told him of her dreams, she had even sent a message to the Judgment chamber, knowing full well how, to obtain their end, the Jews would press him. She knew Pilate well enough to fear that his frank, intrepid nature would be ill-matched against the crafty subtlety of the law-versed Jews.

" Well ? " she asked, without greeting him, in her excitement, " hast thou released Him ? Where is He ? "

" Oh, Claudia, Claudia, blame me not! " he said. " I could not. They would not. They prevailed with me, as those cursed Jews do ever."

" 'T is not true; it cannot be true! " shrieked Claudia.

" What is Truth ? What is Truth ? " murmured Pilate. " Would I knew the Truth."

" What is Truth ? " repeated Claudia scornfully, her eyes flashing with the wrath that stirred her. " What is Truth is this: thou art a coward, a mean, shrinking coward. The Romans were called ever brave, but in all Judæa there is no such coward as thou. For fear of the multitude thou hast struck at God, if He be indeed the Son of God! "

Surely his retribution was coming swiftly, dealt by the hand that could wound the most; for all this man's great love was centred in, and wisely so, his wife.

" Oh, Claudia, Claudia, blame me not," he said again, in a voice beseeching as a little child's. " He blamed me not, for when I said, ' Speakest Thou not unto me ? knowest Thou not that I have power to crucify Thee, and have power to release Thee ?' He answered me, ' Thou wouldst have no power at all against Me, except it were given Thee from above: therefore he that delivered Me unto thee hath the greater sin.' Then, when I heard those words, I tried all I could to save Him; believe me, Claudia, I brought Him forth as a king; I cried, ' Will ye crucify your King ?' And, when they derided me, I said again, 'Behold your King!' Yet they cried only the more, ' We have no King but Cæsar. Crucify Him! Crucify Him!' Then I sent Him to Herod, but he, too, would not condemn Him; and methinks the people would have listened to Herod, but that hell-hound Caiaphas, that suave-mouthed, leprous-souled High Priest, had paid many of the Jews to cry out ' Crucify!' and, for fear of an uproar, and lest the multitude should tear the Nazarene to pieces, I did let them have Him."

22

" Thou wert sore-pressed, truly, Pilate," said the just Claudia, " but yet thou hadst power to release this Man; and now thou wilt see that all our glory will fade away and great misfortunes will befall us, and through endless ages we shall be cursed for this thing which thou hast done; for a dream this night did tell me that He was the Son of God and that He will come with power again upon the earth." Then, changing her tone, she shrieked out: " But why converse we here ? There is yet time. He is not dead. Release Him yet. O Pilate, for love of me, the wife of thy bosom, whom thou sayest thou lovest; O Pilate, noble Pilate, release Him, save Him yet!" And she flung herself at his feet, appealing to him by every loving name.

One faint gleam of almost savage hope flashed up, then flickered feebly in the Roman's eyes.

" Ye know not these vile Jews, they thirst for blood; like dogs, they would lick sores; they have no mercy. If I release Him now, Caiaphas will excite the people and they will rend Him limb from limb. Leave Him to die, Claudia, for 't is the kindest thing that thou canst do. Let Him sleep to-night in heaven."

Awed by his words, Claudia said after him: "In heaven ? Dost thou, too, believe He is the Son of God ?"

And Pilate stood there silent, while his deep-set eyes gazed far beyond the hills to where he knew a cross was being raised against the sky.

As in a vision he saw the bleeding body on the cross. He knew the torture, for he had seen many hanging so; the body, with its weight, tearing the

flesh from the nails that pierced the hands; the
strain of outstretched arteries and nerves; the one
position that never, never could be changed; the
scorching sun beating fierce on eyes and brain, and
the maddening thirst; the swollen flesh, the aching
back, the smarting seams inflicted by the scourge;
the taunts, the insults, the abuse; then the solitude
and the silent agony of death. This for a man; and,
for a God, the awful load of foulest, unrepented sins.
Better, better, to go and pierce Him with his own
hands, than to leave Him to that lingering death.

"Oh, what is Truth? Who will explain? Who
is He? Whence is He?"

Then life's business intruded itself upon these
awful thoughts; a soldier came with tablets in his
hand.

"We would know what thou wouldst have placed
above the cross," he said.

Yes, there was a possibility of avenging the Nazarene, of insulting the whole Jewish nation, of maddening with fury those two high priests. It was the
last sweet moment of Pilate's darkened life; he
would make the most of it.

"Write," he said to the grovelling scribe who
stood cringingly awaiting his commands—"Write,

'JESUS OF NAZARETH THE KING OF THE
JEWS.'"

Then, when the emissary of Caiaphas seemed to hesitate, he said: "Dost hear me? In Latin and in
Greek and in Hebrew shalt thou write, so that all
men and nations can read, 'Jesus of Nazareth the
King of the Jews.'"

And, wondering, the man fled from Pilate's pres.
ence to obey.

The Saviour was now hanging on the cross; the
last drops of agony were being drunk; the cup was
nearly empty. But Pilate could do something to
curtail His sufferings, and he would. His remorse
was maddening.

" Send me hither," he commanded, " Portius and
Tertius, my two most trusted soldiers."

" Go," he said, " to the cross of the—the—the
Nazarene that is crucified to-day, and let Him not
die a lingering death; but, when the multitude press
round, pierce Him with your spears close to the
heart, so that He die and hang not long. Even to
the condemned we may show mercy."

Then again he began to pace his chamber, and
from his heart, unconsciously, there rose a prayer
for light and truth.

CHAPTER XXXVII.

PREPARED for his death sentence, yet now no longer fearing it, Lazarus was surprised at his reception when ushered into the presence of Pontius Pilate.

Indeed, so agitated was Pilate, that he motioned with his head to Claudia to ask the burning questions that lay so close to both their lips.

" Oh, tell us, tell us, noble Lazarus, is He dead ? " she asked.

" I think that even now they are but nailing Him to the Cross, if so be they lose not time in buffeting Him," said Lazarus, his voice trembling with emotion.

" Be seated, I pray thee," said Claudia, seeing how pale and tired he looked. Then she continued: " Cannot we yet save Him ? "

A gleam of hope shot from the eyes of Lazarus, but quickly died. After a pause he said: " Nay, let Him die, fair lady. 'T is but another hour of agony, and then the sweet spirit will have rejoined His Father. Needs must that He should die. He Himself hath said so, and His word is Truth. If thou shouldst release Him now, Caiaphas will by subtlety retake Him. For the salvation of the world He must needs die to bear the sins of all."

" Thinkest thou, then, that He is the Son of God ? "

"Askest thou me, whom the Lord hath raised, whether I believe He is the Son of God?" said Lazarus.

"Wast thou really dead?" asked Pilate.

"Dead? Yea," said Lazarus. "Four days in the tomb, and my spirit departed into Hades."

"Is there, then, another world?" asked Pilate breathlessly; "a world of life and death?"

"Another world in truth," said Lazarus. "A world of light and peace and righteousness and joy for evermore."

"Oh!" Pilate cast himself down before his table and, throwing his hands outstretched across it, placed his head upon them and cried out: "And I have crucified Him! I have crucified Him!"

At that moment in the distance rose a hideous yell—the yell of triumph at sated hate. It fell on Lazarus's ears like sharp-edged stones. He knew it for the death-knell of the Christ. Claudia started, then wrung her hands and cried out: "He is dead! The Son of God is dead!"

Then down on his knees fell Lazarus, and bowed himself to the ground. And now occurred a wondrous thing: the house swayed backwards and forwards, as though it were like to fall, so fearful was its rocking.

Claudia stretched out her hands in awe and horror to her husband, but, the while, a darkness, a solid darkness, with no faint glimmerings of struggling light, had fallen between her and him.

"Lazarus!" she cried, "Lazarus, Pilate, what meaneth this?"

And Lazarus's voice beside her said: "Fear not,

't is but God's earth mourning for the Son of God.
Pray, lady, pray that thou and Pilate may yet
believe.''

Suddenly the clatter of a horse's hoofs was heard
beneath the window. Breathless, a centurion entered and, saluting, briefly handed his report to
Pilate.

'' Didst do as I commanded ? '' Pilate asked.

The centurion, unable to restrain himself, threw
himself on his knees.

'' Of a truth,'' he said, '' I did as thou didst command ; and forthwith from his heart there flowed
two streams, of water and of blood. Further, even
if my words displease thee so that thou shouldst
slay me, I still will say that I do believe that this
was indeed the Son of God.''

Why shouldst thou not believe and live ? '' said
Pilate gently. '' Methinks, as thou dost, that this
Man had somewhat of the divine in Him.''

'' Not part, but all,'' said Lazarus reverently.
Then approaching Pilate respectfully, he added :
'' Dost need me further, noble Pilate, for I would go
and see my Lord's body and tend my women, who
will be bowed with grief ? ''

'' Art not afraid,'' asked Pilate, '' that the crowd
will rend thee ? ''

'' I am afraid of naught,'' said Lazarus ; '' and, if
they rend me, I count such pain but glory to my
God.''

'' Thou talkest like a Roman,'' was Pilate's answer. '' Yea, go, for to go or stay availeth nothing
now. I would that I could help thee, for I fear that
thou, too, and all who loved this Man will suffer

yet. But, should Caiaphas seek to take thee, or to do thee hurt, and I do hear of it, it shall be the worse for him; for, while I am Governor of Judæa, I will protect thee. In my foolishness, but now I suffered this Sadducee to prevail; but it shall not be thus again. By my hand no man again shall die unjustly, for this thing was unjust."

When Lazarus was about to retire, a soldier announced Joseph of Arimathæa, who, on entering, glanced at Lazarus half in astonishment and half in fear that he was a prisoner.

Pilate greeted him with a friendly smile.

" Hail, noble counsellor, what wouldst thou of me ?"

" I would crave of thee the body of Jesus of Nazareth, the Son of God."

" How sayest thou the Son of God," asked Pilate, thirsting for a further understanding of these mysteries, " since it is reported that He is the Son of Joseph, a carpenter of Nazareth ?"

" For the glory of God and the salvation of the world was this thing done," said Joseph. " He is no man—begotten man—for His mother hath known no man; she is yet a virgin (Blessed be she amongst women !); and He is the Son of God."

Pilate paused a moment before he made answer. What if all this were a trick ? What if Lazarus had not been dead ? What if they required the body to perform some pretended miracle of resurrection ?

Doubt, Satan's strongest instrument, that enfolding cloak he throws over the heads of those he would ensnare, so that they cannot see nor hear, nor yet cry out for help, seized him again. Then, turning to the centurion, he said: "Dost swear that this Jesus is dead?"

"Truly I would I thought it not. But He is dead in very deed, and many will bear witness of it," was the centurion's answer.

"Wilt thou still doubt," asked Lazarus, "and forget already the darkness and the earthquake?"

Then Pilate said: "For my own sake said I this; for, if indeed He rise again, I would be sure that there is no witchery and would have others witness of it."

Then he gave leave to Joseph to do what he would with the holy body, and the two men left together.

It was not long before the rumour of Pilate's concession reached the ears of Caiaphas, so he sent a deputation of priests and Pharisees to the Governor, to ask whether he did not fear a repetition of the miracle of Lazarus.

" Sir," they urged, " we remember that this deceiver said, while He was yet alive, ' After three days I will rise again.' "

" Do ye then so fear the vengeance of this Man whom ye have crucified?" asked Pilate. " I wonder not that ye fear to see His face again."

" We would but make certain that His disciples bewitch not the people further," said the cringing group of Pharisees. " We would but have thee command that the sepulchre be made sure until the third day, lest His disciples come by night and steal Him away, and say unto the people, ' He is risen from the dead.' So the last error be worse than the first."

Then Pilate answered them with scorn : " Ye have

a watch; go your way, make it as sure as ye can.
And tell Caiaphas that, on the third day, methinks
the Nazarene will rise again.''

And, shaking their heads and wondering whether
Pilate had in truth gone mad, they hurried back to
Caiaphas and bid him seal the sepulchre, for which
thing Pilate had given his permission.

CHAPTER XXXVIII.

LIKE Pilate, Caiaphas also paced his room, but with what different thoughts! Terror, too, was his, but the terror only of some horrible death, some awful retribution that would fall on him, though its form was hidden from him. This morning he had triumphed, he had wrung the heart of Pilate, but his triumph had not been unalloyed. He knew that both Herod and Pilate despised him for the act, and till he had heard that the Nazarene had breathed His last he had felt a lurking dread of what he knew not. Then how would the people take it? He had seen oft in history that from a national success had sprung a national hatred. The poor, the maimed, the blind, would they form an alliance and make Lazarus their head? Two rulers had disappeared from the council of the Synagogue—Nicodemus and Lazarus; two powerful, wealthy men. And they had sent no word to him. What did their silence mean? For crafty people dread ever silence. They are afraid of secret machinations, of the sudden outbursts of revolutions, of unlooked-for actions, the outcome of cabals. Every one is in league to intrigue against them, because a life without intrigue appears to them impossible. Every one hates them, for they know that in themselves is nothing lovable.

What strange foreboding of horror was this that

haunted him ? What meant this great unrest ?
Once more he saw the twilight scene, the rocks, the
faint blue light 'twixt morn and night. No loving
arms were round him, no sweet voices soothed the
lonely horror of his cogitations. Daughter and kindred and wife, all were subordinated to that all-ab-
sorbing self that had neither ears nor eyes except
for the thing desired, the furthering of ambitious
schemes, the fulfilment of self-seeking dreams.

The hours went on, but none brought the joyful
news that this Nazarene was crucified. What stirring wonders there might yet be betwixt Jerusalem
and Golgotha ! Spies brought him word that Pilate
still kept within his house, apparently much disturbed. A messenger had been sent after the procession that followed the cross. Two soldiers had
been despatched to Golgotha. Wherefore ? What
did it mean ? What hidden plot was gendering in
the heart of the proud Governor ? He was capable
of acting in defiance alike of king and law. What
if he had acquiesced in the crucifixion of the Nazarene only to release Him afterwards ? What if the
Nazarene should come to life again, like Lazarus ?

The night wore on, and the harrowing meditations
of the High Priest ceased only in the morning, when
Annas came, and with him other priests, to discuss
the question of the disposal of the thirty pieces of
silver scattered by Judas in the Temple court, but
since collected. No time should be lost in dealing
with this sum.

As if by mutual consent, no one broached the
subject that lay next their hearts, the condemning
of the Nazarene. Glad of any change that might

divert the current of his thoughts, Caiaphas suggested an adjournment to the Temple, there to debate the point with other Jews; but in this he did but cheat himself, for all he yearned for was forgetfulness.

The animated conversation going on amongst the rabbis and the money-changers who hung about the Temple, and their fevered gestures, were ascribed—and rightly too—by Caiaphas and his companions to the stirring events of the previous day; and the obsequiousness of the greetings he received assured him that the crucifixion of the Nazarene had reestablished the dominion he had feared to lose.

Presently the name of Judas arrested his attention, and he stopped near a little group of gesticulating Jews.

" We are here," he said, addressing one he knew, " to discuss the question of this money."

" Hast heard the news, rabboni ?" replied the man.

" Aye, what news ? These are strange times in the which news doth follow news so fast that one knoweth not which precedeth," answered Caiaphas, not wishing to show his curiosity, yet trembling with excitement.

" Iscariot is dead; he was found hanging in the potter's field this morning; and no one knoweth whether he did slay himself, or was slain by the disciples of that Nazarene who, God be praised, can harm us now no more."

" Dead, Iscariot dead ?" Caiaphas held out his arm and, with feigned indifference, leaned against one of the great pillars of the Temple for support.

Dead, Iscariot dead ! He had scarce grasped the fact when—lo! what was this sudden darkness? Was Caiaphas struck suddenly with blindness, or where were they who had stood around but now? The chief priests, the scribes, the cages of the doves, the little tables, the altar—where were they all? Was this the end of all? Was this Nazarene truly God?

And, panic-stricken, he smote upon his breast and bowed before the God whose Son he had condemned to death. Then the earth beneath him trembled, and the Temple rocked, and he looked to see it crumble stone from stone. The deepest blackness lasted but a moment, and when the darksome pall had somewhat lifted, and the shivering, crouching Caiaphas dared to raise his eyes, he saw that the veil of the Temple had been torn to pieces. The red, the blue, the purple linen hung in shreds, like a flag that had borne the brunt of battle. The cherubim, too, had been cleft in twain between the wings; and the altar, with its golden candlesticks and shewbread and burnt offerings, was exposed to the public gaze, for thousands were crowding in terror at the darkness, regardless of the High Priest's presence.

And thus ran the thoughts of Caiaphas: He was dead, the Nazarene, so said the people; but would His death free him from his shadowy dread, and restore his peace of mind, his power? Or was more to come? Added horror—would He return in glory as He had said?

With teeth chattering with terror, Caiaphas tried to persuade himself that he had been the victim of some trickery, some illusion. But the shreds of the

Temple veil still hung there, mute witnesses of what had been, and the crouching, panic-stricken multitude were living ones; moreover, they must have seen his horror and alarm.

The position was indeed an awful one; but there was no escaping it: he must face it, and endure the penalty; for, if the Nazarene were indeed the Son of God, and if He should return, Caiaphas would find no mercy.

Then, one after another, people came with stories of graves open and risen saints, and heart-rending tales of the last hours of Christ—tales in which terror had lent strength to their imagination. All was confusion and horror and doubt and consternation.

But Caiaphas hurried off the scribes and elders to his house, lest in their alarm they should commit themselves. The rending of the veil was no easy matter to explain away; nor was the darkness (earthquakes, forsooth, were plenteous enough).

" We must speak no word of this in the Sanhedrim, nor amongst the people," enjoined Caiaphas. " Then they will forget, as all else is forgotten. As for those tales of opened graves, I believe them not. Perchance the earthquake did so shake the tombs that, to the terror-stricken people, the clouds of mouldering dust borne upwards by the wind did in the darkness look like shrouded mortals rising to heaven. So must we tell the people, for if the idea of the resurrection do but get abroad 't will be worse even than the preaching of the Nazarene."

" God forbid!" aspired the elders piously. " Already we have suffered enough through this one

Man; and this blinded people must be allowed no more to think and reason, and meet to preach and pray, for the indolent do love to idle and to gossip, and are readily misled.''

Then, lowering his voice, added another: '' Methinks that Lazarus, too, must needs be put to death; else will he follow in the traditions and false doctrines of this Nazarene. Thus peace will be restored in Israel once more.''

'' I know not whether Lazarus be worth the tumult that would ensue. He blasphemeth not, nor calleth himself the Son of God,'' replied the High Priest unctuously. '' It is for blasphemy alone we crucified this Nazarene; for, in all else, He was a righteous man; and 't is ever a hard task to condemn a man, except for blasphemy.''

So spoke the High Priest, Caiaphas. He had cheated the Jews, he had sought to cheat his God, but he could not cheat the scribes and rulers, who, with words of farewell and affected homage, then dispersed.

CHAPTER XXXIX.

SO all was at an end; the Son of God had come and gone, and few had known Him; salvation had been purchased for the world; to be the hope in life, and the solace in the hour of death, of countless thousands yet unborn. The reason for living had been given to humanity. The priceless object of His incarnation had been achieved. The agony of death the martyrdom of life, were over. The great Spirit, released at last, had flown back to its Father.

Torn as they were with grief, the mourning women could not but rejoice that His long night was ended and, faithful to Him in His death as they had been in His life, they now thought only of how best to honour the divine Body they loved so well.

Now that the great agony of watching Him was over, their thoughts turned to Lazarus. Was he, too, now in prison, following in the anguished steps of his beloved Master? With what joy they saw him appear with Joseph, to help them in taking down the body of their Christ! Nicodemus, grown fearless through remorse, helped too, and soon the sad procession wound round the hillock of Golgotha to the garden in which Joseph had hewn out a tomb. How tenderly they bore that lacerated body to its resting-place, the women ever pressing forward, if

23

the beloved head rolled from side to side, or one arm hung over ever so little. They would give Him, dead, all the loving care they fain would have lavished on Him living. With what love they washed the body, then anointed it with the sweet spices brought by Nicodemus! With what gentle, reverent touch they wound round those sacred limbs the finest linen that could be had! In death no one disputed Him with them. He had lived as a carpenter, they might bury Him as a King. It was nearly dark when they had finished their solemn task. The two Marys knelt down, intending to spend the night in prayer, while Lazarus and the disciples watched. A great stone had been rolled before the sepulchre by the disciples.

Meanwhile Martha, ever anxious over household matters and mindful that she had been away from home two days, wended her way to Bethany, both to set matters in order there, and also to prepare fresh spices with which to fill the sepulchre on the Sabbath morning; for they knew not of the guard that Pilate had placed to forbid all access. On her way home in the darkening evening she was joined at intervals by friends, sympathisers, and the curious, all echoing in the cry which consumed her inwardly: " Dost not fear now for Lazarus also ? "

Could she, she wondered, bear the loss of the one she held so dear ? Would it not be doubly hard, now that all the world seemed slipping from her with the death of Him who had been her support so many months ? Then suddenly an idea flashed on her, and she turned in at the gates of Jerusalem, instead of taking the outer road to Bethany. Through the silent streets she walked, and past the Temple, till she reached the door of the house of Caiaphas.

Here she asked to be admitted to the presence of Rebekah, little guessing in her ignorance, poor woman, the fatal consequences that would follow.

She found Rebekah standing by the window, her favourite attitude, looking out upon the crimsoning sky. Her face was troubled, yet no remorse was in her gloomy heart; only a wondering that Lazarus should have disdained her, should have preferred even the death of his Friend to making her his wife; for, in her narrowed vision, she failed to see the world's salvation in the Saviour's death.

On hearing that Martha wished to see her, she was but slightly moved; yet who could tell what wonders might still come about? Fear, that incentive so powerful with the Jews, might have driven Lazarus to seek her help. Thus does a small mind measure others by its own dimensions.

" I would speak with thee," said the somewhat authoritative voice of Martha, for Rebekah had not even heard her entrance. " I would ask a favour for one thou lovest."

Ah, she had been right! Rebekah turned and frowned.

" What dost thou crave ? " she rejoined haughtily; " for I am not one given to kindness."

" Thou knowest that the Master is dead."

" The Master ? which, whose Master ? " interrupted Rebekah. " Meanest thou the Nazarene ? "

" Even so," said Martha.

" Well, say on."

" And it is rumoured amongst the Jews," went

on Martha, her task becoming more difficult as she became conscious of Rebekah's want of sympathy, " that they will also take my brother Lazarus and crucify him." Here her voice trembled.

Rebekah thought for a moment; then she shrugged her shoulders. Yet she had a liking for Martha.

" How can I help thee? What is thy brother to me? How can I stay the Jews?"

" But thou dost love him," urged Martha gently, repeating what to her had become the very essence of truth, that to love much was to overcome every obstacle.

" I did love him," the other answered, shrugging her shoulders, " but, since he doth not love me, it mattereth naught to me whether he be alive or dead."

" Yet surely love needeth but to love," urged Martha, little knowing how wide the compass she embraced, imbued as she was with the Messiah's teaching. " Love desireth but to love."

" That is new teaching which doth savour of the Galilean doctrine," replied Rebekah. " Of such a love I know nothing. But this I know, that, if thy brother will take the proud daughter of Caiaphas to wife, then he need fear nor Jews nor Romans, but be safe always."

Then Martha spoke the words which though she knew it not were later to return to her with all the bitterness of death.

" How can he wed thee, maiden, seeing that he loveth another?"

Words of truth from one who, through daily contact with the Spirit of Truth, could not lie; yet

Martha would have recalled them, when she saw the
burst of rage and bitterness they called forth.

" Loves another!" cried Rebekah. " Thy
brother Lazarus doth love another ? He who, we
thought, did so disdain me because his heart was
given to good works ? Dost speak the truth ? Is
it for this that I must save him, to give him to some
other woman ? By the beard of Aaron, Martha,
thou knowest me not, to ask me such a thing. Perchance I would have given him up to lead a life of
purity and sacrifice. If so be that he believeth that
this Man is the Son of God, he doeth well to worship
Him. But, if the stainless Lazarus can love an
earthly woman, then I will be that woman, or he
shall die. Dost hear, woman ? Either thy brother
Lazarus doth wed me, or he dieth."

Fear and horror fell on Martha. What horrible
perplexity was this ? Would that she had never
come! Of a truth the Lord had said that she was
over-troubled about many things. She had sought
the proud maiden in order to help her brother,
and now it seemed that she had but increased his
peril.

" Who is this woman that thy brother loveth ? "
asked Rebekah scornfully.

" Nay, but I cannot tell thee that, proud maiden.
It seemeth me that I have already told too much.
I will go home, for I am very weary, and at dawn I
must bring spices to the sepulchre of my Lord, for
't is the Sabbath. Farewell, maiden; methinks that
still thy love will triumph over this tempting of the
devil. Thou wilt yet think of my poor brother and
of his two sisters whose lives are bound up in his,

and of her that trusteth him, and, therefore, thou
wilt entreat thy father for him.''

"I care not whether thy brother live or die.
Henceforward he is naught to me but a perverse and
wretched, misguided ruler,'' said Rebekah angrily.
"Now leave me, ere I say that which will grieve
thee more.''   And Martha turned away, and with a
heavy heart regained the road to Bethany.

And, the moment she had left the room, Rebekah, murmured to herself through clenched teeth:
"Would that I knew this woman whom he loveth,
that I might slay her!''

CHAPTER XL.

A T Bethany nearly all the night had been spent
in prayer. Not only were they overwhelmed
with grief at the crucifixion of the Lord, but they
feared also that other terrible events would follow.
Lazarus was conscious that, in a humble way, he
would have to travel in the footsteps of his Lord,
and he was troubled with the thought of how the
Master would wish him to proceed.

A little troop of friends and believers had visited
him that night, and laid before him a plan for his
escape, should his life be placed in peril; and it
seemed to Lazarus that to leave Judæa would be his
only way of continuing to testify to the wondrous
miracles by which it had been proved beyond dis-
pute that the Messiah had indeed visited the earth.
Already steps were being taken by Caiaphas and
Annas to prevent the scribes from making any records
of these events; and, although those of the disciples
who could write had assidiously noted day by day
each event and word and act, still if, as was to be
feared, they should be massacred, who could tell
into whose hands their notes might fall, or how they
might be altered and corrupted ? To one who had
once died, and knew a little of the world beyond the
grave, death held fewer horrors than did life; therefore to leave his home and his beloved country, with

all its tender memories, and thus preserve his life, would be to Lazarus a greater sacrifice than to lay it down.

With the first cold rays of the rising sun that stole into the room in which the three were seated with some of the disciples, their thoughts turned to the sepulchre, and they fell to reflecting how the sweet face looked after its first night of repose. With eager restlessness, Martha set about putting together the spices and essences she had prepared to take to the sepulchre that morning.

A hurried step was heard without the door, and the Magdalene, tired and flushed, but with exultation in her eyes, rushed in.

" The Lord is risen! " she cried. " The Lord is risen! Who then dare deny that He is God ? "

Then, while the others pressed round to listen to her tale, Lazarus called to Peter and John, and said: " Let us hasten to the sepulchre, for I fear some artifice of the Romans. Therefore did they set a seal, to rob the Lord of a King's burial."

And so, still doubting,—as even the redeemed will doubt to the end of time, sitting in darkness and straining through the glass that they themselves have dimmed by superstition, by infidelity, by self-raised complications,—they hurried down the hill. Yes, Lazarus, who himself had risen, could barely accept the rising of the Lord.

The Magdalene called after them in vain. " Nay, if they had but stayed to hear my tale, they had not need to fear or hurry so," she said.

Then, when Mary and Martha and their household questioned her, she told them of her dismay when she had come to the sepulchre and found the body gone, and how, in the semi-darkness, she had not recognised the Lord, till she had heard His voice say: " Mary."

At the memory of this she fell upon her knees and cried out: " Who am I, who am I, that the Master should thus speak to me and say, ' Woman, why weepest thou ?' Oh, Martha, where is now the sting of death, or the grave's bitterness ? All life, henceforth, is one great truth, that riseth like a wall of strength against man's scheming wickedness."

And a great silence fell on all around, in the presence of the certainty of resurrection, the proof of a beyond.

Then, after a few moments, one voice after another clamoured for further details.

" What spake He unto thee ?" asked one. " How looked He ?"

" How can I tell thee ?" answered Mary; " for words do fail me when I think of the love and beauty of that face that is always beautiful. I, in my foolishness, made as though I would clasp His feet in tenderness and love. But while I did so, He seemed to vanish from my touch, and in gentlest tones He said: ' Touch Me not; for I am not yet ascended to My Father: but go to My brethren, and say unto them, I ascend unto My Father, and your Father; and to My God, and your God.' And obediently and silently I came hither, according to His word, to tell the great news to the brethren and to the whole world, that the Christ is risen indeed."

CHAPTER XLI

PALE-FACED, excited, with dishevelled hair, Claudia rushed to her husband's room, with the news brought to her by the slaves.

"Hast heard? He is risen! He is risen!" she cried excitedly.

No need to give name, for Pilate, ever straight-forward, made no pretence of not knowing whom she meant. Yet no terror seized him; rather a look of triumph lit up his features.

"Is it even so?" he questioned calmly.

"Speakest thou thus?" exclaimed Claudia angrily; "dost not fear that some evil shall befall us for this thing?"

"Nay, I fear naught, for naught that can befall me can be worse than the dull ache which gnaweth at my heart, which will ache for evermore." Then, rising from his bench, he exclaimed in a changed tone: "Yet how knowest thou that this thing is true? How knowest thou not that either this Man's followers seek once more to bewitch the world, or that Caiaphas hath not some plot of base deceit with which he too would blind the eyes of the Jews? I will at once to my bath and go myself and see into this thing; and, if it be true, 't is I, Pilate, who will be the first to tell that priest of hell, and mark the grinning infamy of his foul smile of dread. Ah, 't will be sweet to me, and such moments will be rare henceforth.''

" 'T is verily true," said Claudia; " for the Magdalene and Mary have seen Him, and He hath spoken with them; and they say that He hath sent a wondrous message to the whole world.''

Hastily Pilate dressed and left the house without his usual guard.

For all it was so early, he yet found Caiaphas dressed and busy writing, and he could not but admire the power and energy of the man. A great uneasiness seized the heart of Caiaphas at this early, unexpected visit, for, since the condemnation of Jesus of Nazareth, he had felt ever a great restlessness and anxiety he could not account for, a dread of some catastrophe whose nature he could not forecast. Yet, when he rose, he sought to hide his fears.

" How may I serve thee ?" he inquired, his face taking on the smile that so exasperated Pilate.

" Methought I would be the first to tell thee some strange news," said Pilate, in that taunting tone which in one less noble-hearted would have marked the bully. " The Nazarene hath risen! Even now He walketh about Jerusalem, as though thou hadst never hated Him and I had never allowed Him to be condemned. At any moment He may appear to thee and me, and woe betide us both.''

" 'T is a lie!" gasped Caiaphas hoarsely, clutching at his table, yet failing to find it in his perturbation; his fingers seemed to clasp and unclasp the air behind him.

" Thou were ever courteous," answered Pilate,

" but we Romans lie not; we leave that to the Jews, who surpass in that all other nations."

Unmindful of the taunt, Caiaphas stood silent. Could this that he had just heard be true, or was Pilate mocking him ? Or was it some pretended miracle ? Dismay and fear showed on his countenance, for his sense of justice told him that, if God meant vengeance, it would fall heavily on him.

" 'T is some witchery in which thou hast helped," he burst out at last, no longer able to control the torrent of hate and wrath he felt against the Nazarene, Pilate, the whole world. " It is some witchery of thine own soldiers. Therefore didst thou allow Joseph of Arimathæa to take away the body. Thou art a traitor to thy Emperor. Thou hast ever tried to mock me since thou wert Procurator here, and I will write to Cæsar."

" See that thou write in Latin, and not in Hebrew," said Pilate, laughing at the priest's petulance; " and send it not by a Roman soldier. . . . Ha! Ha! thou art indeed afraid, poor Caiaphas, of this carpenter's Son." Then, changing his tone, he added: " Thou wouldst not fear Him so, great Caiaphas, were it not that thou knowest He is the stronger. He is stronger than art thou, be He God or not. His heart is pure and noble, and true and wide, wide as the ocean; and thou, thou art a base, plotting, deceiving little hound of a Jew, with a mind as narrow as that." And with the thumb and forefinger of his right hand he portioned off the tiniest tip of the little finger of his left hand. " And thy soul, if thou hast indeed a soul, is foul, like water into which men have spat; and thou wouldst deceive the whole nation for thy own power's sake, and thou wouldst hound pure-living souls to their destruction, so that thou and thy tool, Annas, may hold in chains each Jewish heart; and, when thou diest—as thou must surely die—to thee it will not matter whether or not there be a resurrection, for thou wilt never rise again, since neither heaven nor hell could hold so base a soul. So now thou knowest, Caiaphas, what I think of thee, and with that I bid thee farewell. Henceforward, except in the Sanhedrim, we shall meet no more, for Romans like not cowards; and, if there be a resurrection, all I pray is that thou and I may never meet at it.''

With these words, Pilate left the room, and the little priest, who was huddled up in his seat, and looking more like ape than exasperated man, and so amazed, so swelling with rage and hate, that voice and tongue refused their office.

And, when Pilate had reached the street, he raised his head and took a long, deep breath, as though he had been inspiring in the High Priest's chamber some foul, death-dealing gas.

CHAPTER XLII.

AS rapidly as possible Lazarus sent messengers from one disciple to another, bidding them assemble at a given place in Jerusalem, in case the Lord should appear to them. He had chosen the house of a trusted friend, and, at the given hour, all, except Thomas, who could not be found, assembled. They came in singly, at short intervals, lest they should attract attention, and be massacred before they could perform their Lord's command to spread the glad tidings of salvation throughout the world. When all had come, the doors were shut and barred; then all knelt, and Lazarus raised a prayer that, if it were God's will, it might be granted them to see the Lord once more; also that they might be quickened by the Holy Spirit, which Jesus had promised should be shed upon them.

And, while he prayed, the room, that had been almost dark, seemed to grow lighter and ever lighter. The lightness was no natural one, for its source was not apparent. It seemed to gather of itself and gradually to form a column of surpassing radiance in the centre of the room. Suddenly, in the midst of it appeared the figure of the Lord.

So sudden and unexpected was His coming, so dazzling was the brightness of His visage, that they all fell upon their faces, half in worship, half in awe.

Then, on the throbbing silence, words arose that were to be treasured up through life and death, till they should be heard once more within the gates of heaven: " Peace be unto you."

And, while He spoke, He raised His hand, that they might recognise Him by the cruel marks of the nails.

Then again, with deep solemnity, He said, " Peace be unto you." And with His hand He pointed to His side, the side which Pilate, out of mercy, had ordered to be pierced. " As My Father hath sent Me, even so send I you."

Then, in the midst of the utter silence, it seemed that He heaved a sigh, and that from those lips there issued some holy essence which, in the semi-darkness, took the image of a golden dove. At the same moment the voice of Jesus rose distinct and clear: " Receive ye the Holy Ghost."

And, at these words, it was as though lips and heart had been smitten with a lightning flash, and a curtain rolled away from before brain and soul. And then a great peace fell on them softly, like evening dew on moss, and Life and Death and Immortality and Faith and Christ had become certainties for evermore. And all the earth seemed alive with whirring, rushing sounds of wings that filled the heart with breezy gladness.

Then, in the gloaming of that spring evening, He led them forth, as heretofore to Bethany, where He had ever loved to be; and, in those last hours of sweet companionship, He unfolded to them many things that they could now the better understand—things that before had seemed mysterious and unreal

—how that each incident of His Passion had been foretold by Moses and the prophets. Then many matters that to them had seemed inexplicable stood out bold and clear before their understanding, amazing them with their simplicity. And then He vested them with power over serpents and evil spirits and to heal disease, and further, to pardon sins and to perform miracles; and He bid them bear true witness of what they had seen and heard, and to preach repentance and remission of sins.

Then from before the eyes of Lazarus there seemed to rise a veil, and he saw with unerring vision that as he had once died to witness to the glory of the Lord, so now he was to live to show it forth.

They reached Lazarus's garden, and there fell in adoring worship at His feet, pouring out their hearts in gratitude for all that He had done for them; and Mary Magdalene, with faced bowed to the ground, cried out: " For my sins, my Saviour, wast Thou crucified; for my sins, for my sins! "

Then, in one last great act of love, He stretched forth His hand and blessed them with a blessing that should protect and guide them for evermore, and stamp them with the seal of heaven.

The faint odours of budding flowers, the gentle breeze that seemed to soften the chill of spring and to waft into it a breath of summer; the dull glow that was neither light nor darkness; a strange burning of dread and expectancy in their hearts; the hush of nature, as if all living things were listening to the choir of angels waiting to welcome the coming of their Lord—all these combined to stamp the scene upon the disciples' minds forever.

One last parting look, and a great tearing of the heart-strings; and then, like a streak of roseate effulgence borrowed from the dying sunset, the Divine Figure floated upwards; and as He rose, His hands, uplifted in one last blessing, showed the imprints of the lacerating nails. And while they gazed with upturned faces to the sky, they sank once more upon their knees, a strange radiance lighting up their faces and shining all around; and a cry went up: " Glory to God, Glory to God on earth ! "

And angel voices echoed : " Glory to God in heaven ! "

And the stupendous act of man's redemption was accomplished.

24

CHAPTER XLIII.

THE Magdalene alone seemed inconsolable at the departure of the Christ. The links between her and the Nazarene had been the strongest that could be forged—those that bind a saved soul to its saviour. He had raised the drooping soul, He had sanctified her the Jews called unholy, He had placed her feet on a sure foundation; and He was associated with the great redeeming joy of her life, the possibility of beginning again—a chance the world rarely gives. She had few relatives, and those she had had cast her off as an unclean thing.

Too many events had supervened since the journey to Golgotha to permit Lazarus to give more than a passing thought to that betrayal of her innermost heart when she had feared that he was being dragged off to condemnation. But now the intimate life with the human Christ was over, and life must needs fall back into its old routine, but with an added hope, a great comfort, a great promise, that would sustain and sweeten it, and make its burden lighter. A great work lay before all who had believed in the Nazarene, had known Him to be the Christ—the work of testifying; and this none so well as Lazarus could perform. And this possibly, nay, almost certainly, would mean death—death in its most hideous and torturing form. On one point his mind was irrevocably fixed, all his possessions should be given to the poor; he would but keep a cottage for his sisters, if so be they would not join him; all else should go, all that he had so greatly treasured. Then what would remain for him to offer to the Magdalene? A great personal love and a share in his Christ-work. That would be all. No thought of self must ever enter either heart; her only temporal reward would be her re-instatement in the eyes of the world.

Her words appealed to every sentiment of chivalry and romance in him, when, at nightfall, she bade farewell to them. " Ye have been very good to me, Martha and Mary," she began, while her tears fell fast. " Ye have suffered me to be with you much, and have loved me for the dear Lord's sake; but I am but a poor sinner and I must come no more. Henceforth I will go about my Saviour's business. I will seek other sinning women and tell them of the Christ, and I will minister to the mother of the Master."

Then, with loving tenderness Lazarus took her hand. " Magdalene," he said, " thou wast beloved of the Lord and favoured by Him above all other women; I too will work with thee, if thou wilt let me. I will sell all I have, and will follow Him with thee. Together we will journey hither and thither, without scrip or purse, and, like our dear Master, we will have nowhere to lay our heads. Everywhere we will testify of Him, but together in the Lord. Wilt have me, Mary, for thy husband?" And in her eyes he saw her answer and the radiant gratitude of her re-awakened soul, that shone like beacons in her lovely eyes.

" Surely I am blessed above all women!" murmured the Magdalene. But, while they spoke, a horse's hoofs resounded on the distant road, echoing freely on the stilly night.

" A messenger from Pontius Pilate," said the servant; and instinctively the Magdalene drew nearer to Lazarus.

" Whom seek ye?" he inquired.

" Lazarus, the ruler," replied the man, making obeisance. Then, drawing his arm through the bridle of his horse, he whispered, looking round: " I would speak with thee privately, for the Governor hath not dared to put this thing on paper. He would warn thee that, ere coming morn, thou do depart; for the chief priests and the Pharisees have heard how that the Christ hath been seen in nine places since His death; and Pilate doth fear greatly that if they find thee they will kill thee."

" Greet the most noble Pilate, and thank him for that he hath warned me; tell him that we will try to depart, if so be that, after prayer, we are minded that our Master Jesus doth so command. But if so be that death should overtake us, tell him that we fear it not, and that we are ever grateful for his remembrance, and will pray for him."

Then, while the soldier was departing, Lazarus turned to the Magdalene.

" Art thou still so minded," said he, " that thou wouldst have me for thy husband? The persecution hath already begun, and henceforth there will be no rest or peace for them who serve the Lord. Art not afraid?"

With a proud, loving gesture, the Magdalene answered : " With thee I fear naught, Lazarus; for the Spirit of God will be with us always, even to the end of the world.''

Then, as the hour was late, she hurried down the hill towards Jerusalem, her heart overflowing with the joy that filled it.

CHAPTER XLIV

ENFOLDED in the intoxicating elation of earthly bliss, that did not crowd out her peaceful trust and thankfulness and adoration as regards the Christ, the Magdalene walked quickly on. Already the thrills of terrestrial joy, for which her earthly heart was still most fitted, were soothing the graver griefs of separation from the Christ, and she sped fearlessly along the by-path of the Jericho road. It was later than she thought. Olive and cactus, prickly pear and pomegranate trees, all were growing grey and dark; and, as now and then she lifted her eyes and tried to pierce the deepening gloom, great shadows rose in front of her, like screens of night-clouds, against which it seemed she must strike her body, till she came close to them and saw their nothingness swallowed up in farther deeps of shadows; and above, the glow, that had seemed like the eternal eye of God, grew dimmer too, and it was really night.

Presently she became conscious of a strange fear —not of earthly things, but of something about to happen. As a new terror crept into her heart, so a voice seemed to whisper, " Fear not! Fear not!"

Almost she felt a supernatural presence walking by her side. Was it fancy, or was there really in the darkness a faint, golden light, like atoms of

heaven-sent glory? Accustomed as she had been
to miracles and incomprehensible events, made be-
lievable only by the assurance of a great faith and
the daily presence of Divinity, little wonder that she
strove to still the beatings of her heart, to hear
whether voice of angel spoke. Her soul and heart
seemed to grow hollow and vaulted and expectant,
as if emptying themselves to make room for some
great presence to hold the voice of God; and yet she
sped on, fearful of she knew not what. Why did
the words of the Crucified Saviour haunt her? The
words He had murmured through His dying agony
to the thief that suffered too: " This day shalt thou
be with Me in paradise! " Why in the darkness did
she see, as it had stood before her on the darkening
mount of Calvary, the beauteous divine face looking
upward ?

For an instant she doubted whether she had sinned
in loving Lazarus. Then all her terrors and her
doubts were brought to a sudden ending at the
sound of a voice close by.

" Woman! " it said. 'T was a voice she knew,
but not a voice divine, nor of a friend, nor yet of
man. A woman's voice, deep with set purpose,
wrung with hate, and hoarse with loathing. " Woman, I would speak with thee! "

Then all the fearlessness of a noble nature depend-
ent on divine support returned.

" What wouldst thou ? Who art thou? " asked
the Magdalene.

" I am the daughter of Caiaphas; and thou, thou
art the affianced wife of Lazarus. Is not that so ? "

" 'T is even so," said the Magdalene, in a sweet,

low voice, all the gladness of that bright reality and her true love ringing in her answer.

She was close now to the dark, veiled woman who faced her. The two stood on the pathway, unable to distinguish one another's faces, barely the outline of each other's figures; only their voices and the faint rustle of their clinging garments proving the presence of two human beings in that solitary spot.

"Dost know that I, too, loved Lazarus, whom thou hast filched from me?" asked Rebekah fiercely.

"Alas! I know that thou dost love him, and I grieve for thee, fair maiden," replied the Magdalene. "But thou wouldst not grudge the poor, sinning, penitent Magdalene one little ray of joy in her sad life. I have loved Lazarus dearly for many years; yet it never seemed to me that I, the harlot, should have such joy as to wed Lazarus; and it never could have been, but that the Lord forgave me and washed me from my sins."

"Thou shalt not wed Lazarus," cried out Rebekah, raising her hand as if to strike the Magdalene. "I tell thee thou shalt not, thou shalt not; I will not have it."

"Believe me, maiden, I feel much for your grief; but, if I wed not Lazarus, he will not wed another; why then be jealous of one so lowly as thy servant Mary?"

"I will not have thy pity," cried Rebekah, beyond herself. "Who art thou to dare to pity the High Priest's daughter? Thou sinning harlot, who wert derided of all men and women, till this half-mad Nazarene appeared and made a pastime of the companionship of sinners, because none other would believe on Him."

" 'T is true I was a sinner and a harlot," replied the Magdalene, with downcast eyes and sweet, sad voice. " *I was;* but there is that in the power of God that can wipe out all sin and set one, with clean feet, afresh along a new path of life, that is all joy, and peace, and faith, and happiness, and love."

"Believest thou this ? " asked Rebekah musingly. Then, with renewed wrath and infinite scorn, she added: " Ah, 't is easy for thee to talk of all this inward joy when Lazarus is thy affianced bridegroom, and he loveth thee; but tell me, if I took him from thee, and if he left thee, or if he died, or if he loved another, what wouldst thou say then ? Wouldst still have inward joy and peace and trust ?"

The night was growing chilly, and a shiver struck the Magdalene's heart at Rebekah's words. She paused a moment to reflect what she would do if the newly opened doors of her heart were shut to again.

If Lazarus should die! It was as if her heart fluttered and fainted within her, and as if from the ebbings of her swooning mind there rose up mystic music on the night air, that only she could hear or understand:

" Yea, I will be with you always, even unto the end of the world."

Then, with strengthened spirit, she raised her head and looked outwards in the gloom, towards where she fancied the eyes of Rebekah were looking for her answer, and she said: "Yea, even if I should lose Lazarus, if he should die, or love another, I would still believe and love the Lord."

While she spoke, Rebekah uttered not a word, and all nature, the creeping things of night, the humming, buzzing things that hang on trees and boughs, all seemed to hush to do obeisance to the soul the Lord had won.

Then, like a beacon from heaven, a faint moon crept out from behind the clouds, so that the two women could just discern each other on the pathway; and the Magdalene looking, saw the face of Rebekah glowing with anger, distorted by a sullen despair and wounded vanity and wrath; and, in her heart, there rose a tender feeling for this woman, who loved and was not loved by Lazarus. And all this time Rebekah's arm was beating with strange, nervous movement beneath her cloak. She found it hard to anger herself with one so meek and gentle as Mary Magdalene; but the fierce, unrelenting, domineering spirit of Caiaphas was strong within her. To be spurned by Lazarus, triumphed over by a harlot, how could so proud a nature brook such ignominy ?

"Am I not as beautiful as thou ?" she asked, turning, while she did so, without knowing it, her beautiful face upward toward the moon. "Why should Lazarus not love me ?"

"Thou art indeed more beautiful than I," replied the Magdalene; "but who can direct love ?"

"I tell thee he *shall* love me," cried Rebekah, growing furious again, like a stormy sea that has been calm during a short lull. "He shall need me, he shall serve me, and, if thou wert not here, I would make him love me. It is thou, thou, who hast beguiled the hearts of thousands of men with thy witchcrafts; thou, who hast united thyself with this prince of darkness that calleth Himself the Christ and is no God at all, who triest by thy foul treacheries to take him from me. I tell thee thou shalt die; or, if thou live and wed Lazarus, then Lazarus shall die—a horrible death; and it will be thy pride, thy foul beguilings, that will have caused it."

"I fear thee not," replied the Magdalene, "for the Lord would not permit Lazarus yet to die; or, if He should, He would surely bring him to life another time that he might testify of Him. Thou art mad, most noble maiden, for love of Lazarus. Be calm, be patient, and forget this thing, and turn unto the Lord."

"Ah, thou canst speak like this, who hast thy soul's desire; but I will not have it to be robbed by thee of Lazarus. I tell thee I will not." And she stamped her feet and gazed close into the Magdalene's face.

"I rob thee not, maiden, since he loves thee not," replied the Magdalene; "and this is no place for thee so late. Should any pass, what would they say to see the proud daughter of Caiaphas in the olive groves at night?"

"I care not what they say, so Lazarus loves me not," Rebekah answered waywardly, her voice ending in a sob. "I care not, I know not; only I know that there is no room on earth for thee and me and him; and one must die. Seest thou this?" and she raised a dagger in her hand; in the moon's pale gleam it looked like a flaming needle. "Seest thou this?"

The Magdalene bent her eyes on it, and a great fear crept over her.

" Well, either thou or Lazarus shall die by this. I would rather it were thou; but, if thou weddest Lazarus, then will I kill him."

Helplessly the Magdalene looked around her; but save where, here and there, the moon half-heartedly lit up a tree, the darkness was profound. In her heart she cried to Heaven for help, for her own thoughts were so bewildered that she failed to realise that a great purpose was being accomplished.

Who was she to wed a man so good as Lazarus ? Why had she ever thought such sins as hers could end with such mad joy ? And Lazarus, what if her love and presence should hamper him along the path he had cut out; what if these two brands, plucked from the fire and united in the fierce flames of earthly passion, should forget—forget their close companionship with the Christ, the Immortal Example, the Stupendous Sacrifice, the gigantic trust He had left behind, the forgiveness, the miracles, the gift of the Holy Spirit, their mission to others ? Then a voice that seemed to her as if the Christ still spoke on earth, a voice that, with its music as of low-pitched organs playing by the side of mountain torrents, brought back the remembrance of a holy adoration that pressed out all possibility of lesser or mere earthly love; that voice spoke to her once more the words, " Greater love hath no man than this, that a man lay down his life for his friend."

" If it must be Lazarus or I," she murmured faintly—for the flesh is very weak; the weaker, when the spirit is the strongest, as if the devil cried out for his own—" If it must be Lazarus or I, kill me, for Lazarus must testify." And she bared her lovely bosom with proud gesture to the poignard, pressing against it that the pain might be the sooner over, that the sharp steel might sever the cords of life with swifter touch; then she sank on to her knees and, as her head fell back, she cried: " Forgive her, Lord, for she knoweth not. She loveth much; forgive her much as Thou forgavest me. O Lord, receive my soul ! "

Then she fell quite back and died, and, as she fell, Rebekah leaned over her and smiled with a hard, triumphant smile, but with the light of madness in her eyes. Then, when the Magdalene moved not, her eyes opened wide with horror, and as the dark red current gushed in a ceaseless torrent to the ground from her white bosom, Rebekah held her hands with horrific terror to her head and watched. At last, once she shrieked; then tore madly through the grove of olive trees towards the home of Caiaphas. And the Magdalene lay dead beneath the dawn-tinted trees, the will of God accomplished. At rest at last.

CHAPTER XLV

" SELL all that thou hast, take up thy cross, and follow Me," murmured Lazarus, while he bent over the dead body of the beauteous Magdalene, now lying on the very couch on which he himself had died.

She had been found close to Jerusalem, stabbed in the heart by some foul hand. None would ever know the quick, hot words, the madness-given strength of the proud woman who had stabbed her in her jealousy. None would ever know how Lazarus mourned his bride. He had sold all that he possessed; had this too been a possession that would have kept his soul back from the great work of testifying? If so, blessed be the Lord who giveth and taketh away; he, too, must tread the winepress alone.

A ship was waiting to take Lazarus and Mary away to where he could preach the gospel unmolested. Simon could not make up his mind to let both daughters leave him in his old age; so it had been decided that Martha should remain with him. The spirit of the Eternal One had shown Lazarus that he would not have been restored to life only to die again at once. The Lord had commanded him to testify. This he must needs do, and, to do so,

382

he must leave Judæa; for, everywhere, a price was offered for his capture.

He had hoped to carry away with him the living Magdalene, but the Lord had willed it otherwise. Perhaps she had deserved a better fate, a rest for all her taunts and trials.

In the beautiful garden of Bethany, where the almond tree and pomegranate were now just putting forth their buds, where the feet of the Lord had so often stood, they buried her, and Martha and Mary combed with loving tenderness the tresses that had wiped the feet of Jesus. And on her bosom Lazarus placed a little cross of cedarwood, the first that had been made in record of the Christ's shameful death; the symbol that was to become the only staff of comfort in the valley of death, that dark, terror-beset ravine that must be traversed; the dark shadow thrown across eternal sunshine. And over the grave they planted the myrtle in token of love, and little cypress trees.

And then the two who had so loved the Lord left Bethany and Judæa for ever, and sailed forth to preach to other nations the great truth of salvation that had been rejected by the Jews.

THE END.

www.ingramcontent.com/pod-product-compliance
Lightning Source LLC
Chambersburg PA
CBHW021531110726
47902CB00004B/828